Praise for Va...

The Filling Station

"The 1921 Tulsa Race Massacre is, shockingly, little more than a footnote in history—because history has always been written by white men. Miller's book, thankfully, reverses that egregious oversight. By seeing through the eyes of two sisters who suffered catastrophic loss, we viscerally learn how this vibrant Black community fought devastation with resilience, faith, and grit."

—Jodi Picoult, #1 *New York Times* bestselling author

"*The Filling Station* is a compelling contribution to the understanding of Black Wall Street and the 1921 Tulsa Race Massacre. The depth of research, coupled with Vanessa Miller's ability to bring these historical events to life, ensures that these stories are not only remembered but resonate with readers. So many of the names and places come to life in a way that makes me have to stop reading and process the fact that this event actually happened, and it happened in my community to people I have known."

—Michelle Burdex, program coordinator
for Greenwood Cultural Center

The American Queen

"Vanessa Miller's *The American Queen* is a rare untold novel showcasing a hidden gem of factual history about North Carolina's Queen Louella of the Kingdom of the Happy Land—the only queen that ruled on American soil. Inspirational and unforgettable, Miller weaves a fascinating story set in rugged Appalachia in a community built by emancipated formerly enslaved men and women."

—Kim Michele Richardson, *New York Times* bestselling
author of The Book Woman of Troublesome Creek series

"The struggles in *The American Queen* resonate with contemporary issues, making the story not just a journey into the past but a reflection of our present and a hopeful vision for the future."

—Rhonda McKnight, author of *The Thing About Home*

"Vanessa Miller's page-turner *The American Queen* takes readers on a winding journey through the horrors and triumphs of the post–Civil War / Reconstruction era to show how a broken formerly enslaved woman transforms into an actual queen over her people. Louella Bobo Montgomery emerges from a Mississippi plantation with a vision of a 'happy land' where her people will live together in peace and with dignity. Turning that vision into a reality, however, tests the very foundations of her faith. *The American Queen* is a moving, heartwarming story that reminds us that all things are possible with faith, hope, love, and forgiveness."

—Kaia Alderson, author of *Sisters in Arms*

"Some books just feel inspired. You feel blessed for having read them. They feel like a gift. This is one of those books. *The American Queen* is definitely a story everyone should know, and a year from now, I have a feeling they will. Put it at the top of your bookstagram reading list."

—Jamie Ford, *New York Times* bestselling author of *The Many Daughters of Afong Moy*

"Miller (*The Light on Halsey Street*) captivates with a propulsive historical based on the true story of a group of formerly enslaved people who founded a utopian society in the Appalachian mountains in the 1860s . . . Readers will be won over by Louella's gumption, optimism, and tenacity. Miller brings to enthralling life a hidden gem in American history."

—*Publishers Weekly*

"*The American Queen* by Vanessa Miller is a rich, multilayered saga of a little-known true story that completely captivated me with one of the strongest and most compelling protagonists I've ever read. The dreams of Louella Montgomery were strong enough to infuse an entire community and carry them on the wings of hope off the plantation. I had to blink several times to come back to the present after finishing the last page of this wonderful novel. Everyone should read this book!"

—Colleen Coble, *USA TODAY* bestselling author

"Regal, self-possessed with inner strength and dignity—that's the portrayal of Louella Bobo Montgomery in Vanessa Miller's *The American Queen*. Miller crafts a stellar image of resilience, giving life to a little-known story of American royalty. There's something special, soul-stirring to read of a woman, a wife, a queen building a space with her husband and found family that makes a community's hope of freedom come true. Everyone should read *The American Queen* and be inspired."

—Vanessa Riley, award-winning author of *Island Queen* and *Queen of Exiles*

"Queen Louella, the American Queen, is a character so richly drawn, she writes the story of American history. Born into slavery, robbed of her mother and family, Louella has no reason to love or be loved. However, the superb Vanessa Miller has created a new world of possibility and the story takes flight. The impossible path to forgiveness is as arduous as the road to freedom is for the enslaved. When Louella decides it's her world, one that she will make her own in emancipation, the sky opens up and rains hope. This novel is a triumph."

—Adriana Trigiani, bestselling author of *The Good Left Undone*

"*The American Queen* is beautifully told, a story rife with struggle, intrigue, and the indomitable spirit of a woman strong enough to carry the weight of a community, bold enough to dream the impossible, and determined enough to fashion dreams into reality. Louella Montgomery is a woman for the ages. I loved traveling alongside her and meeting the people of The Happy Land."

—Lisa Wingate, #1 *New York Times* bestselling author of *The Book of Lost Friends*

"*The American Queen* brings to light another hidden triumph in Black American history. Queen Louella is frankly a woman that everyone should know. Filled with bravery and cultural beauty, this marvel of a novel transported me while educating me on the sheer determination of an emancipated community to not only survive but to also thrive."

—Sadeqa Johnson, *New York Times* bestselling author of *The House of Eve*

The Light on Halsey Street

"Dana Jones is just trying to survive in 1985 Brooklyn, which is a tough task while having a cocaine-addicted mother and a boyfriend who's a petty thief. Her best friend Lisa Whitaker lives just around the block but has a fairy-tale life and dreams of making a difference in her predominately African American Bedford-Stuyvesant neighborhood. One fateful night sets both young women on a path that seems unchangeable—one to prison, the other to college. Jumping ahead in time, Miller (*Something Good*) explores how one bad decision can change a life forever, but she also brings the main characters plenty of chances for redemption. Bedford-Stuyvesant, at once tight-knit and fractured, is practically a main character in this women's fiction offering, and many will recognize similar ebbs and flows in their own cities . . . Friendship and the power of community are the shining stars of this novel, which doesn't shy away from tough issues but also offers a hefty dose of hope and humor. Read-alikes include *Lean on Me* by Pat Simmons and *No One Ever Asked* by Katie Ganshert."

—*Library Journal*

"*The Light on Halsey Street* is an emotional story that takes you on an up close and personal journey across the decades with two friends. The plot is woven with friendship, forgiveness, and faith. An unforgettable read from cover to cover by Vanessa Miller."

—Tia McCollors, bestselling author

"Vanessa Miller's *The Light on Halsey Street* is women's fiction at its finest. Riveting and redemptive, *The Light on Halsey Street* vividly transports us back to 1980s Brooklyn with an unforgettable cast of characters and leaves you with the firm belief that light can truly never be extinguished by darkness."

—Joy Callaway, international bestselling
author of *All the Pretty Places*

"Vanessa Miller set *The Light on Halsey Street* in Bedford-Stuyvesant, New York, but she takes readers on a decades-long exploration of the heart. In her coming-of-age story, two women learn about the impact of bitterness and resentment and the power of love to heal and restore what was lost. Readers will find it hard to put this novel down, and they'll hold on to these life lessons long after they turn the last page. Well done!"

—Robin W. Pearson, Christy Award–winning author

"Vanessa Miller delivers a poignant story of friendship and betrayal, bringing Lisa and Dana full circle, with an uplifting ending that proves there is power in prayer."

—Lacey Baker, *USA TODAY* bestselling author

"Vanessa Miller's latest, *The Light on Halsey Street*, reawakened memories of my own growing up in the neighborhood of Bedford Stuyvesant in Brooklyn, which is a testament to her skill as a weaver of words. *The Light on Halsey Street* is not only a story of times gone by but the resiliency of friendship, family, and faith. This redemptive story of two friends, Lisa and Dana, poignantly demonstrates that we need not be a product of our circumstances and that the power to change is within all of us. Miller has created a timeless tale that will resonate long after the last word is read."

—Donna Hill, author of *Confessions in B-Flat*
and *I Am Ayah: The Way Home*

"Vanessa Miller serves a heartfelt and fulfilling, Brooklyn, New York, literary buffet in this 1980s coming-of-age journey through friendships and hardships, all nourished by 'the Light on Halsey Street.'"

—Pat G'Orge-Walker, *Essence* and national bestselling author
and creator of the Sister Betty Christian comedy series

What We Found in Hallelujah

"Two sisters reunite with their mother in Hallelujah, S.C., in the satisfying latest from Miller (*Something Good*) . . . The result is a potent testament to the power of faith and family in the face of tragedy."
—*Publishers Weekly*

"Three strong women, family drama, secrets, and a setting that works masterfully with the plot—Vanessa Miller is at her best in this book! The complex, nuanced relationships between mothers and daughters captured my attention and drew me in from the very first chapters. This book is a heartwarming treat that will leave readers hopeful and singing their own Hallelujah praise!"
—Michelle Stimpson, bestselling author

"In *What We Found in Hallelujah*, Vanessa Miller so brilliantly tells a heartwarming, page-turning, beautiful story about family secrets, mother-daughter relationships, forgiveness, and restored faith, and I thoroughly enjoyed this saga from beginning to end! So well done, Vanessa!"
—Kimberla Lawson Roby,
New York Times bestselling author

"Vanessa Miller has created a soul-searching story in *What We Found in Hallelujah*. Her ability to weed through the hard topics with grace, humor, and family makes her stories like no other. I was invested in the characters and felt like praising with them in the end."
—Toni Shiloh, author of *In Search of a Prince*

"Vanessa lays a solid foundation for the fictional town of Hallelujah. Her characters are rich in diverse personalities. She layers the plot with an artistic flair that readers race to the finish line for the big 'reveal.' Redemption and reconciliation are sweet in Hallelujah."
—Pat Simmons, award-winning and national bestselling
Christian author of the Jamieson Legacy series

Something Good

"The enjoyable if familiar latest from Miller (*Once Upon a Dream*) follows three women who are connected by a car accident . . . Prayer for 'something good' brings together the three women in an unlikely friendship, changing hearts and restoring marriages . . . Triumph of faith over tragedy will resonate with inspirational fans."

—*Publishers Weekly*

"*Something Good* by Vanessa Miller is a literary treat that captivated me from the first page. This story of three women drawn together by the unlikeliest of circumstances had me sitting back and realizing that no matter our backgrounds, no matter our struggles, when it's for God's purpose, we can come together. With characters that I could relate to and women who I wanted to win, I enjoyed *Something Good* from the beginning to the end."

—Victoria Christopher Murray, *New York Times*
bestselling author of *The Personal Librarian*

"Vanessa Miller's thoughtful and anointed approach to crafting *Something Good* made for a beautiful page-turner full of depth and hope."

—Rhonda McKnight, award-winning
author of *Unbreak My Heart*

"Vanessa Miller's latest novel is a relevant and heartwarming reminder that beauty for ashes is possible. This page-turning read inspires understanding, connection, and hope."

—Stacy Hawkins Adams, bestselling author

"This real-to-life story doesn't shy away from some hard issues of the modern world, but Miller is a master storyteller, who brings healing and redemption to her characters, and thus the reader, through the power of love and faith. I thoroughly enjoyed this book."

—Rachel Hauck, *New York Times* bestselling author

"Vanessa Miller's *Something Good* warms the heart with a vivacious tale of faith, redemption, and renewal. She masterly creates a sisterhood of unlikely friends who realize that there is something good, absolutely wonderful in accepting people as they are and believing they can be better."

—Vanessa Riley, bestselling author of *Island Queen*

"With bright threads of faith, resilience, and finding a way forward where there seems to be no way, Vanessa Miller weaves together the lives of three women in a beautiful tapestry of redemption and hope, friendship and found family. A story that shows, even when we think we've bolted all the doors, something good can find a way in."

—Lisa Wingate, #1 *New York Times* bestselling author of *Before We Were Yours*

"*Something Good* is much better than good. It's great! Vanessa Miller always delivers, and you know you will get unforgettable characters and a redemptive, heartwarming story that readers will find unputdownable. Get ready to laugh and to feel all the feels."

—Michelle Lindo-Rice, Harlequin Special Edition author

"Vanesa Miller's *Something Good* unveils the reality of living with guilt, shame, and the weight of unforgiveness through the lives of three women. This story will offer readers a beautiful perspective of redemptive healing and the measure of peace which comes with a forgiving heart."

—Jacquelin Thomas, national bestselling author of the Jezebel series and *Phoenix*

The
FILLING STATION

ALSO BY VANESSA MILLER

The American Queen
The Light on Halsey Street
What We Found in Hallelujah
Something Good

The

FILLING
STATION

a novel

Vanessa Miller

THOMAS NELSON
Since 1798

Library of Congress Cataloging-in-Publication Data

Names: Miller, Vanessa, author.
Title: The filling station: a novel / Vanessa Miller.
Description: Nashville, Tennessee: Thomas Nelson, 2025. | Summary: "From the author of *The American Queen* comes another important story about love, resilience, faith, and grit"—Provided by publisher.
Identifiers: LCCN 2024041344 (print) | LCCN 2024041345 (ebook) | ISBN 9781400344123 (paperback) | ISBN 9781400350179 (library binding) | ISBN 9781400344130 (epub) | ISBN 9781400344147
Subjects: LCGFT: Christian fiction. | Novels.
Classification: LCC PS3613.I5623 F55 2025 (print) | LCC PS3613.I5623 (ebook) | DDC 813/.6—dc23/eng/20240909
LC record available at https://lccn.loc.gov/2024041344
LC ebook record available at https://lccn.loc.gov/2024041345

Printed in the United States of America

25 26 27 28 29 LBC 5 4 3 2 1

This book is dedicated to my sister, Debra Clark,
who rescued me a few times in our youth.

And to the people of Greenwood, Oklahoma,
who had to rescue themselves from the toll
of death, destruction, and despair after the
1921 Tulsa Race Massacre.

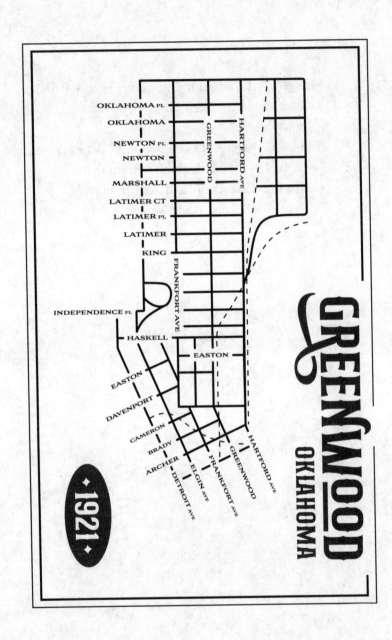

This is a fictional account of actual events that occurred in Oklahoma between 1921 and 1926.

Letter to the Reader

Dear Reader,

I am writing this letter in June 2024, exactly fifty years from the day I almost died. I had gone to a river with my cousins. I was just six years old, and I was amazed at how my cousins walked on the green moss and crossed over to the other side of the riverbank.

I tried to do the same but slipped into the river. My sister and my cousins ran toward the street and began screaming for help. One man, Sergeant John Clark, stopped his car and asked my family what they were so upset about. My sister, Debra Clark, told him, "My sister's drowning."

He ran down to the river, jumped in the water, and pulled me out. They said I had been underwater for about ten minutes. From the newspaper account, it took Sergeant John Clark about thirteen minutes to get me to breathe again.

Here's the thing that got me to thinking this week: I was in dire straits; I couldn't help myself if I wanted to. I thank God that someone came to my rescue. But in the story you are about to read, the Greenwood residents were in dire straits when a white mob came into their community and burned it down and shot hundreds of people as they tried to flee. Why didn't anyone come to their rescue that night? Where were the police? Where were the firefighters?

Where were the city officials who were supposed to help them rebuild after such a disaster caused by hateful humans? Where was the justice system when Greenwood needed it? As you read *The Filling Station*, I need you to keep in mind that this vicious massacre occurred during a time when Black bodies didn't matter.

So please understand that when I use the N-word in my historical novels (a word I would never use when writing a contemporary novel), it is not for shock value. It is to be authentic to the time period and to let the reader step into the shoes of those Black bodies that didn't matter much to those who would use and misuse them. Please also note that during this most unfortunate time in our history, some white residents in Tulsa regularly referred to Greenwood as "Little Africa," so you will see that term as well.

I hope you enjoy *The Filling Station*. I pray it fills you with not just historical truths but a deep appreciation for a resilient group of people who would not be destroyed.

This novel may leave you with questions—for example, after going through the most traumatic experience of your life and being emptied of everything you thought you knew, what will fill you up again? What will you turn to in order to keep moving forward in this thing called life? If you have questions like these, please go to my website, vanessamiller.com, for resources.

This book was a labor of love and honor. I hope you enjoy it.

Vanessa

Part 1

HOME NO MORE

Prologue

Greenwood! Lest you go unheralded, I sing a song of remembrance.

—*Wynonia Murray Bailey, Tulsa Race Massacre survivor*

1905

TULSA, OKLAHOMA

They stood on dried-up land that the authorities in Tulsa deemed good for nothing, worthless enough to sell to Negroes. As far as the eye could see, there was only open land cut by dust-ridden roads.

"I just don't understand it, Ottowa. What can we do out here that we can't do in Noble County?" Emma asked, putting a hand over her eyebrows and looking out at the expanse of the land, trying to see just how far down the way forty acres could be.

Taking his flat cap off his head, Ottowa Gurley, or as most people called him, O. W., tapped the short brim of the cap against his wool pants, breathed in the humid air, then blew it back out into the world. "I can be somebody here. Done run my course in Noble County." O. W. Gurley had taken part in the Cherokee Outlet Land Rush in Indian territory back in 1893 when the white folks in Oklahoma decided they needed money more than the Indians needed all the land that had been promised to them.

He felt bad for the way the Indians had been treated, but not too bad, since they had owned slaves just like the white folks before emancipation. He staked his claim in Perry, Noble County, Oklahoma, like a lot of others who'd come to these parts from the South.

He'd run for treasurer in the town where he'd purchased a plot of land and lost. Then opened a general store and became principal of the town's school. But the prospect of owning more land than he'd ever imagined led him eighty miles from Noble County. To the land that nobody wanted. Well, he wanted it and would gladly take it off their hands.

Still looking out at the land before them, Emma asked her husband, "But why so much? We don't need more than an acre."

"Use your imagination." He angled his foot toward the ground and used the tip of his shoe to etch an X in the dust. "Right here is where the boardinghouse you've been dreaming of will be." He pointed down the way. "I can build another grocery store right over there."

"My goodness, you are just full of grand ideas. But I still don't know what we gon' do with the rest of these acres you done bought."

Scratching his head, O. W. planted a gleeful smile on his face as dust kicked up from the ground and swirled around them in the light breeze. "The white folks don't want this land, but there's a whole heap of Negroes migrating from the South looking for land to buy. I s'pose we got enough to sell."

Emma held on to her long skirt as the wind threatened to lift it. Her eyes lit with the dawning of a new day, a new way of life. "You talking 'bout building our own community, with folks just like us?"

He put his arm around her shoulders and turned her so they were both gazing out toward the vast land before them. "That's exactly what I'm thinking on. Every inch of this land will be sold to colored folk. We're going to build businesses and homes that will be the envy of Tulsa. You just wait and see."

Chapter 1

There had been rumblings on the night of May 31, 1921, that there was going to be trouble in Little Africa. But we hadn't paid much attention to the rumors.

—*Veneice Dunn Sims, 1921 Tulsa Race Massacre survivor*

SIXTEEN YEARS LATER
MAY 31, 1921
GREENWOOD, OKLAHOMA

D id you hear about—"

"I don't like telling tales, but—"

Gossip flowed like a mighty river through Mrs. Mabel B. Little's beauty parlor. Margaret Justice and her younger sister, Evelyn, sat by the picture window, waiting to get dolled up for Evelyn's graduation from Booker T. Washington High School, taking place the next day.

They had been waiting for an hour, but Margaret was thankful they were at the parlor on a Tuesday afternoon rather than Thursday, when most of the housemaids who worked for the white folks in Tulsa had their day off and spent their weekly pay in the business district of Greenwood.

Mrs. Mabel's beauty parlor was a madhouse on Thursdays. But in truth, it was pretty busy five days of the week since she received her certification from Madam C. J. Walker, framed it, and nailed it to her wall for all to see.

"Okay, Evelyn, go over to the washbowl," Mrs. Mabel said as she took the shoulder cape off an older woman who was seated in her styling chair.

Margaret playfully shoved her sister. "I don't know why you get to go first. I'm the one paying."

"That's only 'cause Daddy gave you the money." Evelyn sat down in front of the washbowl and stuck her tongue out at Margaret.

"Maybe I won't pay for your style this week. Leave you here to help some of Mrs. Mabel's stylists wash hair and sweep up the floor."

"You two stop being silly before I tell your daddy." Mrs. Mabel slung a towel across her shoulder, then leaned Evelyn's head back toward the washbowl. "Your sister has a special day tomorrow. When you graduated from college a few months back, I took you first, 'member?"

Margaret laughed. "I was just messing with Evelyn. She should go first since she has to get back to school for the graduation rehearsal."

Mrs. Theola and her daughter, Brenda, were seated next to Margaret. Mrs. Theola's husband owned a diner and a boardinghouse on Archer Street. They lived on Detroit Street a few blocks down from them. Evelyn and Brenda had been the best of friends right up until high school.

Mrs. Theola touched Margaret's shoulder. "Do you mind if Brenda gets in Mrs. Mabel's chair after Evelyn? She has to get back to the school for graduation practice too."

Margaret had been away at Oklahoma Colored Agricultural and Normal University in Langston, Oklahoma, since her sister began high school. But Evelyn had written several letters, telling Margaret how Brenda had turned on her. "If I didn't have to meet up with my daddy directly after this, I'd let Brenda take my place in the chair, but I simply can't spare an extra minute today."

Brenda rolled her eyes, then turned her back to them. Margaret almost felt bad for denying Mrs. Theola's request, but she was right fine with it now.

Margaret glanced out the window as a farmer in a horse-drawn wagon loaded down with produce passed by, then within the space of a minute a Ford Model T with the top pulled back came down the street. The man in the automobile waved at some folks who were walking near the dress shop across the street.

Seeing the wagon and the car share the same road seemed like a conundrum. Like the world was bewitched and between the past and the present. But Margaret wasn't fazed by any of it. Since she graduated from college, her mind was set on what would be and all that she would accomplish before settling down to marry and have a few babies.

Much to her daddy's chagrin, Margaret had accepted a teaching position at Booker T. Washington High School. She would be teaching history when school started up again in the fall.

"I don't believe it one bit. Just some more lies being told," one of Mrs. Mabel's stylists said while putting rollers in her customer's hair.

"He shouldn't have gotten in that elevator with that white woman in the first place. What was he thinking?" another woman in the beauty parlor added.

Margaret turned from the window and listened as the women discussed the latest scuttlebutt. Her daddy was up in arms last night about Dick Rowland's arrest. Said it wasn't no way that boy touched that white woman. Just maybe fell into her when the elevator jerked and whatnot.

Mrs. Mabel lifted Evelyn's head from the washbowl and put a towel around her hair to soak up the water. Evelyn joined in the conversation. "I went to school with him before he dropped out. Seemed like a nice boy to me."

"Never should've dropped out. Just wasting his life out here shining shoes," Mrs. Theola said.

Margaret didn't know the kid, but she hoped he would not soon be hanging from a tree, like her daddy said. "Well, I'm praying for him," she told the group.

Mrs. Mabel lifted a hand to the heavens as she and Evelyn walked to her styling chair. "Keep it up. That boy needs all the prayers he can get."

The other women kept chatting on about Rowland's predicament while Mrs. Mabel heated up the Marcel curling iron after drying Evelyn's hair. Her sister wanted the Marcel waves, which were similar to finger waves, but instead of forming the waves against the scalp, the Marcel curling iron was used to crimp the waves and allow women with longer hair to let their hair hang loose.

When Evelyn turned toward her, Margaret was struck by an overwhelming sense of days gone by and things changing all too fast, kind of like the horse-and-buggy riders and automobile drivers being on the same street.

"What?" Evelyn patted the waves. "You don't like it?"

Margaret's voice caught in her throat. The edges of her eyelids glistened with wetness, blurring her vision. Her sister normally got her hair washed and pressed, with no extra frills.

Evelyn's long hair would hang straight, or she'd pull it into a ponytail.

"She's probably used to you looking so plain Jane that you've rendered her speechless," Brenda said with a smirk.

Margaret bristled at that smirk. Evelyn turned away from the insult without giving as good as she got. How many times had her sister let this turncoat of an ex-friend disparage her? The letters Evelyn sent were always complaints about how terrible Brenda was but never anything about how she set the girl straight. "I love it. But you're beautiful with your hair straightened or crimped." Margaret eyed Brenda, let her lip curl a bit, then turned back to her sister. "You just looked so much like Mama when you turned around, I . . . I . . . You're beautiful, Evie."

Evelyn grinned like a Cheshire cat as she got out of the chair and took off the cape. "Your turn."

Mrs. Theola stood, soon followed by her daughter. "I don't think Brenda and I can wait much longer."

Margaret sat down at the washbowl and loudly announced, "I think I want pin curls this time."

Brenda rolled her eyes again. Threw up her hands. "We'll never get out of here."

Mrs. Mabel pointed to the other workers in the parlor. "I have three other stylists. Brenda can sit in one of their chairs and get her hair done, probably before I'm finished with Margaret."

Brenda sat back down, pulled her mother with her. "We'll wait."

After getting her certification, Mrs. Mabel became so busy that she had to hire three other stylists. But her regular customers refused to sit in any other chair in the parlor. Mrs. Mabel had the touch. People in Greenwood swore that their

hair grew long and thick due to Mrs. Mabel's personal connection with the Lord and that Madam C. J. Walker certification.

An hour later, Margaret and Evelyn left the beauty parlor,
headed home to change for their evening activities. Margaret
breathed in the fresh scent of lilacs and the herbaceous peo-
nies as they walked toward Mount Zion Baptist Church at the
corner of Easton and North Elgin. She waved at Pastor R. A.
Whittaker as he stood at the front entrance of the church.

"Hey, Miss Margaret. Hey, Miss Evelyn. I sure hope to see
y'all at church this Sunday. We'll be having our own reception
for all of you graduates."

Evelyn waved while Margaret said, "Of course we'll be at
church this Sunday. Will you be able to make Evelyn's graduation tomorrow?"

"Wouldn't miss it," Pastor Whittaker told them.

Passing the church, Evelyn said, "My hair will never hold up
all the way to Sunday. Guess I'll be plain Jane again."

Margaret's chest heaved as hot indignation blew out of her
nostrils. She grabbed Evelyn's arm and pulled her to a stop.
"Why do you regurgitate the words of a clown?"

"Brenda said—"

"Don't you dare let that girl's words slip from your mouth
again." Margaret looked into her sister's beautiful brown eyes,
then touched the caramel skin that was so much like their
mother's. Evelyn not only looked like their mother; she had
the same gentle spirit.

"Listen to me and listen good: You are beautiful, and you are
something special. You will set this world on fire one day, and
don't you let anyone tell you different."

Evelyn lowered her head. "Since I was a little girl, all you've
told me is how special and strong I am, but I don't feel that way
at all."

At five seven, Margaret was nearly a foot taller than Evelyn. She lifted her sister's chin with her index finger. "Evie, don't you know how sweet, loving, and caring you are? You can sew like nobody's business. You and Mama . . . y'all the only two I ever seen that can take a piece of scrap material and make it into something chic and fashionable. That's pretty special, if I have to say so myself."

"Speaking of that. I need you to try on the dress I made for you to wear to my graduation." Evelyn grabbed Margaret's hand, and they ran all the way home.

Evelyn and Margaret both had desks in their bedrooms. Whereas Margaret kept her books and papers on hers, Evelyn kept their mother's Singer sewing machine on her desk. The sewing machine had been a prized possession for Velma Justice. She'd tried to teach Margaret how to design and sew her own clothes, but Margaret hadn't been able to get the hang of it, nor did she have the desire to learn.

Evelyn, however, was born with their mother's gift for sewing and clothing design. Glancing around Evelyn's room, Margaret saw dresses hanging from curtain rods, strewn across chairs, laid out on her bed, and stuffed in her closet. "When do you find the time to make all these clothes?"

Evelyn shrugged. "I don't know . . . I sew when I have free time." She giggled. "And I'm graduating tomorrow, so you no longer have to worry that my designs are getting in the way of my studies."

The girls' mother had passed away nine years ago. They'd been devastated and heartbroken. Even though Margaret was only four years older than Evelyn, she had been thirteen at the time and had instantly taken on a mothering role. Someone had to look out for her sister while their dad was working.

"Here. Try this on."

Evelyn handed her a white knee-length sundress with a high waist. Margaret tried on the dress. She loved the feel of it on her skin. Perfect. "How you manage to get my fit just right every time, I'll never know."

Evelyn rolled her eyes. "I have your measurements, silly."

"Thank you. I am going to look lovely in this beautiful airy dress tomorrow."

"The white of the dress looks good next to your brown skin tone."

Margaret smiled her agreement. She'd taken her complexion from her daddy, who was only slightly darker than the brown paper bags they used at the grocery store. "Well, I love it."

Evelyn hugged her sister. "I'm so glad you're back home."

"I'm home, and you'll be leaving soon." Margaret shook her head.

Evelyn took her cap and gown off the bed and put them on. "We have the whole summer before I leave, so let's make sure to spend lots and lots of time together."

Stepping back, Margaret gave Evelyn the once-over. "I can hardly believe you're old enough to graduate." Margaret wrapped her arms around her sister. "I'll miss you dearly when you leave."

Hugging Margaret back, Evelyn said, "I have the best big sister in the world. I love you so much."

Letting the moment linger before she let go, Margaret was once again reminded of Evie's kind heart. She didn't care if her sister gave as good as she got as she drank in the love from Evie's embrace. Regardless of how the world changed, with its automobiles and kids not being kids anymore, she prayed that Evie's heart would remain the same.

Chapter 2

With joy, we once did greet you, but with sadness, we depart, and though we are to leave you, we go with an aching heart.

—*1921 class poem for graduation, Booker T. Washington High School*

After changing into the ankle-length African-print dress Evelyn had made for her, Margaret left the house, heading for Justice for All Grocery Store to meet up with her daddy.

Mr. John Clifton was in his driveway, bent over in front of his drop-top Ford T with a sudsy towel in his hand.

Margaret waved at him. "Getting your car all spiffed up, I see."

"Got to take care of the things that matter," he told her while wiping down his driver's side door.

Mr. Clifton owned the dry cleaner's next door to her daddy's grocery store, and he kept things spiffed and clean as a whistle over there too. Daddy said he was thankful that Mr. Clifton cared about his property.

A little farther down the street, Margaret saw Mrs. Johnson chasing behind one of her five children. The two older boys tried to help, but the three younger were too fast for them.

"Don't y'all want to go out to supper with Daddy this evening?" Mrs. Johnson tried to cajole them.

The Johnsons had a white house with black shutters. She grew red roses in her front yard, which ran up the trellis on the porch. The three-year-old pulled off a petal as she escaped, opened the gate of the wooden fence, and ran out onto the sidewalk, right into Margaret. She wrapped her arms around Margaret's beautiful dress.

Mrs. Johnson's hand went to her mouth. "Oh, my dear Lord, I'm so sorry."

Margaret picked up the rambunctious child and handed her to her mother. "Good evening, Mrs. Johnson." With a giggle she added, "I hope you make it to supper."

"I probably should stay home, but Mr. Johnson has the day off and wants to take us to Huff's."

Mr. Johnson was a delivery driver for C. B. Bottling. He worked long hours, but Mrs. Johnson said he brought home enough money to keep the family in clean clothes and buy new shoes for the children each year, so she was content.

Opening the screen door wide, her husband called out to them, "What's all this fuss out here? Get back in this house and let your mama clean y'all up."

Mr. Johnson was a tall, imposing man. The children stopped running around and "yes, sirred" themselves back into the house.

Margaret continued on her way. She was only a few blocks away from the grocery store. She had worked with her daddy at the store in the evenings and during the summer months before going off to college.

She'd had designs on taking over the grocery store or opening one of her own. But while in college, she began thinking on other businesses like real estate. Mr. O. W. Gurley and Mr.

J. B. Stradford owned buildings in Greenwood, and they leased them out to business owners. That sounded like a good model to follow. But she also liked the idea of owning a place where she could work and be able to help members of the community with their needs.

Confusion had set in so strong that she'd finally told her daddy she would just teach for a spell. That's when her daddy got her a summer job working with Mrs. Loula Williams at her confectionery shop. He thought being mentored by a businesswoman such as the renowned Mrs. Williams would change her mind about "teaching rather than doing," as Daddy put it.

Like many of the business owners in Greenwood, Daddy had taken out a loan from Mr. Stradford to open the grocery store but had paid back every dime a few years ago. Now that he owned the store free and clear, Daddy was expanding the building since he had unused land behind it.

The contractors and the supplies had cost him a boatload of money, but he was confident he'd have the funds for Evie's school fees once the investments he'd made with Mr. Stradford paid off.

A few customers were milling around the store when she arrived. One was in the canned goods section, another in produce, squeezing all the fruit for ripeness. Margaret shook her head. Mrs. Pearl would never change. She was their next-door neighbor and made sure to do her grocery shopping at Justice, but she'd told Margaret time and time again that she wasn't going to be cheated by nobody, not even Henry Justice.

Margaret waved. "Hey, Mrs. Pearl."

Mrs. Pearl waved back at her. "Well, aren't you just the bee's knees. Love that dress."

Margaret twirled around. The dress swung and swayed this way and that, showing off her long, shapely legs.

"Just you be careful not to attract some of the riffraff running in and out of that billiard room down the street," Mrs. Pearl told her.

Since their mother passed, Mrs. Pearl had taken it upon herself to look after them. Margaret loved all the smothered pork chop meals and especially the mac and cheese and fried chicken. But sometimes . . . . "I'm headed out with Daddy today, so I'm sure he'll keep the riffraff away."

Mrs. Pearl turned to Margaret's father, who was standing behind the counter, eyes focused on the newspaper. "Good," she said. "I'm glad Henry will be keeping an eye on you tonight."

Shaking her head, Margaret walked over to her daddy. She looked down at the *Tulsa Tribune* to see what had captured his attention so.

The headline on the front of the paper read, "Nab Negro for Attacking Girl in an Elevator." They'd put that Rowland boy's business in the paper before investigating the incident. What if he wasn't guilty of what they said? But in white folks' minds, colored folks were always guilty.

The *Tulsa Tribune* was not the preferred newspaper in Greenwood. She fancied the *Tulsa Star*, which was published weekly by A. J. Smitherman. That newspaper had warned Blacks of a possible lynching if a Black man was arrested and taken to the Tulsa jail.

Looking into her daddy's transfixed eyes, Margaret figured he, too, was recalling A. J. Smitherman's words after a white mob had forced their way into the Tulsa jail, taken Roy Belton out, and hung him for killing a taxi driver just last year. Smitherman said that if they could so easily exact mob justice and hang a white man, a Black man didn't stand a chance.

Turning the newspaper over, Margaret waved a hand in front of her daddy's face. "Don't think what you're thinking. Lightning won't strike twice in the same place."

Rubbing his eyes, Henry Justice turned to his daughter. "Wish you was right. But that lightning will strike as many times as it wants. And believe me, them white boys are going to hit hard on this one."

"I don't want to think about things like this. Evelyn is graduating tomorrow, and you promised to take me to the Dreamland Theater this evening."

Henry nodded. Put a hand on Margaret's cheek. "You and I haven't been to Dreamland together in over a year." His eyes brightened. "Yes, let's go."

Grinning, Margaret backed away from the counter as her daddy threw a set of keys to the clerk who was restocking the grocery shelves. "Lock up. I'm going to take in a movie with my oldest."

The clerk put the keys in his pocket. "Yes, sir."

The sun sparkled like diamonds as Henry and Margaret walked down Archer, headed for Greenwood Avenue. Margaret wiped the sweat from her brow while passing by fine establishments like Satisfactory Tailoring, Jackson Undertaking, the Earl Real Estate Company, Nails Bros. Shoe Market, and Liberty Plumbing. The businesses in Greenwood supplied needed services to its residents.

The white folks on the other side of the Frisco tracks didn't want Negroes shopping in their fine and upstanding establishments. Their bigotry only fueled the success and growth of Greenwood as colored folks shook the dust off their feet and spent their money with business owners who were only too happy to take their hard-earned dollars. "It's such a beautiful day," Margaret declared.

Glancing up at the sky, Henry nodded in agreement. "Right fine week for a graduation."

"Oh, and, Daddy, don't be shocked when you see Evelyn. She has a new hairdo, and it makes her look so much like Mama that I almost cried."

"Your sister has always favored Velma."

"Yes, but now she looks like the grown-up version of Mama, and I simply wasn't ready for it."

He stopped walking. "Do you think I was ready for you to grow into the woman you are?" Putting a hand to her cheek, he said, "You used to be my little Maggie-Pie. Now . . ." His hand dropped, and they continued down the street. "Things just been happening so fast; I can't keep up with it. Next thing I know you'll be married and off with your own family."

Margaret wondered about marriage . . . and babies . . . and George Martin. They had gone steady all through high school. He promised to marry her when they finished college. But George hadn't bothered to attend her college graduation and had enrolled in the advanced degree program at Straight University in New Orleans, Louisiana. How was she supposed to build a life with a man who preferred being six hundred miles away from her?

"You needn't worry about those wedding bells anytime soon."

Henry put an arm around Margaret's shoulders as they continued down Greenwood Avenue. "I'm gon' have a talk with George. His daddy tells me he'll be in town tomorrow for his annual backyard barbecue."

Lifting her stubborn chin, Margaret said, "I haven't heard from George, so I wouldn't know."

"I'll make George hold up his end of the bargain, you can be sure of that." Henry patted her on the back as if forcing a man to marry his daughter was the grandest thing he'd ever thought of.

Margaret was about to speak her mind on the subject, but they'd arrived in front of the Stradford Hotel. "I need to speak with J. B. about one of my investments. I won't be long."

J. B. Stradford was one of the wealthiest men in Greenwood. He owned a hotel, boardinghouses, and billiard halls. But mostly, he liked seeing colored businesses prosper, so he loaned out money to start-up businesses. Daddy liked that about J. B. Stradford; she guessed that was why he'd started investing with him.

A soft wind blew, billowing her dress behind her. Margaret touched a hand to her head, making sure the pin curls were staying in place. Looking to the sky, she wondered where the wind had come from. It was almost June; wind didn't blow like that when the sun beat down so hot and humid.

She entered the Stradford Hotel with her daddy, taking in the sight of the chandeliers hanging from the twenty-foot ceiling, the waxed hardwood floors, and the flowers that adorned tables in the corridor. People came from all around the country to experience the opulence the Stradford offered.

"Well, well, well." J. B. Stradford stood in the entryway with arms outstretched. His booming voice carried the weight of a man of importance. "I haven't seen Miss Margaret in a month of Sundays. Where you been keeping her?" he asked Henry, then put an arm around Margaret's shoulders and brought her in close for a hug.

"I've been around," she answered for herself. "Just haven't been this far into the business district lately."

O. W. Gurley walked over and gave her a hug also. "It's good to see you, Margaret. You're a credit to Greenwood."

"High praise indeed, coming from you, Mr. Gurley."

A. J. Smitherman entered the lobby of the hotel and approached them with a newspaper folded under his arm. "Gentlemen." He then nodded in her direction. "Margaret."

"Hi, Mr. Smitherman."

He turned away from her, looking hurried, like he needed to get the news out and couldn't abide any distractions.

Her daddy pointed toward a chair just outside of the dining hall. "Have a seat there, Margaret. Let me speak with these men, and then we'll be on our way."

Margaret took a seat as her daddy continued into the dining hall and sat down at a table with three of the most important men in Greenwood. By the way Smitherman threw the newspaper on the table and jabbed a finger at it, Margaret figured they were up in arms about that Rowland boy.

Trying not to poke her nose in her daddy's business, Margaret adjusted her seat so she was looking toward the entrance. That's when she caught sight of Gayle Johnson entering the hotel. She was wearing a pale pink day dress with cap sleeves and a pleated skirt. Margaret stood and hugged her. She hadn't seen her friend since they graduated from college a few months ago.

"I can't believe you're in town. What's the occasion?"

Gayle answered, "Meeting my fiancé's folks this week. I'll stay at the Stradford tonight, then have breakfast with them in the morning."

"I wish I'd known you were coming to town. You could have stayed at our house."

Gayle's eyes danced with delight. She lifted her head toward the chandeliers. "I couldn't resist checking into the Stradford. This place is swanky. I had to experience it on my first trip to Tulsa."

Booker T. Washington had dubbed Greenwood "Negro Wall Street" due to the flourishing business district. Many people traveled to Greenwood just to see how colored folks supported each other and prospered.

There were plenty of working-class folks in Greenwood. But the travelers didn't come to see the washerwomen or the house-maids. They wanted to rub elbows with men like her daddy, O. W. Gurley, and J. B. Stradford and women like Mrs. Loula Williams.

Gayle glanced around the foyer with a stepping-in-high-cotton smile planted on her face. "Just look at this place. Have you ever seen a hotel this fine for Negroes?"

The Stradford was a vision indeed. With fifty-four sleeping rooms, a dining hall, a gambling room, a saloon, and a large hall for events such as live music, it was the grandest hotel for Negroes in all of Oklahoma. Margaret nodded as her daddy walked back over to her. "It's a fine place, indeed."

Henry held out his left arm to Margaret. "You ready to go?"

Looping her arm with her daddy's, Margaret said, "Yes, sir." She waved goodbye to Gayle. "Hopefully I'll get a chance to see you again before you leave town."

"It's hot out here, and this cap and gown is making it worse," said Glenda Jones, Evelyn's best friend since the ninth grade. She wiped the sweat that had gathered on her neck just above the collar of her blouse.

Evelyn laughed at her friend. "I'm savoring every moment. I worked hard to get this diploma, and I can't wait to show it to Margaret."

Evelyn and Glenda were standing outside of Booker T. Washington High School with the other graduating students. They were lined up by the entrance, waiting to practice their march into the auditorium where they would receive their diplomas the next day.

Anna Goodwin, the class president; John Claybon, the class secretary; and Phineas Thompson, the class treasurer, stood at the front of the line. They would lead the procession as all eighteen graduates marched into the school auditorium.

"You act like you're valedictorian. That diploma isn't going to impress Margaret, not when she just graduated with her bachelor's degree," Glenda said.

"Margaret stayed on my case about sewing when I should be studying. My grades have never been good enough for her. But she'll be so happy to see my diploma, she just might cry."

Clarence Jones, Glenda's cousin, was standing in front of them. He turned toward Evelyn. His eyes sparked with a last-chance desperation. "My mom is going to cry when she sees my diploma," he said, then quickly added, "I think the two of us need to grab an ice cream at Williams' Confectionery to celebrate."

Evelyn shook her head. "No can do. My daddy isn't home right now, and I would need to ask his permission before going anywhere."

"She's such a baby." Brenda had been lined up behind Evelyn and Glenda, but the moment Clarence started talking to Evelyn, Brenda hopped out of line and came to stand next to him. She looped her arm around his. "I can go for ice cream." Rolling her eyes heavenward, she added, "I don't have to ask for permission to hang out with friends."

Evelyn's lips twitched and itched to tell Brenda that she was hateful to her for no good reason. She had never wanted anything to do with Clarence Jones. Brenda could have him. But instead, she turned back to Glenda and said, "Tomorrow can't come fast enough. I'm ready to be done with this school."

The door opened, and Principal Ellis Walker Woods, along with a few of the teachers, stepped out. They had been smiling earlier when they first helped everyone line up, but now, worry lines etched their faces.

"What did we do?" Evelyn glanced around. Everyone was lined up, just as Principal Woods requested—well, everyone except Brenda, who still had an arm wrapped around Clarence's.

"I don't know," Glenda whispered out the side of her mouth. "Maybe someone didn't pass the final exam, and they're about to remove them from the line."

Evelyn wasn't the slightest bit worried about that. She may not study as hard as Margaret, but she knew she passed her exams.

Principal Woods raised a hand to get everyone's attention. "Thank you for cooperating with us and lining up as we asked. I am sorry to inform you that we will not be able to continue with the graduation rehearsal. I need everyone to go straight home. There is trouble in downtown Tulsa, and we don't want any of you to get hurt."

Restless teenagers yelled out their complaints.

But Principal Woods was not moved. "Go home. We'll see you all back here in the morning."

Chapter 3

It was reported among white people to go to the county courthouse and lynch the boot-black. This report spread over "Little Africa" and . . . crowds of Negroes began forming.

—*Tulsa Daily World, June 1, 1921*

A little ways down Greenwood, Margaret entered Williams' Confectionery with her daddy. It was a three-level building. Mrs. Loula rented out office space on the third level. She and her husband and son lived on the second level, and the confectionery shop was on the first level. Candy, popcorn, ice cream, beverages, and many more sugary treats were sold here. It was a top hangout for teens and young couples wanting to grab an ice cream cone or a cool drink on hot summer days.

"What flavor do you want?" Henry asked Margaret once they reached the front counter.

Margaret's eyes roamed from one side of the shop to the other. "I don't know if I want ice cream anymore. There's just too much to choose from in here."

"What about some popcorn? You can eat it while we watch the movie."

Henry requested one scoop of vanilla ice cream in a cone while Margaret decided against the popcorn and loaded up on candy.

"Margaret Justice, it is so good to see you, my dear." Loula Williams entered the confectionery shop adorned in a bright red dress that moved back and forth with every step. Several strands of pearls sparkled around her neck. Her long brown hair was pinned up into a bun on top of her head. She was the picture of excellence.

"Hey, Mrs. Loula. How've you been?" The two women hugged.

"You know I'm always right as rain." Loula hugged Henry then turned back to Margaret with hands planted on her hips. "And what's this I'm hearing about you taking a teaching position?"

"Yes, ma'am. I've accepted a teaching position at Booker T. I begin in the fall."

Loula wagged a finger in her face. "Don't forget what I told you."

How could she ever forget? Margaret had asked how Loula had been able to do so much in this day and age. Just as she'd done back then, Mrs. Loula stood in front of her like a force to be reckoned with. Her daddy stepped aside as she looked heavenward with an outstretched, open hand and said, "Margaret, you can't catch some of that magic dust that falls from the sky if you're not aiming for the stars."

Then she snapped her hand shut as if some of the magic had just fallen. She took Margaret's hand, opened it, and released the magic dust into it. "Keep reaching, my young protégée. Don't settle for what the world will give you. Take what you will and leave the rest for them."

Grinning at this force of a woman who stood regal and immovable before her, Margaret made a show of unclamping her purse and putting the magic dust inside. "One thing at a time, Mrs. Loula. We're out for a movie tonight. I have plenty of time to take over the world. Just wait . . . I'll make you proud soon enough."

Loula patted her on the back. "Enjoy your evening. I'm also planning to head to Dreamland to check on things over there." As she was about to walk away, she added, "I pray it will be uneventful with the menfolk getting all stirred up." Shaking her head, she moved on to greet other customers.

"What's she talking about, Daddy?" Then she thought back to seeing her dad huddled together with the men back at the hotel. "What were you talking about at the Stradford? Mr. Smitherman seemed really upset."

Henry frowned. Slapped his hat against his pants. "Sometimes Loula talks too much." He took Margaret by the arm. "Come on. Let's get to this movie."

They left the confectionery and went next door to the seven-hundred-seat theater. The Dreamland was the pride of Greenwood. They were able to see live musicals, theatrical revues, and silent movies. Margaret had spent many afternoons at this theater with George or some of her school friends.

Popping a piece of candy in her mouth, Margaret and her daddy took their seat, marveling at the silent movie on the big screen. Margaret savored her candy and giggled at the funny scenes, then leaned in for some of the other scenes that simply took her breath away.

But in the midst of a giggle, the projectionist stopped the movie and turned on the lights. Margaret turned to her daddy; he shrugged.

A few people yelled, "Turn the movie back on."

Mrs. Loula and her husband, John Williams, the owner of the local auto body shop, stepped onto the stage. Mr. John had been the first Black man to own a car in Greenwood. Now it seemed cars were everywhere.

"We're closing for the night," John Williams yelled out to them. "There's trouble down at the courthouse."

Mrs. Loula clutched her pearls tightly with one hand and shooed them with the other, fear dancing in her eyes. "All of y'all, go home and don't come back out for the rest of the night."

People pushed and shoved to get out of the theater. Margaret lost her shoe and almost toppled over as someone pushed her from behind when she stopped to put it back on. "Hey! Watch out," she yelled, then turned to push back.

Her daddy grabbed hold of her hand. "We gotta go."

Adrenaline raced through her as the two of them scurried down the street. Her mind was scattered as she tried to make sense of what was happening. They had been seated in the theater, laughing and taking in a movie. Before that, her dad had enjoyed an ice cream cone. They held conversations with friends. Now the street was filling with Greenwood residents, running and shouting, trying to get anywhere—everywhere—but there.

"Mommy, I'm scared," a little girl said as her mother picked her up and ran down the street with her.

A man ran out of the billiard hall brandishing a gun. "They done it now. Them white folks 'bout to get the fight they been asking for."

Margaret heard another one say, "They thought they was gon' lynch that Rowland boy without us saying a word about it. Now they know."

Margaret's hand slipped out of her dad's. The air was thick with fear. She spun in circles, her dress billowing around her like a vibrant kaleidoscope of colors. Bits and pieces of words wafted around her as angry and tired-of-being-tired men passed by like bullets being shot out of a gun.

"What's happening?" Margaret's eyes got big. She put her hands over her head, not sure which way to go or what to do next.

Her daddy shook her. "Listen to me. I need you to snap out of it. Go home and check on your sister."

Go home? "Yes! Yes! Let's go home."

The Stradford Hotel was in front of them. Mr. Stradford was standing outside holding a shotgun, looking like he was chewing on nails and ready to spit them out at any trouble coming his way. "Just let 'em try to destroy my property. I got something for 'em."

Her daddy shooed her forward. "Go on home. I got things to do."

Margaret reached for him. Clawing at his arm, she screamed, "No! No! You can't stay out here. Let's go home together."

"Henry, come on! Grab a gun inside and help me hold down the fort." Mr. Stradford waved her daddy over.

"Don't help him, Daddy. Come home with me." Margaret tried as she might to pull her daddy forward. Away from Greenwood Avenue. Away from men with guns . . . away from outrage and "we'll show them." "This isn't your fight. Don't go with them."

Fear crept up Margaret's spine and lodged there like a cancer. Her eyes shifted this way and that. She'd never seen Greenwood in the state it was in tonight. If she let go of her daddy, would she lay eyes on him again?

Slipping away from her, Henry shouted, "I said go. You do as I tell you. Go on home and see about your sister."

He turned his back to her as he obeyed Mr. Stradford's command. "You don't owe him nothing, Daddy. You already paid every dime Mr. Stradford loaned you, so don't be a fool."

In the midst of all the tumult in the street, with people running past her, yelling and screaming, Margaret lost sight of her daddy. She touched her hand to her heart as pain shot through it.

Tears burned Margaret's eyes. Should she follow her daddy into that hotel? The sound of gunfire rang out. Margaret wiped her eyes as the crowd pushed her forward. She wanted her daddy, but her mind turned to Evelyn and the state her sister might be in. She pressed her way through the crowd, made it to Archer Street, then turned right onto North Detroit Street.

The cacophonous chaos outside was suffocating as people rushed around and pushed each other, their voices a deafening blend of noise that she desperately wanted to drown out. Every shouted word felt like a physical blow, each one a reminder of the cruel reality she was trying to escape.

It was as if they were preparing for a war. Men were stationing themselves at the end of her block and around the corner. They all had weapons. And in a way, the sight of the menfolk on patrol in her neighborhood gave her a bit of comfort.

She ran home and unlocked the front door. "Evie?"

Evelyn opened her bedroom door and ran into her sister's arms. "They sent us home from Booker T. We didn't get to practice our graduation march or anything. They say a riot broke out downtown."

"It's terrible out there. I'm glad you're home and safe."

But as Margaret said those words, she could hear the sound of her heart pounding. Her stomach churned and twisted in knots. Was her daddy safe? Were any of them truly safe?

Chapter 4

The wholesale destruction of property, life and limb in
that section of the city occupied by negroes testifies to
a one-sided battle.

—*Maurice Willows, Red Cross Disaster Relief Report*

Margaret and Evie huddled in the living room for hours.
Margaret thought about picking up a book to kill
some time, but the only books on the coffee table were *The
Talented Tenth* by W. E. B. Du Bois and *Up from Slavery* by
Booker T. Washington, and she had read both books numerous
times.

A framed photo of her mother and father sat on the mantel,
just above the fireplace. Where was her daddy? Why hadn't he
come home by now? All the commotion outside was straining
her nerves.

Shuffling footsteps and shouts of "Go this way," or "Check
behind that house," could be heard outside as the men worked
to secure Greenwood. By midnight, the noise quieted down.
Things were calm once again. Her sister glanced over at her
with hope lighting her eyes. "Daddy should be home soon."

"Things have settled down out there. Maybe you should get
some sleep."

Evie pointed toward Margaret's hair. "What are you going to do with that? You've sweated your hair out."

Margaret touched the bouffant puff on top of her head. It was thick and coarse from all the running and sweating. "I guess I'll be a plain Jane and put my hair in a ponytail."

Evie *tsk-tsk*ed her. "None of that negative talk. You are special and beautiful no matter how you wear your hair."

The first giggle since the lights came on at the movie house escaped Margaret's lips. "Don't feed my own line back to me."

A small laugh escaped from Evelyn. But the night had been too stressful to hold much merriment. Evelyn glanced toward the front door. "Everything's going to be okay, right?"

Margaret nodded. "It has to be." Margaret's eyes drooped, and she yawned. Evie went into her bedroom and brought back blankets for both of them.

"I was trying to stay awake for Daddy."

"Well, I'm plum tuckered out." Evie curled up on the settee.

Margaret's head flopped against the arm of the sofa as sleep won the battle. Late into the night she sniffed, rubbed her nostrils. Turning over, dreaming . . . She smelled barbecue on that ancient firepit Mr. Martin used for his annual backyard gatherings. Margaret's multicolored sundress fluttered in the light breeze of the sun-drenched day.

"Fire! Fire!"

The covers were ripped off. Margaret shot up. She turned her head, eyes blinking, looking for the backyard barbecue. She sniffed the air again.

"Get up, girls. We got to get out of this house before that fire latches on and burns us to ashes."

What fire? Margaret rubbed her eyes. Why was Mrs. Pearl in their house? What was burning? Did she smell smoke?

Evelyn peeped out the front window. "People running around outside like the devil chasing 'em."

"It's that green-eyed devil, alright. They out there looting and burning down our homes like thieves in the night." Despair rested on Mrs. Pearl's shoulders and weighed them down.

"Where's Daddy?" Margaret slipped on a pair of shoes and ran through the three-bedroom house, eyes scanning each room for Henry Justice. Her daddy would know what to do.

Mrs. Pearl bit down on her lip. "He must still be out there trying to handle this dustup. A lot of our men been out all night."

Margaret's eyes lit with fire and fear. She ran back into her room. If the house was about to burn down, she couldn't leave her purse. It would be too much of a hassle to replace her passport.

After the war ended in 1918, the government instituted a policy on passports for European travel, and Margaret was saving her money to make such a trip. How else could she teach the children in her class about the world if she didn't experience a bit of it?

She heard Evelyn scream, "I need my clothes."

"You girls better get out here this instant."

"I'm coming, Mrs. Pearl." Margaret pulled the purse strap over her head, letting it rest on her right shoulder while the purse pressed against her left hip, then rushed back to the living room.

Evelyn had a paper bag in her hand. She peeked behind the curtain in the living room again. "I see men with guns." She pulled the curtain closed, eyes bulging, looking like she'd just seen the boogeyman. "What are those white men doing in our neighborhood with guns?"

As if in answer, gunfire went off like rockets going to the moon. Mrs. Pearl ducked and then pulled Margaret and Evelyn down on the floor with her.

"Oh, my sweet Jesus." Mrs. Pearl steepled her hands and called on the Lord.

"What's going on?" Evelyn scooted closer to Margaret.

"Why are they shooting?" The noise outside sounded like firecrackers pop, pop, popping. Margaret's ears perked to screams and folks stampeding past their house. Her eyes went wild as she tried to make sense of the nightmare playing out while they were awake. "We can't go out there."

Mrs. Pearl coughed as smoke billowed like clouds around them. "We can't stay in here either." She pointed toward the ceiling.

Evelyn's pretty brown eyes widened with alarm, her hand jutting upward. A guttural scream escaped her lips, piercing the air like a sharp blade. "Fire!"

"Grab your sister's hand." Mrs. Pearl gripped Margaret and crawled toward the front door, while Margaret kept a tight grasp on Evelyn's arm.

With each movement, the smoke grew thicker and the flames drew closer. The three of them crawled toward the front door like chain links, desperate to escape the inferno that surrounded them. Margaret's heart raced as Mrs. Pearl reached for the doorknob, unsure if it was safe to leave. Should they wait for help or risk facing the unknown dangers outside?

With trembling fingers, Mrs. Pearl opened the door. Margaret prayed they were making the right decision. Mr. Clifton ran over to them when they pulled the door open. "Let me help you get these girls out of here. Them white boys trying to kill us."

"This is crazy." Mrs. Pearl's eyes grew wide as she looked around. "Why they destroying our homes like this?"

Still clad in her multicolored African print dress, Margaret's mind spun wildly. She turned and turned and turned. A white man ran out of Mrs. Marley's house, holding her prized fur coat in the air and yelling, "I'm giving this to my wife."

Should she have brought some items with them? Should she have let Evelyn bring more? What if these thieves took all of Evelyn's beautiful dresses? As her mind mulled going back to the house and sidestepping the flames to get more of their items, a white man kicked in the door of one of her neighbors' homes and threw a fiery torch inside.

Another white man with a torch in one hand, a gun in the other, and evil swirling in his eyes cackled, "We're burning Little Africa down."

It was no secret that the white folks on the other side of the Frisco tracks had been calling Greenwood Little Africa for as long as she could remember. Even though all of the residents had been born right here in America. But being associated with Africa didn't bother Margaret one bit . . . It was the association with hateful men who would do harm to them for the least infraction that left a sour taste in her mouth.

Fear gripped her community as people ran down the street, some holding their hands above their heads, others holding as many of their possessions as they could carry. With trepidation guiding their way, Margaret, Evelyn, and Mrs. Pearl followed their neighbors as white men with guns chased them down the street, away from their homes . . . away from everything they knew.

Mr. Clifton ran back across the street as a white man broke the window on his car and threw a lit torch inside.

Margaret glanced down the other side of the street as the same chaotic scene played out no matter which way she turned.

"Please . . . please don't burn my house!" a woman yelled. "I beg you, don't do this."

The woman's pleas fell on deaf ears. Her house was burning, Margaret's house was burning, Mrs. Pearl's house was burning, and on and on the fire went. Licking its destructive path, taking away everything Margaret held dear. She pulled at her hair as her normally calm and quiet street went up in flames.

"What's happening?" she cried, heart racing, palms sweating. Were they all going to die? Would anyone come to save them? She heard airplanes. Looking into the sky, Margaret prayed that the firefighters had deployed airplanes to drop water from the sky . . . something . . . anything.

But instead of the water Margaret prayed for, black birds fell from those airplanes. They looked like black birds, but fire sparked from them as they hit the ground or punctured the roofs of homes.

Margaret's eyes went wide with stark terror as she realized that no one was coming to save them from this unimaginable horror.

Mrs. Pearl grabbed her arm and pulled her farther down the street. They ran and ran as fast as they could. They were almost in front of Dr. Andrew Jackson's home when he came outside, holding his hands above his head. A couple of white boys, who didn't look to be more than fifteen or sixteen, ran over to the doctor, yelled, "Nigger," then fired shots at him.

Evelyn screamed like terror had a vise grip on her. Dr. Jackson fell to the ground clutching his chest. Staring at one of the boys who shot Dr. Jackson, Evelyn stood transfixed. "Why! Why! Why!" Her screams flowed like a mighty rushing river from her lips.

The boy turned his gun on Evelyn. "You're next," he said, then pulled the trigger.

Margaret shoved Evelyn to the ground, then jumped on top of her sister. Wrapping her hands around the back of her head, she prepared herself for the pain that would surely come when that bullet cut through her flesh.

Chapter 5

The real truth regarding the underlying causes of the short-lived civil war . . . may come to surface in the future. The consensus of opinion . . . places the blame upon the lack of law enforcement.

—*Maurice Willows, Red Cross Disaster Relief Report*

Click. No *bang* . . . *Click.* No *bang*! Margaret's eyes widened with fear and confusion. She leaped off the ground and pulled Evelyn with her. They ran to catch up with Mrs. Pearl as the white boy's gun jammed.

"My clothes." Evelyn reached toward her bag, which had fallen to the ground.

"Leave it!" Margaret screamed, pulling Evelyn forward.

They managed to escape death not once but twice as the night was long on terror and short on mercy. "What do we do? Where do we go?" Margaret's hands cupped her head as another black bird–looking thing fell from the sky onto Mr. Elmwood's house. It caught on fire. Where could they find safety if these things could just drop down and set them on fire?

Mrs. Pearl took hold of Margaret's and Evelyn's hands. "Let's go this way." They turned down East Cameron Street.

It was still dark outside. They had run down so many streets that Margaret didn't know which part of the Negro district they were in. But bullets were falling from the airplanes above them like raindrops. They needed to find someplace to hide.

Passing by a farm on a side of town that wasn't being looted or bombed, Mrs. Pearl pointed to a chicken coop. "Let's go in there."

"Where we going?" Evelyn asked in a singsong voice. The girl was eighteen, but at that moment it was as if she'd reverted back to a toddler with her thumb pressed against her lips like she was about to suck on it.

The chicken coop was in front of them. Mrs. Pearl pointed toward it. "Duck down and go in."

"But it stinks in there," Evelyn protested.

"You want to stay out here and catch a bullet?" Mrs. Pearl shoved the girl forward. Evelyn slumped down to get into the small entry.

Margaret didn't have to be pushed or prodded. She didn't care that the four-by-six coop had nesting boxes and roosting perches for chickens or a hay-filled floor. Bullets were flying over their heads, and that was good enough reason for her to sit in here with the chickens.

Mrs. Pearl closed the door as she entered behind Margaret. "We'll sit here for a while. Hopefully things will calm down out there soon."

Evelyn's face took on a greenish shade, and she put a hand over her mouth and lurched forward. The remains of her supper spilled out onto the hay. The chickens started squawking, moving around like they were spoiling for a fight.

Margaret put a finger to her lips. "Shh," she instructed the chickens. "We don't want to be in here any more than you want us."

"It stinks so bad. I'm going to throw up again."

Margaret put a hand on her sister's shoulder. Breathing in the mixture of vinegar and chicken poop, she prayed she wouldn't throw up. But then remembered that all she'd had in the last hours were pieces of candy.

Sighing, Margaret thought on the night that was supposed to be a graduation rehearsal for Evelyn and a daddy-daughter date for her. They had been out enjoying the business district. Now she didn't even know where her daddy was, their house had burned down, and they were keeping company with stinking chickens.

"What are we gon' do? Where can we go if we don't have a home anymore?" Tears ran down Evelyn's face. She shook like it was February and the cold night air had seeped deep into her bones. "Why did those white boys shoot Dr. Jackson? He never hurt anyone."

"That man ain't never done nothing to nobody. Only wanted to heal. He performed surgery on Black and white folks. Now they done shot him dead." Mrs. Pearl's eyes fluttered with sadness.

Evelyn started crying.

Margaret let her sister lean her head against her shoulder. "We're together, Evie. We'll be okay. You'll see."

Evelyn's head popped up. "We're not okay. And we're not all together. Where's Daddy? What if those white men shot our daddy down like a dog in the street—then what?"

Evie's questions chilled Margaret to the bone. No heat from outside would warm her soul if they couldn't find Daddy.

"Don't talk foolish. Your daddy's fine. We just got to get through this night, and then we'll find him."

The words Mrs. Pearl spoke were hopeful, but the tremble in her voice wasn't. Fear had crept in and snatched away their hope—taken away their ability to believe they'd ever be safe again.

Margaret whispered, "What if we don't find him?"

Mrs. Pearl pulled the girls into her arms as chaos ensued all around them. "Hush now. We're safe in here. And we'll find your daddy when daylight comes."

But the screams outside and the pop of guns going off belied any sense of we-gon'-be-alright that Mrs. Pearl tried to exude. The screams didn't stop until daybreak. As the light broke free of darkness, Mrs. Pearl pressed an ear to the wall. She opened the door and waved them over. "Let's get going."

Evelyn hesitated. "It might not be safe yet. Maybe they forgot about this street and are coming for it this morning."

Margaret pulled her sister toward the door. "We can't stay here. We need to find Daddy."

Evelyn wrenched away from Margaret. "No! No!" She ran backward until her body was pressed against the wall, next to the roosting perch. The chickens fluttered their wings like they were getting ready to fly the coop. Margaret's eyes flashed concern at the way Evelyn was acting. Mrs. Pearl had had to shove her into the coop, and now she was refusing to leave.

"Help me get her," Mrs. Pearl said as she moved past Margaret over to Evelyn.

Mrs. Pearl pulled on one arm, and Margaret grabbed the other. Evie was shaking so badly that Margaret almost wanted to let her stay, but she couldn't separate from her sister and be left wondering what had become of her too.

"Let me go. It's not safe out there."

They'd always felt safe in Greenwood. Black folks in this community were homeowners, business builders, and peace-minded people for the most part. She and Evelyn visited with friends and attended yard parties during the summer. They slept in their comfortable beds at night without fear that someone would invade their community and set it on fire. Never would she have seen something like this coming, even in her most terrifying nightmare.

Evie's feet dragged on the ground as they pulled her out of the chicken coop, then Margaret wrapped loving arms around her sister and didn't let her go until she stopped shaking. "We're together. We're going to be alright." Margaret spoke those soothing words, but deep down, she didn't know.

They started running down the street, stopping every few steps to check their surroundings. When they reached the train tracks, other Black folks were there, moving down the tracks like ants fleeing Greenwood. Margaret eyed her surroundings, looking at all the people who'd once been calm and cool as they went about their daily business. They were now letting fear of things unknown guide them farther and farther away from what once was.

She wanted to stop and yell at them. This wasn't right. They shouldn't be letting those awful men run them away. They needed to go back, find Daddy, and fight. Somebody had to fight against this evil.

But they kept walking. They were almost to Golden Gate Park near 36th Street when a group of Black men ran toward them with hands waving in the air. "Stop! Stop! The airplanes are back, and they're shooting us down up yonder."

Another man yelled, "Get off the train tracks!"

Screams . . . that was all Margaret heard for miles and miles. Other people's screams mingled with her own as they scattered like roaches at the break of day. Margaret held on to Evelyn's hand. They ran to 36th Street. The crowd pressed against them. Slowly she turned her head as a truck with soldiers pulled up.

"Where's Mrs. Pearl?" Margaret asked Evelyn.

Evelyn's head swiveled from one side of 36th Street to the other. "I don't see her."

Across the street, soldiers dressed in green army fatigues and black boots climbed from the back of the truck. The soldiers grabbed hold of some of the men and women as they tried to escape the air attack. Margaret's eyes widened. She tapped Evelyn's shoulder and then pointed as one of the soldiers took hold of Mrs. Pearl and put her in the truck.

"What are they doing? Where are they taking her?" Evelyn took off running toward the truck.

Margaret ran after her, pulling her sister into her arms and holding her tight as the truck sped off. "No, Evie. Mrs. Pearl wouldn't want them soldiers to take us too."

Evelyn stretched her hand out toward the departing truck. "B-but . . ."

"But nothing. Come on. We've got to go." Margaret glanced back, all the while wondering why soldiers were in Greenwood rounding up people. Were they really and truly at war? Was the whole United States of America as well as the white men in Tulsa against them?

War had been declared on Greenwood, just as if they were Germans. African Americans had been labeled the enemy. Death and destruction had rent them asunder, and Margaret was completely undone . . . unsafe in the country of her birth because of the hue of her skin.

They walked for hours, heading to a place they knew not. The dust of the road clung to their clothes as tears streaked down their faces. Yesterday they had all the comforts their father could provide. Today they didn't even have a place to lay their heads. Margaret looked to heaven. The sun unapologetically shined as if something was bright and wonderful about the day. She lifted fisted hands, shaking them as her nostrils flared.

"What kind of evil have You loosed on us?"

"Stop!" Evelyn pulled Margaret's arms back down and ducked as if lightning was about to strike. "Don't question God."

"Who . . . who am I supposed to question, if not God?"

"I don't know," Evelyn whined, "but I'm tired. I need to lay down."

"Me too." Margaret wiped at the tear running down her face. Her throat was dry, and the sun was scorching the back of her neck so badly, she feared that heatstroke would be the next enemy to contend with.

They had run away from Greenwood with a crowd of people, but with each twist of the road, some in the crowd went one way and others went another. Now she and Evelyn were walking down a dusty road alone. "We've got to keep going."

There was no place to stop. For miles and miles, all they'd seen were trees and the dust of the road. What were they to do? Rest among the twigs and thistles?

They passed the city limits of Tulsa and entered one of the small surrounding towns. A chill went up Margaret's spine as she and Evelyn stood in front of a posted sign that read, *Nigger, Don't Let the Sun Go Down on You Here.*

There were plenty of sundown towns in Oklahoma. Her daddy had told her, "It's not good for a colored man to be on the road at night. And he better not run out of gas, I can tell you that much." He told her that white folks snuck out at night, looking for Negroes to lynch.

"Do we need to turn around? They don't expect us to go back to Greenwood, do they?" Evelyn's eyes were wide with fear.

Glancing around, Margaret told her, "It's daylight, so I guess we're okay to come through here. But we got to keep walking till we come to another town—no resting here, okay?"

"I'm tired," Evelyn whined.

"Keep walking." Margaret grabbed Evelyn's hand and pulled her forward; they picked up the pace. Felt like they'd been walking for days. The soles of Margaret's shoes were wearing out with all the miles of rocks and dust they'd treaded over. The sun kept beating down on them like an angry foe, and still they walked.

When they had gone far enough that they'd almost cleared the sundown, her breathing eased, she let Evelyn's arm go, and they slowed their pace.

"Where are we?" Evelyn looked around, eyes bloodshot.

"I don't know. Hopefully we're getting close to a Negro town." There were several Negro towns in Oklahoma. Folks had left the South and headed to Oklahoma after being told that colored folks could buy land here—could make something of themselves.

They heard the loud roar of a car coming down the street. Thoughts of *they're coming for us* swirled around Margaret's head. Her heart beat so fast, it was about to bust out of her chest. She grabbed Evelyn's arm again and pulled her off the road. They hid within a forest of tall trees. The car sputtered past them. Evelyn hugged a tree, then slid down behind it.

Margaret watched as a white man drove past them. A few seconds later a horse and carriage passed by with another white man holding the reins. White men with cars and horses and planes and guns were everywhere. Her hands trembled as she leaned against a tree. Was there anywhere they could be safe from the kind of terror white men caused?

Blinking twice, she tried to refocus her eyes as her vision blurred. Her arms were heavy, legs wobbly. She wanted to sit down next to her sister and take a nap. But she couldn't take the risk of them falling asleep and being wakened by soldiers, carting them off to God knows where.

"We're homeless, you know that, right?" Evelyn sniffed as if she was about to cry again.

Margaret had never been homeless. Could never have imagined what that felt like. But as they sat on the ground, surrounded by tall trees that kept the sun from beating down on them, she imagined that being homeless was like wandering aimlessly with no place to go, withering in the sun, and then finding comfort in the shade of a tree.

Her belly growled. The homeless didn't concern themselves with the importance of three meals a day. Sighing, Margaret said, "Are we in a nightmare, or is this really happening? Maybe we should go back home later tonight."

"They set our house on fire, Margaret. They set Mrs. Pearl's house on fire, and they shot Dr. Jackson. I don't think they want us there anymore."

"But why? What did we do to them?" Margaret shook her head. Confusion and bewilderment had become constant companions. But she knew one thing: They couldn't sit in this forest of trees with no food or water for much longer.

Standing, she pulled Evelyn back to her feet. "Let's keep going. There has to be something down the road, or why else did the car go that way?"

"It was only one car." Evelyn rolled her eyes. But she followed her sister anyway. "I'm hungry."

"Me too."

They walked another mile down the road. Margaret tripped over a broken branch as her legs started to give out on her. She didn't think she could go another step, then Evelyn lifted her hand and pointed. "Look, sissy, isn't that the Threatt Filling Station?"

Margaret's eyes lit like Christmas lights dangling from a tree. Her father had driven their automobile to this filling station every time the family went on a road trip. He'd told them that the Threatt Filling Station was where Black folks could refuel their cars without fear of harassment or jealousy from white folks not wanting them to have nice things.

It was a place where they could be safe. And right now, that was the most important thing in the world. She wanted—no, needed—to feel safe again.

Chapter 6

The original shooting took place at the county jail on the night of May 31st, the actual burning, pillaging and destruction was consummated during the daylight hours of June 1st.

—*Maurice Willows, Red Cross Disaster Relief Report*

Margaret had never been so happy to see the Craftsman bungalow–style structure that looked like a home but actually served as a store for travelers to grab items like snacks, a loaf of bread, or a soda pop to take with them on the road.

They stood behind a mound of trees, looking toward the Threatt Filling Station as Mr. Allen Threatt Sr. rolled a tire from behind the store and laid it down next to the black 1919 Model T. His customer stood next to the car door staring at the wheel and shaking his head.

"I just bought this car last year. Them tires should last longer than this."

The filling station had calibrated glass globes on top of the pump. Those globes had fascinated Margaret the first time her daddy brought them here. The amount of gas Daddy requested was pumped up into the globe. When the pumping stopped, the gasoline was let out of the globe and flowed into his tank as if by gravity alone.

Mr. Allen ran his hand along the side of the tire. "It's pulling away from the rim. Looks like your inner tube is busted too."

"Wrong time to have a flat with them white boys setting fire to Greenwood and shooting at anything moving."

Mr. Allen put the jack under the car and lifted the left side of it off the ground. He then put a wood block underneath the car. "Where was the police while all this was going on? That's what I can't wrap my mind around."

"From what I hear, some of them white men flying around in them airplanes, shooting at us, was law enforcement."

As they stood behind a tree not far from the filling station, Margaret could hear Mr. Allen talking with his customer. The customer was fair-skinned—from the short distance she couldn't tell if he was white or Black. Was he trying to get Mr. Allen to say something bad about them devils who burned down their homes so they could come out here and do the same?

Mr. Allen filled the inner tube with air and then stuffed it inside the tire. He placed the tire around the rim, then used both his hands to fit the tire to the rim.

Once the tire was properly mounted, Mr. Allen put more air in the inner tube, then connected the tire rim to the metal piece that was connected to the wooden spokes. He stood and wiped his hands. "You're all set."

"How much do I owe you?"

"Can't see taking your money while doing a good deed for someone in need."

"You deserve your pay."

Mr. Allen shrugged, lifted his hands. "Not today. Just remember me when you get back on your feet."

The man tipped his hat. "You're a good man, Mr. Allen."

He got in his car and pulled off. Margaret then started flailing her hands and yelling, "Help! Help! We need help!" Margaret had tried to be strong for her sister, but now that they were nearing the Threatt Filling Station, she could pretend no more.

"Help!" Evelyn yelled as they inched closer and closer.

Wiping his hands on his overalls, Mr. Allen turned, lifted a hand to shield his eyes against the sun. "Who's out there?"

They were crossing the street to get to Mr. Allen when Margaret saw a tall man wearing overalls approaching them. As she turned toward the man, the world started spinning, and Margaret lost her footing. "Oh no!" She tried to use her hands to brace her fall but ended up on her back, rolling around in the grass by the trees they had been hiding behind.

"Margaret, oh my goodness." Evelyn reached a hand out to help her up.

Margaret lifted her hand, but it fell back to her side. She was spent. Couldn't move from this spot if she tried. "Go on without me. Get to safety," Margaret told Evelyn.

"Are you crazy? I'm not leaving you." Evelyn screamed, "Help! Help us!" Margaret stretched out on the ground as if the grass had tied a web around her. "Something's wrong with my sister. Please help us."

Why couldn't she get up? What was happening to her?

The boots coming toward them shook the ground. Fear gripped Margaret, froze her to the spot. She heard the man say, "I've got her, Mr. Allen."

Get up! The words swirled around in her head as the man came closer. What if those boots belonged to one of those men with guns and airplanes that dropped bombs on people?

Margaret turned toward Evelyn. "Help . . . me up. Got to get out of here."

"Where we going? You said we'd be safe here." Evelyn's eyes flashed fear as she tried once again to pull her sister off the ground.

Margaret gripped Evelyn's arm and tried to lift herself up, but her legs weren't working. Then strong hands lifted her from the ground. "Wait! Wait! Put me down."

Evelyn yelled toward the filling station, "Help us!"

Mr. Allen told the man who was carrying Margaret, "Take them to the farmhouse. I'll meet you over there—just let me close the station down."

Evelyn hurried to catch up with the man. "He said to take us to the farmhouse. Please don't drop my sister. She's feeling poorly."

He swung around with Margaret slung over his shoulder. "You girls from Greenwood?"

"Yes," Evelyn answered. "We ran for our lives."

"I figured as much." He continued walking. "A couple others found their way here. Mrs. Alberta will take good care of you. Don't worry about anything. Your sister just needs some rest."

"My legs feel better. I can walk now," Margaret told him.

"Don't be stubborn. Just let me carry you to the farmhouse."

"She's not being stubborn." Evelyn kept up with them, almost running at times. "Margaret fell and hurt her legs."

"Well, you're out of harm's way now, so calm down."

Who was he to tell them to calm down? He had no idea what they had been through. His arms were strong and unyielding. He was big and much taller than her, but if her strength suddenly came back, Margaret would give him a good wallop for talking to her like a child who needed to be scolded for acting out.

When he put her down on the porch of the farmhouse, Margaret adjusted the dress that she had loved, with its vibrant colors. It now had tears and holes in unseemly places. Shame caused her to place a hand over her side to cover the slit that exposed her dirty skin.

"Thank you," she said without looking at him. She then grabbed Evelyn's hand and knocked on the front door.

Chapter 7

Wounded people turned up at Muskogee, Sapulpa, and other adjoining towns, and as far north as Kansas City.
—*Maurice Willows, Red Cross Disaster Relief Report*

When the woman who answered the door saw Margaret and Evelyn standing on her wraparound porch looking like the world had swallowed them up and spit them back out, she put her hands on her hips, looked heavenward, and said, "Lord, I thank You for bringing these two beautiful young women out of that terrible ordeal."

Margaret's nose wrinkled. God couldn't have been helping them . . . That didn't make sense. The God she'd been taught about in Sunday school didn't sleep or slumber. So how did a massacre such as this catch Him unawares? Why would He have to guide her and Evie out of Greenwood rather than stop those evil men in the first place?

"God don't make mistakes, Maggie-Pie." Her daddy's voice boomed in her ear as if he was standing next to her right now, rather than where he'd actually said those words: at her mother's grave, the day they shoveled dirt over her casket.

"You poor dears. I'm Mrs. Alberta." She opened the door wide. "Come on in this house." She was tall and thin with a kind caramel face. "Y'all hungry?" she asked as they stepped inside the spacious home.

Evelyn touched her belly. "My stomach's been growling for hours."

There was a staircase just to the left of the front door. Hardwood floors in the entryway. But what stuck out most to Margaret were all of the framed photos that hung on the wall. Mr. and Mrs. Threatt's photo was on one wall. Below their photo was one of a baby. On another wall were several photos of people Margaret didn't recognize, but each and every one of them made her wish she had snatched the photo of her parents off the mantel before the fire took hold.

A tear rolled down Margaret's cheek. She averted her eyes as they walked past the photo wall and into the dining room. Mrs. Alberta seated them at the dining room table with enough chairs for ten people. Two other families from Greenwood were at the table with them, sharing horror stories of the melee.

Mr. Dorsey, who lived over on North Elgin Avenue, and his wife and three children hungrily ate the potato soup that Mrs. Alberta gave them. His hand shook each time he brought the spoon to his mouth. "Never seen anything like it. Ambushed like that."

Veronica Jones, whose family owned the furniture store on Cameron Street, rocked back and forth, hands crossed around her belly. "It wasn't right . . . wasn't right what they did to us. We done lost everything."

The Joneses' furniture store was burned down just like their homes. Those evil white men wanted to stamp out any remembrance of what colored folks had built in these parts. Businesses that had taken years to build had been snuffed out in one night.

"Shh, shh." Mrs. Alberta came running into the dining room, wiping her wet hands on a dish towel. She turned up the radio. "Judge Martin is speaking about the riot."

"Wasn't no riot—that was an ambush and a massacre, and they know it." Mr. Dorsey slammed a fist against the table.

Through the radio they could hear Judge Martin: "Tulsa can only redeem herself from the countrywide shame and humiliation into which she is today plunged by complete restitution and rehabilitation of the destroyed Black belt. The rest of the United States must know that the real citizenship of Tulsa weeps at this unspeakable crime and will make good the damage, so far as it can be done, to the last penny."

Veronica perked up. "He's going to help us. Praise God, they're not going to let them demons get away with what they done to us."

Judge Martin was the former mayor of Tulsa, Oklahoma. According to the radio announcer, Judge Martin had just been elected chairman of some group of businessmen who vowed to restore Greenwood from ashes to its former glory.

"I don't want to go back home. It's too dangerous," Evelyn said, then wrapped her arms around herself as if needing warmth.

Margaret turned frustrated eyes on her sister. "There's no home to go to, Evie. You're worrying about impossible things."

Evie's lips quivered. Hands smacked against her face as the floodgates opened and doused everyone around the table with an ocean of grief. "But Judge Martin said 'complete restitution.' That means homes will be rebuilt, right?"

"That's what it sounds like to me," Veronica said, then pumped a fist in the air. "Somebody needs to restore our homes."

Evie's head dropped to the table in despair. Margaret pulled her sister into her arms. Regret for the harsh words she'd spoken to Evie hung in the air between them. "I know you're scared. We'll figure something out. But first we need to find Daddy. He'll know what to do."

Mr. Dorsey's head popped up, eyes filled with horror. He opened his mouth, then bit down on his lip and turned from Margaret.

Did he know something? Had he seen their father? She wanted to ask, but she wasn't sure if her heart could handle the truth she'd glimpsed in his eyes. Margaret stood and pulled Evie to her feet. Evelyn needed to lie down, but there was nowhere to rest. No home to shelter in.

As if reading her thoughts, Mrs. Alberta wiped her hands with the cloth she held and told them, "I've made up Davie's room for you and your sister."

Margaret shook her head. "We can't take your son's room. Evie and I can make a pallet on the floor. We just need some blankets."

"I won't hear of it. You all have suffered too much. The least we can do is provide a place to sleep. Davie will sleep in the room with his brother."

The Threatts had three boys, the youngest just a few months old. They also had five bedrooms, several outbuildings, and a store where others could sleep, should anyone else from Greenwood find their way here.

"Thank you," Evie said. "I just can't deal with anything else right now."

"We appreciate your hospitality," Margaret told Mrs. Alberta.

"Follow me, my dears." Mrs. Alberta took them upstairs, where the kids' bedrooms were. She gave each of them a warm hug and left them to get settled.

"I feel terrible laying in this bed with our dirty clothes on." Evelyn bit down on her lip. "Daddy would've thrown a fit if someone laid on our beds without washing and putting on clean clothes."

"We don't have any clean clothes. We'll just have to wash out our clothes along with these bedsheets in the morning." Margaret looked down at her tattered dress. "What am I going to do with this?"

"You want me to see if Mrs. Alberta has a needle and thread? Maybe an old shirt or skirt she don't want anymore? I can patch it for you."

"Not tonight." Margaret's head pounded so badly, all she wanted to do was close her eyes and forget about the last eighteen hours. But Evie wasn't ready to fall asleep.

She lifted on her elbow. "Where you think them army men took Mrs. Pearl? You think we'll ever see her again?"

Eyes filling with buckets of sadness, Margaret wiped a hand across her face. "I don't know." Resting her head on the pillow, she let the tears sink into the fabric of the pillowcase. "Go to sleep. Hopefully we'll learn more about Mrs. Pearl and Daddy tomorrow."

By morning, another family made their way to the Threatt family farm. Mr. Allen brought the Stubbinses from Archer Street into the dining room as everyone ate breakfast. Mrs. Alberta had collected their clothes and given Margaret and Evie old housecoats that had belonged to her mother to put on.

Margaret never thought she'd be grateful for a hand-me-down housecoat. But she was so thankful to be getting her clothes washed that this housecoat felt like some of the finery she'd seen at Elliott & Hooker over on Greenwood Avenue. Or even some of the dresses Evie made.

Mrs. Alberta had biscuits and gravy and creamy grits on the table, along with milk that her oldest son had squeezed from their cow. Evie leaned close to her. "Is it okay to eat, or do we have to wait?"

Margaret whispered back, "Not sure." Their dad had instilled proper manners in them. They never ate anything at someone else's table before saying grace or unless the cook invited them to get a plate.

Miss Veronica wasn't thinking about good manners. She filled her plate, and the others followed suit. Margaret hunched her shoulders, grabbed two plates, handed one to Evie, then commenced putting a nice fluffy biscuit on her plate and smothering it with the thick gravy that had chunks of sausage in it.

As they sat around the table eating breakfast, a pang of guilt hit Margaret so hard that she pushed her half-eaten plate away. "This isn't right. How can we sit here eating as if nothing is wrong? I don't know what's become of my daddy or Mrs. Pearl. I can't sit here and act like life is still normal."

"Nothing's gon' be normal for us again, young lady," Mr. Dorsey said. "But you're right. We shouldn't be sitting here. We need to be checking on our property."

Mr. Stubbins scratched his head. "What property? Everythang I own's gone up in flames over a flat-out lie. That Rowland boy didn't mean to touch that girl, and they know it."

None of it made any sense to Margaret. Her daddy was always talking about the goodness of God, but where was God's goodness in this? "I have to find my daddy. Can any of you help me? His name is Henry Justice—he owns the Justice for All Grocery Store."

Mr. Stubbins turned toward her. "If he ain't at the hospital, he might be over at the fairgrounds. I hear that's where them soldiers took a lot of menfolk the other night."

Mr. Dorsey chewed on a biscuit and turned his head from her.

"Fairgrounds." Evie scrunched her nose. "Why'd they take 'em over there?"

The tall man who'd carried Margaret to the farmhouse stepped into the dining room with a biscuit in his hand. "I listened to the news last night," he told them. "They say some general by the name of Barrett swooped into town and declared martial law. Rounded up all the Negroes and stuck 'em over at the convention hall and a couple of other places like the fairgrounds."

Mrs. Alberta entered the room carrying a pan of scrambled eggs. "You all haven't met Elijah. He's our head farmhand." He didn't look like an Elijah to Margaret. More like a six-foot John Henry, with those muscles and the overalls he wore.

Mrs. Alberta continued, "They treating Black folks like refugees . . . can't even leave without identification."

Evie turned to Margaret with horror-stricken eyes. "You think Daddy's trapped at one of them places and can't get out since his ID cards were burned up in the house?"

Margaret put a hand over her sister's. Her voice filled with determination. "I don't know, but I plan to find out."

Chapter 8

Refugees were being driven under guard to places of refuge.

—*Maurice Willows, Red Cross Disaster Relief Report*

Evelyn stayed at the Threatt farm while Elijah drove Margaret back to Greenwood. Her first order of business was to find their father.

Mr. Dorsey and Miss Veronica sat in the back, whispering until Mr. Dorsey shouted, "Alright, alright." He then tapped Elijah on the shoulder and said, "My good man, can you pull over so I can discuss a matter with you?"

Elijah pulled into a cornfield a few miles outside of Greenwood. He and Mr. Dorsey stepped out and began speaking in whispers as they moved away from the car.

Margaret glanced back toward Miss Veronica. "Is something wrong?"

Miss Veronica patted her on the shoulder, then looked out the window. "Let the menfolk figure this out."

Margaret had no patience for whispers in the wind. She didn't care about anyone's secrets. She was along for the ride to find her father and figure out what happened to Mrs. Pearl.

But what could she really do to help? She was only twenty-two years old, just barely out of college . . . hadn't even started her teaching position yet.

Thinking of her teaching position brought on other questions. Could she still take that job? Where would she stay?

Elijah and Mr. Dorsey got back in the car. They continued their journey to Greenwood. Silence and an ominous dread of what lay ahead guided them forward.

Oh Greenwood . . . Greenwood. Margaret's heart bled as they reached their destination. The town that had once been a beacon of light had been dimmed by the fires of hate. Soot and debris clung to the once-beautiful homes that were now nothing more than rubble, bricks and debris strewn on the dusty roads.

"We'll have to get out here. I don't think I'll be able to drive Mr. Allen's automobile any further."

Margaret trembled at the thought of walking the same streets she'd run for her life on just a couple nights ago. Was it safe to be here? Would those evil men attack them again?

Elijah put a hand on her arm. "You okay?"

Breathe in, breathe out. "I'm okay." *Breathe in, breathe out.* "I'll be okay . . . one day, right?" She looked at him, hoping he had the answer she sought.

Mr. Dorsey and Miss Veronica opened the back door and stepped out of the car.

"Look what they did to my beloved Greenwood." Veronica put a hand to her face and cried a thousand sorrows.

Margaret tried to be strong, but her chin quivered. The pitying way Elijah stared at her when he asked if she would be okay didn't help matters. How was she to know if she would ever be okay again? Her hands wouldn't stop shaking, and that spinning feeling was taking hold of her again. She put a hand to her head. Oh Greenwood. Poor, dear Greenwood.

"Let me get the door for you." He got out of the automobile and rushed around to the passenger side. As he opened her door, Margaret wanted to slam it back shut. But this was Mr. Allen's automobile; just as Elijah didn't want to destroy the tires by driving over all the debris in the streets, she couldn't damage the automobile when Mr. and Mrs. Threatt had been as good as gold to her and Evie.

She got out and leaned against the automobile. *Breathe in . . . breathe out.* She repeated that a few times, then gathered her bearings as her eyes roamed the distance. She was at the corner of Greenwood and Archer. George Martin's house used to be on the left-hand side of the street. The spot where his house used to be was empty, except for the smoking wood planks scattered on the ground.

Margaret put a hand to her heart. This was all so terrible. She prayed that Mr. Martin was okay. She and George had talked about marriage. Her father and Mr. Martin had expected them to marry. But how could she think about such things now, when neither she nor George had a pot to pee in or a window to throw it out of.

"We best be getting on down the street," Mr. Dorsey said.

Looking at the empty space that used to be Mr. Martin's home—the home where she'd kept company with George on numerous occasions—caused a tear to roll down her face. How could this be real? How could everything be gone? This place was nothing like the Greenwood she knew.

Miss Veronica blew her nose and headed off for East Cameron Street. Mr. Dorsey's house had been three streets over, so he headed that way.

"Did you live near here?" Elijah asked, bringing Margaret back to the moment.

She pointed to the left of where they were standing. "My house is about four blocks down that way."

They began their trek down the dust- and brick-covered road. Bricks that had been blown off homes and businesses. The eerie silence spoke volumes to Margaret. This community had been so vibrant and bustling. They were always doing, always going, always moving as if the drumbeat accompanied every which way they swayed.

But today, there was no such movement. Tents had been erected on the sidewalks in front of the rubble that used to be homes. Men, women, and children sat under those tents. Desperation clung to them as dust clung to the ground around them.

Margaret wrapped her hands around herself, rubbing her arms, trying to infuse warmth into her body on this sweltering hot and gloomy day. "Everything is so out of place." Her eyes shifted one way and then another. Nothing made sense anymore.

"Looks like a war zone to me," Elijah said.

When they crossed the street and turned the corner, Margaret glanced around Detroit Street, where she'd lived since she was seven years old. She tripped on a wood plank that was in the road and almost fell. Elijah grabbed hold of her.

As he held her, Margaret saw the rusty nails sticking up from the wood. Her hands went to her mouth as the debris mixed with day-old trash caused a rumbling in her stomach. She gagged and heaved the contents of her stomach.

Elijah patted her back. "Let it all out. Just let it out."

Wiping her mouth with her shirtsleeve, Margaret righted herself. She looked away from Elijah as shame enveloped her.

"Thank the Lord. Chile, I thought I lost y'all forever."

Margaret swung around as she heard the familiar voice of Mrs. Pearl. She wrapped her arms around her neighbor and held on to her as if letting go would tear her whole heart out. "I was so worried when those soldiers took you."

"I was worried too." Mrs. Pearl stepped out of the embrace. "But in truth, I probably should've stayed at that convention hall. Now that I'm here, I'm stuck laying under a tent while we're trying to figure out what to do with all this rubble."

"Don't say that. Them soldiers had no right pulling you off the street as if you didn't belong in your own neighborhood."

"Well, right or not, they did it. They's still plenty of folk being held like prisoners of war. I was lucky enough to have my identification card on me, so they said I was free to go . . . go where was what I wanted to know." Mrs. Pearl stuck out a hand and pointed at the destruction before them.

Tears formed in Margaret's eyes. She touched her heart as a deep pain threatened to topple her.

Mrs. Pearl nudged Margaret. "Who's this fine gentleman standing next to you?"

Margaret wiped her eyes and glanced in Elijah's direction, noting his chocolate-coated skin and his soulful brown eyes. "This is Elijah Porter. He works on the Threatt farm over in Luther."

"I know where the Threatt farm is. They the ones that own the only filling station friendly to us Negroes in these parts."

Margaret turned to Elijah and pointed toward the rubble to the right of where Mrs. Pearl had pitched her tent. "That's our house." Most of the homes on the street were completely destroyed. Their house was in shambles as well. All that was left of it was the brick foundation and half of a wall.

No roof, no wood siding, no sofa or love seat in the living room. Just the bricks that formed a barrier for all the dirt, debris, and tree branches that had made their way into what used to be a home.

"I'm so sorry, Margaret."

Tears swam down her face as she walked toward the rubble. Seemed like all she knew was tears. "Sweet Jesus, where is the mercy?"

Elijah rushed to her side. "You can't go in there."

She wiped the wetness from her face. "I have to. There might be something salvageable. My daddy would want me to at least try." Elijah helped her step over the brick foundation. They moved pieces of debris from one side to the other.

Margaret found the spot where Evelyn's closet used to stand. Rubble and scorched pieces of cloth lay in the debris. Nothing that resembled any of the beautiful dresses Evelyn had created. Tears threatened to fall again, but she sniffed and searched through the rubble, hoping she would be able to bring something of use to her sister.

But nothing was salvageable in Evie's room. Margaret's eyes widened in horror as she stepped on a piece of her sister's Singer sewing machine. The thing was made of cast iron, so Margaret had thought it was unbreakable. Tears . . . tears . . . tears as she discovered how wrong she had been. "Nooo!"

Startled, Elijah grabbed hold of Margaret's arm. "You okay?"

Jabbing a finger toward the broken pieces on the ground, Margaret tried to talk through her storm: "Evie . . . will be . . . destroyed. Mama's sewing machine is gone."

Elijah bent down. He shoved a few things out of the way and then picked up pieces of the sewing machine. When he stood back up, he showed the items to Margaret. "Better that Evelyn have a piece of the machine she cherishes than nothing at all?"

The spinning wheel and a piece that had the name Singer on it with the red eye design Singer was famous for were in his hand. Margaret was like those pieces . . . broken.

She was lost and hopeless. Needed her daddy and didn't know where he could possibly be. She leaned her head on Elijah's shoulder and let the tears roll. "Everything is falling apart. I don't know what to do."

"Things seem bleak right now, but things will get better."

"I need my daddy." Margaret lifted her head from Elijah's strong shoulder. She wiped her face with the back of her hand, then glanced around, as if remembering the reason for coming to Greenwood. She made her way back to Mrs. Pearl.

"When did you come back to our street?"

"Last night. The Red Cross brought these tents. A few of the neighborhood men set it up for me."

"Have you seen my daddy? Has he been here looking for us?"

Mrs. Pearl's head leaned to the left as if in thought. "Been wondering about your daddy. He's probably at the hospital. I hear tell the Red Cross done set up a hospital for coloreds over at Booker T."

Margaret's eyes closed. She touched her hand to her heart, trying to wrap her mind around the fact that Evie hadn't been able to graduate at her high school, and now it was being used as a hospital. The shame of it all sent ripples of hate through her whole being. Her hands fisted at her sides. "I just want to smash something."

Mrs. Pearl waved a hand at the devastation before them. "Everythang already been smashed 'round here, chile. So set your mind on finding your daddy."

It took a minute to steady her breathing as hot anger burned through her. Daddy . . . she needed to find her daddy. "You didn't see him at the convention hall?"

Mrs. Pearl shook her head. "They took some of the ones they rounded up to the fairgrounds. You might check there. But I'd start at the hospital."

"The hospital?" Margaret rubbed her chin. "You think Daddy got hurt?"

"Why else isn't he here?" Mrs. Pearl patted Margaret's shoulder. "You go down to that hospital and check on your daddy."

Margaret turned back to Elijah. "I need to go over to Booker T. It's now a hospital."

Elijah put a hand on Margaret's shoulder. "The thing is . . ." His throat made a loud scratchy sound, and he tried again. "The thing is . . . M-Mr. Dorsey was with your father when a group of men tried to protect the community."

Margaret remembered the look on Mr. Dorsey's face when she mentioned needing to find her daddy earlier that morning. Like he knew something but wasn't spilling the beans. "And . . ."

Elijah turned his back to her, took a couple of steps, then turned back. Those soulful eyes torched her with the intensity she saw there.

Hands in pocket, he said, "I'm having a hard time figuring a way to tell you this." Pulling his hand out of his pocket, he placed it on her arm.

Margaret backed away. She didn't want to know what Mr. Dorsey told Elijah. Standing in the midst of the rubble that used to be her home, Margaret didn't know what she would do if one more thing went awry.

"Your father didn't come home the night of the attack because . . ."

She put her hands to her ears, but she still heard Elijah say, "He was shot, and they lost track of him."

She gave a sharp intake of breath as her world shifted from being her daddy's little girl to being something she didn't recognize. She stood in a place she didn't want to be . . . had to find her way back. She put a hand on Elijah's arm. "I'm walking over to Booker T."

Chapter 9

I can never erase the sights of my first visit to the hospital. There were men wounded in every conceivable way . . . Was I in a hospital in France? No, in Tulsa.

—*Mary Elizabeth Jones Parrish, Tulsa Race Massacre survivor*

You have a Singer?" Evelyn's eyes widened in delight as she ran her hands along the side of the black sewing machine with a spool of thread on the top and a spinning wheel on the back. It was like her mother's.

She would sit next to her mother and watch as she cut fabric and then sewed the pieces together to make something grand out of what had looked like nothing.

"I make clothes for my boys when I have time," Mrs. Alberta told her.

Evelyn's eyes clouded with sadness. She bit down on her lip. "Wish I could show you some of the things I've made on my sewing machine."

Mrs. Alberta put a hand on Evelyn's arm. "These sewing machines are sturdy. I bet yours survived the fire."

Evelyn could only hope for such a blessing. But right now, she was more focused on whether her daddy survived.

Her nerves were getting the better of her as she waited for Margaret to come back to the farm with word. But in truth, even if her daddy was at home waiting for them, Evelyn didn't think she could stomach going back to Greenwood.

Thoughts of moving to New York months before she was to begin design school swirled around her head. Would she be able to get her diploma to show proof that she graduated? Would her daddy let her move to New York this summer? Would he understand that she could not, would not go back to a place that had so thoroughly terrorized her?

She went outside as images of Dr. Jackson being shot and falling dead in the street took hold of her again. She'd looked into the crazed green eyes of his killer. The madness she saw on that boy's face chilled her. Wrapping her arms around herself, she walked through the field. Several men were out, plucking the cornstalks for harvest. She ignored the stares as she passed by them.

Lifting her eyes to heaven, she silently prayed, *Please, please let Margaret find Daddy.*

Why had her daddy been so compelled to go into Tulsa and take up a fight they had no chance of winning? And why hadn't he been home when their house went up in smoke?

Daddy was all she and Margaret had. She'd gladly give up her sewing machine and all the dresses she'd designed, as long as Margaret came back with Daddy. "Did you hear me, God? I just want my daddy."

"Please, I'm trying to find my daddy. Can you tell me if he's here?" The hospital for Greenwood residents had been burned to the ground. Since the Tulsa hospitals were for whites only, the Red Cross opened a hospital to help the men and women who had been injured in the massacre.

The worker behind the desk lifted a pencil and notepad. "What's his name and his injury?"

"Henry Justice." Margaret glanced over her shoulder at Elijah before adding, "They say he was shot."

The woman got up from her desk. "Let me check. I'll be right back."

Elijah stepped forward. He put an arm around Margaret's shoulders. The gesture brought her a small bit of comfort. She turned to him, a smile creasing her lips. "He's here, I just know it. Daddy's going to be alright." Margaret's head bobbed up and down with her conviction.

"I pray he's here."

"He has to be." Margaret expelled a deep, long-suffering sigh. "If he got shot like Mr. Dorsey said, then he would need a doctor, right?"

But the worker came back and said, "As far as I can tell, we don't have a Henry Justice here."

"But he has to be here. Maybe you missed him." Margaret took several steps toward the curtain the worker had just come from behind. "I'll find him." She rushed behind the curtain before anyone could stop her. A mix of black and white wrought iron beds were lined up against all four sides of the room. They were all twin beds except for the two cribs that were also in the room.

The men, pallid and still beneath the crisp white sheets, let out low, guttural moans that echoed through the sterile hospital room, each one an embodiment of pain and sorrow. The men's suffering seemed to permeate the very air around them. It was a scene of quiet agony, a stark contrast to the bustling conduct and get-up-and-go attitudes these men once exhibited in their beloved Greenwood.

Looking to her left, Margaret groaned inwardly as she saw a man with half his face burned, another with a patch over his eye. On the other side of the room, an amputee had his knee in a sling; his leg hung down, but his foot was missing. Wails of pain spilled from that side of the room.

Margaret's heart stopped in her chest. She jumped, her hand instinctively flying to her chest as her gaze fell upon the man lying in the bed next to the amputee. A cold chill gripped her spine. His eyes were empty, as if his mind had been transported to a distant and desolate place. Overwhelming despair emanated from him like a dark cloud suffocating his soul. And again, she wondered, where was the mercy? What kind of world was she living in, where people caused such human suffering as this?

"You can't be in here," the woman told her as she and Elijah followed Margaret into the room.

As hard as it had been, Margaret had looked each man in the face. Her father wasn't there. "Do you have another room? He could be in a coma or something."

"Ma'am, we have seen about eight hundred wounded men and women from Greenwood. But we have logged every victim with gunshot wounds, and your father isn't here."

A man from one of the beds yelled out, and the woman went to him. Pain lodged in Margaret's throat and escaped on a sigh. "I'm sorry. I didn't mean to disturb anyone."

Elijah grabbed her arm and moved her out of the room. "Let's go check out the Tulsa County Fairgrounds. Maybe he's there."

Margaret had her doubts about that, but they drove over there anyway. The fairground was north of Archer Street and Lewis Avenue.

Men, women, and children stood outside the three-story brick building near the entrance, not moving, not going anywhere or doing anything in particular. Hopelessness rested on their shoulders. Sadness and confusion weighed them down.

Several white men in army fatigues held rifles as they stood outside with them. Margaret didn't know if they were protecting them from further harm or holding them prisoner.

"I'm looking for my father," she told one of the soldiers.

"Name?" he asked without looking her way.

"Henry Justice."

Turning to the left, the man hollered to someone who was seated at a table closer to the building, "We got a Henry Justice?"

The man at the table looked through a few pages, then lifted his head and shouted, "Not here."

"Margaret! Hey, Margaret, tell these men that you know who I am so I can get out of here," Mr. Clifton yelled to her.

"Of course I know you." She turned back to the soldier. "That's Mr. Clifton. He owns the dry cleaner's next to my daddy's grocery store."

"He already told us about his shop. We're waiting on someone to vouch for his character."

Margaret's eyebrow arched upward. Indignation flowed through her vocal cords. "I just did."

The soldier set his full attention on her then. "Unless you want to join him, I suggest you go on your way."

Disgust for a world that could hold people who'd just experienced the worst tragedy of their lives like prisoners of war filled Margaret's nostrils. "But he needs to go check on his business. Why won't you let him out of here?"

Elijah grabbed her arm and pulled her away. "Let's get going. We can't stand around here."

"But . . . but . . ." She tried to pull back.

He leaned closer to her. "I'll pick you up and carry you out of here if I have to."

She stopped struggling and walked back to the car with Elijah. But her heart cracked with each step they took. "My daddy's dead, isn't he?"

They were sitting in the car. Elijah had his hands on the steering wheel. He took them off and turned to her. Pressing his lips together, he looked at her as his chest heaved. "I think so."

"Then where is his body?" Margaret exploded, glancing around the streets, seeing all the debris that had been left from the massacre but no bodies lying in the street as they had been a couple of days ago. Someone had moved the bodies, but where did they take them? Where was her daddy?

"God don't make mistakes, Maggie-Pie." Who was making all these mistakes? That's what Margaret wanted to know.

When Margaret came back to the farm later that day and put the broken pieces of the sewing machine in Evelyn's hand, the pain was indescribable. But it was nothing compared to what Margaret said next.

"I searched all over for Daddy." Her sister lowered her head as her eyes filled with tears. "I don't think he's ever coming back to us."

A strange sudden calm descended upon Evelyn. Like she was disconnected from the moment. This was someone else's life . . . someone else's pain. "What are you saying? I don't understand."

Margaret hesitated a moment. Sucked in some air. "I think . . . Daddy's . . . dead."

"No, no, no!" Evelyn screamed. "What do you mean, you think? Did you search hard enough? Did you look everywhere?"

Without waiting for a response, Evelyn lashed out. Swung at the air. Connected a blow against Margaret's arm. Anything to make the pain leave her body.

"I did. I looked everywhere." Margaret absorbed the blow. "They moved all the dead bodies that were on the ground the other night. So we don't have a body as proof of his death. But you know Daddy. Nothing but death would keep him from coming back to us."

Margaret's words cut so deep, Evie crawled within herself and died a little. She threw the cast-iron pieces of her sewing machine to the ground and ran back inside, climbing the stairs to a room she wasn't yet comfortable in. With its blue blankets and blue rug on the floor.

Her room in Greenwood had frills, and it was girly with a lavender bedspread, lace curtains, and her sewing machine. As grateful as she was for Mrs. Alberta giving them a place to rest, she didn't belong in a boy's room with toy trucks, a train set against the wall, and blue blankets.

Evelyn collapsed onto the bed. She sobbed until day blended into night. She cried until she heard Margaret's gentle footsteps approach her. She was torn between wanting to be alone and needing someone to comfort her. When Margaret sat next to her and pulled her into a hug, a mix of relief and frustration flowed through her. Evelyn didn't know if she wanted to push Margaret away or hold on to her tightly.

"I'm sorry I left you here in sorrow by yourself all day." Margaret shook her head. "Daddy would not have approved of my actions."

Through the pain, a smile creased Evelyn's lips. "'You girls stick together.'" Evelyn deepened her voice as she gave a good Henry Justice impression.

Margaret laughed, her eyes dancing on a memory. "He was so mad when I refused to take you to the movies with my friends." Now it was Margaret's turn to mimic their daddy. "'Maggie-Pie, friends come and go, but you Justice girls stick together.'"

Wiping the tears from her face, Evelyn added, "I not only got to go to the movies that day, but you bought me an ice cream cone too."

Margaret nudged her sister, then held out her pinky finger. Sniffing and wiping away an errant tear, Evelyn wrapped her pinky finger around Margaret's. "I won't ever forget it again, Evie. We Justice girls stick together."

The floodgates burst open once more, unleashing a torrent of tears as the sisters fell into each other's arms. Their bodies shook with sobs. They mourned the loss of their old life, but they clung to each other fiercely, knowing that together they could weather any storm. Nothing would ever be the same again, but they had each other, and that was enough to give them strength amid the chaos and devastation.

Chapter 10

Where were the police? Where was the fire department?
Why the temporary breakdown of City and County
government?

—Maurice Willows, Red Cross Disaster Relief Report

W hat are we going to do? Where will we live?" Evelyn
asked while she and Margaret prepared to go downstairs for supper.

Margaret shook her head. There were so many things she
didn't have answers to anymore. "We're together, and that's all
that matters."

They hugged again. When they parted, Evelyn asked, "I'm
not going to design school, am I?"

The tears that flowed down Margaret's face served as the
answer to confirm that Evelyn's dreams had died with their
daddy. The salty drops traced a path through the dust and dirt
on Margaret's face, leaving behind glistening trails as they fell.

"Daddy's money was tied up in investments. He'd just paid a
contractor a lot of money to expand the grocery store, so unless
that man is willing to give the money back, I don't know what
we're going to do."

Evelyn broke. Sobs wracked her body, revealing the depth of her grief, the heaviness of her loss. It was as if the very air around them had grown thick with sorrow, suffocating any remaining glimmer of hope.

With red-rimmed eyes, Margaret and Evelyn left their room and timidly entered the dining room for supper. They stood against the wall, waiting for others to join them, not wanting to take a seat that had not been offered.

Mrs. Alberta came into the dining room carrying a pot. She sat it in the middle of the table, then turned around. She jumped, put a hand to her heart at the sight of Margaret and Evelyn standing against the wall. "I didn't know you were in here. You girls scared the dickens out of me."

Margaret rushed over to the woman and helped to steady her. "I'm so sorry. We didn't mean to scare you. We were just waiting for the others to come down for supper so we'd know where to sit."

Mrs. Alberta waved that notion off. "Go on and take a seat. It's just going to be Mr. Allen and the kids with us tonight."

Glancing around the room, Evelyn asked, "But what about Mr. Dorsey and his family? Or Miss Veronica?"

Margaret added, "I thought I saw Mr. Stubbins when I arrived back a couple of hours ago."

Mrs. Alberta nodded. "The Red Cross provided tents for them, so they wanted to be in Greenwood to work on their homes."

Evelyn's hands trembled. She turned to Margaret. "I can't go back there. We don't even have a home. What are we going to do?"

"Calm down, Evie." Margaret pointed to the dining room table. "Mrs. Alberta fixed supper. Let's sit down and eat with the family."

Evelyn sat down as Margaret suggested. Her body shook as tears rolled down her face.

Margaret took the seat next to her sister. She put a hand on Evelyn's shoulder and tried to soothe her. "I promise we'll figure something out. Just stop crying, okay?"

Margaret could hear Mrs. Alberta and Mr. Allen whispering in the kitchen. She hoped that Evelyn's crying wasn't disturbing them. She would hate for these kind people to think poorly of them.

When Mr. Allen sat down at the head of the table and Mrs. Alberta came back into the room and placed a bowl and spoon in front of each of them, Margaret didn't care what was in that pot—she was going to eat it and thank them for it.

"We have beef stew tonight," Mrs. Alberta said, glancing over at Evelyn with concern etched on her face. "I know it's hot outside, but I thought we could use something hearty."

Evelyn wiped the tears from her face and lowered her head. Mr. Allen said grace. They ate in silence until the delectable spices from the gravy in the beef stew caused Margaret to hum and smack her lips. Mrs. Pearl was the best cook she knew, but even her gravy paled in comparison to what was going on in her mouth. "Mm-mm-mm."

Mrs. Alberta smiled. "I'm glad you're enjoying the meal."

"It's delicious," Margaret told her, and Evelyn agreed.

Mr. Allen cleared his throat, put a hand on the table. "Mrs. Alberta tells me that you girls aren't too keen on going back to Greenwood and living in one of them tents."

Another tear rolled down Evelyn's face. She put her spoon in the bowl and wrapped her arms around herself.

Margaret put a hand on her sister's shoulder. "Evie has been severely traumatized by everything we endured while escaping that massacre."

With compassion in her eyes, Mrs. Alberta turned to Margaret. "I'm sure you've been traumatized as well."

Margaret nodded, pursed her lips, praying she wouldn't start crying and make her hosts more uncomfortable than they already were with the way Evelyn was acting.

"Well, if it's alright with you girls, the missus and I want to offer you a home for as long as you need it."

Evelyn exploded with, "Oh my goodness!"

Margaret lifted a hand. Her daddy wouldn't want them to be a burden to anyone. "That is very thoughtful, but we can't abuse your kindness."

Mrs. Alberta put a hand on the table. "You're not abusing anything. God has blessed us with everything that we have. And we want to be a blessing to you and your sister in your time of need."

The tears came then. Margaret didn't even try to wipe them away. She stood up and hugged Mrs. Alberta and then Mr. Allen. "We won't be any trouble, and I promise we won't overstay our welcome."

Evelyn was so overcome by their kindness that she could barely speak. She did hug Mr. and Mrs. Threatt and finally said, "Th-thank y-you."

Margaret sat at the dining room table reading an article in the *Tulsa Tribune*. It was hard to believe a week had passed since she'd eaten at her dining table in Greenwood. And now, apparently, Governor James B. A. Robertson had come to Tulsa after the riot and tried his best to restore order. Before he returned to the capital, he requested an inquiry into events, especially concerning the part that the city and the sheriff's office played in the massacre.

State Attorney General Sargent Prentiss Freeling initiated the investigation. According to the newspaper, the investigation would begin today, June 8. The jury would be selected by June 9—tomorrow.

Anger filled Margaret's lungs. She showed Mrs. Alberta the article when she sat down at the dining table next to her. "How much of an investigation could they have done this fast?"

Mrs. Alberta blew out a puff of air while shaking her head. "Not much, that's for sure."

"If the city and the sheriff's office were involved in killing my daddy and destroying Greenwood, then I want them to pay. They can't play around with this investigation."

Mrs. Alberta put a hand on Margaret's arm. "It just breaks my heart . . . Sometimes I am truly disgusted by this country."

Judge Biddison expected that the state attorney general would call numerous witnesses, both Black and white, due to the large scale of the so-called riot. She didn't know how she would get there, didn't know where she would lay her head. "I'm going back to Greenwood. I'm getting on that witness list. They need to know what them white folks done to us."

If her father was still alive, he would have been the first to testify. If her daddy truly was dead, she wouldn't let his death be for naught.

The next day Elijah drove Margaret to the courthouse. Her stomach did flip-flops as her nerves got the better of her. "You think my testimony will do any good?"

"It's got to." Elijah pulled the car into a parking space down the street from the courthouse. "What those arsonists and killers did to the Greenwood community was pure evil. I have to believe justice will prevail."

Her family's last name was Justice, but would they receive any? "If the sheriff was involved . . ."

Elijah put his finger to her lips. "Don't do that . . . don't doubt yourself. God's going to set this right."

God . . . The word rolled so easily off Elijah's lips. He must have never had a problem that God couldn't solve. Margaret had gone to church every Sunday morning. Served on the youth advisory board and believed every word the preacher said about the Bible. But God had let her down. Turning away from Elijah, she got out of the car. He followed her as she walked down the street.

Anger sparked in the eyes of several of the Black men and women she passed on her way to the courthouse. The devil had wreaked havoc in Greenwood, and Elijah's God hadn't done a thing about it. Now she was going to see if the court system would give them their due. But in a country where colored folks didn't see much justice, Margaret wasn't sure if she was hoping and wishing in vain.

The Tulsa County Courthouse was on the corner of Sixth Street and South Boulder Avenue. It was a massive building that had been constructed with Yule marble. Large and small windows framed in by art deco–style carvings and bricks decorated all three levels.

Walking up the steps of the courthouse, Margaret took in the three archways on the front and sides of the building that paved the way to the entry. Just above those archways, on the second level, were six marble columns that spoke of the weightiness of the building.

Once inside the courthouse, she and Elijah were instructed to walk down the long corridor to get to the area where the hearing was being held.

State Attorney General Sargent Prentiss Freeling was seated at a table, taking down the names of witnesses. He had thin lips,

white hair, and long fingers. After adding her name to the witness list, he told her, "I've got your name down. Can't promise
we'll get to you today."

She sucked in her breath, feeling thick layers of sweat coat
her skin. "How long will you be holding the hearing?"

"Don't know that either." He pointed toward the wooden
benches in the corridor that were already crowded with Greenwood residents, sweating in the stifling hot building. "Just have
a seat, and we'll call you when we can."

As they made their way to the benches, Elijah ran a hand
across his forehead, wiping away the sweat beads that had
formed. "You might not be called to the witness stand for several days, depending on the list of witnesses the attorney general
has," he pointed out.

Margaret squeezed into a small free spot on the bench, then
used her hand to fan herself. But the meager breeze did nothing to cool the smoldering heat within. She wiped the sweat
that dripped from her forehead and then put her hands in her
lap. "I'll stay as long as it takes."

"How will you sleep or eat?"

She hadn't thought about those things . . . only testifying and
telling the jury what those hateful men did to her family. She
couldn't just go to her home and come back tomorrow. Elijah's
question brought to light, once again, all the things, big and
small, that had been taken from her. "I—I don't know."

Elijah wiped his forehead again as his gaze traveled to the
unfriendly-looking guards and the ever-growing tension in the
room. "I can't just leave you here by yourself."

They had only expected this to be a day trip. Elijah was needed
back at the farm; she understood that. But she was needed here.
She had a story to tell. And she wasn't leaving this courthouse
until she told it.

"Margaret . . . Margaret Justice, is that you?"

She swiveled to the left. And there he was. George Martin, one of the handsomest boys in all of Booker T. Washington High. The man who might have been her husband if he hadn't up and decided to go to college all the way in New Orleans.

"Hey, George." She stood and hugged him. As the warmth of his body connected with hers, she was comforted. George was familiar; he'd been a part of the Greenwood that she knew, not the rubbled mess it had become. "My daddy told me you were coming to town. I'm just sorry it had to be at such a terrible time."

Sadness creased the corners of his eyes. "I didn't arrive until the day after. Those soldiers swooped me up and took me to what I would describe as an internment camp . . . acted like us Black men weren't even citizens of this country."

"I searched for my daddy at one of those places. They wouldn't let Mr. Clifton go, even after I vouched for him."

"They're treating us like animals." His nostrils flared. "A white man had to vouch for me."

Margaret's eyebrows scrunched so tight her forehead crinkled. "Did you know the white man who vouched for you?"

"Never saw that man a day in my life . . . said I looked like a good boy and I spoke well enough. Plus, I had my school ID on me." Puffs of air blew from his nostrils as he lifted three fingers. "Took me three days to find my daddy at the Red Cross hospital."

"Mm-mm."

Margaret heard Elijah clear his throat. Remembering her manners, she turned to him. "I'm so sorry, Elijah. I didn't mean to ignore you. Let me introduce you to a childhood friend." She then turned back to George. With a wave of her hand, she said, "George Martin, this is Elijah Porter."

While the two men shook hands, George chuckled. "A childhood friend, huh? We were sweethearts all through high school."

Could she really call George her sweetheart? He had gone on about his life after high school . . . That hadn't been so sweet to Margaret.

"I'm very sorry for all your recent troubles," Elijah said to George.

The two men stood on either side of Margaret. One looking as strong as Samson and the other as meek and mild as a history professor.

"I can hardly believe that all my father worked for is gone. He might not be able to attend this hearing, but I'm going to stay until this judge knows what we've suffered."

"I'm staying too," Margaret told him and then turned to Elijah. "You don't have to worry about me. Go on back to the farm. I'll stay here with George."

Chapter 11

Let the blame for this negro uprising lie right where it belongs . . . and any persons who seek to put half the blame on the white people are wrong and should be told so in no uncertain terms.

—*Tulsa Mayor T. D. Evans, June 14, 1921*

A night of sleeping on a bench in the hallway of the Tulsa Courthouse had proven to be more of a challenge than Margaret imagined. Lifting from the hard, wooden bench, she pressed a hand to her back and rolled her head from side to side to get the kinks out. The only saving grace was that she had George with her.

George had spent most of the previous day telling her about New Orleans and how much he preferred it to Oklahoma. But now as she stretched out her arms and leaned forward, he asked, "Is your dad stuck in one of those camps?"

Her heart constricted. She rolled her neck again. Sat down and let out a long-suffering sigh. "We looked for him at the hospital and at the fairgrounds. Mrs. Pearl had already told me that he wasn't at the convention hall." Margaret shook her head. "We haven't been able to find him."

"I hate to hear that."

Margaret wiped the wetness from around her eyes. "They say he got shot. We think he might be dead." Her hands went up, then flopped back into her lap. "Nobody has produced his body, so we don't know for sure."

"The sad thing is, you'll probably never know. From what I heard, they dumped a bunch of dead bodies in unmarked graves at different places around town. But nobody knows where those graves are."

Margaret's hand went to her mouth. The wood creaked as she stood back up and ran outside. A gust of hot air assaulted her whole being as she burst through those heavy doors. She kept going until she reached the tree that was to the left of the front doors of the courthouse.

The leaves provided no reprieve. But she didn't care. She'd rather take in the hot, sweltering heat of the day than be smothered by the blazing inferno of injustice that colored folks endured for no good reason at all. Could her father's body have just been thrown away as if it was nothing and meant nothing to his children? Were people in this world really that cruel?

"I'm sorry. I probably shouldn't have told you that." George walked up behind her and put a hand on her shoulder. "Never thought I would see anything like what's been done to us. And to think, my dad left the South thinking it would be better for us in Tulsa."

"Same thing my daddy told my mom when they left Alabama. Negroes was being lynched and crosses being burned in their yards. He packed us up and came here." Margaret watched the men and women who looked like her walking in and out of the courthouse. Not a smile on any of their faces. Eyes downcast, shoulders caved inward as if they'd been beaten and didn't know if they could get up before the final count.

Two white men stepped out of the courthouse. One of them pressed a finger to his nose. "It smells like death in there. Why do they let them darkies stink up the courthouse like that?"

Margaret caught a whiff of her underarms and took a few steps away from the courthouse, wrapping her arms around herself.

"We can't go too far. We might be called to testify any minute," George told her.

She nodded to the white men by the entrance. "They think we stink." She lowered her head and turned away from him.

George balked at that. He pointed an accusatory finger toward the courthouse. "If they hadn't burned down our homes, we'd have somewhere to bathe. So the shame is theirs, not ours."

One of the white men threw his cigarette to the ground and approached them. "You talking to me, boy?"

He got in George's face, nostrils flaring as if he was angry at them for being angry about their maltreatment.

Head lifting ever so slightly, George said, "Are you one of the men who burned down the Greenwood neighborhood?"

"What if I am?" the white man said boldly and brashly as his friend joined him.

Margaret stepped in front of George. She lifted a shaky hand. "He wasn't saying anything against you. Please . . . we don't want any trouble."

"Then why don't y'all go home? Why y'all keep coming down to this courthouse, stinking it up and whining about your lot in life?" jeered the man who'd pressed a finger to his nose in front of the courthouse.

"Have a good day, gentlemen." Margaret tugged on George's arm, then pulled him back into the courthouse.

"Why'd you pull me away? Those animals needed every bit of the tongue-lashing I wanted to give them."

Margaret nodded. "They deserved it. But you weren't here the night they destroyed our beloved Greenwood. You didn't see how . . ." Her voice got caught in a tangle of emotions. She exhaled. "I didn't want them to shoot you right in front of the courthouse and then claim they were doing their civic duty by killing another N—"

"Those men should be in jail. Not standing outside degrading us further. But it's the same old way it's always been. When you're white, you're right, and if you're Black, you get arrested for what the white folks did."

George made that statement as if it was fact. Margaret wondered what she had missed. "Who got arrested?"

"You haven't heard?"

They sat back down on the bench. "I've been in Luther, staying over by the Threatt Filling Station before I came back here to testify."

George blew out hot air. His eyes rolled heavenward. "The Tulsa police arrested O. W. Gurley and accused him of causing the riot."

"What? How? They think he asked those white men to storm our neighborhoods, guns a-blazing, with airplanes bombing our homes and businesses?"

"They say Gurley told the Greenwood men to go to the courthouse to stop them white folks from lynching that Rowland boy. Say if he hadn't done that, them white boys wouldn't have gotten so riled up."

"But what about those men who stormed our neighborhood? Why didn't they arrest any of them?"

George clasped his hands together. "It gets better." Expelling a puff of air, he continued, "Now the police say Gurley told them J. B. Stradford and A. J. Smitherman were the ones who incited the riot. So they released Gurley, then went and arrested Stradford and Smitherman."

Margaret's eyes flashed fire. "This is crazy. It makes no sense."

"You and I know it. But they needed to pin this on somebody. The white man throws rocks and hides his hand while Black men get scapegoated for their crimes."

"Shame on them." She looked heavenward. *"God don't make mistakes, Maggie-Pie."* She clamped her hands over her ears, trying to get that lie out of her head.

"I used to love Greenwood. Now I hate this place." George pounded his fist against his leg. "Hate that I brought Brenda all this way just to have her sleep in a tent."

"Who's Brenda?" Her eyes darted about with questions.

"Brenda's my fiancée. I brought her home to introduce her to my father. She's at the hospital with him now."

George had a fiancée. He hadn't said a word while he talked about New Orleans yesterday. The nonchalant way he just blurted it out stung more than she wanted to admit. She'd never imagined that George's staying away meant that he'd found someone else. But life was full of mishaps and miscalculations.

"Well," was all she got out.

She turned her head as the door to the courtroom opened. Mr. Clifton walked out. He'd always been a proud and confident man. Nice suits and hats. And his car with the top that could be let down that he drove around Greenwood in the summertime impressed many in their neighborhood.

The clothes he wore now were dirty and unkempt. Stubbly hair was sprouting on a chin that had always been clean-shaven. She jumped out of her seat and rushed over to him. "Mr. Clifton, what did they say in there? Are they going to do something?"

His shoulders folded inward. He patted her arm as he lowered his head. "Those white folks in there are no better than the ones who set fire to our homes."

"But they called this investigation. Surely they'll see what was done to us wasn't right."

The whole world couldn't be against them. Somebody had to fix this dastardly wrong that had been done to them.

Mr. Clifton shook his head and ambled his way out of the courthouse like he had nothing to do with the rest of his day. No business to tend to and no car to let the top down on and drive wherever he pleased.

Margaret wiped the sweat from her forehead as she turned back to George. "Did you hear him? He thinks we're all sitting around this hot courthouse for nothing."

George's lip curved slightly. "He's lost everything. You can't expect him to be his normal self. He probably doesn't know where his family's going to sleep tonight. Coming here to testify probably discouraged him all the more."

The longer she sat in this courthouse, talking with George and watching the people come and go, the more discouragement settled on her shoulders like a bird perched on a tree branch. People who used to have the world in their hands now looked as if the world had caved in on them. And hadn't it?

"Margaret Justice." A man holding a clipboard held the door to the courtroom open.

It was her turn to tell of the horror she'd witnessed the night everything changed for them. Gulping down the fear that wiggled its way up her throat, she lifted a hand. "I'm Margaret."

Chapter 12

While "Little Africa" was still burning . . . while "dead" wagons were carrying off the victims . . . the fiendish looting, robbing and pillaging was still in progress.

—*Maurice Willows, Red Cross Disaster Relief Report*

No! No!" Evelyn lifted her hands and grabbed the gun from that green-eyed devil. She ran over to Dr. Jackson. Put her hand to his wound. "You're going to be okay," she said as she pressed and pressed and pressed against his wound. But it wasn't enough. Blood oozed from his back, his leg, his head . . . and flowed down the street so thick and heavy it turned into a river of red, devouring everything in its path.

Evelyn desperately thrashed her arms, trying to stay afloat. Panic rose in her chest as the river grew deeper and more powerful, threatening to consume her entirely. She cried, "Help!" but so many people were being consumed by the river that she wondered if anyone would be able to help them.

"Margaret!" she yelled. "Where's Dr. Jackson? Where's Daddy?" Evelyn searched as far as the eye could see, but Margaret had disappeared too. She flapped her arms again and again, trying to keep the blood from entering her mouth. Dr. Jackson floated by her and kept right on floating down the way.

She stopped thrashing against the current so she could reach out and pull the doctor back to her. All at once, the realization that she couldn't swim paralyzed her. She sank and kept on sinking into an abyss of blood and death. She opened her mouth to scream, but it filled with blood.

"Wake up, child. You're having that awful dream again."

Evelyn felt her body shake. The blood . . . the blood was all over her. She jumped out of bed, flailing her arms until she realized that there was no blood . . . she wasn't drowning. And Mrs. Alberta was standing in front of her, holding on to one of her arms.

Grabbing her chest with her other arm, panting and gasping for air, Evelyn cast her gaze wildly around the room. Mrs. Alberta sat her down on the bed. "Put your head between your legs and breathe."

A couple of deep breaths, and Evelyn's breathing was back to normal. She sat there with her elbow on her thigh and her hand pressed against her forehead. "I hate that nightmare . . . Hate seeing that evil boy. But I can't get him out of my mind."

Mrs. Alberta sat down next to her and put an arm around her. "It'll get better." She rubbed Evelyn's back. "I promise it will."

"When?" was all Evelyn had the strength to ask.

Margaret had come to Tulsa to tell her truth but quickly learned the prosecutor wasn't interested in the death and destruction of everything she held dear.

"A lot of witnesses seem to have trouble recollecting what truly happened the night of the riot. Do you have things right in your mind?"

Margaret shifted in her seat, let out the words that had stuck in her head for the last two days. "The horror of that night still lives in me, sir. I could never forget what they did to us."

"And when you say 'they,' are you referring to the Black mob that got this whole thing riled up?" the prosecutor asked her.

She left the courtroom as dejected as the others she'd witnessed in the last couple of days. Now she needed to check on their home. Deep inside, she had hopes that when she made her way to where their house once was, her daddy would be there, clearing out the trash and debris and wood planks that had settled in their yard.

As she walked toward Detroit Street, the sight of tent after tent gave her pause. This was no longer the place she remembered. No hustle and bustle from the neighbors. No pep in anyone's steps. The people seemed lost, walking around as if in a daze. Undoubtedly they were stuck, trying to figure out what to do about the mess before them.

Even though the tents alarmed her, she was thankful the Red Cross had brought them to their community. At least the people had something over their heads while they worked to clear out their yards and rebuild their homes.

One of the tents was like a teepee with a nine- or ten-foot-tall peak at the top. It sloped downward and then flared out on all four sides. It appeared to Margaret that they could stand in the middle of the tent but had to slink down or crawl around the sides of it.

Another style of tent was more of a square box that went straight up about five feet, then sloped upward, like a pointy hat, about another two feet. This was the kind of tent she saw in front of Mrs. Pearl's yard the day Elijah brought her to Greenwood to search for her daddy.

Piles of trash were visible on every curb and corner, over-flowing and spilling onto the street. Flies buzzed around the rotting food and garbage. The once-tidy neighborhood looked unkempt and unsanitary.

A putrid stench hung in the air, a mixture of sour milk, spoiled meat, and decaying vegetables. It was a smell that per-meated everything, clinging to clothes, hair, and skin. Sighing deeply, Margaret kept walking.

When she turned onto Detroit Street, then went a couple more blocks, she noticed there was now a tent in front of her daddy's yard just like the kind Mrs. Pearl had. The tent hadn't been there a few days ago. A fire of possibilities lit within her soul. She quickened her pace as hope dared to break through her despair.

Had her daddy been found? Did he put the tent up in front of their yard? She swung the screen door and ran inside. The tent was no more than eight by eight, like the slave cabin her daddy's daddy had once lived in. A mattress was on the floor on the right side of the tent. A small table with a chair was on the left side. Wood planks had been laid on the floor, making it possible to walk on an even surface. But with the mattress and the small table and chair, there was barely enough room left to turn around.

At least the screen door on the tent would keep out the flies that were buzzing around the trash outside. But that was all that was in the tent. Henry Justice was not inside.

Margaret sat down in the chair and slumped. Then she heard the creak of the screen door and turned around, eyes grow-ing wide. Mrs. Pearl walked in. She was smiling, but Margaret couldn't make her lips return the greeting.

"Has Daddy been here?" she asked. "Did he put this tent together? Did he find us a mattress?"

Mrs. Pearl came to her, gently put a hand on her cheek. "No, dear heart. Your daddy didn't do this."

Margaret said, "Oh," as if a whoosh of air had been pushed out of her. She lowered her head. Heart break, break, breaking.

Mrs. Pearl took Margaret in her arms. "I wish he was here too."

Sweat beads formed on Margaret's forehead and upper lip. Wiping them away, she glanced around the small space, trying not to let the tears that had been loosed by her short-lived hope spill out. "It's like an oven in here."

"I've been sitting my chair outside my tent during the heat of the day, but it stinks so bad out there that sometimes I just stay in my tent and sweat it out."

They stepped outside, and the odor of rotted fish swam up Margaret's nose and gagged her. "That smells terrible."

"I'm hoping I'll get used to it."

"I don't want to get used to this. I want my house built, and I want the trash picked up like it always has been." She wanted her daddy too. But she didn't think that wish would come true, so she let it drift on the currents of the rancid air they were forced to breathe in.

"I think you need to go back to them filling station people until we get the insurance money and can build this place back up." Mrs. Pearl pointed toward the tent. "That nice fellow of yours is the one who put the tent up for you and brought the mattress by here. Said he'd be back tonight to see if you were still at the courthouse."

Confusion danced in Margaret's eyes. She glanced at the tent, then asked, "Elijah?"

Mrs. Pearl snapped her fingers. "That's what he told me . . . Elijah."

"He did this . . . for me?"

"Said you might be looking for a place to sleep depending on how long court held over."

Kneading the dough for biscuits as she helped Mrs. Alberta in the kitchen, Evelyn found her mind turning over thoughts of Margaret being run out of that courthouse, or worse yet, shot dead for daring to show her face in Tulsa.

"Shouldn't Margaret be back by now?"

Mrs. Alberta stirred the soup in the large pot. "Elijah said there were a lot of witnesses. And anyway, he went back down there to check on her, so stop worrying."

"I just don't want those evil men getting hold of her."

One of the field hands knocked on the back door. When Mrs. Alberta opened it, he handed her a basket of eggs. "Figured you'd be wanting some eggs soon enough."

Smiling at him, Mrs. Alberta said, "Thank you. I'm almost out." She opened the refrigerator and put the eggs inside, then turned back to the man who was still waiting by the back door. "I could use some more milk when y'all milk them cows."

"Sure thing." He tapped his hat to her, closed the back door, and headed back to the field.

"How much do field hands get paid?" Evelyn asked, looking at the man's departing form from the kitchen window.

"Not enough for all the hours they work in the hot sun, that's for sure."

Finished with kneading the biscuits, Evelyn wiped her hands. "I don't think I want to work in the hot sun all day."

Mrs. Alberta turned to Evelyn, a look of wonder on her face. "What's got you thinking about field work?"

Evelyn bit down on her lip, then said, "I need to earn money so I can pay my way to design school."

Mrs. Alberta had been slicing freshly made banana nut bread. She put the knife down and gave Evelyn her full attention. "I don't believe you mentioned anything about design school. Is that where you were going this fall?"

"Yes, ma'am. I've been accepted to the New York School of Fine Art and Applied Art. My daddy told me that since Margaret was finished with school, it was my turn." Evelyn let that last word out on a that-was-the-way-it-was sigh.

Looking up, Evelyn caught Mrs. Alberta wiping away a tear. "Don't cry like that. I didn't mean to make you sad."

Mrs. Alberta waved her concern away as she put two pieces of banana nut bread in a basket with some fried chicken and rice with gravy. "So how's a job going to help you?"

"I figured if I could get a job, maybe I could earn enough money to get myself to college by fall. Maybe even give you and Mr. Allen some money for boarding us."

"Me and Mr. Allen do well enough without you and Margaret having to pay your board and keep."

"Me and Margaret, we're not takers, ma'am. My daddy taught us better than that."

Mrs. Alberta nodded, wiped another tear from her face, then handed the basket to Evelyn. "Take this food to Mr. Allen. When you get there, tell him that you're applying for the position at the filling station."

Evelyn's eyes lit up. "You think he'd hire me? I used to work in my daddy's store, so I could be of use stocking his shelves."

Mrs. Alberta nodded, then shooed Evelyn out the door. As Evelyn headed toward the filling station, swinging the basket and dreaming of all the money she would save toward college, Mrs. Alberta yelled out to her, "If he says he don't need no help at the filling station, tell him that I just quit."

Chapter 13

Thirty-five city blocks were looted systematically, then burned to a cinder, and the twelve thousand population thereof scattered like chaff before the wind.

—Maurice Willows, Red Cross Disaster Relief Report

True to his word, Elijah returned to Greenwood later that evening. With sweat dripping from her face, Margaret opened the screen door to greet him. The grin she received told Margaret that he was relieved to see her.

"What? You thought they'd gobble me up at the courthouse?"

Taking off his hat, he told her, "Wasn't worried about that at all. I knew you'd bite back."

She didn't feel much like biting or fighting today. Her body still ached from sleeping on that hard bench, and her heart ached from everything else. "Well, I'm all worn out from trying to stand up for what's right at that courthouse, against folks who didn't care a lick."

"Maybe something was said that got through to the jury."

"We can only hope," Margaret told him. But in truth, she was just about all hoped out. "Thank you for putting this tent together for me. I have never seen one with an actual screen door attached."

Elijah nodded. "The screen door was a part of the package. These tents are built to handle all types of weather."

"It certainly holds in the heat."

Elijah looked out at the mounds of rubble in her yard, then back at her. "Well, I came to see if you wanted me to take you back to the farm for a spell. But if you'd rather stay here to be closer to George—"

"George?" Her eyebrows knitted together in a perplexed expression. "Why would I want to stay here for George?"

"I thought maybe . . ."

If Elijah was fishing to see if she still had designs on George, he was being very clumsy about it, so she decided to help him out. "George is engaged to be married, and it's not to me. So we are not sweet on each other."

"Oh." He turned back to the pile of rubble, ducked his head. Like he was trying to hide in plain sight.

Margaret stepped outside. She was wearing the same clothes from the day Elijah dropped her at the courthouse. The pungent order wasn't only coming from the neighborhood, but from her unwashed body as well. She folded her arms across her chest. An errant wind blew. A nauseating smell drifting up her nose caused her to cough.

"Mrs. Pearl thinks I should go back to the filling station until we get everything settled with the insurance company."

Eyes wet with compassion, Elijah told her, "To be honest with you, I could barely sleep last night thinking about you being here, having to handle all of this"—he waved an arm toward the pile of rubble—"on your own."

"Can't handle nothing till we get that insurance money." First plan of action once the insurance money came in was to hire someone to remove all the debris from their yard. She wasn't a day laborer and didn't want to work that hard.

He nudged his head toward the car. "Let me take you back to the farm. I'll bring you back once you have things settled with your insurance company."

"I must look terrible." She turned away from him, wrapping her arms around her chest, wondering if he was repulsed by the smells.

But Elijah shook his head. "What I see is a woman determined to survive. And that's a beautiful thing in my sight."

"Hey, pretty lady, can you come pump my gas today?"

Evelyn rolled her eyes. She went back inside the store just a few steps away from the gas pumps. She'd been working at the filling station for two weeks now. Another day, another ogling customer. She sold accessory items inside the store like bread, canned goods, and snacks. On hot days like today, customers wanted a cold soda pop.

She sold them whatever they needed and also took payment for the gas Mr. Allen pumped. It was a small bungalow-like building, but it was spacious enough for customers to walk around and collect their needs.

"Evelyn don't pump gas. That's my job," Mr. Allen told the man as he lifted the pump from the handle. He pumped five gallons of gas, then stuck his hand out toward the customer. "That'll be one dollar."

Leering in Evelyn's direction, the customer waved his dollar in the air. "I'll pay her."

He started walking toward the store. But Mr. Allen put a hand to the man's chest, stopping his forward motion. "You'll pay me, or you'll find somewhere else to get your gas if you can't be respectful."

The man shoved the dollar in Mr. Allen's hand, then got in his car and slammed the door. "Didn't mean no harm. Just wanted to introduce myself to the pretty lady."

A lot of the men who stopped at the filling station didn't mean no harm. But they were twenty or thirty years older than Evelyn. And Margaret would have her hide if she entertained men old enough to be their daddy.

Why these men were always ogling her was a mystery to Evelyn. She looked dreadful in her Threatt Filling Station shirt and overalls. Wished she could design some new uniforms for the filling station. But if she did, would Mr. Allen even use them once she left for college?

Evelyn preferred dresses and church hats. But even if she still had her nice dresses and hats, she wouldn't be able to wear them to the filling station, not with the kind of grimy work she was doing.

"How am I supposed to change a tire without getting my nails dirty?"

Mr. Allen took the handkerchief out of his pocket, wiped the sweat from his forehead, and scowled at her. "You're wearing overalls and worried about your nails? Maybe you should be working with the field hands; then your nails will really get dirty."

"I don't like digging in the dirt either." Evelyn scrunched her nose. The whole idea of working in the dirt or changing tires . . . What had become of the life she was supposed to have?

Looking up from the tire he was working on, Mr. Allen said, "If you don't want to do the work, then why are you here?"

Evelyn poked her lip out. "That's not fair, Mr. Allen. You know I need the money."

"Girls," he muttered under his breath. Then he said, "If you need the money, then you need to work. Now get down here so I can teach you something useful."

Evelyn liked Mr. Allen. She was thankful he'd given her a job. So even though this was not what she imagined doing with her life, she got down on the ground and let Mr. Allen teach her how to change a tire, or at least how to blow up the inner tube and then fit it to the outer rubber part of the tire.

After that, she took her place behind the checkout window until her shift was over. On nice sunshiny days, folks needed gas to get from here to there. And having lots of customers made the day go by faster.

"Suppertime," Evelyn announced as she hopped off the stool. Her favorite time of day. Mrs. Alberta's pots were filled with love and goodness. She grabbed her purse and was headed back to the farm with Mr. Allen when she noticed the automobile that had pulled in for gas about an hour ago was now parked behind the filling station.

She pointed toward the car and said, "Something's up with those people. They came into the store earlier and grabbed a bunch of food like they was headed on a journey, but they didn't go nowhere."

Looking up at the sky, he said, "It's about to get dark."

Evelyn glanced back at the automobile. "You should say something. What if we leave and they break into the store?"

He turned her away from the filling station and nudged his head toward the farm. "Come on, Mama's cooking, and I want my portion while it's still hot."

Evelyn scratched her head. "You're not going to make them leave? What if they stay all night?"

They crossed the street, walking through the field toward the farmhouse. "I take it you didn't travel much outside of Tulsa with your daddy."

Evelyn shook her head. "We took a few trips, but he was always so busy with the store that we didn't spend a lot of time visiting or traveling."

"Well, I have traveled with my family enough to know that no colored man wants to be on the road with his family or by himself at night. Too much can happen to a man and his family that folks can claim wasn't the way it actually was in the dark of night."

While Evelyn was noodling on that, Mr. Allen added, "Sometimes people just need a safe place to rest when traveling these unfriendly roads. Not many places where folks who look like us can get lodging."

Evelyn had experienced danger while in her own home, but she'd never given much thought to the dangers people like her faced while driving from one place to the next. "So you let them sleep on your property?"

"As many as need to," he answered. "I'd rather they rest up a few hours at the filling station than injure themselves after falling asleep while driving. Or trouble come their way in the dark of night."

"When people were down on their luck where I come from, my daddy used to let them pick up groceries and put it on a tab. I watched him tear up Mrs. Pearl's tab after her husband passed on."

"Your daddy sounds like a good man."

Evelyn nodded. "He was." They were silent for the rest of the walk, but thoughts churned in Evelyn's mind. Thoughts about the evil she'd witnessed in Greenwood and the goodness of people like her daddy and Mr. Allen.

When they reached the farmhouse, just before going in, Evelyn turned to him. "You know what, Mr. Allen? I think God must put people like you and my daddy on this earth to balance out people like that terrible white boy who shot Dr. Jackson and those men who burned down our home."

She hugged the man who had provided a safe place for her and Margaret to land after experiencing the most horrific event of their lives. "Thank you."

She then opened the door and went inside but noticed that Mr. Allen didn't follow. When she turned back, he was wiping his eyes. The aroma of rice, beans, and fried chicken wafted from the kitchen to the entryway. She left Mr. Allen to recover himself and headed to the kitchen.

With the *Tulsa World* newspaper in her hand, Margaret paced the floor of her bedroom while Evelyn sat on the bed waiting for Margaret to explain why she kept saying, "I don't believe it. I don't believe it."

"What does it say? Did the grand jury indict those men or not?"

Blacks and whites had been interviewed for twelve days in front of that all-white grand jury. Margaret had hoped that the jury would have compassion for them—would understand their great loss—but in the end, they had been no more compassionate to them than the men who had terrorized their neighborhoods.

Crumpling the newspaper up, Margaret told her sister, "They didn't indict even one of those white men."

The jury blamed the riot on the so-called Black mobs that tried to stop a lynching, totally ignoring the white mobs that destroyed everything they held dear.

They poured salve on their guilt by noting that law enforcement officials had failed in preventing the massacre. But law enforcement hadn't just failed to stop the massacre; they participated in it.

Margaret was undone. She didn't know what to believe anymore. Didn't know who to trust or what to do with her doubts and fears.

"How they just gon' let those men go? They killed our daddy." Evelyn sat on the bed with her arms wrapped around her legs as Margaret balled that newspaper so tight, it could be used for the next baseball game on the Threatt property.

Margaret threw the wad of paper to the floor. "They don't care about our losses, just care about our skin color."

"But Daddy—"

"Was a thug . . . to hear that prosecutor and the jury tell it."

Unfolding her legs, Evelyn scooted to the end of the bed and let her legs dangle off. "Our daddy wasn't a thug. He just didn't want those white men lynching that Rowland boy for something he probably didn't do in the first place."

"Of course he wasn't," Margaret agreed. "Daddy was a good man. But that jury didn't care nothing about that. All they cared about was not sending their white neighbors to prison for crimes they committed."

Margaret's chest heaved as she stood looking out the window. Looking out at a farm that was not her home. Looking out at the people who worked the farm, who had all been kind to her and Evelyn. She was thankful that she and Evelyn were able to stay with the Threatts. But her resolve to fight had not changed. Those people would not get away with what they'd done to them. She just had to figure out her next steps.

"Makes me sick." Evelyn shook her head. "How can human beings turn a blind eye to what those bloodthirsty savages did to us?" Evelyn sighed, put a hand under her chin. "I don't ever want to go back to Greenwood."

"We have a home that Daddy worked hard to build. And I cannot . . . I will not let them take everything from us."

Margaret's eyes shone with fire as she settled in her resolve. "I just got to figure some things out." Like where was she going to sleep while working on their home? That tent was not appealing to her in the least.

"But what if those hateful men come back? What then?"

Seeing the fear in her sister's eyes, Margaret sat down on the bed, put an arm around Evelyn's shoulders. "I know you're scared. I am too. But we can't let them win."

Like a whisper in the wind, Evelyn told Margaret once again, "I don't want to go back."

Rocking back and forth as if soothing a crying baby, Margaret planted a kiss on top of Evelyn's head. "I love you, my sweet sister. Things will get better for us—just you wait and see."

Chapter 14

The number of dead is a matter of conjecture. One estimates the number of killed as high as 300, other estimates being as low as 55.

—*Maurice Willows, Red Cross Disaster Relief Report*

Seated at the dining table, a plate of mashed potatoes and meat loaf in front of her, Margaret lifted her fork, mouth watering for a taste of Mrs. Alberta's delicious food. Coming into the dining room, Mrs. Alberta placed a letter on the table next to her plate. "This came for you today," she said.

"A letter? For me?" Margaret put down her fork and picked up the envelope. Not many people knew that she and Evelyn were staying with the Threatt family. When she saw that it was from Mrs. Pearl, she pushed her plate aside and opened it, hoping that there was finally news about her father.

> I hope this letter finds you and Evelyn well. I've rarely had an idle moment since you left. The Red Cross is providing some assistance but believe that we should work for whatever is given to us.
>
> I don't want to trouble your mind with all the goings-on here. But the authorities in these parts

have noticed that you aren't in your tent and haven't signed up for any of the work duties. I don't want to see you lose your home as I have been asked repeatedly by the Red Cross if you have abandoned the place.

And one more thing to add to the pile of dung being flung at us. My insurance claim has been denied. So you need to find out what's going on with yours.

At this point, I don't know if we will be able to rebuild our homes, but while all of that is being sorted out, most of us have decided to live in our tents, to prove to the city of Tulsa that we have not abandoned our property. I'm thinking you might need to do the same.

Love you and Evelyn dearly,
Mrs. Pearl

Margaret put down the letter, scooted her chair away from the table, and went outside. She sat down on the porch steps and wrapped her arms around herself as she tried to process the things her friends in Greenwood were enduring.

"What's got you so troubled? Your supper's getting cold."

Mrs. Alberta sat down next to her. Margaret leaned her head on Mrs. Alberta's shoulder and cried a multitude of sorrows.

Patting her back, Mrs. Alberta said, "Cry it out, chile. Get it all out."

"They burn down our homes, and now they trying to stop us from rebuilding." Margaret wiped the storm from her face and sat back up.

Mrs. Alberta pursed her lips. Put her hands in her lap. "Life is full of injustices. I pray every day for things to get better for my children."

"I don't know how to pray anymore," Margaret confessed, still wiping tears from her face. "I loved God, I really did. I just don't understand why He hates us so much."

"No, no. I'm not gon' let you say that." Mrs. Alberta shook her head. "God don't hate us."

Margaret lifted a hand, let it flap back in her lap. "I can't stay here no more."

Mrs. Alberta's eyes widened. "Now wait a minute. I might disagree with you, but that doesn't mean you have to leave."

"I'm not upset with you." Margaret took Mrs. Alberta's hand in hers and squeezed it. "I have to go back to Greenwood. Them city officials trying to steal away what's left of my daddy, and I can't let them do it."

Putting a hand to Margaret's cheek, Mrs. Alberta said, "Let your heart lead you."

"But Evie don't want to go back." In truth, the only thing in Margaret that wanted to go back to Greenwood was the great big old space in her heart for her daddy. She wouldn't let all that he worked for be for nothing. But living in a tent, surrounded by the awful stench and conditions, wasn't what Margaret's dreams were made of. And she knew for sure that Evie wouldn't be able to handle it.

"You go and do what needs doing to protect your daddy's legacy. Evelyn can stay here with us. She's already working at the filling station." A slight giggle escaped Mrs. Alberta's lips. "Although Allen wouldn't say she's doing much work."

"My daddy used to say the same thing about that girl. She'd go to the grocery store to stock the shelves and mix up everything. He said he was better off doing it himself."

Margaret laughed at the memory of her daddy being so frustrated after one of Evelyn's attempts to restock the shelves. She was grateful for the moment's respite from sorrow. Hugging Mrs. Alberta, she said, "Thank you."

Fireflies, watermelon, and baseball filled the night and brought a reprieve from all that would come on the morrow. Margaret sat in a folding chair holding Mrs. Alberta's baby while Evelyn ran around the back side of the field catching fireflies and putting them in glass jars with the Threatts' oldest sons, Ulysses, David, and Allen Jr.

The boys were having the time of their life, laughing and diving after flying bugs as if they were leprechauns chasing after a pot of gold. Evelyn clamped the lid on one of the jars and danced around the back of the field with the boys like she was reliving her carefree childhood with them.

Allen Threatt, Elijah, and the other field workers gathered in the open field, throwing the ball and swinging that bat as if they were in the Negro League. While patting baby Alonia's bottom to settle him down, Margaret watched Elijah grab his bat and make his way to home base.

"You want me to take him?" Mrs. Alberta held her hands out when the baby started squirming.

"No, I've got him. You go on and cut up that watermelon. My mouth's been watering for a slice." Baby Alonia wanted to get down and crawl, but Mrs. Alberta thought he was too young to be let loose on the grassy field. Margaret hadn't seen much grass in Greenwood the last time she was there, or had she just missed it? Had the debris and trash covered the grass, making everything dull and gray?

"I'll take care of the watermelon." Mrs. Alberta pointed to Alonia. "Don't let him down."

"I won't." Margaret stood and bounced Alonia on her hip. He was eight months. Ate cornbread and mashed potatoes, so he was weighing heavy on her hip. But Margaret kept bouncing him.

Elijah was at bat. Mr. Allen was the pitcher. "We got the big boy to strike out now." He wound his arm around, preparing to throw the ball.

Elijah yelled back at him. "Just come on with it." He twirled the bat and positioned his feet. Mr. Allen threw the first ball so fast that Elijah barely had time to swing before the umpire yelled, "Strike one."

Margaret pointed toward the field, leaned her head toward Alonia. "Look, your daddy is getting ready to strike Elijah out."

Elijah's back was toward Margaret, but he turned and said, "I heard that. Now you're about to eat them words."

Margaret put her hand over her mouth and backed away from the field as Elijah lifted the bat and swung it hard, connecting with the ball and sending it sailing in the air so far that Elijah walked to each base and then got his home run before the ball was found for the next player up to bat.

"Did you see that?" Margaret punched her fist in the air several times as she adjusted Alonia on her hip. "Home run!"

Joy! She felt joy for Elijah. Joy for easy days watching a baseball game as the sun hung low in the sky. Joy at bouncing this baby boy on her hip even as she wondered about the day she might have her own husband and baby to care for. But how could she wonder about such things with the mountain before her?

"You said I was going to strike out," Elijah reminded her when he sauntered over to her and flexed his arms, showing off his muscles.

She pointed toward the baby. "I was just trying to distract Alonia. It wasn't looking good for you, though."

Elijah laughed. "That first ball did come in fast, but I got him."

Mrs. Alberta walked back over to them. She handed Margaret a slice of watermelon, then took the baby out of her arms. "You did good with Alonia. Thanks for giving me a break."

"He was no trouble at all. I like babies." Margaret took a bite of her watermelon.

Mrs. Alberta turned to Elijah. "Did Margaret tell you she's planning on going back to Greenwood?"

Elijah's eyes widened as he glanced over at her. "She did not."

Thinking on the way she looked and smelled the last time Elijah rescued her from Greenwood brought a sigh floating on the wind. "I don't want to go back so soon, but the mayor is trying to take our homes. I've got to fight for what my daddy built."

Mr. Allen called to Elijah. "You playing ball or chatting with the pretty lady?"

"I'm coming," Elijah called over his shoulder, then asked Margaret, "Can we talk later tonight?"

Margaret nodded, but as Elijah headed to the field, Evelyn tapped her on the shoulder and swung her around. Her sister put hands on hips. "Did I hear you say something about Greenwood?"

Margaret hadn't wanted Evelyn to overhear their conversation. She'd planned to discuss her decision with Evie after the baseball game. "I was going to tell you."

Evelyn pursed her lips. "Why are you going back to that horrible place? You told me about the flies, the trash, the tent . . . Don't you remember all of that?"

Margaret looped her arm in Evelyn's and began walking back toward the house with her. "Don't be cross with me. If there were any other way, believe me, I would wait until things were better in Greenwood. But it's just not possible to wait."

"I'm not going back. I'm working for Mr. Allen so I can earn money for my college classes," Evelyn told her in no uncertain terms.

Margaret prayed that Evie would not always feel this way about Greenwood. As nice as the Threatt family had been to them, and as nice as everything was here, Greenwood was still their home. "Mrs. Alberta has already assured me that you can stay right here with them. I hope you can earn enough money for college, but don't get your hopes up."

Evelyn stomped her foot. "You went to college. I deserve to go too."

"Of course you deserve to go. I just don't know if we'll have enough money. The insurance company has been denying claims, so we might need every dime we can spare to fix the house."

"Come to New York with me. I can go to design school and you can find a teaching job."

Margaret shook her head. She could never run off and leave her father's business unfinished. The things that mattered to him now mattered to her. "I need you to promise me something."

Margaret and Evelyn stood looking at each other face-to-face. "While I'm in Greenwood, I want you to listen to Mrs. Alberta and Mr. Allen."

Rolling her eyes, Evelyn said, "I'm eighteen. I know how to take care of myself."

"You think you know. You've led a sheltered life. So listen to me when I tell you to stay out of trouble while I'm gone."

Evelyn unfolded her arms. Her eyes took on sadness. "Don't go, sissy. I can't bear the thought of you suffering like that."

Smiling, Margaret tried to put on a brave face. "It won't be so bad. And Mrs. Pearl is there, so I'll have company."

Evelyn pursed her lips.

"I'm doing this for us." Margaret lifted her pinky finger. Evelyn hesitated but then wrapped her pinky around Margaret's. "Justice sisters stick together."

Evelyn tightened her grip on Margaret's finger as she said, "Then don't go back to Greenwood. Stay here and get a job. That way we can save enough money to get our own place. Maybe you can come to New York with me when I start design school."

"I have to go." Margaret pulled her finger away and stepped back. "You just mind your manners."

Chapter 15

Negroes are a servant class of people and there is no reason why the women should not work as well as the men.

—*Head of the Tulsa Reconstruction Committee*

To keep the reeking odor of human waste, sweat, and garbage from assaulting her nostrils and leaving a vomit-
inducing taste in her mouth, Margaret draped a scarf around
her face as she worked.

When she arrived back in Greenwood last week, she was
told she needed to check in with the Red Cross so she could
receive some supplies to cover basic needs in her tent, like a
pot, pan, bowl, and spoon. A pillow and blanket for her mattress.

The counselor at the Red Cross told her she would be assigned to a work detail for any items received. Margaret thought
she would be assigned to teach the children but instead found
herself on meal duties.

She and several other women created a firepit on the side of
the street a couple of blocks up from where her tent was and
directly across from a huge pile of trash. They set up two tables
next to the firepit to handle food preparation. She put the rice
and butter beans in bowls that still had the stain of yesterday's
beans in them.

The water that was delivered in jugs and pots was to be used sparingly, so she prayed that no one would get sick from anything she served. "Come and get it," she called out to the men who were digging ditches for the sewage.

There was no relief from the odors that permeated Greenwood. Even the night breeze carried with it the stench of human waste and rotted garbage. When she closed the door on her tent, sweat like a waterfall trickled down her face, making her just as miserable as the smells outside. The dawning of a new day brought no reprieve from her troubles.

Work. Everyone had to keep their heads down and work. Fear that the Red Cross might take their tents or not supply the promised lumber to rebuild their homes was ever on their minds. Even the children had to work for the schoolbooks the Red Cross provided.

The head of the city's Reconstruction Committee had stated, "The Negro is a servant class, so they must work for any relief they receive."

In all her life, she had never felt like a "servant class." Her daddy had raised her and Evelyn to believe that they were exceptional and could do and be anything they wanted. He'd said, "Them slavery days over, so nobody's gon' tell my girls what they can't do in this world."

"How you doing, Mr. Clifton?" she asked as she handed him a bowl of beans.

His face and clothes were caked in dirt. He was a long way from the dry cleaner who kept their clothes clean and pressed. "My back hurts, but don't nobody care about that." He took the offered meal. Turned to find a seat. The slump in his back was pronounced as he held on to the bowl with one hand and rubbed his lower back with the other.

Mr. Johnson lived a few houses down from them on Detroit

Street. He grabbed a bowl from the table without so much as a thank-you or a backward glance. Mr. Johnson had always been friendly, with kind words for her and Evelyn.

Back in the comforts of the Threatt place, Margaret had romanticized the idea of living in a tent and protecting her homestead. But the place was nothing like the prosperous area she grew up in, with stately mansions next to modest well-kept homes and businesses. Men and women who walked straight and proud down the streets of Greenwood with a pep in their step and a wave to folks passing by.

Now it was more a shantytown or a war-torn area where bombs had exploded, leaving dust, debris, and calloused hands in their wake.

When she was done with her work assignment, Margaret walked to the insurance office just outside of Greenwood where her daddy had made his monthly payments faithfully for over a decade.

On the way, she passed tent after tent, folks sitting outside on stumps, wiping sweat from their heads, others pulling trash out of the yards and carrying it to the side of the road. The menfolk would come by to pick up the trash that families laid on the side of the road as part of their service to the Red Cross. Most times, though, the trash sat for days on end before someone could get to it.

Mrs. Mabel B. Little walked the streets with a Bible in her hand, yelling out, "Hold on, Christian soldiers. God's gon' fix it. We shall rise again."

Mrs. Johnson sat in front of her tent with three of her children at her feet. They all looked hungry, but she raised a hand in praise. "Thank You, God. Come see about us."

"Oh, He will—just keep the faith," Mrs. Mabel said as she headed on down the street.

Margaret knew Mrs. Mabel to be a God-fearing woman, a faithful church member. But Mrs. Mabel had lost her home and her beauty parlor. Her husband had lost his café, so how could she still walk the street with that Bible talking about how God was going to fix things for them? Margaret shook her head and kept walking.

The farther she moved away from Greenwood, the more the stench dissipated, and she pulled the scarf down as she crossed the train tracks . . . the same tracks she'd run for her life on the day the airplanes came and started shooting at them.

Her heart raced as she looked up at the sky. Ducking as if something might drop on her, she got off those tracks as fast as her feet would carry her. She had a mission this afternoon, and nothing was going to stop her. Opening the door to the insurance company that her daddy had trusted, she shook the shameful correspondence she'd received a couple of days ago in the redheaded secretary's face. "I demand to speak with someone about this. How do you expect me to rebuild my home if y'all won't pay the insurance claim?"

"Ma'am, there's no one here for you to speak with." The woman smugly pointed toward the paper in Margaret's hand. "The correspondence tells you everything you need to know."

"But this says y'all won't pay due to rioting in the neighborhood."

The woman folded her arms and nodded as if enough had been said.

But that wasn't any kind of an explanation as far as Margaret was concerned. They had it all wrong. Surely this matter would be resolved once she enlightened them. "White men came into our neighborhood and bombed it. Threw lit torches into our homes. We were running for our lives when those men crossed into our neighborhood and caught us unaware."

The woman pursed her lips. "Every insurance company in the state has reviewed this incident, and no one is paying for what you people brought on yourselves."

"How did we bring any of this on ourselves?" Margaret's voice rose. "We didn't do anything to any of those men. One of them tried to shoot me, and I'd never seen him a day in my life before that night. Now my home is destroyed, and I haven't seen hide nor hair of my daddy since, and y'all say we did it to ourselves."

When the woman didn't respond but kept staring at her as if she was the troublemaker and was getting what she deserved, Margaret's hand shook with the correspondence as she waved it back and forth. "You won't get away with this. You're going to pay out that claim . . . We paid your company for over ten years. You're going to pay!"

She kept shouting those words until a white man in a black business suit with a crisp white shirt and a nice clean white handkerchief in his jacket pocket stepped out of his office and jabbed an angry finger toward the door. "You get out of here this instant, or I'll get the law on you."

Looking down at the dust-ridden cotton dress she'd purchased from the secondhand store, then back at the clean suit, clean shirt, and clean hands of the man threatening to get the law on her, she had a sinking feeling that men like him always won, while people like her and Mr. Clifton and Mrs. Pearl would always strike out.

"Call the law on yourself," she told him as she let the insurance correspondence drift from her hand to the floor. She left the office as despair clung to her like a wet blanket.

A few blocks away from the insurance company, she put the scarf back over her face. But as she passed the area where rotted food had been dumped, the odor penetrated the scarf, causing her to gag.

When the gagging stopped, she crossed the street only to see two children crouched next to their tent like animals relieving themselves outside. The tears came then. She tried to wipe them away and think on better days, but nothing was going right for them. It was like the whole neighborhood had fallen into a pit and couldn't claw their way out no matter how they tried.

In the week she'd been back home, she and Mrs. Pearl had only been able to spend a couple of hours a few nights clearing out the debris from their homes. Those efforts didn't seem to put much of a dent in the work needing to be done. The Red Cross had promised lumber and supplies, but they had to clear the area themselves and figure out how to rebuild their homes with no money to hire help.

What was she doing? Could she really rebuild their home and her dad's business with no money? And no help? Had she overestimated her abilities?

Margaret rounded the corner to Detroit Street with serious thoughts of throwing in the towel taking root in her mind. This was too hard . . . too much. But if she gave up, where would she and Evie live? They couldn't impose on the Threatt family forever.

Rolling up her sleeves for the work at hand, she pressed forward and wiped the tears from her face even as her heart beat heavy. But as she arrived at her house, Margaret's eyes lit with delight. Elijah had come back and had brought three other men with him. Two were working in Mrs. Pearl's yard, and Elijah and the other man worked in hers.

She couldn't help herself. Margaret hugged him and kissed his cheek. "I can't believe you're here. How did you know I needed help?"

With hands at his waist, feet planted firmly on the ground, and a smile of appreciation for the kiss on his cheek, he told her, "Seems to me a lot of folks need help in these parts."

Margaret looked to the sky. "I hope it doesn't start raining before y'all can haul some of this stuff away."

Elijah looked up, eyebrows furrowed. "There's not a cloud in the sky."

"Can't trust the calm," Margaret told him. "The rain could come just like that." She snapped her fingers.

"Well, Mr. Allen is allowing us to spend two days a week down here. So if it does rain, we'll finish tomorrow what we don't get done today."

"Mrs. Pearl, did you hear that?" Margaret turned to her left as the woman walked over to them. "We've got help!"

"It was a blessed sight to see them," she said.

Elijah went back to work, pulling tree limbs and the broken pieces of her life out of the rubble and setting them on one of the two wagons they'd brought with them. A blessed sight indeed. When Margaret had arrived back in Greenwood, not much of the debris had been removed from Mrs. Pearl's area. A few men had been helping her right up until the Red Cross demanded that they dig ditches, haul trash, and do whatever else the city refused to do since no one wanted to set foot in Greenwood anymore.

The men in the neighborhood were simply too exhausted with the backbreaking work they were forced to do for twenty-five cents a day. When the day was done, they couldn't even remove their own debris, so helping others had been put on hold.

"How did it go with them shysters on the other side of the tracks?" Mrs. Pearl asked.

Margaret's shoulders lifted, then fell on a heavy sigh. "They took Daddy's money for all them years, but now they say they're not responsible to pay out the insurance money."

"It's a lot of that going around. Everybody else I've talked to is having the same problem. Go see Buck Franklin. He and

I. H. Spears been working to help with all this insurance fraud business."

Buck Franklin hadn't lived in Greenwood but a few months. He and I. H. Spears had opened a law office on Greenwood Avenue. Their office was destroyed during the massacre like many other businesses, but they had set up a tent and were still hard at work for the people in the community. "I'll go see him in the morning," she told Mrs. Pearl, then started pulling from the mounds of debris in her yard and throwing the stuff onto Elijah's wagon.

But Elijah was having none of it. "Go sit down with Mrs. Pearl. You two need to take a rest. Let the menfolk handle this tonight."

Margaret's eyes shone with unshed tears. She didn't know what she had done to deserve a friend like Elijah, but she was grateful. "Okay, but at least let us rustle up a meal for y'all."

"I could eat." He smiled. Rubbed his belly as he went back to work.

"You can always eat," Margaret joked. "That's why your head's so big."

He then flexed his big arms. "Nope. That's why I'm so strong."

"Whatever. Just get over there and scoop that rubble with those strong arms." Margaret sat down next to Mrs. Pearl, laughing and grinning. Elijah's arrival in Greenwood had proved to be just the balm she needed.

Chapter 16

We charge that . . . on the 7th day of June 1921, the
above named defendants . . . passed and approved a pur-
ported ordinance, attempting to extend the fire limits of
the City of Tulsa.

—*Joe Lockard vs. T. D. Evans, fire ordinance lawsuit*

O. W. Gurley had designed the forty acres of land he'd
purchased with short but substantial blocks. None were
more substantial than Greenwood Avenue. You could walk
from the one hundredth block to take in a movie to the three
hundredth block for a nice meal in a matter of quick-stepping
minutes.

Block after block, there had always been something to do,
with two movie theaters, restaurants, a bakery, a confectionery,
grocery stores, churches, beauty parlors, and barbershops. Anything that was needed could be found on Greenwood Avenue
or on nearby Archer Street. But today, the only people open for
business as far as the eye could see were Attorney Buck Franklin
and Attorney I. H. Spears.

Their law practice had been at 107$^{1}/_{2}$ Greenwood Avenue.
Like most businesses in Greenwood, it had been burned down
as if its very presence offended. Mr. Franklin and Mr. Spears's

tent had a wide opening in the front, the floor lined with clay bricks. The tent had just enough space for a large desk that was shared by the two attorneys and their secretary, Effie Thompson, along with mounds and mounds of law books.

I. H. Spears was seated on one side of the desk, Buck Franklin on the other. Effie Thompson was seated at one end of the desk with a typewriter in front of her. She was taking dictation from Mr. Spears when Margaret approached, so she went to Mr. Franklin.

"Good day, sir. My name is Margaret Justice. I live over on Detroit Street, and I was told I needed to come see you about my daddy's insurance company refusing to pay out our claim."

Buck put the law book he was reading on the desk and gave her his full attention. "We're working on these cases. Seems like the insurance companies have decided Negro business is bad for their bottom line."

Putting a hand on her hip, Margaret said, "They already killed my daddy. I'm not gon' stand aside and let them destroy everything he built. They need to pay."

Buck stood, eyes filled with compassion. "I'm very sorry to hear about your father. A lot of good men lost their lives during that massacre. I myself was detained at the convention hall for several days, for no other reason but that I was a Black man living in Greenwood."

"That's the truth of the matter," Margaret said. The compassionate way he spoke took a bit of the bite out of her anger. She exhaled, took her hand off her hip. "Our people have suffered through things I never would've thought possible since slavery's been abolished for nearly sixty years now."

He patted her on the shoulder. "Things look bleak now, but as long as the spirit of the community remains, we will rise again."

Margaret wanted desperately to believe that. She hoped to rebuild and live in a thriving community again. But as each day passed, she questioned the reality of her hopes and dreams. "Do you think you can help us? I don't know how we'll be able to rebuild our home and my daddy's business without that insurance money."

"I'm going to do my very best," he assured her.

Margaret was about to ask how long the process might take when Joe Lockard came storming into the tent. With fire and retribution in his eyes, he barked at them, "Now, I was willing to put my name on this lawsuit against the city, but you boys have to keep me up on things. When are we getting moving? I just saw a developer scouting around my property. And if y'all don't hurry up and do something, I'm going to jail for shooting that man."

Joe Lockard was a well-respected businessman in Greenwood. He owned The People's Café near Tulsa's Frisco train depot and last year was elected president of the board of directors of an investment company. Margaret didn't know what kind of investments they were dabbling in, but her daddy spoke highly of Mr. Lockard.

Mr. Franklin told her, "Give your information to Effie." He pointed to the woman behind the big desk that the three of them were sharing. "I. H. and I need to speak with Mr. Lockard."

The three men stepped outside of the tent, but Margaret could still hear Mr. Lockard reprimanding the lawyers. "How am I supposed to rebuild my business with this fire ordinance the city is trying to pull over on us?"

Margaret hadn't heard anything about a fire ordinance, but she didn't like the way Mr. Franklin brushed her off to speak with Mr. Lockard. Yes, Mr. Lockard was an important man in this community, but she and her daddy's business were important too. Did she need to take her grievance to another law firm?

"Pay him no mind," Effie whispered. "Mr. Lockard is normally good natured, but they just found his brother stretched out over by the airport with a bullet in him."

Margaret's hand went to her mouth. "Eddie?" she whispered. "He's dead?"

Effie nodded. "I'm afraid so."

Eddie Lockard was a nice man. He'd waited on her and Evelyn a few times when they'd eaten at The People's Café. He couldn't have been more than ten years older than her. Margaret's eyes closed as the heavy weight of loss penetrated her heart. Joe's pain was her pain.

"Give me the name of the insurance company and any other information you have. We'll make contact with them."

"Are you sure you all have time for my claim? This matter is just as important as Mr. Lockard's matter."

Effie lifted a pile of paper from her desk. "And just as important as all of these claims as well. Mr. Franklin and Mr. Spears have their work cut out for them, but we're working day and night to get all of us some justice."

Nodding, Margaret provided Effie with the name of the company and her daddy's information. As she was leaving the tent, two other residents of Greenwood approached and lodged a complaint with Effie.

They were in for an uphill battle, but they had to fight. She didn't know if she could put her hope in Franklin and Spears, but she desperately needed something to go right. She caught sight of Mrs. Loula and Mr. John Williams, whose movie theater, Dreamland, had been a couple doors down from where the law office had been. She rushed over to Mrs. Loula. A smile crept across her face. She hadn't seen her since the night of the massacre.

But Mrs. Loula was in no mood for chitchat. She trampled through the rubble that had once been Dreamland. "They want bricks," she shouted as she bent down and picked up several bricks, brought them to the street, and dropped them there. "We got bricks. And we'll rebuild Dreamland with all the bricks we can find. Just let them try and stop me."

Mrs. Loula went back to the rubble and gathered more bricks. "Darling, get out of there. Let the men we hired for this task gather those bricks," John Williams said.

"No! No! They want bricks. I'm going to show them some bricks."

Mr. John took off his hat and wiped the sweat from his forehead. He turned to his son, Willie. "Get your mother. She's overwrought with all this heat."

Margaret asked Mr. John, "Who wants the bricks?"

Shaking his head, he tightened his lips as if annoyed by the whole matter. "The mayor of Tulsa put in this fire ordinance against us. Say we can't rebuild unless we do it with bricks."

Margaret's eyes exploded with the anger that shot through her whole being. "But people 'round here can't even afford wood planks, let alone bricks. How can they do this to us?"

"I don't think these city officials care one way or the other." Willie brought Mrs. Loula away from the rubble. Mr. John grabbed hold of her arm and placed her in the car. "We'll see you another time, Margaret. Have a good day."

She waved at them. Mrs. Loula didn't seem to notice that she was there at all. Margaret glanced up at the sky. It had been threatening to rain for a few days now. She needed to get back to her tent, but before going home she stopped in front of the lot that used to be Justice for All Grocery Store on Archer Street.

Her only focus had been on clearing out the lot for the house so they could rebuild it and have a place to lay their heads. But if this fire ordinance was going to get in the way, she needed to make sure she had all the bricks necessary to rebuild the grocery store when the time came.

Walking through the rubble on her daddy's property, she saw sticks and wood pieces but few bricks. She bent down to pick up a couple of them. In her estimation, the bricks should have been on top of the rubble since they made up the outer layer of the building. But where had all the bricks gone?

She stood on top of the pile of what had been her daddy's lifework, bricks clutched in her hands as her eyes traveled the distance. Shooting daggers at everyone and anyone who walked by. Someone had taken those bricks. The lot to the left of her daddy's grocery store had been a restaurant; to the right was the dry cleaner's. Both lots had been cleared. Had one of them stolen from them?

"Where's my daddy's bricks?" she yelled as people passed by looking like they didn't know nothing about nothing. But somebody had to know something. Bricks didn't just disappear.

"I need those bricks. You can't just go around taking what don't belong to you." The passersby kept ignoring her as they went about their way. No one cared about the things that concerned her. Everyone around here was too focused on their own pain.

Her hands fisted over the bricks she held. "I won't let you down, Daddy. No fire ordinance or thievery is going to stop me. I promise you that." She spoke her declaration on a whisper and let the wind glide her words all the way to the heavens, where her daddy must now reside.

As she walked back to Detroit Street with bricks in hand, the rain came. She and Mrs. Pearl were within days of getting all of the debris hauled off and having their lots cleared. Margaret lifted her head to the sky. As the raindrops fell on her face, she shook a brick toward heaven. "Not even You will stop me. I will right these wrongs."

Mrs. Mabel could walk the streets of Greenwood preaching about the goodness of God all she wanted. Until He came down from His comfortable seat above those clouds and helped them, Margaret would sooner trust in the bricks she could see than an invisible God.

It rained for three days. The ground stayed wet two days after the rain left. Trash piled up and the smells intensified in such a manner that Margaret's scarf did little to quell the stench. The air was tinged with the musty scent of debris and the sharp tang of burnt wood. The faint aroma of wet and sweat lingered. Yet determination fueled her every step.

She borrowed a wheelbarrow and went back and forth to the grocery store, obsessed with finding every brick she could before any more thievery took place. She had lived in Greenwood most of her life. Never thought twice about having her back turned before.

But the smoldering anger and the oh-woe-is-me attitude resulting from having to clean up after such extensive damage on their own, as if they were spoiled children who needed to be taught a lesson about destroying their good stuff, was wearing on everyone. Trust in humanity, in good prevailing over evil, was being singed from her memory.

Her daddy's store would be rebuilt, and like Mrs. Loula, she would give the city all the bricks she could find.

Sifting through wood pieces, plaster, and trash, she kept going until she came upon a brick here and a brick there. Each time she found one or two, she carried them over to the wheelbarrow, then went right back to work.

At one point she found a piece of one of the shelves that held the canned goods and other items. Then she found a swollen can of green beans, and it broke her. She sat down among the remains of her daddy's dreams and let the tears fall, mixing with the dirt and sweat on her face. The dust in the air coated her tongue, making it feel dry and gritty.

"We'll have none of that," Elijah said as he walked through the mounds of debris and sat down next to her.

Her head jolted upward. She wiped away the tears. Sighing as a lump of pain settled in her chest like a heavy weight she couldn't shake off, she told him, "You weren't supposed to see me like this."

He put an arm around her shoulders. "You don't have to be strong for me. Remember, I'm the one with the big head and muscles."

A bit of a laugh seeped out before the anguish of the moment squelched it. "I'm glad you're here."

"Me too." He stood up, wiped off his overalls. "Now what can I help you with?"

Chapter 17

Survivors of the Tulsa Race Massacre, brought suit against Defendants seeking abatement of the public nuisance caused by Defendants' unreasonable, unwarranted, and/or unlawful acts and omissions that began with the Tulsa Race Massacre of 1921 and continue to this day.

—*Randle v. City of Tulsa (decided: June 12, 2024)*

The August heat was unbearable. Evelyn wanted to find a river and dunk her whole body. She might even dump a bucket of water over her head once she got off work. But for now, she got on her knees, putting candy and fruit on the lower shelves. It was cooler the closer she was to the floor.

A customer entered the store. Evelyn was so hot, sweaty, and uncomfortable, she didn't want to get up. She turned to greet the customer, and her eyes lit with long-time-no-see joy when Mr. Jones from Elgin Avenue stepped in to pay for his gas. She jumped up and hugged him. "Oh my goodness. I'm so happy to see you."

"Evelyn." He hugged her back. "The girls have been sick with worry about you. We didn't know what had become of you."

"I've been worried about Glenda and Abigail too. Can you give them a hug from me?"

"You can give it to them yourself. They're out in the car."

A grin spread across her face. She hugged him again, then ran out of the store to find her friends. She and Glenda were in the same graduating class. Abigail was a year behind them. The three of them had spent countless hours talking about college and all they would do with their lives after high school.

Glenda wanted to be a teacher, and Abigail had her sights on becoming a nurse. Evelyn had made a few dresses for her friends, and they knew she'd been dreaming of being a designer since the first time she used her mother's sewing machine.

Mr. Jones owned a Chevrolet FB-50 Touring car. It had a green base with a black top and front. Mr. Jones gave ten-cent rides to folks who needed to get from one place to another but didn't have nothing but their feet to get them there. She spotted it at the pump. Flailed her hands as she rushed over to the automobile. "Glenda! Abigail!"

The girls were seated in the back. Their heads swiveled toward her as she approached. The three of them screamed. Glenda and Abigail got out of the car and wrapped their arms around Evelyn, and the girls jumped around as if they hadn't seen each other in years rather than a couple of months.

"Calm down, girls. Everyone can hear you." The woman seated in the front passenger seat glanced around as if mortified, and maybe even a bit nervous about the attention the girls were attracting.

"Good afternoon, Mrs. Jones. I hope you're doing well," Evelyn said as she and her friends let go of each other.

"I'm making it the best I can, Evelyn. It's good to see you," Mrs. Jones said in a rote manner. Like she was saying the words she knew, but they had become foreign to her.

Evelyn turned back to her friends. "Is your dad driving you to school? Are you excited to be leaving town?"

Glenda's smile faded. She shook her head. "No money for school. We're busy with work assignments the city officials said we had to do in order to receive help from the Red Cross."

Abigail chimed in, "I even have to work to get books for my studies at Booker T."

"I heard about that. It's plum disgusting what these city officials are doing to make things worse for the good folks in Greenwood. Margaret is down there now. God only knows what she's dealing with."

"Daddy say if it's the last thing he does on this earth, he gon' make sure them white folks don't do no more damage in Greenwood," Abigail said.

"Abigail and I are helping Daddy rebuild the store and our home. I'll probably work at the store until I get married or something," Glenda told her matter-of-factly.

Abigail then hugged Evelyn again. "Is your daddy with Margaret in Greenwood?"

Evelyn felt that hug way down to the pit of her belly. She blinked several times, turning away from Abigail. Sucked air through her teeth and then blew it out. "No, we haven't seen him since the night of the attack." Evelyn couldn't bring herself to say the word *dead*, so she pressed her lips together as her chin quivered.

Glenda put a hand on her arm. "I'm sorry, Evelyn."

Turning back to her friends, she waved off their concern. "I'm okay. I'm very grateful to the Threatts for taking me in and giving me this job."

Mr. Jones got back in the car. "Come on, girls. We want to get back home before nightfall."

Glenda explained, "Daddy took us on a drive so we could get out of the neighborhood and clear our minds a bit."

"Where's Margaret?" Mrs. Jones asked.

"She's back in Greenwood trying to rebuild our house."

Mrs. Jones's brows furrowed. "I haven't seen her. But I've been so busy working at the hospital that I haven't seen much of anyone except for the ones falling ill from the deplorable conditions we're forced to live in."

Mr. Jones started up the car, the girls waved at Evelyn, and then they drove off.

As Evelyn waved goodbye, a deep heaviness overtook her. Nothing was the same anymore. Nothing was the way it was supposed to be. It had been good to see her friends, but discovering that college was no longer an option for them and hearing Abigail mention her father had opened a floodgate of emotions. The storm glistened, then rolled down her cheeks like fragile crystal beads. Touching her lips, it tasted of salt and sorrow.

Needing to breathe and not feel so confined, Evelyn left the house later that night and headed back toward the filling station. It was Friday night, and Mr. Allen was barbecuing for the folks who were traveling from near and far for the baseball game that would be played tomorrow in the open field.

Picnic tables were set up behind the filling station. A jukebox was plugged into the outside outlet. Louis Armstrong was blowing his trumpet as "St. Louis Blues" blasted from the jukebox. Lights were strung from one tree to another on both sides of the platform stage that had been constructed from wood planks.

People were milling around. Women snapped their fingers, men tapped their feet. Evelyn had never been much of a dancer.

But she was feeling the vibration of the beat and snapped her fingers too.

Mr. Allen put his spatula on the table next to his barbecue pit and walked over to her, wagging a disapproving finger. "Did Alberta tell you it was okay to be down here at night?"

The sun was setting, but it wasn't even eight o'clock yet. "Come on, Mr. Allen. I'm almost nineteen. I just want to enjoy the music and eat one of your famous burgers."

"One burger and then you go back to the house with Alberta." He stomped back over to the barbecue pit and flipped the burgers.

He almost sounded like her daddy. It was Friday night, and as grateful as she was to Mr. Allen, she had the desperate urge to let loose . . . to feel something, maybe even a little joy. Evelyn's foot tapped to the music as the smell of chicken, hot dogs, and burgers wafted from the grill.

"Dance with me." Jerome, one of the regulars at the filling station, grabbed her arm and pulled her toward the platform stage, where a few others had already started dancing and gyrating.

Evelyn wasn't sure about her movements at first. Her daddy had never allowed her and Margaret to go to the local dances. But as "Dardanella" by Louis Armstrong started playing and hips started oscillating, she followed suit. Before she knew it, she was laughing, dancing, and having a good time.

> Oh, sweet Dardanella,
> I love your harem eyes.
> I'm a lucky fellow to capture such a prize.

The music drew her in. The lady next to her started doing the Charleston with her dance partner. On the other side, dances like the foxtrot and the Black Bottom were executed to perfection. Tapping her feet and swaying to the music, she told Jerome, "I don't know how to dance."

"Of course you do. It's all about rhythm. I ain't never met a Black woman who didn't have rhythm."

Putting her hands on her hips, she laughed at that, then turned to walk off the stage.

Jerome took her hand. "Here, let me show you." He put her left hand over her right, did the same with his. "Now you do what I do." His left knee came up, and he brought his hands down to touch his knee, then did the same with the right knee.

Evelyn followed suit.

"Yeah, you're getting it." Jerome then lifted his hands, jerking them in one direction and then the other as his feet shuffled.

Feeling the groove, Evelyn shuffled her feet too. She learned not only the Black Bottom but the Charleston as well. Her stomach started growling, so she got off the dance floor and grabbed the burger that Mr. Allen laid out for her.

She wolfed it down and then grabbed a hot dog. "You having anything?" she asked Jerome.

Instead of grabbing a burger, he laughed at her. "You go on and eat. I can see I'll have to save up my pennies if I want to take you out."

A date. Was he asking her out? Margaret couldn't complain about Jerome; he was only a few years older than her. Before she could answer him, Mr. Allen stepped in between them. That's when Evelyn noticed that not only had the sun gone down, but the moon was rising.

"Time for you to go on home," Mr. Allen said. His eyes were set and piercing. A look that brooked no back talk.

"I'd better get going," she told Jerome.

"Wait." Jerome grabbed her arm. "You can't rush off like that. I wanted to teach you another dance."

Mr. Allen wouldn't relent. "A young girl shouldn't be out this late. You go on to the house like I told you."

"Maybe next time." Jerome released her arm. "Mr. Allen's right. I best be getting to the house."

Evelyn left the filling station and headed for the farm like she was told. But Mr. Allen couldn't stop her from doing the Black Bottom in the field. She danced all the way to the house and found herself smiling and giggling as she used to with her friends before life turned on them.

She made up her mind right then and there that she would not allow her light to be dimmed any longer. One day she was going to drive down that road in front of the filling station and go wherever the wind blew her. And if she saved up enough money, that wind might just blow her to design school.

When she reached the farmhouse, she could still hear the beat of the music. She didn't need Jerome to teach her another dance; she was dancing to her own beat. She felt alive again . . . and nobody was going to take this feeling away from her.

Chapter 18

The girls . . . who could not purchase their school books were furnished with work . . . thus enabling them to pay for their books.

—*Maurice Willows, Red Cross Disaster Relief Report*

I f anyone would've told her that a farm boy would become like air and water to her, Margaret would have laughed in their face for spouting such an outright lie. But when Elijah was around, Margaret was able to see light . . . better days ahead. In this whole wicked world, she had found someone she could depend on.

Sweeping the dust and debris away after Elijah and his men hauled the last of the wreckage from her and Mrs. Pearl's plots of land, Margaret tried to think on ways she could show Elijah just how much she appreciated his kindness.

It was now the last week of September. They'd endured four months of nightmarish days in Greenwood. Things were finally turning around as three judges just ruled in Attorney Buck Franklin's favor. Mayor Evans wouldn't be stealing Greenwood away from them with his cooked-up fire ordinance that had been put in place so the developers he was in cahoots with could build some fancy new buildings.

Two wagons pulled up in front of her and Mrs. Pearl's tents. Margaret glanced over at Mrs. Pearl. She leaned on her broom as if she needed it to hold her up. "You alright?"

Mrs. Pearl coughed. "I'm fine." She pointed toward the wagons. "Looks like the Red Cross finally bringing our supplies."

"Just in time." Margaret put down her broom and ran out to greet the men who were unloading lumber, nails, and all sorts of roofing supplies needed to rebuild the house. Smiling, Margaret told them, "You all couldn't have come at a better time. We just cleared out the debris. It's ready for you to begin the build."

One of the men jumped down from the wagon. He hollered instructions to four other men who started pulling the supplies off the wagon. He then turned to Margaret and held up two clipboards with a few pages attached. "I have supply orders for Mrs. Pearl Brown and Miss Margaret Justice."

Her eyes lit with excitement as she glanced from the clipboards in his hand to the men who were pulling long, thick pieces of lumber off the wagon. "I'm Margaret. Mrs. Pearl is right there." She pointed toward the woman who was still standing in the cleared lot, holding on to her broom.

He handed Margaret the clipboards. "All of your supplies are listed on these pages. Once my men get the stuff off the wagon, I need you to look everything over and then sign here." He pointed to the signature line on the paperwork.

The insurance companies had denied their claims, but the Red Cross had finally come through for them. "I'll look everything over and then get out of your way."

As the supplies were being dumped in her yard, Margaret noticed that Mrs. Pearl still hadn't moved. She held up the clipboards. "They have your work order. You'd better check off these supplies before they start the build."

Mrs. Pearl put down her broom and inched her way toward the wagons. Margaret checked off the supplies as she went through the long list. Mrs. Pearl had sat down in front of her tent with her clipboard in hand. Something wasn't right with her today. Margaret didn't want to slow the workers down, so she grabbed Mrs. Pearl's clipboard and reviewed her supplies as well.

It took about an hour to review all the materials and sign off. Once she handed the clipboards back, she asked, "When do you all get started? Will our tents be in the workers' way?"

Taking the clipboard from her, he shook his head. "I don't know what you've been told, but our only assignment is to drop off these supplies."

Confusion danced in Margaret's eyes. "But I—I don't understand. Who's going to build the house if you all aren't going to do it?" They didn't have money to hire anyone. The Red Cross had been their last hope. When they showed up with the supplies, Margaret had been so thankful that they'd held to their end of the bargain. But she should have known better.

"You people are resourceful." He waved a hand from one side of the street to the other. "Look how you've cleared out the place. Surely you people can get together and build these houses."

The way this white man kept saying "you people" told Margaret all she needed to know. Once again, the mayor and the Red Cross officials had determined that Negroes only needed the bare minimum. She was so tired of proving her somethingness to people who thought they were less than nothing.

Margaret walked away from the man in a huff. "Did you hear that, Mrs. Pearl? We got to fend for ourselves yet again."

"Don't surprise me none," Mrs. Pearl said, then bent forward as a coughing spell took hold.

The men got back in their wagons. Margaret rushed over to Mrs. Pearl. "I knew it. You're not okay." Margaret touched the woman's arm and forehead. "You shouldn't have been out here sweeping. You have a fever."

"I do?" Mrs. Pearl asked, eyes glassy, face flushed.

Margaret had been so busy clearing out the debris from the house and the grocery store that she hadn't noticed any signs of sickness with Mrs. Pearl. Now the woman could barely stand up.

"Lean on me. I'm taking you back inside so you can lay down."

"B-but . . ." She pointed toward her empty lot. "I got to sweep. Gotta find a plumber . . . electrician." She glanced up at Margaret, tears threatening to rain down her face. But the glass walls around her eyes locked them in, trapping her pain inside like a cage. "They not gon' help us. You know that, don't you?"

"Ain't nothing new." Margaret tried not to sound bitter as she pulled Mrs. Pearl from her seated position. But the jab of "you people" settled in her chest like a cancer. She was so tired of being devalued and seen as unworthy of help yet also expected to be "the help" for others. She had a degree. Was supposed to be a teacher or running her own business like her daddy and Mrs. Loula, but the officials in Tulsa had made her a cook.

Looking out at the wood, pipes, nails, and the like that lay scattered on the ground before her while Mrs. Pearl leaned heavily on her arm, Margaret wondered how on God's green earth she was now to become carpenter, builder, plumber, electrician, and caregiver. The taste of frustration lingered on her tongue, like a bitter aftertaste from constantly trying to complete tasks she had no experience with. The flavor of overwhelming defeat consumed her. She shed the tears that couldn't get past Mrs. Pearl's glassy eyes.

Mrs. Pearl reached up and wiped away her tears. "Don't you pay these people no mind. We got too much work to do to worry about them."

Margaret took Mrs. Pearl inside her tent and placed her on the cot as gingerly as possible. Her skin was hot like she'd lain next to a burning fire all night long. Margaret left the blanket at Mrs. Pearl's feet. Sweat dripped from her body like a running faucet. "You're going to be okay. Just need a tonic."

Margaret stepped outside the tent and looked down the street. Where would she get the tonic for Mrs. Pearl? Greenwood used to have several pharmacies and doctors. Just a little ways down the street, she saw the plot of land that used to be Dr. Jackson's house. Her daddy had received a tonic from Dr. Jackson for her mother that winter she first took ill.

The tonic didn't help her mother, but she had to try something for Mrs. Pearl. That fever wasn't anything to play with. Running down the street, she stopped at Mrs. Johnson's tent. "I need a tonic for Mrs. Pearl. Do you know where I can get one from?" Margaret asked.

Mrs. Johnson stepped outside. She had a wet rag in her hand. She used it to wipe the sweat dripping from her face. "Not anymore, I don't. But if you find someone, please get a few. Two of my boys got the fever, and they done gave it to me."

"Oh no! I'll see what I can do."

Wiping her forehead with the wet rag, Mrs. Johnson said, "It's not just us. A lot of people have gotten sick 'round here. We ain't got no doctor, just the Red Cross, for all the good that's doing."

Sickness had snuck into Greenwood like wild weeds, putting a stranglehold on the progress they were making. Margaret's hands went to her head. Fear clenched her heart. What would they do if this thing kept spreading? The unsanitary conditions in Greenwood had taken a toll. Now more people were getting sick, some had died . . . and still they had to fend for themselves.

The Red Cross gave with one hand and took with the other, so Margaret wasn't happy about going to them for help. Especially after they were just told they would have to build their homes with no help from contractors. But what else could she do?

She went to the hospital and rushed over to the reception area. The woman behind the desk looked harried, like the day had been long even though it wasn't yet noon. "I need help. People on my street have taken ill."

"A lot of people are ill. We don't have any empty beds," the woman told her.

"What about medicine? Do you have anything I can give them?"

The woman stood with three clipboards in her hands. "Have them put a cold compress on their heads and drink plenty of water."

"But the water in Greenwood is contaminated. How's that going to help anybody?"

"It's either that or bring them in here and have them wait until we get an empty bed."

The woman walked away from the desk and went behind the curtains without saying another word to Margaret. Frustration mounted. Her mouth opened for the scream she wanted to let out. Then the door opened, and a man carrying a woman in his arms stepped in, yelling, "My wife needs help! She won't wake up. She's burning with fever!"

She wouldn't be getting a tonic or anything else at the Red Cross hospital. She would have to go get Mrs. Pearl and bring her back here. By the time she got back to the tent, Mrs. Pearl had pulled the covers up. "I need to get you to the hospital."

Margaret took the blanket off of her and watched as she shook like a leaf in the breeze. Her clothes were drenched with sweat. Margaret put the blanket back over her. "You've got the chills. You're going to need some water with all this sweating."

As much as Margaret hated to give Mrs. Pearl the contaminated water they had been forced to drink, she doubted the woman would be able to get on her feet so they could get to the hospital if she didn't replace some of the fluids she'd already lost.

They didn't have cold water. But both Mrs. Pearl and Margaret had a pitcher they refilled with water when the water containers were set outside by the meal preparation tables. Mrs. Pearl's water pitcher was on her small table. It was half full. Margaret looked around for some type of cloth. But she didn't see anything.

"I'll be right back." Margaret ran over to her tent and tore a piece of cloth from a skirt she'd received from the Red Cross. As she was headed back out of her tent, she glimpsed her pitcher; it was almost full. She took the pitcher and the cloth back to Mrs. Pearl's tent.

"We gon' get you all fixed up. You'll see. In no time at all, you'll be right as rain." Margaret bent down next to Mrs. Pearl. She poured some of the water from her pitcher onto the cloth, wiped the sweat from Mrs. Pearl's face, and then placed the cloth on her forehead. She hoped the moisture from the lukewarm water would help bring down the fever.

Mrs. Pearl moaned and pulled the covers up under her chin, shaking like something had put the fear of God in her. Margaret grabbed a cup and poured some water in it. She lifted Mrs. Pearl's head, and the older woman's sweat trickled down Margaret's arm. The heat from Mrs. Pearl alarmed her, and even though she kept pulling the cover up, Margaret threw it off.

"Drink this." She wished she had a fresh sip of the water at the Threatt farm to offer. But this was all they had. Some of the water dribbled from Mrs. Pearl's mouth and down her chin..

"I hope some of that water went down your throat. I need you to be able to get up so I can get you to the hospital." Then Margaret had a thought. She went back to her tent and grabbed one of the cans of soup they'd been given. She started a fire between her and Mrs. Pearl's tents and warmed the soup.

Using some of the water from her pitcher, she cleaned the bowl and spoon as best she could. Poured the soup in it and went back in to sit with Mrs. Pearl. Margaret prayed that Mrs. Pearl hadn't pulled that cover over her body again.

When she reentered Mrs. Pearl's tent, Margaret was happy to see that the blanket was still at the foot of the bed. As she got closer, she noticed that sweat was no longer dripping off of Mrs. Pearl. Maybe the water had done some good. "I've got some soup for you. We'll get this food in you, and then I'll get you down to the hospital."

Getting back down on the floor next to the bed, she held the bowl in one hand and tried to lift Mrs. Pearl with the other arm. Margaret's eyes widened in stark fear as she leaned closer and heard the shallow breathing.

"Wh-what's wrong?" Mrs. Pearl's eyes fluttered as if they were trying to close, but she was fighting it with her last bit of strength.

"Stay with me," Margaret begged and begged and begged. "Stay with me." But Mrs. Pearl's body shook violently, then went still.

Her eyes closed and stayed closed. The bowl fell from Margaret's hand as she wrapped both arms around the woman who had looked out for her and Evie after their mom died. "Nooo! You have to get better."

She wasn't moving. Margaret laid her back on the bed. She needed to get help. She stood up, touched her hands to her head. Heat . . . heat radiated from her scalp. The room started spinning and spinning. "Help! Help!" Margaret yelled. "We . . . need . . . help!"

But just like all the empty promises of aid and support they had received, the help would come too late and be insufficient to mend her shattered heart. The weight of grief and loss pressed down on her like a heavy burden, suffocating any hope of healing.

Margaret's legs wobbled. She went down on her knees. She could hear the echoes of screams and smell the smoke from the burning buildings, haunting memories that lingered in the air. In this town where tragedy would not be still, love and loss mingled together until they strangled all the little bits of hope that had accumulated.

This wound ran deep, cutting through every fiber of her being, leaving behind a jagged emptiness that could never be filled. As she lay next to Mrs. Pearl, she felt like she was drowning in a sea of grief, desperately reaching out for hope. But all she could see was darkness and despair, no light at the end of this endless tunnel of sorrow. No amount of help or pity could undo the trauma inflicted upon her and her loved ones. It was a sore that remained open, a wound that would forever remind her of the atrocity that had taken everything from her.

Part 2

HEALING AND FILLING

Chapter 19

All that fire, rifles, revolvers, shot guns, machine guns and organized inhuman passion could do with thirty-five city blocks with its twelve thousand negro population, was done.

—Maurice Willows, Red Cross Disaster Relief Report

When's she going to wake up? She's been out for two days." Evelyn doused a cloth with cold water, wrung it out, and placed it back on Margaret's forehead.

Mrs. Alberta patted Evelyn's back. "Stop worrying, chile. Margaret's fever broke an hour ago. She'll be coming around soon enough."

Evelyn sat on Margaret's bed. She held on to her sister's hand, praying that Mrs. Alberta's estimations would come to fruition. Didn't know what she would do if she lost Margaret along with everyone else who was dear to her.

"Come on." Mrs. Alberta tugged on her shirt. "You've been by Margaret's side all night long. You need to eat. You'll be no good to your sister if you faint from hunger."

"But what if she wakes up and I'm not here?"

"I'll stay in the room while you go fix yourself a plate. But I don't want you coming back to this room until you've eaten."

Mrs. Alberta put a hand under her arm, lifting her from her seat. "Don't argue with me. Go eat."

"Yes, ma'am." Evelyn walked to the door, turned, and stared at her sister. "Wake up, Margaret. You can't leave me too."

"She'll get better."

Evelyn prayed that Mrs. Alberta was right. Margaret was improving. She would come back to her. This wasn't like Mama or Daddy or Mrs. Pearl. God couldn't be that cruel. He just couldn't be.

Putting a hand over her mouth to stifle a sorrowful moan, Evelyn did as she was commanded. Mrs. Alberta made the best rice and gravy she'd ever eaten. But today her tongue didn't dance over the spices in the gravy or the hunk of pork meat. She wolfed the food down, drank a glass of water, then ran back upstairs.

"Did she open her eyes?" Evelyn asked as she entered the room again.

Mrs. Alberta's head fell backward as she laughed. "You weren't gone but a few minutes. Give her some time."

"She can have all the time she wants once she wakes up." Evelyn took the cloth off Margaret's head and dipped it in cool water again. She wiped the cloth across Margaret's mouth. Her lips were dry and flaky.

"Let me get something to put on her lips." Mrs. Alberta left the room.

Evelyn sat back down on the bed. She placed the cloth back on Margaret's forehead. "I know your fever is gone, but I don't want it to come back. So if this cloth is too cold, you'll simply have to wake up and take it off your head."

Evelyn's chin quivered. She sniffed. "Come back to me, sissy. I don't think I can make it without you."

Loss, loss, loss was the evil she'd been dealt. What more would the horrible events of that night take from her? Her chest heaved as an avalanche of sorrow tumbled out of her, and she cried, "Please, wake up!"

Her eyelids felt as if they'd been glued together. Mouth dry like cotton. She licked her lips.

"Did you see that? She's waking up!"

Margaret heard the excitement in Evelyn's voice, and it confused her. Had someone brought her sister to Greenwood? Had she been sleeping? Her pulse raced. She blinked several times as her eyes opened. Looking around, she prayed that Mrs. Pearl was with her.

Evelyn sat on the bed holding her hand while Mrs. Alberta and Mr. Allen stood to the side of the bed, looking down on her as if she possessed an answer to a question they hadn't asked. "How did I get here? Where's Mrs. Pearl?"

Evelyn patted her hand, pursed her lips together, then told her, "Elijah brought you home."

Home? Her home was in Greenwood. She needed to be there to find workers who could help build their home and the grocery store. Needed to . . . "Was Elijah able to get Mrs. Pearl to the hospital?"

Evelyn bit down on her bottom lip. Her eyes filled with that wish-things-were-different kind of sorrow. She wiped at her eyes as the pain leaked onto her face. "I thought I had lost you too. I didn't know things had gotten so bad down there."

Margaret had been so busy with the load of work that she had become numb to the conditions in Greenwood. In her estimation, things had been getting better, but sickness had not only taken hold in the community; it seemed like it dragged her a country mile and then dumped her in a field of rubbish.

Margaret squinted, put a hand to her head. "My head hurts."

"Let me get something cold to put on your head," Mrs. Alberta said as she rushed out of the room.

Looking toward the door as Mrs. Alberta scurried away, Margaret saw Mr. Allen standing there with a scowl on his face, like her pain was trouble to his soul. It reminded Margaret of her daddy and how he would do anything to take away her and Evie's pain. A tear drifted down her cheek. She turned away from him.

But just as she tried to situate her mind on things that didn't bring her pain, Elijah bounded into the room. "I was told our patient woke. Had to see it for myself."

Moving her lips around, trying to get rid of the cottony feel in her mouth, she swallowed. "Elijah?"

He came and stood in front of the bed. "Hey, Margaret. We've been praying for you to get better. Mrs. Alberta told me that your fever is gone."

Mrs. Pearl had a fever. She'd been so hot that nothing Margaret did took away the heat. "You found me?"

He nodded. "Brought you back here to Mrs. Alberta. I figured she could get you fixed up."

"Where's Mrs. Pearl?"

Elijah's eyes clouded with sadness just as Evie's had when she asked her about Mrs. Pearl. But he didn't evade the question. He told her, "I'm so sorry, Margaret, but Mrs. Pearl died."

A throbbing from way down deep took hold and beat a path to her heart. "Nooo!" She turned away from Elijah as silent sobs wracked her body. Part of her wanted to cling to him and cry on his shoulder, while another part wanted to push him away and bury herself in the blankets. She knew . . . in her heart she knew, but hearing the words hit harder than she could have imagined. She was so tired of losing and losing and losing.

Evelyn wrapped her arms around Margaret as the deluge flooded down her face. The two rocked back and forth together. Once again, their pain mingled and melded into a collective sorrow that wouldn't let go.

Later in the week, Margaret had regained a bit of her strength. She got out of bed and sat on the porch, looking out at all the green grass and beautiful trees with orange leaves swaying in the light breeze. The clouds hung in the sky, refusing to let the sun break free. Just like things kept getting in her way, not allowing her to reach her goals.

A chill went through her. She pulled the shawl tighter around her shoulders. Margaret wasn't ready to take off running yet, but she was thankful that she was getting better. Knowing there was still so much to be done, but she didn't have the strength to do it, was the worst part of the healing process to deal with.

"Penny for your thoughts."

Margaret's head popped up. Elijah was flipping a penny as he came up the walkway and sat down on the porch steps next to her. He had on his overalls. The front pocket had been torn and flapped in the breeze. "Where you been?"

"Greenwood."

She folded his torn pocket inward to stop it from flapping. "That's how you tore your overalls?"

"Wasn't paying attention when I picked up a two-by-four and got it caught on a nail."

"Who are you Good Samaritans helping now?"

"We decided to build Mrs. Pearl's house. Buck Franklin will see if she has family somewhere who'd like to live at the property once we're done."

Margaret's eyes watered. Her heart expanded at Elijah's words. Even though Mrs. Pearl was gone, somebody cared enough to do what was right by her. There wouldn't be another empty lot left for them to mourn over. Someone would be able to live . . . truly live in that house. "Thank you for doing that. You are a true blessing."

Elijah wiped her tears as they dropped from her eyes. "I don't want you fretting about anything. Just stay here and heal up."

"But I have to get back to Greenwood." Her body had given in to the sickness that had overtaken the community, but no matter how weak and tired she felt now, she couldn't let her daddy down. Couldn't be the one to leave an empty lot for the community to mourn over.

Elijah placed a hand on her shoulder. She was amazed at how gentle his big, calloused hand was as it pressed ever so softly against her collarbone.

"I told you not to fret. Me and the boys gon' build that house for you and Evelyn. When we get finished, your house will be the envy of Detroit Street."

A smile creased her lips, but she told him, "I don't need anything fancy. Just the regular house my daddy built up for us. Just put it back to right, and I'll be happy."

"Consider it done."

For a long moment, she didn't know what to say or do. Elijah had become such a blessing in her life. There were so many things she wanted to say to him, but no words could truly express how she felt. She averted her eyes from Elijah's, patted his front pocket. "Evelyn will fix you up. I'll make sure of it."

Chapter 20

"Race Riot" it has been most generally termed, yet whites were killed and wounded by whites in the protection of white property against the violence of the white mob.

—*Maurice Willows, Red Cross Disaster Relief Report*

It was Thursday, November 17, 1921, and Evelyn had turned nineteen. She and Margaret agreed not to make a fuss about her birthday. Mrs. Alberta had been so kind to help Margaret recover that they couldn't bother her for more. So she didn't get a cake or anything.

Didn't matter much anyway. Evelyn didn't want to blow out candles without her daddy right there to tell her how much he loved her.

She lay in bed with her eyes shut tight as she tried to block out the noise telling her that nothing would ever be the same again. When she finally did open her eyes, she was late and had to run all the way to the filling station.

"Girl, if you don't want this job, I can find somebody that do," Mr. Allen barked at her as she stepped inside the store. "I got a flat tire to fix, but I had to stay in the store, cashing customers out."

Was she about to get fired on her birthday? Would he throw her out of the house as well? Hearing Mr. Allen yell at her made her miss her daddy all the more. Her lip quivered. Tears rolled down her face. "I didn't mean to oversleep. I-I'm sorry."

"Wait a minute." Mr. Allen waved a hand. Stood and put an arm around her shoulders. "Now hold on, I wasn't trying to make you cry."

"I-I'm sorry for crying." Putting a hand over her face, she pleaded, "Please don't fire me . . . Please don't put us out. We don't have nowhere to go."

Patting her shoulder, he put his hat on. "Shouldn't have been so harsh." He pointed toward the cash register. "Get to work. I'll go fix that tire."

Sometimes when the teachers at Booker T. corrected her, she would bristle and then settle down. But since the massacre, rebuke felt like a gun to her head, which was causing her emotions to be all over the place. She wiped her face, then sat down on the stool next to the cash register. Why did she keep messing up? Mr. Allen didn't deserve this from her. Sighing, she got to work. "Some birthday."

Customers came in and out of the store so much that Evelyn didn't have time to think about turning nineteen. Many arrived from surrounding towns, getting ready for the Negro League baseball game between the Oklahoma Giants and the Tulsa Black Oilers that would be played in the empty field owned by Mr. Allen tomorrow afternoon.

Mr. Allen told her that as soon as he had extra time on his hands, he was going to turn that piece of land into a full-fledged baseball field, and then the Negro League would play there all the time.

The day had swept by like a crisp winter's breeze. She was about to call it quits and go back to the farmhouse when Jerome came into the store and swung her around. "Hey, pretty lady. What you doing tonight?"

Nothing, same as every night, she wanted to say, but she gave him a sly smile and asked, "What you got in mind?"

"Got paid today." He took a few dollars out of his pocket and waved them around. "Figured I'd take you to get a meal and do some dancing."

Margaret would tell her not to go. She'd tell her to stay away from Jerome and his slick talking. But it was her birthday. So she leaped into Jerome's arms and hugged him. "Let me go home and get dressed. I'll meet you back here."

"Meet me at the Threatts' juke joint in two hours. I need to get out of my work clothes."

Evelyn didn't need two hours and didn't understand why Jerome did either. It was Friday. It was her birthday, and she was ready to party. It wasn't every day a girl turned nineteen. Somebody should know . . . somebody should care. Her daddy would have cared. He would have brought her a great big ol' cake to celebrate. Probably given her a beautiful bracelet or a colorful scarf.

She was going to dance. She was going to smile and remember that today was a good day. Margaret wasn't in their room when she got home, so she didn't have to sneak around. After tossing a few items on her bed, Evelyn decided on a hand-me-down dress that Margaret had found at a church giveaway.

The dress was red with fringes at the hem. It was fine for an evening out, but if Evelyn had designed it, she would have started the fringes at the waistline and let them flow all the way to the hem.

As she glanced at the windowsill where she kept the broken pieces from her Singer sewing machine, a tear leaked from her eye. She wiped it away. No thinking about the things she'd lost. It was her birthday, and she was going to enjoy herself.

Evelyn crept down the steps and escaped out of the front door as fast as she could to avoid her big sister's glare of disapproval. Jerome was not at the juke joint when she arrived, but the music was playing and she caught sight of a woman in the middle of the dance floor. She had on a lilac dress. It was a V-neck with fringes from the top of the shoulders all the way down to the knee-length hem.

As she danced, the fringes swished and swayed with the movement of her hips. The dress itself was a melody. Evelyn frowned as she glanced down at her polyester dress with only one layer of fringes at the very bottom of the dress. The designer should be run out of business.

"You lookin' mighty fine tonight," Big Willie, one of the farmhands, said and then swung her around as Mamie Smith sang "Crazy Blues." Evelyn's feet beat a path along the dance floor. The fringes at the bottom of her dress swayed. But it was nothing like the swishing of the lady's lilac dress.

Big Willie started two-stepping the Black Bottom, and Evelyn joined in. Before she knew it, she was laughing and enjoying life.

She swung around, and then Big Willie pulled her closer to him. That's when she felt a tap on her shoulder. Mamie Smith sang:

I ain't had nothin' but bad news.
Now I got the crazy blues.

Glancing to her left, she saw Jerome standing behind her, scowling like he'd missed his supper. He pulled her away from Big Willie. "Didn't I tell you to wait on me? Why you on the dance floor shaking it up with this dumb field hand?"

"Hey, who you calling dumb?" Willie stepped closer to Jerome.

Evelyn stretched out her hands, putting one on Jerome's chest and the other on Big Willie's. "Calm down, boys. It's my birthday. Let's have a good time. Okay?"

"You wasn't s'posed to be having no good time without me," Jerome huffed.

The day started off bad with Margaret telling her not to mention that it was her birthday. She finally let go and allowed herself to revel in the simple joy of the moment, but then Jerome barged in and ruined the last few hours left in her day. Smiles and good times were off-limits, even on her birthday?

Mrs. Alberta was expecting her fifth child. Margaret hated seeing her struggle to keep up with her four boys while carrying another life and ministering to her needs as she healed. She was thankful that each day brought more healing to her body. Being a help to Mrs. Alberta was pleasing to her soul.

Ulysses left the house to help Elijah in the cornfield. And with David being six and Allen Jr. five, Margaret decided to work on letter writing with the boys while Mrs. Alberta took care of her eleven-month-old son, Alonia Marion. But David was having none of it.

"I want to go to the filling station and help Daddy. Why I got to be cooped up in the house?"

"You don't know how to write your letters. Don't you want to show the kids at school what a big boy you are?"

He frowned at Margaret. Put a hand under his chin and pouted.

Allen Jr. lifted his paper and excitedly announced, "Look, I wrote an *A*."

Margaret clapped and jumped as if he'd brought home all excellent marks on his progress report. "You did! You did!"

Mrs. Alberta was in the kitchen making beef stew. She came into the dining room and placed the chocolate cake that she'd made for last night's supper on the table. "Let me see."

Allen showed his mother his paper, and she gushed over his accomplishment. Then David said, "I can do it too, Mama." He scratched an A on his paper, then showed it off.

"Good job." Mrs. Alberta hugged both her boys. "I'd say you've earned some playtime outside."

Margaret lifted a hand. "But I had a few more things I wanted to show them today."

Mrs. Alberta put Margaret's hand down. "You've done enough. It's Friday, and you deserve some time to yourself."

What did she need with time to herself? There was nothing else she had to do but help with the kids. From what Elijah told her, no work was being done on her home in Greenwood. She was starting to wonder what was taking him so long to get started.

Then she remembered what today was. She pointed to the cake. "Can I have a slice of that?"

"You sure can." Mrs. Alberta took the glass topper from over the cake and sliced a piece of the moist, chocolaty confection with buttercream icing on top. Margaret smiled as she thought about quietly singing "Happy Birthday" to her sister, then presenting her with this scrumptious cake.

But when she went to the room she and Evie shared and saw the clothes strewn on her sister's bed with no sign of Evie, Margaret had a sinking feeling that Evie had gone off and done something foolish. And for the first time since coming back from Greenwood, Margaret wondered if she had lost her footing with her sister while she was off trying to rebuild their home.

Chapter 21

The Red Cross records . . . eight definite cases of premature childbirth which resulted in death of the babies.

—*Maurice Willows, Red Cross Disaster Relief Report*

Margaret checked for Evelyn behind the filling station, but Mr. Allen wasn't grilling out tonight. When she came around to the front, she heard a commotion over by the juke joint. Big Willie and Jerome were dusting it up while Evelyn yelled and flailed her arms. "Stop acting so pigheaded! Y'all don't need to fight. It was just a dance."

"Evelyn!" Margaret clutched at her heart, then rushed over to her sister, pulling her to the side. "What are you doing out here in the middle of a fight like that?"

"I'm trying to stop these two lunkheads from ruining my birthday," Evelyn yelled out so the men could hear her.

Margaret gave her sister a once-over. Looking at her from head to toe, patting her arms and shoulders. "You could have been hurt . . . You aren't hurt, are you?"

Evelyn tried to push Margaret away. "Will you stop?" She headed back in the direction of the fight.

Big Willie and Jerome were circling each other. Margaret pulled her sister back again. "You're not going over there."

"Somebody has to talk some sense into them."

"Not you." Margaret held on to her arm.

Evelyn struggled to get away from Margaret as Jerome swung at Big Willie. Willie was big, but he wasn't slow. He dodged the punch, then landed one that knocked Jerome back. As he stumbled and grabbed hold of his jaw, Elijah stepped up.

"Men, stop this foolishness." He put a hand on Willie's shoulder.

Big Willie had been advancing on Jerome, getting ready to land another punch. But when Elijah touched him, he stopped. "You men know better than to act like this. If we fight each other, where will we get the strength to fight our true enemy?"

"It wasn't me, Elijah." Willie flapped his big arm in Jerome's direction. "He come in there"—he pointed toward the juke joint—"pulling on Evelyn and calling me dumb."

Rubbing his jaw, Jerome muttered, "Evelyn was s'posed to be waiting on me. She had no business dancing with you like that."

Elijah turned toward Jerome. "What does your wife think about you spending time with Miss Evelyn?"

"Wife?" Evelyn's eyes bugged as she looked to Jerome for answers.

"Quit meddling, Elijah," Jerome said with a wave of his hand.

Margaret poked her sister on the shoulder. "You catting around with a married man." She then lifted her eyes to heaven, put a hand to her forehead. "My mama would wear you out with a stick for doing some mess like this."

"She was my mama too. And I'm not catting around with nobody." Evelyn pointed toward Jerome. "He asked me out, and since you wouldn't celebrate my birthday, I figured I'd come down here and have some fun."

"This looks like loads of fun." Margaret grabbed a fistful of Evelyn's sleeve and pulled her away from the juke joint. "You coming home this instant."

Margaret started walking so fast, Evelyn stumbled over a few rocks trying to keep up with her. "Let me go. I don't have to do what you say anymore."

Having none of it, Margaret held on tighter. "Oh yes you do. We're all that's left, and I'm not letting you destroy your life with some no-'count riffraff."

Evelyn pulled free and glared at her. "What life? I'm stuck working at the filling station when I should be designing clothes." She snatched at the fabric of her dress. "Instead of wearing these hand-me-downs."

Margaret blinked rapidly. She sucked air through her teeth. "Why, you ungrateful little brat. I'll have you know, I spent my last few dollars getting you those clothes."

"You told me they came from the church."

"Some came from the church. And the rest I purchased with my own money."

"Ladies, ladies, please don't be cross with each other. I just broke up one fight. I don't know if I have the strength to break up another."

Margaret put her hand on her hip and addressed Elijah as if she were talking to one of Mrs. Alberta's kids instead of a full-grown man. "Nobody's fighting over here. Please get your nose out of where it doesn't belong."

Evelyn gasped. "Margaret! That's no way to talk to Elijah. He's been nothing but good and kind to us."

Elijah patted Evelyn on the shoulder. "Thank you, but Margaret has been cross with me for a couple of weeks now."

"I'm not cross with you. It's just that we were finally making progress, and then the rain . . . and then Mrs. Pearl got sick . . . then . . ."

"Then you got sick," he reminded her.

"I wasn't that sick. I could have rested a few days and then kept working on the house." That wasn't true, but she needed to plead her case.

He put his thumbs beneath the straps of his overalls and rocked back and forth. "We field hands don't have as much book learning as you city girls. But when a girl is running a fever and passes out, I'm gon' think she's sick."

Margaret pointed an angry finger at him. "Not funny at all, Elijah. I know you're more educated than you let on. What I don't know is what you're running from. But there is definitely a reason why you're hiding away on this farm."

The devilish grin on his face went lopsided. His hands dropped to his sides. "I apologize, Margaret. I shouldn't have made fun of you." His head lowered as he walked away from them.

Evelyn pursed her lips and folded her arms while glaring at Margaret.

"What?" Margaret shrugged. "I didn't do anything."

"You hurt his feelings."

Margaret couldn't deny the truth of that statement. She saw how Elijah's face had changed when she accused him of running from something. She rushed over to him, tapping his shoulder. When he stopped, she said, "I shouldn't have been so mean. I had no right to accuse you of anything when I don't know much about you in the first place."

He stared at her a moment. Rubbed his chin. "You could get to know more about me if you really wanted to."

Margaret stepped back. "How am I supposed to do that while chasing after the Threatt boys and"—she pointed toward Evelyn—"my sister?"

"Don't put me in that," Evelyn insisted. "I have nothing to do with why you won't give Elijah the time of day."

She wanted to shush her sister. She wasn't avoiding Elijah, had just been busy. There was nothing between her and Elijah. They were friends and that's all . . . that was all she could give place to.

"Why are you ignoring me lately? I make really good fried chicken. If you'd allow me to cook for you, you'd see," Elijah told her.

"I have no reason to ignore you. As you said, I've been sick, and I'm just getting back on my feet."

Looking into her eyes, Elijah took her hand. After a pregnant pause, he said, "Have supper with me, Margaret."

She pulled her hand back. "I told you, I'm too busy."

"I'll watch the Threatt boys so you can keep company with Elijah," Evelyn told her.

"Any more excuses?"

Elijah was staring at her with those luminous brown eyes. Why did he have eyes like that? And why did she wilt beneath his gaze? In that moment, Margaret found a question to which she wanted to discover the answer. "Okay. I'll go out with you. But your fried chicken had better be everything you say, or I'll let everybody know that you tell lies."

Elijah laughed at that. "Guess I'd better not burn it this time."

Chapter 22

While the National Association of Negroes have agreed to [finance some tent houses], it is improbable that they will carry out their agreement unless some white guiding hand is present.

—*Maurice Willows, Red Cross Disaster Relief Report*

Elijah came calling on her the following Thursday. He picked her up at the Threatt farm. Mrs. Alberta handed Margaret a shawl. She wrapped it around her shoulders, and then Elijah took her down a path that had not been tilled or plowed. There was just lush green grass and big tall trees as far as the eye could see.

"A picnic, huh?" An easy grin crept across Margaret's face.

"A picnic is perfect." Elijah spread out a blanket, then placed the basket he'd brought with him on it. He took Margaret's hand and helped her sit down. "We both love the land, so why shouldn't we enjoy the great outdoors while getting to know each other?"

Margaret glanced over at the trees that were a few feet away. The leaves were off the branches, but the trees were still tall and imposing. The blades of green grass lightly swooshed in the November breeze. "It's beautiful out here."

"I'm just thankful I was able to get an afternoon off."

It took Elijah a whole week to make good on his promise of letting her sample his fried chicken. "Have you been back to Greenwood? Is Mrs. Pearl's house finished?" She actually knew the answer to that question. Mrs. Alberta had told her the men had finished Mrs. Pearl's house two weeks ago. What she didn't know was why they hadn't started on her house as he'd promised.

"I didn't mean to keep your mouth watering for so long, but yes, I was back in Greenwood for a few days working on the Johnsons' house. We want to make sure she and those kids have a roof over their heads before it gets too cold."

Most of Mrs. Johnson's five kids had taken ill during the outbreak, and her husband's back had given out on him while digging those ditches. It was good that Elijah helped them. She tried to be thankful that the Johnsons had someone like Elijah on their side.

He removed the cloth from the top of the basket. The smell of fried chicken wafted in the air, causing Margaret's stomach to grumble. Licking her lips, she let the shawl fall to her waist. "Let me see this chicken you've been bragging about."

Elijah pulled out a plate of crispy fried chicken and a container of potato salad. "Got to be honest; Mrs. Alberta gave me some of her leftover potato salad. But I fried this delicious chicken myself."

"I'll be the judge of whether it's delicious or not."

He nodded. "Yes, ma'am. It's for you to judge." Elijah made Margaret's plate and slid it over to her. He then blessed the food.

Margaret lowered her head for the blessing but glanced up when his prayer turned to . . . "And, Lord, if You don't mind, look down on Margaret and her sister. They've endured so much pain, I'd consider it . . ."

Prayer time at church had been a balm to her soul before the massacre. But after witnessing so much of the horror this world could inflict, she just couldn't put her faith in earthly prayers and a heavenly God listening to them. She put a hand on Elijah's arm. "You don't need to pray for us."

His head jolted backward. He stared at her for a moment, then unsteepled his hands. "I didn't mean to offend you. I just know what your kind of pain feels like, and I know God can fix it."

"God didn't have to let it happen in the first place. Then He wouldn't have to fix it." She heard the bitterness in her voice but could do nothing about it. Her mother taught her to pray, took her to church every Sunday morning. After her death, her father continued the Sunday morning ritual, but no more. She was tired of believing in something she couldn't see, feel, or touch.

"I've been where you are. I know how anger at unthinkable tragedy can cause bitterness toward God. But one day He came into my heart and removed all the bitterness. I wish the same for you."

Margaret cut her eyes at him, then took a crispy chicken leg off her plate and stuffed her mouth with it. Her taste buds delighted as the seasoned flakes danced on her tongue. "Oh my, oh my, oh my." Wiping some of the crumbs from the side of her lips, she pointed toward what was left of the chicken. "You cooked this yourself?"

"Sure did. It's my grandma's secret recipe." Elijah tapped a finger to his head. "I promised her I wouldn't forget it."

"Your grandma must be proud. A gentleman and a cook."

Sorrow dimmed the brightness in his eyes. "She never got to see me grow up. But she was happy that I learned some of her recipes."

"What else can you cook?" Margaret finished her chicken leg and started on the potato salad. An errant wind drifted their way, lifting one side of the blanket and almost turning the basket over. Margaret lifted her shawl back over her shoulders.

Elijah steadied the basket as the wind blew past them. "Oh, I can poach some eggs and make a roast and potatoes that'll make you lick your lips."

Margaret grabbed a chicken thigh off the plate and proceeded to eat while staring out at the trees. There was something about the way Elijah smiled, the way his eyebrows dipped close to those dark brown eyes. It caused a flutter in her stomach.

Why was she attracted to this man? He was all wrong for her. She shouldn't be wasting his time like this. While in Greenwood, she had allowed herself to believe that Elijah was what she needed. But they had nothing in common. Putting her chicken down, she wiped her hands on the blanket. "Thank you for fixing this delicious meal, Elijah, but I really need to figure out what's going on with the house. If you're too busy with the other homes, just let me know."

"It's not that—" he began, but Margaret cut in.

"Then what is it? I think it's wonderful that you're helping the Johnsons, but Evie and I need our home too."

"And we will get to your home, I promise. I just don't think you need to be in Greenwood right now."

Her forehead crinkled as her eyebrows arched upward. "What's that supposed to mean? You don't think I can handle it? I was out there for two months, and I managed to stay alive, thank you very much."

Elijah lowered his head, eyes downcast. "You got so sick. I don't want you there until all the homes are rebuilt . . . don't want you dealing with the sewage system backing up and creating a mess of sickness for everybody."

"You think I'm some weak little girl who needs a big strong man to lead the way." Pushing her plate away, Margaret stood, hands fisted at her sides. "I'm grateful for your help, but you don't get to tell me what's what."

He stood up and towered over her. "Don't be so bullheaded. I'm only thinking of what's best for you."

"Well, you're not my daddy, so I'll worry about what's best for me if you don't mind." She turned away from him. Started her trek through the field to get back to the farm. She'd put her trust in Elijah, and he'd let her down. She didn't know why she was so angry or why she was surprised. Everything she'd come to know and trust had let her down in some form or fashion.

Looking heavenward, she cursed the sky above for the shining sun that promised warmth while really there was a chill in the air.

"Margaret, wait . . . don't run off like this." He threw the plates back in his basket and pulled the blanket from the ground as he ran to catch up with her. He reached out for her arm, but she pulled away.

"Leave me be, Elijah. I know what I have to do. I'll be going back to Greenwood to find someone who can help me rebuild my father's house."

"I don't think you're weak," he yelled. "You're one of the strongest women I've ever known."

Margaret stopped. Turned back toward him, tapping her foot. "Then why don't you think I can handle the conditions in Greenwood, especially since things have gotten better down there?"

"It's not that you can't handle it. I'm the one that can't take it. My stomach knotted up every time I left you down there."

She appreciated Elijah's concern for her, but he didn't get to decide how she lived her life. People wanted her to move on, just forget about Greenwood, but how could she do that when everything her daddy worked for was there?

"You didn't see it before the massacre. Greenwood was a prosperous place. It was a place where colored folks lifted their heads with pride." If it was the last thing she did on this earth, Margaret was determined to do her part to help Greenwood rise again.

"I've got another week of work with the Johnsons, and then me and the boys will get right on your house." He stuck out his hand. "You can count on me, Margaret."

She had thought he was the salt of the earth. But all his hem-hawing around rebuilding her home had made her wonder. She shook his hand and then said, "I'll ride down there with you in two weeks. I should be well enough by then to help with the building."

He grinned at her. "Don't trust me, huh?"

"It's not personal. I don't trust nobody anymore."

Chapter 23

It came! It came!" Evelyn ran through the house, clutching her package to her chest as if she'd received a precious gift. She'd spent most of her earnings from the filling station, but that didn't matter. With each weekly pay she realized that she'd never be able to save the five hundred dollars needed to start school. The fall semester had come and gone, winter was on their heels, and the most she'd been able to save was twenty-five dollars.

Mrs. Alberta was in the kitchen. Evelyn's excitement bubbled up with every step. When she reached the kitchen, she waited for Mrs. Alberta to turn in her direction.

Mrs. Alberta stood at the counter cutting potatoes. She glanced over her shoulder and smiled at Evelyn. "What's got you so excited?"

Evelyn lifted the package to eye level, then pressed it against her chest again. "My fabric came."

Putting down the knife, Mrs. Alberta wiped her hands on her apron. "And I suppose you want to use my sewing machine."

Shyly, Evelyn said, "Only if it's okay with you."

Mrs. Alberta's eyes sparked with merriment. "Well, go on. You know where the sewing room is."

Evelyn didn't need further encouragement. She took the stairs two at a time, then ran down the hall to get to the sewing room. She tore open her package and the crepe, chiffon, and ribbons of fringes poured out of the package as images of the dresses she would design danced around her head.

Scissors, pins, pencils, and thread were all she needed. Evelyn didn't follow patterns for the dresses. She put her fabric on the floor, penciled the lines, then cut until the design of the dress fit the image in her mind.

It took a few hours to cut out patterns for two separate dresses. One would have fringe and the other would be a dropped waist with a creeping hemline. Sitting down at the sewing machine, she got to work.

An unexpected tear ran down her cheek as she imagined her mother seated next to her, guiding her hand through the turn of the fabric and straightening it so the stitches wouldn't get hung up.

She closed her eyes as memories rushed in like a tidal wave, threatening to drown her. Burying her face in the fabric on the sewing machine, she balled her fist and slammed it against the table. With each strike of her fist, she released bits and pieces of the pain that consumed her. The door to the sewing room opened, and Margaret stepped in. "Hey, you okay?"

Evelyn lifted her head. Wiped the tears from her face. "Sorry. I didn't mean to disturb you."

"You don't need to apologize." Margaret walked over to Evelyn. "You were thinking about Mama, weren't you? I knew this sewing project would be too much for you."

With pursed lips that held in her sobs, Evelyn nodded. Her mom had been gone ten years, but Evelyn's heart still broke whenever she dared to remember the days when she and Margaret had a family. When they were nurtured and cared for.

There was a chill in the house on Sunday morning. Margaret pulled the covers up to her chin, thankful that she would have a day of rest. She was just about to turn over and close her eyes to get a little more sleep before lying around in her pajamas when Evelyn strutted into their room wearing one of the dresses she'd made earlier in the week.

It was a cream-colored dress with a dropped waist and a V-neck that dipped too low for Margaret's liking. "Why are you up so early this morning?"

"Mrs. Alberta's taking the boys to church. I'm going with her."

"She takes them to church every month. You never went before." The Threatts owned sixty acres of land. Mr. Allen built his filling station, farm, store, and restaurant / juke joint on the property, but no church. Once a month a traveling preacher stopped by and used the restaurant for church service.

Straightening a crease in the front of her dress, Evelyn told Margaret, "I didn't have a dress suitable to wear."

Margaret popped up, eyes brimming with condemnation. "That dress is not suitable for church. It's too tight. I don't know what's got in your head, but Daddy would never let you step foot into church showing off all your curves like that." She walked over to the dresser they shared and pulled out two dresses. Neither had a V-neck and one buttoned all the way to the neckline. "These dresses are perfect for church."

Scrunching her nose, Evelyn turned away from the offering. "I'm sick to death of hand-me-downs. Daddy let me wear the clothes I designed, so stop being a bore."

Her words were like a slap in Margaret's face. She'd had fifteen dollars in her purse when she and Evelyn escaped the massacre. She spent every dime ensuring that she and her sister had clothes on their backs. For Evelyn to dismiss what she'd done hurt like a scab being pulled off before the wound healed. "How can you be so selfish? I bought you socks, undergarments, and clothes until I'd spent every penny."

Evelyn rushed over to her sister and hugged her. "I didn't mean to hurt you or to sound ungrateful. I just want to wear something that makes me feel special . . . something that feels like me."

Margaret put the dresses back in the dresser and sat down on her bed. "I know you prefer to make your own clothes. But . . ." Margaret's words trailed off as her mind took her back to the day she walked through the rubble that used to be their home.

If there had been any clothes left, they had been covered in soot or torn beyond repair. Evelyn loved those clothes, but what could she do? Emotions rolled through her like tumbling bricks. She wished for the thousandth time that her daddy was there. Evelyn needed guidance, and she was a poor substitute.

Evelyn wiped the tear that rolled down Margaret's face. "None of that today. Get dressed and come to church with us."

Margaret didn't want to go to church. Didn't want to listen to that traveling preacher talk about a God she couldn't trust. But her sister was wearing a dress that would cause the angels in heaven to blush. And these earthly men didn't seem to have any God-given shame. "Give me ten minutes."

Margaret went back to the dresser. She took the blue dress that buttoned up to the neckline that she had purchased for Evelyn, slung it across her shoulder. "I'll wear it, since it's not good enough for you."

"Didn't say it wasn't good enough . . . I just like my own creations." Evelyn let her hands flow from the top of her dress to her waist.

Her sister had skill, Margaret could admit that. But it wasn't right to snub her nose at a perfectly good dress. Second-, third-, or fourth-hand, it had been purchased out of love and care.

There were about twenty-five people in attendance at the church service. More people attended the Friday night dances Mr. Allen had behind the filling station. But the preacher didn't seem bothered by the empty chairs.

He stood behind the wood podium wearing a shirt and tie, a pair of suspenders attached to his black trousers. He put his spectacles on and opened his Bible.

He began by reading 1 John 4:16–17.

"And we have known and believed the love that God hath to us. God is love; and he that dwelleth in love dwelleth in God, and God in him. Herein is our love made perfect, that we may have boldness in the day of judgment: because as he is, so are we in this world."

He shut his Bible and then started preaching like he had only a short time to convince them of God's love before the world blew up on them again.

Turning to her left, Margaret saw Elijah seated three chairs away from her. His eyes bored into her as if he was hoping and praying that her heart would connect with the l-o-v-e delivered by the preacher, but he didn't know or understand the pain and anger that filled her heart and left no room for anything else.

She tuned out the preacher and turned away from those eyes of Elijah's that seemed to read her thoughts and her every misery. When service was over, all Margaret wanted to do was flee as far away as she could from Elijah, the preacher, and the God who only dwelled among them on Sunday mornings. Where was He the rest of the week?

Evelyn was holding court with Carter Jones. He drove a truck and made stops at the filling station about once a month. Margaret walked over to them and put a hand on Evelyn's arm, trying to hurry her along.

"You are a delight for my eyes this morning, Miss Evelyn. I sure hope you're hungry. I'd like to take you for a bite to eat."

"She is hungry," Margaret told him, "but Mrs. Alberta got up bright and early this morning to cook for us. So she won't be able to go anywhere with you."

Evelyn cut her eyes at Margaret. She turned to Carter. "I can't let Mrs. Alberta's meal go to waste. But it was nice of you to offer."

"I'll be back in town by the end of the month. Maybe we can go dancing or something?"

"I'd like that," Evelyn told him as Margaret twined an arm around hers and tried to rush out of the church.

Elijah stood at the door talking to the preacher. Margaret tried to squeeze behind him and escape without saying her goodbyes to anyone.

"It was sure good to see y'all in the house of the Lord this morning," Elijah said as he swung around in their direction.

"Why, thank you, Elijah." Evelyn unraveled her arm. "Margaret told me about that fried chicken you fixed. Best she's ever had. Isn't that right?" She nudged Margaret forward.

She glared at Evelyn, then turned back to Elijah. "The fried chicken was good. But I'm surprised you're here. Thought you'd be spending your free time in Greenwood like you told me."

She gave him a look that said, "I knew you wouldn't be true." Margaret didn't trust anything she couldn't see, feel, or touch. Not anymore.

"The boys and I have planned it out. We're starting on your house next weekend. A couple of the Johnson kids are going to help now that we've finished their house." He put a hand on her shoulder. "No need for you to come to Greenwood. Just let us get the job done."

Her nostrils flared as she bristled. Once again, he was trying to keep her away from Greenwood. "You don't get to run my life, Elijah. I'm a grown woman."

A parishioner gave Margaret the eye as she walked past them. Elijah moved her away from the door. "Let me walk you home, and we can talk further about this."

Those eyes. He looked at her in such a knowing manner, as if he grieved with her . . . like they shared the same secret. "You don't have to walk me." Margaret latched onto Evelyn's arm again. "My sister and I will be fine."

"Oh no we won't." Evelyn backed away from Margaret. "I'm not walking anywhere with you." She took off running.

"Evelyn, you get back here!" Why was her sister so insufferable? She had been such a sweet and loving girl. But lately Evelyn had been changing, and Margaret didn't like it one bit.

"Mrs. Alberta invited me to supper. It's no trouble at all to walk with you to the farmhouse."

She didn't want to walk with Elijah. Didn't want to hear one more person give her an excuse as to why something that should've been done wasn't being done. Didn't want sky-high promises that fell flat down here in the real world. "Don't worry about me. And don't worry about the house. I'll get back down to Greenwood and finish it myself."

Elijah sighed, then nodded as he backed away from her bitterness as if it had tentacles and would latch onto him.

She walked away, leaving him to watch the steps she took toward the farmhouse without him. She didn't need anything from Elijah Porter. Didn't need one more broken promise to deal with.

Elijah thought she was too frail and needed time away from Greenwood. But what she needed was not to let her daddy's sacrifice be for nothing.

Chapter 24

The raw goods have been furnished, power sewing machines have been provided and the women required to manufacture their own quilts, comforters, cot pads, sheets, pillowcases and pillows.

—*Maurice Willows, Red Cross Disaster Relief Report*

Seated around the table, passing the dishes of baked chicken, greens, and macaroni and cheese, Margaret felt trapped with Elijah on her left side, staring at her as if he was trying to read her thoughts again. And Evelyn on her right, shooting daggers every time she turned in her direction.

Margaret was mortified by the way she spoke to Elijah after church but couldn't bring herself to open her mouth and apologize. She doubted that her daddy would think highly of the way she'd treated a man who'd been nothing but good and kind to her.

"Mm-mm-mm. I hate to admit it, but your baked chicken is better than my nana's." Elijah took another bite and moaned as he chewed.

"Well, I'm sure your nana's chicken was plenty good enough," Mrs. Alberta told him, then lifted a finger. "I almost forgot about my pie."

As Mrs. Alberta rushed out of the dining room, Margaret tried to concentrate on her own plate, but her eyes kept shifting from Evelyn to Elijah. Something inside her was unsettled. She wasn't sure if being in church today for the first time since the massacre was troubling her, or if it was the change she was seeing in her little sister.

Before she had time to contemplate the matter, Mrs. Alberta came back into the dining room and put a pecan pie in front of Elijah. She grinned and offered him a slice. Elijah's face turned to stone.

He pushed the chair back and stood up. "Supper was wonderful." He patted his stomach. "I doubt I can eat another morsel."

Margaret doubted Elijah's stomach was bothering him. Something else stopped him from taking a piece of that pecan pie, and Margaret needed answers to the puzzle that was Elijah. She excused herself from the table and followed him out the front door.

"Hey, why you leaving so fast?"

Elijah turned toward her, eyebrow jutted upward. "Well, the lady speaks."

"Of course I speak. Anyone who's listening can hear me."

"You couldn't be bothered to talk to me at the supper table. Acting as if you'd rather sit anywhere else than beside me."

How did he do that? How could one person read her so well? She folded her arms against her chest. "I didn't have a problem sitting next to you. Evelyn is mad at me. Her anger made me uncomfortable is all."

He laughed. "Okay, have it your way."

Elijah started to walk away, but Margaret stopped him. She had been sore with him about the house, but that didn't change how good he had been to her from the moment he carried her to the farmhouse. He was hurting, and she needed to be there for him like she needed to breathe. "What flustered you so? Why'd you leave like that when you were clearly enjoying the meal?"

He bit down on his bottom lip, his eyes shadowed with sadness. "What makes you think there's more to me than what you see?"

Stepping down from the porch and walking closer to him, she said, "You talk real big, but you're hurting. I can see it in there." She pointed at his eyes.

"I'm nothing special. We all been hurting 'round here."

Putting a hand on his arm, Margaret leaned closer. "Tell me your story. I need to know how you still believe in the love of God with all the pain I see in your eyes."

Sighing, he said, "Take a walk with me."

Margaret looked back, making sure Evelyn wasn't standing at the front door watching her walk off with Elijah. She didn't want to give the girl any ideas. "Okay."

They walked through the front yard and into the field. Elijah raised his head to the sky. "Warm day out for it to be so close to December."

Margaret lifted her head toward the sun that radiated down on them. "It's a nice day. Wonder how long that'll last. We'll probably get hit with a snowstorm in the morning."

Elijah stopped and looked at Margaret a moment too long for her comfort. She turned away. "Why do you do that?"

"Do what?"

"Why do good things turn bad with you so quickly? It's like you can't take a moment to breathe in the air without wondering what terrible thing you'll have to endure next."

Margaret's head snapped. She blew out a puff of air. "Can't really judge a person unless you take a walk in their shoes."

He took her hands in his. "I've been where you're at. And it's a terrible dark place. I thank the good Lord that he didn't let me stay in my darkness."

A raging inferno of anger boiled up in her and exploded all over Elijah. "How dare you say something like that! You could never know the kind of pain I suffer with . . . each and every day of my *life*!"

Tears rolled down her face. She panted as she continued. "They took everything from me!" She beat at her chest as she added, "And left me empty."

Elijah pulled her into his arms. He rubbed her back, trying to calm her. But she would never be calmed again. The things that had been done to her and the people in her community shouldn't have been done to animals, and yet no one paid for what they did. No one even looked her in the eye and said sorry. How could she forget? How could she forgive?

Her chest heaved as she continued to pour out her sorrow. "It's too hard to go on, but I keep getting up . . . I–I can't let my s-sister down. I can't let my daddy down."

He pointed toward a wooden table that was just beyond the field. "Come sit with me."

Margaret wiped the river of tears from her face. The downpour continued, so she wiped her face several times before sitting down across from Elijah. Inhaling and exhaling, she thought she had finally calmed down, but she wasn't prepared for what Elijah had to tell her.

"My mother died giving birth to me. My grandmother was the only mama I knew," he began as his eyes took on a faraway look, as if he was excavating the deepest, darkest parts of his memory. "My grandmother was the best cook in our county. She took care of me by selling meals and baked goods.

"One day this white woman ordered a pecan pie from her. She was all excited. According to my grandmother, this white woman was important. The people in Mississippi listened to her. So my granny thought making this pie would bring more business our way.

"But the woman was short on money and couldn't pay when I delivered the pie." Elijah closed his eyes, blew out hot air. "I remember that day like it was yesterday . . . the smell of that pie . . . how much I wanted a slice of it . . . how upset my grandmother was when I came home with no money.

"'These white folks don't get no free labor out of me. Them days is over.'" Elijah ran a hand through his hair. "She went back to that woman's house, knocked on the door, and demanded her pie back.

"The woman turned red with embarrassment. Told my grandmother to get off her porch. I was just ten years old when that happened, but as we walked home together, I got a sick feeling in the pit of my stomach. I knew no good would come from a Black woman standing up for herself in Mississippi."

He was silent so long after that statement. Looked like something was eating at him and tearing his insides apart. Elijah's fist slammed against the picnic table. He stood and walked to the outer edge of the farm, facing the filling station.

Margaret didn't follow him at first. When white folks were involved in putting an uppity Negro in her place, what came next was the kind of pain that changed people. The hurt would burrow so deep that it couldn't be plucked out so it didn't hurt no more—it crippled and left everything dead inside.

She wasn't ready for Elijah's pain. But the way his shoulders shook made her feel responsible for unleashing the storm. Margaret went to him. She put a hand on his back. "I'm sorry for making you think on things like this."

He took in a long-suffering breath. Turned to her. She wanted to reach up and wipe the wetness from his face, but then he said, "They burned her . . . They burned down our house and burned my grandmother alive, all for the price of a pecan pie."

She felt it now. The pain that Elijah carried was familiar. White folks left an inferno of heartache, and no one paid the price for the evil done to Black bodies. Wrapping her arms around him, she wept like his pain was her pain.

Elijah pulled away from her and wiped his face. "Seeing that pie caught me off guard, but I'll be okay."

"Why do you have to be okay? What happened to your grandmother was the vilest thing ever . . . Now imagine that being done to a whole community of people." Margaret let out a puff of air. "None of us will be okay, not ever again."

"We owe it to the living to try."

Her chest heaved. She sighed. "That night in Greenwood was like living through the worst terror anyone has ever seen. I thought those responsible would pay for what they did." She bit down on her lip, kicked at a twig on the ground. "I want to put my daddy's house and his business to rights to show them that they didn't break us. We ain't never gon' be broken. Not by the likes of them."

She shook. Wrapped her arms around her body when a chill went up her spine as she thought of all the hate that she hated those people with. She wanted justice for what was done to her daddy . . . for what was done to her community. How could she ever turn this hate over to God when not one of those white men paid for what they did?

"I walked around with so much anger for years after my grandmother's death. But the day I discovered God's love for me, that was the day I determined to release the hate from my heart."

"I don't understand you, Elijah Porter. God doesn't love us." She pointed from him to her and back again. "Not us. Black folks aren't meant to know love . . . only pain."

"I couldn't disagree more." Another tear drifted down his cheek. "The day I first saw you, when I picked you up and carried you to the Threatt farm, I knew that God had brought you here so I could show you love."

She almost tripped on the uneven ground as she took a step back, scratching her head. "What can I do with love when this world is so full of hate?"

He reached his hand out to her. "Let me teach you to love. Let me help ease the pain."

Shaking her head, she kept backing away from him. "I won't love another person. Not as long as God allows evil to destroy everything I ever loved." She turned and ran away from him and the love he spoke of. She ran to the farmhouse where she didn't have to think about love or fear. She went to her room, where she was safe from the troubles of the world.

Chapter 25

The labor necessary to rebuild or build the tent house
was supplied by the family or their Negro friends.

—*Maurice Willows, Red Cross Disaster Relief Report*

I don't think I've ever been to this restaurant. Thanks for
bringing me here." Evelyn's date was Tommy Brooks. He was
a baseball player trying to get into the Negro National League.
She'd met him at a dance that had been held in the back of the
filling station a week ago.

Tommy's dark skin, wavy hair, and dapper dress coat caught
Evelyn's eye. Margaret told her to stay away, but that was the
opposite of what she wanted to do. Tommy took her to a diner
just outside of Tulsa that served Negroes. Evelyn had been
afraid to go to a place that was only about ten miles away from
Greenwood, but Tommy gave her courage that was sorely lacking within her.

She kept looking out the window, trying to see if any mobs
were coming up the street to set the place on fire or shoot them
as they made their escape. But the street seemed quiet, and the
waitress and the cooks were going about their business as if
bombs hadn't been dropped on the Greenwood community
less than six months ago.

Life as she knew it was over, but for Blacks outside of Greenwood, not much had changed. She couldn't fathom how everybody was just going about their business as they pleased, no worry on them. Seemed to her that colored folks had perfected the no-worries look. But deep down, their insides were in a constant state of trembling, never truly at ease with the world around them. The facade was a survival mechanism, a shield to protect against the harsh reality of their existence. Wasn't that what she was doing herself?

"Anyone as pretty as you shouldn't be frowning so much."

"Was I frowning?"

He pointed toward the window. "You keep looking out there as if someone is coming to get you." He laughed.

"It's not funny." Her eyes shifted toward the window again. She whispered, "White men in this town did come after us. I watched them kill a man who lived down the street from where I used to live."

Her body shook as if an ill wind had blown into the diner. "Margaret wants me to move back to Greenwood with her, but I could never do that."

Tommy put a hand over hers. "I'm sorry. I shouldn't have made light of your fears. I'm not from here and wasn't in Oklahoma when all that went down." He shrugged. "I hardly hear anyone talking about it, so I guess I don't know much of what happened."

Ducking her head like she was trying to hide in plain sight, Evelyn told him, "Colored folks afraid to speak on it. They might come after us again if we make too much fuss."

"I shouldn't have brought you here. We can go if you want."

The waitress came to the table. She set pork chops smothered in gravy with mashed potatoes in front of Evelyn and fried chicken with macaroni and cheese and green beans in front of

Tommy. He would have to pay for the plates whether they ate them or not. "We can stay. I'm fine."

But Evelyn was a long way from fine. A long way from finding her way back to what she used to be . . . what she used to believe. Glancing back out the window, she saw a school building across the street. It put her in mind of Booker T. Washington and that awful day they were sent home from graduation practice.

"I lost you again." Tommy waved a hand in front of Evelyn's face.

She blinked, ran her hands over her eyes. No sense crying over spilled milk. Thinking on the past did her no good. All she had was today, right now. She needed to live for now, not what was or would be. She plastered a smile on her face. "You haven't lost me at all." She cut into her pork chop and savored the taste of it. "Mmm, this is good. Thank you for bringing me here. I never even knew this restaurant was so close to Greenwood."

"I've eaten here a few times when I've traveled this way."

"And how long do you intend to be in Oklahoma?" She jutted her fork toward the mashed potatoes after taking a quick bite. "Delicious."

"My parents found a plot of land not far from Luther, Oklahoma. My daddy thinks there's oil on the land, so I've been helping him dig in certain spots, kinda secret-like." He leaned closer to her, lowered his voice. "Don't want the white folks in these parts to get wind of what's what before we can stake our claim."

"Smart thinking," Evelyn told him. "They tried to become guardians of Mr. W. A. Rentie's son, Roy Rentie, after he struck oil."

"My dad told me about that." Tommy laughed. "Said Mr. Rentie told that white man, 'The day you become guardian of my children is the day you die.'"

Chewing a piece of pork chop, then wiping her mouth with the napkin, she said, "Mr. Rentie didn't play. But he got arrested. Thank God he was able to take those men to court and win his case, or they would've found a way to steal his money."

Tommy shook his head. "Just not right what they let these people get away with."

Evelyn's heart hurt when she allowed herself to dwell on the kind of things white folks got away with, so she changed the subject. "An oil man, huh?"

Tommy's lip twisted to the left. "Naw, that's my dad's wishful thinking. All I've ever wanted was to play baseball. And I'm going to get my chance, just wait and see."

He said it with such confidence, like a man who never had his plans blow up in his face. Evelyn admired that about him. Wished some of his ability to believe in good things could rub off on her. She lifted her water glass toward him. "Well, I wish all your dreams come true."

But when she said those words, she had no idea that his dreams would pull away her last thread of hope.

Chapter 26

We never saw my stepfather again . . . My stepfather was a strong family man. I know he did not desert us. I just wish I knew where he was buried.

—*Otis Granville Clark, Tulsa Race Massacre survivor*

*L*ook *at your fine self, coming in here toting all them packages and expecting me to wrap 'em for you."* Velma slung the dish towel *over her shoulder. Dried her hands on her long wool skirt and then took a few packages from under Henry's arm.*

"These girls are expecting those dolls they saw in the window at my store. And you told me yourself that they needed more socks and undergarments."

"You're a good man, Henry Justice." Velma kissed her husband and *then set the packages down next to the Elizabethan chair in the living room.*

Henry sat on the sofa and pulled Velma onto his lap. "You haven't been feeling well lately, or the Christmas shopping would've already been done. I had some things at the store, so I grabbed them this morning."

"I'll have you know that I'm up making pancakes. Feeling well or not, our Christmas tradition will go forth."

The two snuggled in each other's arms before Velma stood and propped her hands on her ample hips. "I hope you brought wrapping paper too. I don't have very much left from last Christmas."

"The girls won't care if these presents get wrapped. You go finish breakfast, and I'll call them out here."

Margaret's bedroom door had been cracked ever so slightly. From her vantage point, she could see her parents and those packages. She was twelve that Christmas but still noticed the loving way her daddy took care of her mother.

They had questioned why their presents weren't wrapped, but as their mother experienced deteriorating health the following year, becoming rail thin and barely being able to get out of bed, they would have another Christmas of unwrapped presents and Margaret would be the one to cook the pancakes. That had been their last year of Christmas with pancakes.

God had taken her sweet mother. And then the devil took her daddy. Margaret would not make peace with either of them. So this Christmas morning, when Evie came back into their room and the smell of pancakes drifted in the air, Margaret said, "Close the door."

"Mrs. Alberta made pancakes."

Margaret turned her face to the wall. Resigning herself to lie in bed until the new year rolled in. If someone had told her she could hurt more than she had after losing her daddy and their beloved home, she wouldn't have believed them. But these holidays were making them look like ungrateful guests in the Threatt home.

During the Thanksgiving meal, Margaret noticed Evelyn's hands shaking. Her sister backed away from the table and the family gathering. Leaning against the wall in the dining room, Evie panted and panted and panted.

Mrs. Alberta came to her. "Oh my goodness, not again."

"What's happening to her?" Margaret's heart raced. She rushed over to Evie. The last time she saw Evie in such a state was when she and Mrs. Pearl tried to get her out of that chicken coop. "Calm down, Evie. What's wrong?"

Mrs. Alberta pulled out a chair and sat Evelyn in it. "Bend your head down."

Mr. Allen put his hand on Margaret's shoulder, pulling her backward. "She'll be okay. Step aside so Alberta can help her."

Margaret was so focused on Evelyn that she didn't realize Mr. Allen was talking to her until he started pulling her backward. Margaret reached an arm out to Evelyn. "I need to help her."

"Just wait. Stand here with me." His hand around her shoulder had a calming effect. Margaret relaxed a bit.

"Take deep breaths like I showed you before," Mrs. Alberta said. She then put a hand behind Evelyn's head and lowered it.

Evelyn did as she was commanded. Her breathing settled, and she stood back up. "I'm sorry." A tear drifted down her face. "I need to lay down."

Margaret had made a plate for her and one for Evie, then followed her sister to their room. Evie hadn't been able to deal with Thanksgiving in their new environment. The Threatts were wonderful people, and they hated offending them, but there was no helping the matter. Now Christmas was here. Pancakes were on the menu, and Margaret was undone.

"Did you hear me? Mrs. Alberta wants us to come down for pancakes."

"You go. I don't eat pancakes on Christmas."

Evie walked over to the bed and sat down next to her. "Don't shut me out. I know how you feel about pancakes, but Mrs. Alberta told me to get you out of this room."

Margaret's eyes watered. She rubbed her face. "I can't go down there. I'm surprised you can."

Putting an arm around Margaret's shoulder, Evelyn said, "I haven't had a panic attack since Thanksgiving. Mrs. Alberta has made me feel so at home here. I'm actually excited about having pancakes with them this morning."

Her sister didn't have the same aversion to pancakes on Christmas Day as she did. Margaret understood so thoroughly now why that pecan pie bothered Elijah so much. Memories . . . "You go eat. Enjoy Christmas. I just need a little more time. The holidays have destroyed me this year."

"Mrs. Alberta said she was coming up here if you don't come down for breakfast."

Margaret didn't care. She wasn't getting out of this bed. Christmas had come and crushed her very soul. Tears rolled down her face like melting snow flowing down a hill.

Evie wrapped her arms around Margaret. Crying with her sister, she said, "I won't go back down either. I'll stay here with you."

She couldn't, wouldn't ruin this day for Evie. "No, don't let my bad mood take Christmas from you." Margaret wiped her face and then wiped the tears from Evie's face as well. "Go downstairs and enjoy your day."

"But I don't want to leave you by yourself . . . not when you're so sad."

Margaret blew her nose. "I'll be alright. I just need this day to go away. And I don't want to talk about it anymore. Go downstairs already, okay?"

"What if I asked Elijah to come sit with you?"

Margaret shook her head. "Not today."

Standing up and walking toward the door, Evie said, "Okay, I'll give you some space today. But all bets are off tomorrow."

Spending time with Elijah wasn't the worst thing she could do. But she wouldn't lay her ill temper at his feet today. Especially since every time she saw him lately, she thought about how the bad weather had brought a halt to the work on her house. Several homes in Greenwood had been put back to rights and families were living indoors rather than in tents during the winter, but there were still plenty of homes that hadn't been finished before winter set in.

Maybe she would feel different about Christmas if she and Evie were back in Greenwood and conditions there were just as they had been before the massacre. What good was Christmas when there was so much suffering in the world?

As the new year rang in, Margaret found herself sitting at one of the wooden tables behind the filling station with Elijah. "I'm glad you finally came out of the house. The fresh air will do you some good."

The crisp January air caused Margaret to button the top of her wool coat. She gave Elijah a weak smile. "I didn't know getting through the holidays would be so hard." Sighing on an unwanted thought, she told him, "I laid in bed on Christmas wishing the day would just be over already."

Elijah took her hand in his. Margaret exhaled as if the very act brought her comfort.

"It was Thanksgiving for me," he said in a quiet tone, then looked off like he was trying to find something meaningful in the trees just beyond them. "To my grandma, food was love. We made some good memories in the kitchen, especially during Thanksgiving."

"Evie struggled with Thanksgiving. Then the closer it got to Christmas, with all the snow and no work being done on the house . . . I just got the blues."

"We were able to work on the house this weekend. We'll get it done, I promise you that."

Elijah was a good friend. He and the Threatts were the only good things to come out of everything she and Evelyn had endured. But her heart wouldn't let her forget about the things they had lost. "How did you get over losing your grandma?"

"I don't think you ever really get over losing someone you love. But each year that passes takes a bit of the sting away."

Margaret didn't know if she believed Elijah. Didn't know if her heart would ever heal from the pain that had been inflicted on them for no good reason at all.

"Hey, whatcha doing out here?" Evelyn asked as she came over to the table where Margaret and Elijah were sitting.

"I needed some air. Elijah and I decided to sit out here and wait for Mr. Allen to start barbecuing." There was always something happening over by the filling station—a barbecue, a party, or kids playing baseball in the field across the street.

Margaret rarely hung out over here, preferring to stay close to the farm or in the house. She feared for Evie when she stayed out too late either at a party behind the filling station or over at the juke joint.

"I just got off work. I'm going home to change."

"Change? For what?" Margaret's antenna went up.

"Got a date."

"With who? Not that guy who's just passing through?"

Evelyn let out an exasperated sigh. "His name is Tommy, and he just got a job working on the new highway that's being built right in front of the filling station, so I'll be seeing a lot of him."

Margaret leaned back, pursed her lips. "Well, I guess you told me."

Evelyn turned toward Elijah. "Tell Margaret to leave me alone. I have a right to enjoy my life."

Elijah lifted his hands. "You're not getting me in the middle of this."

Evelyn stomped her foot. "I'm nineteen. But Margaret keeps acting like she's the boss of me."

Margaret folded her arms, her lips tightened.

Elijah then told Evelyn. "I'll tell you what—bring this fellow to church on Sunday, and I'll see what I think of the young man."

Evelyn laughed. "You're an old soul, but Tommy is just two years younger than you. So I don't think you can call him 'young man' like that."

Margaret slammed her hand on the table. "I don't care if he's a young man or an old man. You need to watch yourself with all these men you've been keeping company with. Daddy is probably rolling over in his grave." Margaret shook her head as the pain of still not knowing where her daddy was buried seeped in and tortured her soul like the cut of a thousand blades. "Wherever that is." The pain of what-they-did-to-us was ever present, and she didn't know how to move past it.

Evelyn yanked her arms in a downward motion as steam blew from her nostrils. "You're just a grouch, Margaret Justice. You take that back, or I'm not going to speak to you for a month."

Why had she said that to her sister? They both ached over not being able to find the place their daddy had been buried. Evelyn was old enough to go out on a date. However, Margaret was still her big sister and worried about her choices. But her words had cut.

Taking a deep breath, Margaret parted her lips for the apology she knew was due. "Sorry. I shouldn't have said that. But you're just too impetuous for your own good."

"Impetuous or not, Daddy was proud of me," Evelyn yelled at her sister. "He was proud of both of us, not just you." With that, Evelyn turned and ran across the street and kept going until she was out of sight.

Sometimes the hurting hurt without meaning to. Wasn't right . . . just was. Margaret was ashamed of herself. Wished she could change the world and make it not so cruel. But it, too, just was what it was.

Elijah got out of his seat and walked around to Margaret's side of the table. He put an arm around her shoulders.

She looked up at him. His eyes filled with so much compassion for her that she couldn't speak; all she could do was sit with her pain and accept the fact that somebody in this god-forsaken world cared about the swamp water she traversed in just to get through each day.

Chapter 27

People [were] running down the road near the Midland Valley Railroad tracks; many were headed to the Section Line near Pine, or to the Peoria area, or to parks or other hiding places.

—*Nell Hamilton Hampton, Tulsa Race Massacre survivor*

Where'd you get an automobile from?" Evelyn asked when Tommy pulled up at the farmhouse to pick her up. He'd told her that his car had broken down and he didn't have the funds to fix it.

"Just get in. I want to show you something."

Evelyn's hands went to her hips. "Not getting in no stolen car. You can forget that."

"I ain't no thief. My daddy let me borrow his automobile." Tommy got out of the car and opened the passenger door for her. "Get in before I change my mind."

"Where we going?" Evelyn slid into the passenger seat. It was an older Model T Ford, but it cranked up and drove like the newer models. Evelyn leaned back in her seat, waiting for answers.

"You'll see," was all he said.

But twenty minutes later, Evelyn squirmed as the skyline of Greenwood came into view. She glared at Tommy. "Why you doing this? I don't want to go back to that place."

With his hands on the wheel, Tommy stayed focused on the traffic in front of him. "When I saw how terrified you were at being so close to Greenwood that day I took you to lunch, I figured you hadn't been back since that awful night you and your sister ran for your lives."

"Why would I ever want to go back there? They killed a man right in front of me. Would have shot me too if his gun hadn't jammed." Then she whispered, like if she said it out loud it would be too true, "They killed my daddy."

Tommy kept driving.

She put her hand on the door. "Turn the car around. Take me back home."

"Greenwood Avenue is the next block over. Let me show you something."

Evelyn put her hands over her face and lowered her head. Why had she gotten in this car without knowing where she was going? "It's too hard, Tommy. I don't want to see what they did to us."

Margaret's reports of their hometown had been hard enough to hear. She couldn't bear seeing the people she once knew, who'd walked the streets of Greenwood with such pride, now penniless and homeless.

He turned onto Greenwood Avenue. "Open your eyes, Evelyn. The people here have not given up, and neither should you."

What else could the people of Greenwood do but give up? Their lives were destroyed. Even Margaret had come back to the farm barely clinging to life. Tommy didn't know what he was talking about. He wasn't there, hadn't seen what happened to them.

He parked the car. "Will you take your hands off your face and get out of the car already?" He opened his door and got out.

Evelyn wanted to scream at him. She pulled her hands from her face to see what he was doing. And that's when she noticed that he had parked in front of what used to be the Dreamland Theater. Margaret told her that the building had been completely demolished. But either her eyes were deceiving her or she was looking at the very theater her sister had been in the night the massacre began.

It looked like the same theater that she herself had spent many hours of enjoyment in. But it couldn't be the same building. Getting out of the car with wonderment in her eyes, she turned to Tommy.

"They're rebuilding." He gave a sweeping motion with his arm. "Brick by brick, they're putting the business district back together."

"But Margaret said . . ." Her words trailed off as she turned and looked from one side of the street to the other. Not many of the businesses appeared to be open just yet, but work was being done. The place she'd grown up in was coming back to life. The neighborhood had indeed been demolished, but the heart—the beating, vibrant parts—of Greenwood could never be destroyed.

"If this don't beat all." Evelyn walked over to the Dreamland Theater and peered through the window. The walls were up, but nothing else was in the building yet. It looked like progress to Evelyn. She couldn't wait to get home to tell Margaret.

Then she realized that she'd been thinking of the Threatt farm as home, when her home was really and truly in Greenwood. She turned to Tommy and said, "Take me to Detroit Street."

But Detroit Street complicated things for her. She went from the highest of highs at seeing the resurrection of the business district to the lowest of lows when she saw several homes being rebuilt on Detroit Street while others sat in ruins. She pointed to her house as Tommy drove toward it. "Pull over."

Tommy did as requested, then parked the automobile. "Is this where you used to live?"

"Yeah." She walked over to the house and peered in as she did at Dreamland. Although the outer elements of the house were rebuilt, there were no walls inside the house. No kitchen, no bedrooms. It was just a box and nothing like the home she remembered.

Elijah and a few men from the farm had been working on the house, but Evelyn hadn't asked any questions. Hadn't wanted to know. This place and all the evil that had been visited upon them had become part of the nightmares that haunted her sleep.

Tommy was standing next to her as her eyes danced with memories. "We had a three-bedroom home. My dad used to fry the best catfish you've ever tasted in our kitchen. I used to design dresses for me and my sister and sew them in my room." She lifted a hand and pointed to the left, where her bedroom had been. "My sister sat in the living room reading books in the evenings."

"I'm sure you had a fine house."

"It was." Her eyes watered as she turned away from the shell of what once meant so much to her. "It really was . . . but nothing is like it used to be."

The front door to Mrs. Pearl's house opened, and a woman hurried over to them, waving a hand as if to shoo them away. "Get away from that house. It's not abandoned. The owners are coming back."

Evelyn walked between the two houses toward the woman. She had on a housecoat and slippers, hair in curlers. Mrs. Pearl never would have come out of her house in her bedclothes. She had style and sass. Evelyn felt her eyes watering from missing the woman who had loved on her and Margaret since they were kids. "Who are you?"

"Never you mind who I am." She put a hand on her hip, wagged a finger at them. "Y'all ain't getting ready to squat over here."

Tommy stepped between Evelyn and the housecoat-wearing woman. "Pipe down." He pointed toward Evelyn. "She's the owner of this house."

Pursing her lips, the woman gave Evelyn the once-over. "What's your name?"

"Evelyn Justice." She then pointed to the house. "Henry Justice was my daddy. He built this house for us."

The woman stuck her hand out to Evelyn. "I'm Rose Freeman. Pearl was my aunt."

Evelyn shook hands with the woman. "I'm glad family was available to take over Mrs. Pearl's home. That's what my sister Margaret plans to do with my daddy's home."

"Got to keep it in the family; otherwise them city officials will take even more from us."

It wasn't the city officials who gave Evelyn pause. They had to do their dirt in the light of day with the court system. But those white men in Tulsa who did their dirt late at night when everything was quiet and peaceful, they were the ones who shivered her bones.

Putting her mind on other things, Evelyn said, "I wonder how long it will take them to get the interior walls up and section off the rooms."

Rose nodded toward the house. "They had to stop when the weather turned cold. But they've been back over there the last couple of weeks. Got the roof up and everything."

Evelyn walked back over to the house and looked through the window again. Honestly, she didn't know if she should be happy or sad about progress on the house. She glanced down the street. Homes were being rebuilt on both sides, but the lot where Dr. Jackson's grand home had stood was still empty. "Why hasn't anyone rebuilt Dr. Jackson's home yet?"

Rose shook her head. "I couldn't tell you. I've only been here a little over a month."

Touching a hand to her heart, Evelyn reminded herself to breathe in and breathe out. Tears trickled down her face. Her body shook all over as her mind's eye replayed running down this street and the green eyes of that awful boy who shot Dr. Jackson, then turned his gun on her.

Tommy pulled her into his arms. "Sweetheart, don't do this to yourself. Things are getting better around here. Now stop this."

"I shouldn't be here. It's too much for me," she wailed. "I used to walk down this street, visiting my friends. Waving to Dr. Jackson when he arrived home." She shook her head. "This isn't the home I knew."

Rubbing her back, he said, "I'm sorry. I thought it would make you happy to see the progress in Greenwood and to know that angry mob didn't destroy your community."

She heard his words and saw the progress, but none of it soothed her. Jabbing a finger toward her chest, she said, "They destroyed me."

Tommy put her back in the car. He got in on the driver's side. Evelyn put her head in her lap as sobs wracked her body, causing her shoulders to shake. Her hair fell in disarray, wet with tears and clinging to her face.

As Tommy headed toward Luther, taking her back to the farm, Evelyn realized that she didn't want to go back there. She didn't want to see Margaret or talk to her about the rebuilding of their home. She needed time and space. She put a hand on Tommy's arm. "I don't want to go to the Threatts' place."

"Where do you want me to take you?"

She didn't know how to answer that. There had been so many places she wanted to go, so many things she wanted to do . . . design school . . . travel the world . . . see women proudly wearing her designs. But none of that would ever happen now, and she was utterly lost. "I just want to stay with you a while longer."

He eyed her. "You sure about that?"

"Take me with you, Tommy. I need to be with you." Evelyn needed to be anywhere that didn't cause her to think about all that she had lost . . . all that she still longed for. And if that was in Tommy's arms, then so be it.

Chapter 28

Going back to Greenwood was like entering a war zone. Everything was gone! . . . I'll never forget it. No, not ever!

—*Ernestine Gibbs, Tulsa Race Massacre survivor*

W here have you been?" Margaret demanded when Evelyn came waltzing into their room the next morning.

"Out." Evelyn grabbed a washrag, a towel, and her uniform for work.

"Out where? Did you spend the night with Tommy?" Margaret's mouth hung open in shock. Then anger took over as she stood with hands on hips. "Do you know how worried I was? I didn't get an ounce of sleep, thinking something terrible happened to you."

"Well, it didn't." Evelyn smirked at her sister. "Nothing terrible happened to me last night . . . All the terrible, awful things have already happened."

"What's going on with you, Evie? Something is different about you this morning."

"I don't know what you see this morning. I'm the same Evie I've been since you decided that hopes and dreams were for other people."

"I never said that."

"'You can't go to design school, Evie . . . Give up on all your dreams, Evie . . . Just keep working at the filling station . . . Oh, and move back to that awful place with me, Evie.'"

Margaret walked over to her sister and searched her eyes, as if looking for something, anything that would explain why Evelyn was so cross with her. "Did Tommy give you . . . drugs or something?"

Evelyn laughed in her face, then pushed Margaret away. She was about to walk out of the room but turned back to Margaret. "Nothing is wrong with me. I'm standing up for myself is all. And I'm not moving back to Greenwood."

"Where is all of this coming from?" Margaret tapped her foot, eyes focused on her sister. "As lovely as they are, you know we can't stay with the Threatts forever."

"Tommy drove me over to Greenwood!" Evelyn exploded. "I saw our house. Saw Mrs. Pearl's house, with her niece living in it." Evelyn's hands jerked downward and fisted. "Saw Dr. Jackson's lot is still empty. How can I go back there and see that empty space every day?"

Margaret released a heavy, deep sigh. The pain she saw on Evelyn's face could only be identified by those who'd experienced that awful night of terror. Months had passed with no further assault from those wicked men, but the terror remained in them. She understood her sister's pain but would not be deterred. "Daddy built a home and a business in Greenwood. I won't run away from it. I won't dishonor him by turning away from all he fought for."

"He was my daddy too." Evelyn blew out an exasperated breath.

"Then why don't you act like it? Why aren't you concerned about the things that belonged to him?"

"Those things are in Greenwood. And I don't want to live in that town again after that so-called judge and jury refused to convict those wretched men for their crimes."

"But don't you see, Evie, that's why we and others need to rebuild. We need to show the world that evil didn't win." Margaret's face stiffened with her conviction. "If it's the last thing I do, I'm going to show them that our daddy's life mattered. He will never be erased, not as long as Greenwood lives on."

"And what if they come back? What if they destroy our property again? Where's the money going to come from to rebuild another time? No sense paying insurance on the house. We know they won't pay out."

Margaret prayed that Buck Franklin's law firm would get them some justice with those unscrupulous insurance companies. They had won the rezoning case against the city, and hardly anyone thought that a Black lawyer would win anything in a Tulsa court.

But win they did, and old Mayor T. D. Evans had to go find some other land to steal away. "Somebody is going to pay for what they did, whether it's the insurance companies or the city, you just wait and see."

"I'll believe it when I see it," Evelyn retorted.

Margaret turned away from her sister and busied herself with folding the clothes she had washed the night before. "Go get dressed. You're going to be late for work."

Evelyn huffed, hit the wall with her fist, and then stormed out of the room.

Margaret put the shirt she was folding in her lap and sighed as she stared out into the hallway of a home that was not hers. A home that was full of love but not the love she wished for.

⊫═ ═⊨

"I thought I told you about coming to work late," Mr. Allen said as Evelyn tried to sneak past him.

"I had a few complications, but I made it. Nothing to get out of sorts about." Evelyn opened the door to the store as Mr. Allen finished pumping a customer's gas.

He followed her into the store. "I'll be the one to decide if your being late is a problem or not. And I say it's a problem, 'specially since you didn't bring yourself home last night."

Evelyn put her head in her hands. "Not you too. What age do I have to be before you and Margaret let me be grown?"

Mr. Allen leaned against the wall. Put his hands in his pockets. "I know I'm not your daddy. But you need to be careful. Can't just be running 'round with any and every man that sends a smile your way . . . Folks'll start flapping their gums."

Averting her eyes, she told him, "Yesterday was really hard for me. I just lost my head is all, but I hear you."

"Good." He nodded, then went back outside.

Mr. Allen reminded her of Daddy. A man of few words, but when he spoke, she and Margaret took note. Evelyn bit down on her bottom lip. Maybe folks were flapping their gums about her. Maybe Margaret had a right to be upset.

The first customer came into the store and paid for his gas and soda pop. Evelyn busied herself with stocking the shelves. By midmorning, she found herself staring out the window at the road that lay before them, wondering how far that new highway stretched and whether, if she could get hold of an automobile, she would be brave enough to find out.

Evelyn jumped out of bed and ran down the hall with her hand clamped around her mouth. Thankful the bathroom door was open, she ran in and put her head over the toilet as the contents of her stomach spilled out.

"You caught a flu bug or something?" Margaret stood behind her, rubbing the sleep from her eyes.

Flushing the toilet, Evelyn washed her hands and rinsed her mouth out with water. She turned to Margaret, still feeling flutters in her stomach. "Don't know. Maybe the corn soup was bad."

"But you threw up a few days ago too. Can't be the corn soup."

The room shifted as Evelyn tried to respond. She bent down on a knee and turned back to the toilet.

"I'm getting you to a doctor." Margaret helped Evelyn stand.

Evelyn rinsed her mouth, then washed her hands again. "I don't want a doctor. Just want to lay down."

She was tired. Had been tired since the beginning of February. It was now March and nothing had changed. Evelyn lay back in bed and pulled the cover up to her shoulders.

"Let me get you some toast with butter. Maybe that'll settle your stomach."

Something was wrong with her . . . She didn't feel normal. Didn't like the same foods anymore. Nothing tasted the same. "I don't want anything."

Margaret stood in front of Evelyn's bed. Tap, tap, tapping her foot. Eyes squinted like her brain was working overtime. Evelyn rolled over and faced the wall. She had never felt this way before, but she remembered her tenth-grade teacher describing the things she was currently dealing with . . . She needed to talk to Tommy.

Tommy was on cloud nine when she met up with him later that day. He was all aflutter about a letter he received from the Dayton Marcos, a Negro League baseball team that was based in Dayton, Ohio, but played other teams throughout the United States.

"You can't possibly be going all the way to Ohio. You just took that job with road construction. Thought you were going to help build that new road."

Tommy waved that thought off. "I don't care nothing 'bout no Route 66. I'm a baseball player. Time for me to get back to what I do best."

"But what about me?" Evelyn thought she meant something to Tommy. Thought he loved her—at least those were the words he'd whispered in the dark.

"I won't be gone forever. When my season is up, I'll come back home."

"What am I supposed to do? Sit around and wait on you to get tired of baseball?"

He pulled her into his arms. "Don't be like that. You mean the world to me. But I can't give up on my dream of playing in the Negro League. I've been hungering for this chance, and now it's here."

"But . . ." She didn't know how else to say it but to spit it out. "I'm pregnant . . . with our child."

He let her go. Stepped back. "Is this some kind of trick to stop me from leaving?"

"I wouldn't trick you like that. I've been feeling poorly for a month, missed my period. Started throwing up a week ago. Can't be nothing else but a baby."

The air was thick with the scent of sweat and tension; it hung heavily around them. Tommy's eyelids squeezed shut, his mouth twisting into a pained grimace. When he looked at her again, his eyes were hard, set. "I'm not gon' let you ruin this for me."

Those eyes that had filled with joy when he saw her now despised her. "I'm not trying to ruin anything, but we got a baby coming, and I need you."

He shook his head. "Not giving up on my big break."

Sucking air through her teeth, Evelyn put her hand on her hip. "Dreams don't just walk down your street. I got 'em too." She waved a hand, indicating the area around the filling station. "But this what I been left with." She touched her belly. "And this what you and me been left with. We got to figure on what we need to do for this baby."

His eyes shifted one way and then the other. Like he was hesitating on a thought. But he turned from it. His shoulders pulled inward as he walked toward his father's car.

"Tommy . . . This ain't no time to be stubborn. We got to make plans."

"Can't," he yelled back.

Tears sprang to her eyes. "Can't what? We don't have a choice."

Standing by the automobile with his hand on the door, he looked as if he was caught between want-to and no-can-do. The latter won. "I gotta get the car back to my dad."

The fool that she was, Evelyn sat behind the filling station for an hour waiting for Tommy to come to his senses and drive back to her. Tell her to pack her bags and come to Dayton with him. But as night began to fall, she faced facts.

She was on her own.

Making her way to the house, Evelyn sniffed the air. Smelled like rain would soon be mingling with her pain. How could she face Margaret? She couldn't bear hearing her sister say, "Daddy is rolling over in his grave." Again.

When Margaret uttered those words a few months back, the pain was almost unbearable. But now she felt nothing but numbness. Life wasn't fair to people like her. Maybe she was never supposed to be born. And if she wasn't supposed to be born, then maybe her baby shouldn't be in this godforsaken world either.

Chapter 29

Tulsa was a booming oil town and people were always coming to Tulsa. Hotels, restaurants, entertainment places. . . . And then came the riot!

—*Clarence Bruner, Tulsa Race Massacre survivor*

Margaret, come in here. This man from Tulsa wants to talk to you."

Margaret was in the backyard with the boys using the cornstalks and potatoes to teach a lesson on vegetation. Mrs. Alberta held the screen door open with one hand and pressed against her back with the other hand. She was almost six months along, and her belly was big as a watermelon.

Margaret told Ulysses, David, and Allen Jr., "Okay, time for a break. Y'all can run around the yard, but don't get in Mrs. Alberta's way." Margaret did her best to take some slack off of Mrs. Alberta. With baby number five coming, she needed all the help she could get.

The boys ran off, and she went inside. A white man with wire-rimmed glasses was seated at the table. He wore a navy blue suit and tie. Nobody on the farm wore a suit and tie except one Sunday a month.

Margaret glanced over at Mrs. Alberta and then back at the man seated at the table. He stood, stretched out his hand. "Hello, Margaret. My name is Matthew Lions."

Her hand trembled as she looked in the face of a man who looked like the men who came into their neighborhood with guns blazing, shooting men and burning down homes.

When she didn't shake his hand or respond, he said, "I'm here with good news for you and your sister."

"You found my daddy's body?" Margaret didn't consider that good news, but her heart hurt every time she thought about Henry Justice in some unmarked grave that they just dumped the dead in with no thought that their family might want to visit and lay flowers from time to time.

He averted his eyes. "Ah, no, I don't have any information concerning your father. But my company has noticed that you have not started the rebuild on his grocery store."

"And . . ." Margaret wrapped her arms around her chest. The fear she felt was dissipating as this man's lips parted to say something about anything that belonged to her daddy.

He opened his briefcase and took out a stack of papers. Put them on the table. "I work for a developer. We're interested in buying property in the Greenwood Business District. Especially abandoned property."

She jolted as if punched when he said those words. She hadn't abandoned her daddy's store. Just had to take one thing at a time. Hearing it from this white man sounded to her ears like she had let her daddy and all the dreams he'd ever dreamed slip away.

Anger boiled in her and brought her claws out. "Were you with those men the night they burned down our homes and businesses?"

He vehemently shook his head. "No, ma'am. I can assure you, I was not. I just recently moved to the area when my company decided to build in Tulsa."

He might not have been in Tulsa for the massacre, but he was in business with those vultures who tried to swoop in afterward and take away their right to rebuild. Margaret sat down across from the man. She glanced at the papers. "What's that about?"

"This?" He picked up the papers. "We took the liberty of writing up a contract. You'll see that everything is aboveboard, and we're willing to pay you five hundred dollars for the plot of land on . . ." He glanced at the papers once more. "Archer Street."

Margaret didn't know if she was more offended by this man's presence or by this offer. "So in your estimation, the full measure of a man's worth is five hundred dollars?"

He stammered, "I-I wouldn't presume to know how much your father was worth to his family. This offer is strictly about the plot of land owned by your family."

"No, thank you, Mr. Lions."

He couldn't look her in the eye . . . or just didn't want to. "I wouldn't make such a hasty decision before reading the contract. I assure you this is a good offer considering there's nothing there but the land."

"And whose fault is that?" Margaret jumped out of her seat. How dare this man tell her the property was devalued since the building was no longer on the land when white men like him were the ones who burned it down. "No, thank you," she said again, but this time with more force. She opened the door. "Take your papers and leave."

Matthew turned to Mrs. Alberta. "Ma'am, if you have any influence, I implore you to help her see the benefits of signing this contract. No one else will offer this much for a property in such disrepair."

"Get out!" Margaret screamed. Her fingers fisted with the aching desire to lash out. But fear of what-comes-next squelched the fight in her. Mrs. Alberta had opened her home to them; she wouldn't repay her by doing anything to bring retribution on them.

"You heard her, mister. She wants you to leave." Mrs. Alberta came and stood next to Margaret as they ushered him out the door like a bad wind.

Pacing back and forth, Margaret clenched and unclenched her fists. She turned to Mrs. Alberta with anger spilling over. "I wanted to hit him." Her fist beat the air. "Pummel him for insulting my daddy's memory like that." Her fist unclenched. "But I'm such a coward."

She pointed outside as the man got in his automobile. "Men like him have made me and my sister afraid, and I'm sick to death of fearing what they might do." She plopped down in a chair and hung her head, ashamed of not extracting some measure of the justice that was surely due them.

Mrs. Alberta sat next to Margaret and put her hands over hers. "You and your sister experienced something that only the devil himself could have orchestrated. So don't you dare hang your head low when fear rears its head."

Margaret's daddy had always commended her on being strong after her mother died. She'd had to be strong. Daddy and Evelyn had fallen apart. If she didn't cook and clean for them, they would have wasted away.

"I've never been called fearful. But the first sight of that man and my hands started trembling."

"I understand you better than you know. When Allen first told me that he wanted to move from Alabama to Oklahoma to get us a piece of the land that had opened up here, I was as scared as a mouse scurrying away from a hungry cat.

"But then we bought all this land, nearly a hundred acres, and built our farm, the filling station, the restaurant . . ." Mrs. Alberta smiled as she added, "Allen is even making way for a baseball field."

Margaret's eyes gleamed with excitement. "A couple teams have already played in the open field, but it will be a blast to have an actual baseball diamond."

"I think so too. I love watching the Negro League and can't wait to have them here." Mrs. Alberta lifted a hand. "But the point I'm trying to make is that although I was fearful in the beginning, we have built a legacy for our family. Something they can point to and say, 'This is ours,' for years to come. And that has been worth a mountain-load of fear."

A chill went down Margaret's spine. Legacy was important. Her daddy tried to build a legacy for his children and instill something in her and Evelyn. "I'm happy for your family, Mrs. Alberta, but it feels like I've been dumped in the wilderness with no strength to plow my way out. The house is just about ready. But before I can settle in good, I've got to figure a way to build that store back up before some vulture snatches the land from me."

Mrs. Alberta patted Margaret on the back as she stood. "Sometimes even the strong get weary. Gotta just put it in God's hands."

Margaret wanted to ask how in the world she was ever supposed to put anything in God's hands when He had dropped the ball on so many things that mattered to her. But she left the kitchen and went upstairs with those thoughts in her heart.

She sat down on her bed, looked around the room. Exhaled. Something had to give. She'd been moving in slow motion since getting sick. She had to stop letting people put fear in her about what might happen if she went back to Greenwood too soon. Either she was going to fight her way through or everything was going to wither away like leaves falling from a tree, becoming scattered and useless.

She got up, walked down the hall to the bathroom, and turned the knob, thinking only of relieving herself. Hurrying over to the toilet, she caught sight of Evelyn in the claw-foot tub.

She was about to sit on the toilet when a steady, rhythmic dripping caught her attention, and she realized it was blood. Blood . . . from Evie's arm. She couldn't move, her body paralyzed as her mind tried to comprehend what she was seeing. Fear and confusion rushed through her. Was Evie hurt? Did someone attack her? *But who would attack us here? We're safe here.* She needed to run for help. No, she couldn't leave Evie in this state.

Margaret moved toward her sister. "Nooooo!" She grabbed a towel from the rack, got on her knees, and wrapped it around Evie's arm while screaming, "Help! Help!"

Evie's eyes were closed. Her head leaned against the tub. Margaret touched her. She was warm. She hit Evie's face with the palm of her hand once, twice, and then again. "Wake up, Evie. Come back to me. Come back, sweetie."

"What happened?" Mrs. Alberta ran into the bathroom.

The knife was on the floor next to the pool of blood. There was no denying this. "She slit her wrist. Please help us." Margaret shook her sister again. "Wake up!"

Evelyn lifted her head, then leaned it against the tub again. Her eyes were slits, but that was enough of a sign for Margaret. "Stay with me, Evie. Stay with me."

"I'll get the doctor. Keep holding that towel against her wrist."

Mrs. Alberta left the bathroom while Margaret stayed put, holding the towel tight against Evelyn's wrist. "I'm not going to let you go. I need you here with me."

Tears ran down Margaret's face as she exclaimed, "Don't you know that I need you?"

"I-I'm sorry," Evelyn managed to get out before her eyes closed again.

"No!" Margaret screamed. "Don't you die. I'll never forgive you if you die like this."

Chapter 30

Kind Sir: This comes to express . . . the profound gratitude not only of every Negro in Tulsa, but throughout the civilized world wherever there is a Negro.

—*Letter from Louella T. West and Pastor J. S. West (A.M.E. Church) sent to Maurice Willows, July 1, 1921*

D r. Hampton bandaged Evelyn's arm and put her in bed, prescribing rest and a watchful eye. He didn't have to tell Margaret twice. She wasn't going to take her eyes off Evelyn until she found out what had gotten into her sister.

Evelyn slept the night away. The next day, she cried and kept her face to the wall. Margaret allowed her some time, but on the third day she said, "Are you ready to talk to me? I don't understand why you did this."

Evelyn didn't respond. But a tear ran down her face before she turned away.

"Talk to me, Evie. I can't help if I don't know the problem."

A beat of silence, then, "I'm scared." Evelyn's voice sounded childlike. "You said Daddy would roll over in his grave with the way I've been acting . . . I didn't want to believe something like that could be true, but you're right."

"No!" Margaret leaped from her bed over to Evelyn. Why had she said those awful words to her sister? Was she the reason Evie tried to kill herself? "I was wrong for saying that. Daddy loved you. There is nothing you could do that would cause him shame."

"I wish that were true, but I've really done it this time." Evelyn put her hands over her face.

Looking at the bandage on Evelyn's wrist sent shock waves of fear up Margaret's spine. Her mind turned to the pool of blood on the bathroom floor. Shame had caused that. No more shame. Margaret pulled Evelyn's hands from her face. "We're survivors. And survivors don't quit."

Evelyn put her hands back over her face and tried to turn away. But Margaret pulled them down again. "You don't have to hide from me. I'm your sister, and I love you. Pleeease . . . talk to me."

On a deep sigh, Evelyn asked, "Ever wonder why God allowed us to survive if nothing was going to go right in our lives again?"

Was this about design school? If Margaret had the money, she would send her off and wish her well. Anything, everything but seeing her wrist wrapped like that. "Look, Evie, I would have been distraught too if Daddy hadn't been able to send me off to school. But life can still be good for you."

"I'm pregnant," Evelyn wailed and then fell into Margaret's arms. "Life will never be good for me again."

Air whooshed from Margaret with the force of Evelyn landing against her chest. She wrapped her arms around her sister, closed her eyes. And even though she didn't trust that God cared to help them, she prayed for the right words to say.

Evelyn pulled away. Her eyes held questions, like she was waiting for Margaret to pronounce judgment. "Wha . . . How . . . Are you sure?"

"I've missed my cycle for the last two months. And you've seen me throwing up."

The throwing up . . . Margaret knew it wasn't food poisoning, but in her wildest imagination, she wouldn't have come up with this. "Is it Tommy's baby?"

"Of course it's Tommy's. Do you think I sleep around?"

"No, no." Margaret lifted a hand. "That's not what I think." Then she asked, "Did you tell him?"

Evelyn nodded and the tears came again. "He's been called up to the Negro League, and he thinks I'm trying to hold him back from his dreams."

Margaret put a hand to her chest. "He said that."

"He doesn't want me or the baby." Evelyn wiped the drizzle from beneath her nose. "People are going to think I'm some sort of trollop. I can't bear that . . . I don't know what to do."

"Killing yourself is not the answer." Margaret stood and paced the floor while tapping her chin with her index finger.

"What else am I supposed to do? I'm so scared. I can't do this on my own, and Tommy wants nothing to do with us."

"I knew he was a dolt when I first laid eyes on him. Wish you had listened to me . . ." Margaret stopped herself, went back over to Evelyn, and sat down on the bed again.

She took Evelyn's hands in hers. "I'm scared too. Been scared for a while now. But we can't give up. I promise, we'll get through this together."

The sisters hugged and cried in each other's arms as they had been doing since they lost everything. But this cry was different, for Margaret settled in her heart to do everything she could to protect her daddy's legacy. Henry Justice would soon have a grandchild coming into this world. What would Margaret and Evelyn tell the child about its grandfather's legacy?

✢ ✢

"What's got you so quiet this evening?" Elijah asked as he and Margaret walked the fields while he inspected the crops.

She kicked at the overgrown grass in the field. "Got a lot on my mind today. Evie and I have our backs against the wall, and I don't know what to do."

They took a few more steps. Passing by the cornfield, Elijah asked, "Anything I can do?"

"I don't even know what *I* can do." She put her hands on her head and closed her eyes. Then on a long-suffering sigh she told him, "My sister's distraught." Margaret glanced around, making sure no one else was in listening distance, then whispered, "She tried to kill herself."

Elijah's hand went to his heart. He stared at Margaret, saying nothing, as if he was at a loss for words. She saw compassion in his eyes. But that didn't take away the anger in her heart. "I knew that Tommy was no good. But to leave a woman to bear the shame of having a child with no husband, that is the lowest."

"I'm so sorry, Margaret. I didn't know."

"This all took me by surprise. My little sister has so much potential. She should be in college. But she'll be stuck changing diapers and listening to folks whisper about her." She sucked in air, rubbed the back of her neck. "I have to find a way to help her."

"Evie is getting a raw deal. Makes me want to go find Tommy and knock him around."

"I'd like to belt him a good one myself."

They kept walking and talking and looking at the crops. All the while Margaret's thoughts alternated from how she could help her sister to what she could do with her daddy's property that would honor his legacy.

She told Elijah, "I'm thankful for all the work you've done on the house."

He nodded. "It should be ready for you in a couple of weeks."

A house was good and a business was better, especially if they were going to take care of a child. "A man came to see me about my daddy's store. He wanted to buy the land, but I'm not selling. Wondering if you can help me find someone to rebuild it for us?"

"I could probably scrounge up a few willing workers."

That put a smile on her face. After all the work Elijah had already done in Greenwood, she hadn't had the heart to ask him to work on the store. But the work needed doing. She didn't want any other developers getting thoughts in their heads about something that didn't belong to them.

When she went back home, Evelyn was still lying in bed. Her eyes were hollow with sadness. "Hey. Mr. Allen is barbecuing behind the filling station tonight. Heard there's going to be dancing. You want to go?"

Evelyn frowned at Margaret. "You hate when I go to those parties. Why would you even ask me something like that?"

Margaret exhaled, sat down next to her sister. "You look so miserable. I don't want you giving up on life."

Sighing, Evelyn said, "Tommy will be leaving soon. I best stay put in case he comes looking for me."

"Don't do this to yourself. He probably already left town."

Red-hot anger exploded in Evelyn's eyes. "Why would you say that? How do you know?"

Margaret rolled her eyes. "Isn't that what men like him do— get what they want from innocent girls, then run off to find their next conquest?"

A tear drifted down Evelyn's face. "Baseball is all that matters to him. I was such a fool." Evelyn laid her head on her pillow and cried.

Margaret's heart broke for her sister. Evelyn didn't deserve this. If her parents were still alive, Evelyn would have been away at design school, chasing her own dreams rather than running around with the good-for-nothing men in this area. There had to be something she could do to help her sister . . . had to be something.

Then she decided to broach the subject that she knew wouldn't be music to Evelyn's ears. "The house will be ready in a couple of weeks. We should move back to Greenwood. Elijah's going to help me rebuild Daddy's business. Then I'll be able to take care of you and the baby."

Evelyn kept crying. "I don't want all of my friends knowing that I became a mom before getting married. People will think I'm easy."

"Stop crying, Evie. We have to do something. And we can't stay here and bring the Threatts another mouth to feed."

Margaret's words just made Evelyn cry all the more.

"Okay, calm down. Give me a little time. I'll figure something out."

"I'm not ready to be a mother. I don't want this baby. I need to find someone to give it to."

Margaret never imagined that Evelyn wouldn't want her own child. Maybe she was just talking out of her depression. Or maybe she was thinking on ending her life and the baby's again so she wouldn't have to deal with the consequences. Margaret couldn't, wouldn't lose anyone else in their family. She stood, ten toes planted on the floor. "I'll take the baby. I'll raise it as my own."

"But you're not married either. You can't raise a baby on your own."

"You let me worry about that." She stuck her hand out to Evelyn. "Do we have a deal? You have the baby, and I'll raise it as my own."

Evelyn hesitated. "But people will think poorly of you. I can't do that to you."

"I'll get a husband, Evie. Just tell me that you won't try to kill yourself again." Margaret stuck out her hand again. "Let's shake on it."

Evelyn stared at her sister's hand a moment too long. Margaret moved her hand closer. Evelyn took it, shook, then said, "I promise."

Chapter 31

In 1997, the Oklahoma Legislature passed House Joint Resolution 1035, which established the 1921 Tulsa Race Riot Commission ("Commission") and tasked the Commission with developing the historical record of the racial violence that transpired in the Greenwood community of Tulsa, Oklahoma, between May 31 and June 1, 1921.

—*Randle v. City of Tulsa (decided: June 12, 2024)*

hy do you have my dress on?" Evelyn asked when she walked into the bedroom. She had a glass of water in her hand and sipped while watching Margaret put on red lipstick. Her sister had on the same flapper girl dress that she thought was inappropriate for Evelyn.

"There's a party behind the filling station tonight."

Evelyn spit out the water. "What? Why would you go to that party? In that dress?"

"I told you . . . I'm going to get a husband." Margaret ran a brush through her hair and then pinned it on top of her head.

Neither she nor Margaret had been to the beauty parlor since they'd left Greenwood. They'd learned to wash and curl their own hair. It didn't look as nice as when Mrs. Mabel did it, but it was the best they could do on the farm.

"You can't be serious. You think some man you barely know is going to fall in love and offer to marry you"—Evelyn snapped her fingers—"like that?"

"You're not the only one who can catch a man's eye. Besides, I'm not empty-handed. We have a home and a business that can be rebuilt. A husband can run Daddy's business, and we can raise the baby."

Evelyn didn't like this idea. "You said Daddy's business is a legacy for the baby. What if this husband of yours wants the business for himself?"

"Will you stop worrying and let me handle this?" Margaret put on her shoes and walked out of their bedroom.

Evelyn ran her index finger across her bottom lip. She needed to think. When Margaret told her she was going to get a husband, she assumed she would ask Elijah to marry her, not go off and find some man who'd do the deed just to get what they had to offer.

What about love? What about Margaret's happy ending? She couldn't let her sister ruin her life with some man who didn't care about her. Evelyn had already done enough of that.

She ran out of her room and down the stairs. Margaret was about to step off the porch. Evelyn opened the front door and yelled, "Wait!"

Margaret turned around. Tapped her foot against the ground and put a hand on her hip. "What now?"

"What about Elijah? He's a good man. If you marry him, I wouldn't feel as if I'm ruining your life."

Something in Margaret's eyes told Evelyn that her sister had considered Elijah.

Margaret shook her head. "He's tied to the farm. We might be in a fix, but I can't ask Elijah to change his whole way of life."

"He should be the first person you talk to about this."

Margaret opened her mouth, then shut it.

"I know you like him."

Margaret waved a dismissive hand in the air and then walked off.

Evelyn stomped her foot and blew air from her nostrils. She couldn't bear the thought of Margaret throwing herself at just any old man when Elijah was perfect for her. She wouldn't allow it. For the first time in the week since she'd tried to take her life, Evelyn left the farmhouse.

She went in search of Elijah. Evelyn checked over by the crops in the field, but he wasn't there. She then ran over to the restaurant by day, juke joint by night, right across the street from the filling station.

Elijah was seated at a table in the back of the room. His Bible was open. The sight of that Bible gave her pause. She almost turned and walked back home, but he glanced up. Closed the Bible and waved her over.

"I saw you studying, thought I should let you be."

"Absolutely not. Please sit down." He pointed to the other chair at his table. "I was just getting a little reading in."

"Back in Greenwood, Margaret and I went to church every Sunday. I used to read my Bible during Sunday school, but I never just sat out in public reading." Evelyn glanced around at the other folks in the restaurant. A man and a woman were seated at the table across from them, and two men sat eating at the table behind Elijah.

"It's no secret that I love God." Elijah laughed as he added, "Just reading His Word while I eat some supper."

Evelyn smiled at him. Elijah was the kind of man Margaret needed in her life. She looked to heaven and said a silent prayer. *Lord, can You give Elijah enough love in his heart to marry Margaret?*

"How have you been?" he asked.

After issuing her plea to God, she turned back to Elijah with her truth. "Haven't been doing so good. I'm all torn up inside over what my folly has done to Margaret."

"Your sister is concerned about you, but she'll be okay."

"No, she won't. She's got it in her head that she needs to find a husband. She'll take anyone as long as he will let her be a mother." Evelyn put a hand on her stomach. "This is all my fault." She lowered her head, tears glistening in her eyes.

Margaret had never had time for the dance halls and whatnot. She'd been too busy keeping up with her studies and planning out her future. Now, as she stood next to the dance floor watching the couples gyrating across the floor, she wished she had taken the time to learn a few dances.

Mr. Allen walked over and handed her a burger, then scowled at her. "As long as you've been at the house with us, you've never attended one of these parties. What's gotten into you?"

"Nothing. Just hanging out."

He pursed his lips together and harrumphed.

A guy who'd been eyeing her while he'd danced with another woman came over to Margaret. "Look at you, all dolled up." He held out his hand. "Let's dance, hotsy-totsy."

"Margaret don't want to dance," Mr. Allen said, still scowling.

The man retracted his hand, then went to the other side of the platform stage and found another "hotsy-totsy" to pull onto the dance floor.

Margaret protested. "Mr. Allen, how do you know I didn't want to dance?"

"Not with him, you don't." He pointed at the sandwich in her hand. "Eat your burger and then go on home. Alberta will skin me alive if I let another one of you girls run wild over here."

With that, he walked back to his firepit. Margaret wasn't trying to run wild. She was trying to find a man who was looking to get hitched. She bit into her burger as she tapped her foot, trying to figure out how she would hook a man with Mr. Allen scowling and running them off.

"What's a girl like you doing in a place like this?"

She heard the rich baritone. Closed her eyes as the sound of his voice sent shivers running from the thick veins in her calves all the way up her spine. As she turned in his direction, she caught sight of those denim overalls and that straw hat he wore while working in the field. He was a farm boy through and through. "I could ask you the same thing."

"Who, me?" Elijah jutted his thumb toward his chest. "Oh, I was just sitting over at the restaurant studying my Bible when a little birdie came and told me about this harebrained scheme of yours."

Margaret's face burned with embarrassment. She put a hand to her cheek. "She didn't."

"She did." Elijah stepped back, stared at Margaret. Looking her over with intent and purpose.

She folded her arms in front of herself. "What are you looking at?"

"From the first moment I saw you with your hair scattered all over your head, clothes covered in dust, worry lines stretched across your face, I knew you were beautiful." His head tilted to the right, eyes dancing with curiosity. "But this . . . You're breathtaking."

A hand went to her hip as a knot formed in her throat. When the knot loosened, she said, "You like women in flapper dresses, huh?"

Elijah shook his head, pointed at her. "I like you."

Blushing, she turned away and stuffed more of the burger in her mouth before she said something stupid. She didn't have time for Elijah or what she felt for him. She needed a city boy so she could take him back to Greenwood and rebuild her daddy's legacy.

Elijah deserved a woman who could love him real good. Margaret didn't have it in her. All the love she had—all the love she could've given—had been beaten out of her. What good was love when it broke your heart?

He gently took her hand, then got down on one knee, looking up at her with eyes that spoke of care and concern. "If you'll have me, I'll marry you."

Margaret snatched her hand out of Elijah's grip. She leaned forward and whispered, "Get up. I won't ruin your life, too, with a scheme that's born out of necessity rather than love."

Elijah didn't need to be saddled with an instant family and no promise of love. He deserved love and all that love had to give.

Getting off his knee, he stayed close to her. "A lot of marriages begin out of necessity, Margaret. Love will come. The important thing is that I have no doubt you are the woman God has for me."

"God makes mistakes—you know that, don't you?"

Elijah put his arms around Margaret and pulled her onto the dance floor. As a slow song serenaded them, he pulled her close. The scent of lavender and lemon filled her nostrils. Warmth spread through her body as if a golden light was glowing from within, radiating outward and filling the space between them with heat.

"We're not a mistake. Just give me a chance," he whispered in her ear.

"You belong on the farm. Evie and I have to go back to Greenwood." Evelyn would not be able to stay in Luther after having the baby, not if they were going to convince others that the baby belonged to Margaret.

Elijah put a finger under her chin as they rocked with the slow beat of the music. "I belong with you. I'll be a father to the baby and a husband to you."

She paused. Tried to reason things out in her mind. Could this work? Was it right? Could Elijah accept a loveless marriage?

Chapter 32

My relatives had come to Oklahoma to get away from racism, violence and death in Tennessee.

—*Wilhelmina Guess Howell, Tulsa Race Massacre survivor*

Elijah and Margaret sat down with Mrs. Alberta and explained their need for a quick wedding. "I had a feeling that girl was with child. But after we found her in that tub, I was afraid to ask."

Margaret nodded her understanding. "I thank you for your discretion."

Mrs. Alberta clasped her hands together. "Well, looks like we've got a wedding to plan."

Margaret jumped out of her seat and hugged Mrs. Alberta. She kissed the woman on the cheek just as she would have done if Velma Justice had been standing in front of her getting ready to plan her wedding. "Thank you."

Mrs. Alberta waved that off. "Don't think on it. I'm happy to do it. Besides, the way I keep having these boys, this will probably be my only chance to plan a wedding for a daughter."

Margaret hugged her again. Coming to the Threatt farm when they did had been just what she and Evie needed. She was thankful for this family and would miss them dearly when they moved back to Greenwood.

As the two women ended the embrace, Margaret touched Mrs. Alberta's swollen belly. "And from the way you're carrying this one, I've got a feeling you're about to have your first daughter."

Mrs. Alberta smiled at the thought of a girl but then said, "It'll be what it will be. It's of little concern right now. We've got a wedding to plan." Mrs. Alberta went to the stairs and hollered up, "Evelyn, get down here."

Elijah clasped his hands together. "What do you need me to do?"

Mrs. Alberta told him, "Show up—that's it and that's all." She waved a hand toward the door. "You get out of here and let us women take care of this wedding."

Elijah leaned forward and gave Margaret a quick peck on the cheek. "I'll get back to the field since I'm not needed here."

A flutter went through her when he pressed his lips against her cheek. What was going on here? Was she falling for Elijah already? Or was it just pre-wedding emotions? "Okay. I'll see you later."

Evelyn bounded down the stairs. She looked from Margaret to Mrs. Alberta with questioning eyes. "Did I do something wrong?"

Margaret's heart hurt for Evie. Her sister looked for judgment in every eye, every word that was spoken to her.

Mrs. Alberta didn't address her question. "Chile, come in this kitchen with us. We've got a wedding to plan, and I need you to make the dress."

A mile-wide grin shone on Evelyn's face. She rushed over to Margaret and hugged her. "It's Elijah, right? Please tell me he found you in time."

Margaret nodded. "He found me, thanks to you running your mouth."

"One day you'll thank me for blabbing. He's a good man, sissy."

"Okay, let's sit down at the kitchen table. We have a lot to discuss." Mrs. Alberta took her seat at the head of the table, then rubbed her belly and exhaled.

Margaret glanced in her direction. "Are you okay?"

"Baby kicking." Mrs. Alberta laughed. "None of my boys kicked this soon or this hard."

Taking her seat at the table, Margaret grinned. "Told you . . . this one's a girl."

Evelyn's eyes grew big. "Is it still kicking?"

"I'm not feeling anything else."

"Does it feel weird when the baby kicks?"

Mrs. Alberta leaned forward and put a hand over Evelyn's. "It's not that bad. I don't want you to be scared. It's just a natural occurrence."

Evelyn turned to Margaret, accusation written on her face. "Now who's running their mouth?"

"Of course I told her. You and I have never delivered a baby. We're going to need Mrs. Alberta's help to pull this off."

Patting Evelyn's hand again, Mrs. Alberta said, "Your secret is safe with me. Don't fret over anything. You're not the first girl to get in this kind of trouble."

As long as there were men like Tommy in this world, she wouldn't be the last either. Margaret wished that Evelyn had listened to her and steered clear of that scallywag, but all of that was water under the bridge now.

The wedding took place behind the filling station one week after the three women sat at the kitchen table planning the event. Mrs. Alberta decorated the stage with flowers and lanterns. About twenty people sat in the wood chairs as Mr. Allen escorted Margaret down the aisle.

"Here Comes the Bride" played softly in the background. The fluttering in her stomach started up again. Was she truly doing this? She was only twenty-three years old. Did she know enough to be someone's wife?

Margaret wore a long white dress with lace at the top and on the sleeves. The dress had her feeling like a princess. Evelyn stayed up three nights in a row to make it for her. Margaret was just thankful there were no fringes anywhere on the dress . . . Evelyn loved fringes.

Here comes the bride . . .

Elijah stood in front of the stage. He wore a black jacket and suit pants with a white shirt and red-and-black tie. *Handsome* and *refined* were the words she would use to define the man she was about to marry. He pressed his Bible against his chest as his eyes locked with hers. Was she ready? Could she make him happy?

They reached Elijah, and the music stopped. At six foot five, he was almost a whole foot taller than her. She lifted on her tiptoes to whisper in his ear, "You look nervous."

He whispered back, "I've never been married before. Wasn't prepared for how beautiful you would be."

Those flutters started in the pit of her belly at the way he looked at her. Was he just being kind, or did Elijah really think she was beautiful? She averted her eyes as Mr. Allen stood before them and welcomed the guests. He then proceeded to state the wedding vows.

Margaret and Elijah stood just below the platform stage, repeating after Mr. Allen and saying their "I dos."

"I now pronounce you man and wife." Mr. Allen then winked at Elijah as he added, "You may kiss your bride."

Elijah took Margaret in his arms, leaned down, and kissed her like he'd waited all his life to connect his lips with hers. Margaret was breathless when they parted. Elijah lifted their hands in the air as they turned to face the guests.

"I got me a wife!" he shouted, then picked Margaret up and swung her around as if her mere presence had made him the happiest man alive.

Collard greens, cornbread, and baked chicken were served to their guests. Mr. Allen turned on the lights above the dance floor, and then came the music. Elijah and Margaret walked onto the platform stage for their first dance as husband and wife. Ethel Waters's "Kiss Your Pretty Baby Nice" was playing, and Margaret got lost in the music.

Little boy, your fascinating style,
Why, it just gets me going when I see you smile.
Ooh why, you're so pleasing, oh, but you're teasing.

"You're so beautiful," Elijah told her after swinging her around, then pulling her back into his arms.

Her face flushed red. "You already said that."

"I'm telling you again. You'll be hearing it a lot from me from now on." He kissed her.

She was married . . . really and truly married. But this was going to take some getting used to. "Thank you for marrying me, Elijah. I'm forever in your debt."

They rocked left, rocked right with the music. "You don't owe me a thing. I'm honored to be your husband. And I'm going to do everything within my power to make you happy."

"Yeah, I know, but . . ."

Elijah put his index finger under her chin, lifted her face toward him. While they looked into each other's eyes, he said, "It's you and me against the whole wide world now, Margaret Porter."

Her eyes widened at the sound of her new last name. It didn't quite fit just yet. All her life she had been Margaret Justice. Things were changing . . . had changed too quickly. She needed to catch up. "You've done so much for me. How can I not be in your debt?"

She thought about the way Elijah gave of his time to rebuild her home. And to help others in Greenwood. A look of wonder crossed her face. "I didn't expect to meet a man like you in my hour of need, but you were there, and you've been here for me every step of the way. I didn't see it at first, but from this day forward, I'm yours."

He bent down and kissed her again, in front of God and everyone else. Claiming her to be his. "And I'm yours."

Chapter 33

What had previously been a prosperous, peaceable and fairly well-ordered Negro business and residential district . . . was transformed into a burned and devastated area.

—Maurice Willows, *Red Cross Disaster Relief Report*

Elijah had a small two-bedroom house at the back of the farm. Margaret moved in the day of the wedding. Evelyn moved in with them a month later. Mrs. Alberta told her that Evelyn could stay at her house, but Margaret couldn't see burdening them further, especially with the baby on the way.

Margaret and Elijah fell into an easy groove. She would get up early and fix his breakfast, he would go off to work in the field, and Margaret would work at the Threatt house.

But at night, when the work was done, she and Elijah would sometimes talk for hours about whatever they fancied. Tonight, Margaret couldn't sleep. She tossed and turned until Elijah rose up on an elbow and looked down at her with worry lines creasing his forehead. "You okay?"

Wiping the sleep from her eyes, she told him, "Just restless, I guess."

"Something troubling your mind?"

She thought on it, sighed, and then told him, "Guess I've been letting Evie's fears about Greenwood get to me."

"Does the thought of moving back there still terrify her?"

"She struggles terribly with what happened to us. But I don't know how else to help her. Our plan is a good one. She'll stop working at the filling station when her belly grows big."

"Are you sure she'll be okay being cooped up in this house for months?"

Margaret adjusted the pillow below her head, turned on her side to face Elijah. "She doesn't have a choice. She doesn't want anyone to know about the baby, so she'll have to sit still. We can't even move to Greenwood until the baby comes."

"The house is ready," he told her.

"We got another six months before that baby comes. Meanwhile, my daddy's business remains in jeopardy of being snatched up by them developers."

Elijah lifted a hand. "Don't let that trouble your mind. Me and the boys framed everything out. So the city officials and anyone else lurking around looking for plots of land to snatch up can see that the Justice for All Grocery Store is being rebuilt and will soon be open for business again."

She leaned toward him and flung her arms around him in a tight embrace. The feeling of gratitude radiated from her as she held on, not wanting to let go. "You've been so good to me. I'm so thankful you came into my life."

"I'm thankful for you too," he said as they pulled apart.

Overcome with emotion, she said, "I mean what I say, Elijah. When I went back to Greenwood, I thought nothing would stop me from rebuilding our house and my daddy's business. But so many things got in my way. If you hadn't showed up when you did . . ." Her words trailed off as a lump settled in her throat.

His big strong hands gently rubbed the small of her back. She swallowed, loosening the lump. "What can I do for you, Elijah? What would make you happy?"

His hand moved from the small of her back to her face. Eyes pierced through her as if capturing her very soul. "The only thing I need in this world is your love . . . Just love me. That's all."

He said it as if it was a simple request. As if the very act of love hadn't been the cause of heartache since time began. As if love could be turned on and off so the hurting stopped when the object of affection was no longer around to receive it.

"You don't have to say it yet. I just want you to know I'm not going to be satisfied until I have your whole heart."

"Isn't that a bit greedy?" she teased. "I mean, won't our children deserve some of my heart too?"

Elijah's hand moved up her leg and rested on her belly. "Children, huh? You can't be thinking of another baby before Evelyn delivers our first."

She shook her head. "No, but I do hope we will be blessed with more children. And I want them to know how hard their daddy worked to rebuild something for us, just like Mr. Allen has built something for his children."

"That sounds mighty sweet . . . sweet indeed."

"And so are you." She leaned forward and planted a kiss on his soft, full lips.

She would give him her full heart if it weren't so scarred and bruised. The best she could do in the right here and now was give herself to him.

Looking at her like a man full of thirst, he pulled her gown over her head and laid her against the mattress. "I love you . . . you know that, don't you, Margaret?"

Evelyn buttoned her work shirt, then touched her belly. She was about four months along, and her stomach was getting round and full. She'd made a few jackets and sweaters that helped cover her growing belly, but she would have to quit her job by July. She doubted she'd be able to hide her belly into August.

No more dancing, no more parties, no more working with Mr. Allen at the filling station. Felt like she would be giving up on life. What would she do in the house for months on end, with no one to talk to but Margaret and Elijah?

One thing was for sure: She wasn't going to be any further burden on them. She'd saved every spare penny she made the rest of May and all of June. She would contribute to the groceries and the keeping of the house. Elijah and Margaret wouldn't carry the full weight of her folly. She would even make clothes for the baby. It was the least she could do for what they were doing for her.

Stepping out of her bedroom, she entered the front of the house where Elijah sat at the table reading his Bible. Evelyn had never known anyone who prayed and read the Bible as much as Elijah. Not even her daddy, who was a religious man who made sure they were in church every Sunday.

He smiled at her as he closed his Bible. "Good morning, my hardworking sister. You're heading off to the filling station awfully early this morning."

"And you're up early reading your Bible, as usual, I see." Evelyn put on her jacket and was about to walk out the door.

Elijah lifted the Good Book, looking at it as if it was a treasured possession, as he told her, "This is my filling station."

Her hand was on the doorknob. She let it drop. "Huh?"

"I'm not trying to confuse you." Elijah grinned at her. "You work at a filling station where people pull in to put gas in their automobiles so they can get where they need to go." Lifting the Bible again, he added, "That's how I feel about this book. When I read it, I'm fueling my spirit and my soul so I can get through the day, the week, the month. Some days are harder than others, but my filling station gives me the fuel I need to get to the other side of trouble."

Evelyn was taken aback. She put a hand to her heart. "I never thought of my body needing something pumped into it in order to deal with life."

Placing the Bible on the table, Elijah clasped his hands together. "I want you to promise me something."

She didn't respond yay or nay, but he had her attention.

"Whenever you're feeling down or uncertain about anything, I want you to take a moment to pray. Let the Lord fill you up with His wisdom and understanding about the matter."

"And you really think prayer will do that?"

Elijah nodded. "If you let it. See, God is a gentleman. He will only come where He is invited."

Evelyn opened the door. "I best be getting to the filling station. Don't want to get Mr. Allen's blood boiling so early in the morning."

"You have a good day, Evelyn. I'll be praying for you."

Evelyn smiled as she walked out the door. Somehow she felt comforted by Elijah putting her on his prayer list. She hadn't prayed much since the massacre, but maybe that was the exact thing she needed.

Placing her hand on her belly, Evelyn glanced heavenward. She didn't much like looking up at the sky anymore. Every time she looked up, she thought of those black birds, which turned out to be bombs, being dropped on their neighborhood, like the whole of the United States had gone to war against their forty-acre community.

What she learned from that night was that there were no fair fights in America for Negroes. Now her brother-in-law was telling her to pray. But did God care? Was He listening?

She didn't know what she believed anymore. Elijah believed so strongly that he gave her pause. There was something she wanted—no, needed—from God. She turned her head from the sky, lowered it, and made her petition. "God, if You're listening, can You please make sure that this baby grows up happy? Give him or her a chance to go after dreams. Don't let this baby waste away like a dried-up vine."

While Evelyn was taking Elijah's advice, Margaret stomped into the kitchen with puffed-out jowls. She slammed pots and pans on the stove as she prepared to make her husband's breakfast. She'd been standing by her bedroom door when Elijah admonished Evie to pray in order to fill up her soul. What good was prayer when God wasn't all that interested in what concerned colored folks?

Elijah came up behind her as she slammed the bag of grits onto the counter. "Did I do something to upset you, my love?"

He wrapped his arms around her, pulled her close. The scent of soap and the ruggedness of the man mingled with thoughts of the tenderness he'd shown her last night, and she softened. "I don't mean to be cross with you."

He released his hold and turned her to face him. "But you are. Can you tell me why?"

"I . . . I . . ." He took her hands in his. She sighed, then spoke her mind. "What good is filling Evie's head with nonsense about praying and reading the Bible going to do for her when she's carrying a baby and the daddy done run off?"

"Well, Mrs. Porter, that's where you and I differ. I don't consider prayer and the Bible nonsense, but I understand why you do, so I'm just going to pray on it and let God show you Himself." He released her and stepped out of her way.

Margaret put her hands on the counter, closed her eyes, and exhaled. She wished she could believe in things with the abandon that Elijah did. Wished she had that thing the preachers called faith, but she didn't know if she could ever put her trust in God again. The truth of the matter was, she now believed in hate and evil and things that haunted her in the night.

Chapter 34

Brick and stone stood out in ghastly relief against a background of ashes, cinders, twisted iron and steel, charred autos . . . Household implements, ruined junk was scattered about.

—*Maurice Willows, Red Cross Disaster Relief Report*

Mrs. Alberta had her baby boy on July 6, 1922. Evelyn's jackets and sweaters carried her through the last week of July. She was then forced to quit her job at the filling station. Mrs. Alberta gave Evelyn a few dresses and nightgowns to wear around the house. Evelyn was thankful for the borrowed clothes. She did not want to waste the money she had saved buying dresses that she'd only wear a few months. And she certainly didn't want to sew any more outfits that she wouldn't be able to wear once the baby came.

Evelyn was so ready for this baby to come. She'd done nothing but sulk around the house for the last three months. She'd locked herself away like a prisoner in Margaret and Elijah's house. And she was counting down the days until she could bust out.

Elijah had left the farm and was in Greenwood working on rebuilding the grocery store by day and staying in the house on

Detroit Street at night. Margaret stayed behind so as not to cause wagging tongues when she arrived back in Greenwood with a baby, since she didn't have the growing belly as proof of life.

Evelyn wanted to ask Margaret if she was happy with Elijah, but she didn't know if she could live with herself if Margaret was just as miserable as she was. Her sister could've done a lot worse than Elijah—like some of the guys Evelyn had run into ever since they left Greenwood.

She didn't understand why her ability to discern good men was so far off. Or why she couldn't find someone more like her daddy, a hardworking family man with love in his heart.

Blowing out a puff of air, Evelyn threw off the covers, got out of bed, and sat down in front of the sewing machine Mrs. Alberta had loaned her so she could make clothes for the baby. Her child would never know her as anything more than Aunt Evie. But each time she saw the baby wearing one of the items she made, Evelyn would know in her heart that she'd made it with love.

Her belly rubbed against the table while threading the needle. She lifted from her seat, positioning herself just above the sewing machine. An ooze of wetness streamed down her leg. At first, Evelyn wondered if she had urinated on herself, but then a sharp pain doubled her over and took her breath away.

When Evelyn was able to speak again, she screamed, "Margaret, I think the baby's coming!"

The door to her bedroom swung open. Margaret rushed into the room. "Are you sure? Are you hurting?"

Evelyn pointed downward. "I-I think my water broke."

"Okay, okay, okay." Margaret circled around the room a couple times. "You sit back down and let me dress the bed."

They had decided that Evelyn would have the baby in the house and only Margaret and Mrs. Alberta would know anything about the delivery.

"I can't sit down. My stomach's hurting something awful." Tears rolled down Evelyn's face.

"Don't cry. Give me a minute and I'll have the extra blankets on the bed." Margaret worked fast but not fast enough.

"Arrrgh!" A pain shot through Evelyn's body that was so sharp, she crumpled to her knees. Sweat trickled from her forehead.

"Here I come." Margaret threw a layer of plastic on the bed and then the last blanket. She grabbed Evelyn's arm and helped her stand. They slow-walked over to the bed. Evelyn sat down on the edge, and Margaret lifted her feet and placed them on the blanket. She then took a towel and wiped the sweat from Evelyn's face. "Lay here and rest a minute. Let me get Mrs. Alberta."

Evelyn grabbed hold of Margaret's arm. "Don't leave me."

"I don't want to leave you, but I've never delivered a baby before."

Evelyn's face contorted. Her eyes squeezed shut. Hands gripped her stomach as if trying to hold in the pain. "You've never been a mother before either. Are you ready for something like this?"

"Don't go having second thoughts now. Elijah and I are married. It makes sense for us to take the baby."

Evelyn's breaths came in short gasps, each one accompanied by a low moan of pain. The scent of sweat and fear filled the air around her. She grabbed hold of Margaret's arm. "What if you have other children? Will you still want this baby?"

"This baby will be my first, and I'll never treat him or her any different. I promise you, sis, this baby will have our love."

Evelyn's head flopped against the pillow. Sweat beads formed on her forehead again. She wiped them away. Her child would be loved, and she would not have to hold her head in shame.

This was the right thing to do. But Evelyn's heart broke with each contraction. She was getting closer to the time the child inside of her would disconnect from her and latch onto Margaret.

Evelyn didn't know what tomorrow would bring. But she prayed that God would fill her heart with joy and give her the ability to see something good in this life. *Fill me up, Lord.*

"It's a girl! Oh my God. Look at her!" Margaret's eyes widened as she watched the baby girl enter the world into Mrs. Alberta's arms.

"Hand me the scissors."

Margaret handed over the scissors. Then Mrs. Alberta cut the umbilical cord. "Take her to the basin. Let's get her cleaned up," Mrs. Alberta told her.

"I want to see her." Evelyn reached out for the child.

Mrs. Alberta shook her head. "We need to clean her up first."

Mrs. Alberta gave Margaret a stern look and nudged her head toward the basin. Then in a low voice she said, "Take *your* baby."

The baby was placed in Margaret's arms. The moment she felt the warmth of the child, Margaret was mesmerized. She'd never known she could love someone so much without even trying.

She walked the baby over to the basin, placed her in warm water, and wiped her down. She then cleaned out her mouth and an explosion of this-must-be-love flowed through Margaret's heart. Tears welled up. "She's so beautiful. I can't believe she's mine."

Evelyn started crying, held out her hands again. "Just let me see her. That's all I'm asking."

Margaret wrapped the baby in cloth, then turned to her sister. The tears and the hunger she saw in Evelyn's eyes caused her to hold the baby close to her bosom a moment longer.

"Please," Evelyn cried out.

Fear clenched Margaret's heart. Would Evelyn snatch this joy from her? Would she claim the child for her own? Time stood still as Margaret placed the baby in Evelyn's arms. She stepped back and allowed her sister a moment with the child.

Wiping the tears from her eyes, Evelyn stared at the baby as if she was trying to imprint this moment in her mind forever. Glancing over at Margaret, she said, "She looks like Daddy, doesn't she?"

Margaret glanced over Evelyn's shoulder. Smiling, she said, "Well, I'll be. You know what I think? We should name her Henrietta."

Evelyn nodded as tears flooded her eyes again. "Henrietta is perfect."

As Margaret took the baby from Evelyn, it seemed like a thousand regrets swam up from the depth of Evelyn's innermost being. The wail that came from her sister sent chills up Margaret's back. Caught between Evelyn's regrets and her love for Henrietta, Margaret stood frozen.

Didn't know if she should give the baby back or run away from her sister's pain. Margaret's heart was a tumultuous sea of conflicting emotions. She felt the sharp sting of agony at her sister's tears, but she couldn't help but be overwhelmed by waves of joy.

Henrietta started crying. The sound mixed with Evelyn's moans as the battle between joy and agony tore at Margaret's soul. Holding the baby with one hand, she put the other to her head. "What am I supposed to do, Evie? Your tears are breaking my heart."

"Take your baby to your room, Margaret. Your sister will settle down."

Mrs. Alberta's voice shook something in Margaret. Yes, this was her baby. Evie would want the best for Henrietta, and she planned to make sure this baby had a good life. She rushed out of the room, sat down on the sofa, and rocked her baby to sleep.

Elijah brought the wagon to the house a week after baby Henrietta was born. He hugged Margaret but only had eyes for Henrietta when he entered the house. "She's so small. I want to hold her, but will I break her?"

Laughing at him, Margaret put the baby in his arms. "Be gentle. Just cradle her."

Elijah slowly rocked her as his eyes filled with the kind of love new life inspires. "Is she really ours?"

Margaret laughed at him again. Laughter felt good after all the tears she and Evelyn had shed. Thankfully, her sister had stopped crying and was providing the milk needed to feed Henrietta. "She's ours."

Sighing like a man truly content with life, he said, "I can't wait for you to see the house and grocery store."

Margaret pointed toward the boxes that lined the walls of the living room. "I spent the week packing all of our things. Once you get them loaded on the wagon, we should be ready to go."

All Margaret had wanted since the day they arrived on the Threatt farm was to go back home to Greenwood. She thought she would be elated, but her heart broke into a million little pieces after Elijah packed the wagon and they rode up to the farm to say their goodbyes.

Mrs. Alberta came outside with baby Edmond in her arms. Ulysses, David, Allen Jr., and Alonia bounded down the stairs after their mother. Elijah took Henrietta out of Margaret's arms and helped her down from the wagon. He then helped Evelyn down.

Hugs, hugs, hugs went round and round. "I'm going to miss you two," Mrs. Alberta said when the merry-go-round of hugs ended.

With tears flowing down her face, Margaret told her, "My heart hurts, and we haven't left you yet."

Evelyn kissed Mrs. Alberta on the cheek. "Thank you for everything."

Mrs. Alberta handed Margaret baby Edmond and then put her hands on Evelyn's shoulders as she looked deep into the girl's eyes. "The way you can thank me is to go out and live the best life you can. Don't look back . . . Just sparkle so bright that no one will ever dim your light again. Promise me that."

Evelyn sniffed.

Mrs. Alberta shook her. "Promise me."

Nodding, Evelyn finally said, "I promise."

As Margaret handed baby Edmond back to Mrs. Alberta, she whispered in her ear, "The next one will be a girl."

Giggling, Mrs. Alberta said, "You get out of here with that. These five boys is enough."

Since Mr. Allen wasn't at the house, they stopped by the filling station before heading to Greenwood. "Y'all done came here and stole off my best worker," Mr. Allen said after they hugged him.

Elijah shook hands with Mr. Allen. "Big Willie will do a fine job for you."

"I know . . . I know. You trained him up good. I just hate seeing y'all go."

"Don't you worry," Evelyn told him. "When I get an automobile, I'll be coming here to fill it up, so you will see me again."

"You'd better not be riding no fancy-pants man in that car when I see you, or I'm going to take a stick to you."

They all laughed. Then Margaret told him. "You and Mrs. Alberta have become like family to us. This is not goodbye. Save a seat at the table for us. We will come back for Sunday supper one of these days."

"I'm holding you to that," he said, then abruptly turned and walked away from them. His hand went to his eyes as if he were wiping dust away.

"Let's load back up," Elijah called out to them.

They had been run out of Greenwood. All they possessed had gone up in a blaze of fire. The devil himself had taken their father from them. The insurance companies had refused to pay out the claims. The city officials had tried to steal away their land, and sickness had taken hold as they worked to rebuild. But none of it had quelled Margaret's desire for home.

Greenwood was forever her home. It was the place her daddy taught her that she could do anything she set her mind to. He believed that she would become an entrepreneur even while she had her mind set on teaching.

She looked heavenward and silently told her daddy, "You're getting your wish, Daddy. Elijah and I are going to run that grocery store of yours." She rocked the baby in her arms. Pulled the blanket away from her face and let the sun kiss her skin. "This granddaughter of yours might just run the whole world when she grows up. I'm going to see to it that she believes she can."

Elijah flapped the reins. "Giddyap. It's time to go home."

Part 3

GOING HOME AGAIN

Chapter 35

A conservative estimate . . . places the losses on buildings, business stocks, household goods and personal property, at three million, five hundred thousand dollars.

—*Maurice Willows, Red Cross Disaster Relief Report*

Opening the front door to their home on Detroit Street was like entering unfamiliar territory. The walls were sectioned off in the same manner as before. They had a living room, kitchen, dining room, bathroom, and three bedrooms.

Somehow, Margaret expected to see the furnishings that had been in their home before the massacre. It had never occurred to her that things would be different. A walnut-framed, gold-upholstered sofa and settee adorned the living room. An oak dining table with six matching chairs was in the dining room.

"Where did you get this stuff?"

"I bought some of it, and some was given to us by the church," Elijah told her.

"What church?" Evelyn wanted to know after opening the door to her bedroom and finding a bed and chest of drawers.

"Vernon A.M.E. I've been helping Reverend DeLyle rebuild the church when I have free time, and they blessed us with most of the furnishings for the house."

"Now you're rebuilding a church? When do you ever rest?" Margaret didn't know how she felt about Elijah spending his free time down at the church. But when she opened the door to Henrietta's room and saw the handcrafted baby bed on one side of the room and a dark oak spindle-back armchair with a seat cushion against the wall, she grinned uncontrollably. "Well, isn't this the cat's meow."

"Hot dog! I knew you'd like it." Elijah laid Henrietta in her new bed. He then took Margaret's hand and walked her down the hall to their bedroom.

Margaret's eyes twinkled with delight as they entered the room she would share with Elijah. There was a high-back walnut headboard for their bed along with a chest of drawers that had a wide mirror attached. But what beat all for Margaret was the walnut double armoire cabinet. "I doubt I have enough clothes to fill one of those things."

"Once Evelyn gets her hands on another sewing machine, she'll have that armoire filled for you in no time."

She walked over to it and opened the double doors. An iron rod hung at the top of the armoire, allowing her to hang her dresses. There were a few scratches on the inside of the left door, the only indication of its former use. "I've never owned an armoire before." She smiled at Elijah, then turned back to the beautiful armoire. "I will treasure it."

He came up behind her. She felt the heat of his presence and turned to face him. They'd been apart from each other for two months, and she had ached for him every day of his absence. He pulled her into his arms, and she took in his manly scent and exhaled.

"You're home, my love. It's done," he told her.

God help her, but being "his love" mattered to her. She basked in it as they closed the door and made use of that beautiful bed. Coming home didn't feel the same as when she'd been away at college and then opened the doors to greet her daddy and sister. She and Elijah now had the bedroom that had once belonged to her parents. Those were big shoes to fill, and she hoped they were up for the task.

What a godsend stumbling onto the Threatt Filling Station had been. And what a godsend Elijah had been when she collapsed from exhaustion. If he hadn't been there to carry her to the farmhouse that day, she might have lost herself. She wanted just to drift away on many occasions after the massacre. Why hadn't she?

Was it like Elijah had said? Had God been looking out for her and Evie, guiding them to the filling station? Margaret still didn't understand Elijah's theology, though. If God was looking out for them, why did He let them get trampled on in the first place?

She doubted she would ever have peace about what had happened to them. Doubted she would ever fully trust God again after that terrible night. But one thing was for sure: Her people didn't give up so easily. Being back in Greenwood was a testament to that.

Later that day, Margaret went through a stack of mail that Elijah had saved for her. Most of it was advertisements from businesses that had reopened. But in the middle of the stack, there was an envelope for Evelyn. It was from New York School of Fine Art and Applied Art.

Since Evelyn got pregnant, they hadn't talked about design school. Curious, she ripped open the envelope and read it. The correspondence was short and to the point. They were sorry about the troubles they had faced in Greenwood and wanted to know if Evelyn was still interested in attending school.

But that school was all the way in New York. There was no way Evie could go to design school and leave her to the care of Henrietta on her own. The baby had only been birthed into this world a week ago . . . No, now was not the time. She stuffed the letter back into the envelope and put it in her purse.

After going through the rest of the mail, Margaret decided to take a walk through the business district of Greenwood. As she walked by Mrs. Pearl's house, memories of that last day with her flooded her mind. If she hadn't run to the hospital but instead spent more time applying a cold compress to Mrs. Pearl's forehead, she might have been able to get that fever down.

"I'm so sorry," she mumbled as she looked at the house that Elijah and his friends had built. Mrs. Pearl would never know. But Margaret was thankful that the house was rebuilt. It deserved its place in Greenwood.

As she kept walking toward the business district, thoughts of Mrs. Pearl consumed her. The woman didn't have any biological children, but she'd stepped in and helped her daddy raise his daughters after their mom died. Margaret would forever be thankful for Mrs. Pearl's kindness. And even though she beat herself up with questions of what more she could have done to help the woman in her time of need, she was thankful that Mrs. Pearl hadn't been alone. She had been right there with her until the end.

She made it to Archer and then turned left on North Greenwood. That's when she recognized the true damage that had been done to them. While other buildings had been rebuilt, none of O. W. Gurley or J. B. Stradford's buildings were being rebuilt. The two men who had helped so many others start businesses in Greenwood had been run out of town.

A. J. Smitherman, the publisher of the *Tulsa Star*, was no more either. His building hadn't been rebuilt, and the newspaper hadn't circulated since right before the massacre. The police and city officials had ruled him a troublemaker and the instigator of the massacre. After being arrested along with O.W. Gurley and J. B. Stradford, each one of them fled Tulsa, never to return.

No one in Greenwood blamed them. They'd never receive justice in a city like Tulsa. So, one by one, three pillars of the community had fallen.

A smile crept across Margaret's face as she stood in front of Dreamland. This theater had been the premiere business in these parts. Margaret's heart overflowed with joy to see it back in business.

The building stood proudly at 127 North Greenwood Avenue once again. But the fact that her business was back up and running had not been enough to pull Mrs. Loula out of the depression she had sunk into.

Tears threatened as Margaret looked into Mrs. Loula's dead eyes. She was seated in a chair against the wall on the first floor of Dreamland while her husband and son took care of customers.

"I wish I had known you were feeling poorly." Margaret dabbed at her eyes with a handkerchief. "I shouldn't have stayed away so long. Should've checked on you." Mrs. Loula had been good to her. Being a female entrepreneur was a high achievement, and she'd shown Margaret ways to handle herself in business. Taught her things her daddy couldn't since he didn't know what it was like to be a woman trying to excel in this man's world. But Mrs. Loula knew.

"It's good to see you," she said in a monotone way. Like she was saying the words, but the person, the vibrant being who had once been Mrs. Loula, wasn't really there.

Willie came over to Mrs. Loula and helped her out of the chair. "Come on, Mama. Let me take you home so you can rest."

Mrs. Loula slowly moved past Margaret while her son held on to her arm. She stopped, touched Margaret's shoulder, and said, "You go live your life. Don't give me a second thought."

Mrs. Loula had always been so spirited and an inspiration to everyone in Greenwood. Those hateful men hadn't just taken her daddy away from her and Evie; they'd tried to snatch the hope out of Greenwood.

As far as Margaret was concerned, the fourth pillar to fall in their community had been Mrs. Loula. Women in Greenwood looked up to her. She had courage. Her businesses did better than most of the men's businesses, and she inspired other women to build something of their own. Who would do that for the women now?

With a heavy heart, she left Dreamland and headed toward Justice for All Grocery Store. The men who destroyed Greenwood and left Mrs. Loula in a pool of depression should have to pay for their crimes. When would justice come to Greenwood?

"Hey, pretty lady." Elijah waved at Margaret as she got closer to the store.

She gave Elijah a kiss, then walked inside the store, looking from one wall to the other. Wood planks lay on the floor, needing to be put together so they would have shelves.

"I put in an order for some canned goods and other non-perishables, so we best get these shelves put together."

He stood ramrod straight and saluted her. "Yes, ma'am. At your service, ma'am."

Laughing, she said, "You think you're funny." She got down on her knees in front of the wood piles. "But you're not."

"I think the lady doth protest too much." He got down on the floor with her, and they went to work with hammer and nails.

They worked on those shelves for several hours. When they finally stood up from the floor and dusted off their pants, Margaret heard Elijah's stomach growling. "Let's go home so I can feed you."

Stepping outside, Margaret looked across the street at the empty space that used to be a restaurant. Mr. Stanley hadn't been able to rebuild his business after being injured during the massacre. He and his family decided to go back down south.

"Hey, we were just having a good time. What's with the sad face all of a sudden?"

"Just thinking on the way things used to be in the business district and how much has been stolen from us."

She waved at the resilient men and women who walked down Archer Street on their way to support the businesses in the area. Ever since Jim Crow laws took hold in Oklahoma and white folks decided they didn't want Negroes shopping in their stores, colored folks spent their green dollars in the Greenwood Business District.

The sad part was, white folks hated that the businesses in Greenwood prospered in the face of their racism. But she was part of a community that kept rising from the ashes. That fact made Margaret proud. Greenwood was home and would forever be home to her and her family.

While Margaret and Elijah were at the store getting it ready to be reopened, Evelyn stayed home with Henrietta. Her hands shook like leaves falling from trees as she walked through the house.

Why was she here? Why did Margaret make her come back to Greenwood? She was safe at the Threatt farm, but how safe was she in Greenwood? Evelyn inched her way to the window at the front of the house. She pulled the curtain back and stared at the nearby homes and the people walking by. All seemed calm, but her memories of the last day she lived in this house, on this street, were anything but calm and soothing.

Screams. People running. Fire. *"Please . . . please don't burn my house!"*

Backing away from the window, Evelyn pressed her hands against her ears. Those sounds . . . the terror on replay in her head. She couldn't stay here if she was going to be tormented by these memories.

Why had she promised Margaret that she would move back here? Greenwood was no longer her home. "I can't stay."

Evelyn rushed to her room and threw her clothes back in the bag she'd brought with her. Her mind scattered with thoughts of fire, fear, and evil men who kill just to kill. She ran back into the living room. Her hand on the doorknob. Plans of hitchhiking all the way back to Luther, Oklahoma, danced in her head, drowning out the invasion of screams and flames and death.

Just as she opened the door, the sound of Henrietta's whimpers rose from the nursery.

She had a foot on the other side of the door. Margaret would hate her, but if she stayed here, she'd go mad.

The fussing from the other room rose in pitch.

Then, as if in slow motion, what was real and true caused her to step backward and close the door. Her head turned toward the baby's room. *Henrietta's crying.* She dropped her bag. What was she thinking?

Evelyn rushed to the nursery. The little thing was squirming, kicking her feet and punching at the air as if the whole world had angered her. "Me too, Henrietta. Me too," she said as she picked the baby up.

She'd forgotten to pump the milk from her breasts this morning, so milk had leaked out and was trickling down her shirt. Margaret didn't want her feeding Henrietta from her breasts but preferred that she bottle the breast milk and then feed the baby.

Henrietta's cries turned into wails.

It couldn't be helped today. This baby wanted to eat. Evelyn unbuttoned her shirt and let the baby suckle from her breast. As she did so, she traced the lines of Henrietta's face. When she was born, Evelyn thought she looked like their daddy. But now she saw traces of Tommy . . . and of herself.

"I gave birth to you. I can't be your mommy, but I love you anyway." Tears ran down Evelyn's face. She'd come close to leaving her little girl. Had forgotten her responsibilities as she allowed fear to take hold.

The baby calmed down as she continued to suckle. "You need me, don't you? I'll always be here for you." Wiping tears from her face, Evelyn added, "You'll never know that I'm your real mommy, but you'll always have my love."

Thinking back to Mrs. Alberta making her promise to live without looking back, she said, "I promise you this, Henrietta. You can count on me."

Chapter 36

The picking up of fragments, the relief of human suffering—the care of the sick . . . This kind of a task is not spectacular, and therefore the local or general public knows too little about it.

—*Maurice Willows, Red Cross Disaster Relief Report*

The biggest surprise about being back in Greenwood was running into Gayle Johnson, her friend from college, who was now Gayle Murphy.

"So you and Dale Murphy got married after all," Margaret said as she and Gayle sat down for lunch at the West Archer Lunchroom.

"It wasn't the elaborate wedding we had planned. It took weeks for Dale to get out of that internment camp since he worked for his father and didn't have a white employer to vouch for him."

"I don't know why I was so shocked when I first heard about how our Black men were being treated. Like the only good Black men in Tulsa were ones who had white employers. But the ones who owned their own business or worked for a Black employer . . . they were the bad Negroes, and if let out of those camps, they might decide to attack for the inhumane way they were treated."

"America the beautiful," Gayle sneered.

"The land of the free, unless you're colored or Indian and in the way of what these white folks want to do."

Gayle shook her head. "I never imagined that moving to Tulsa would be this way. My spirit was as low as could be after getting married while standing on the sidewalk in front of the rubble at First Baptist Church. But there was no way I was going to leave Dale here to repair all the damage by himself, with his father taking ill the way he did. And I couldn't sleep in that tent with him without making things legal."

Thinking back to her nuptials brought a smile to Margaret's face. "I got married behind a filling station, and I didn't even bat an eye at the location. Mrs. Alberta decorated it for us, so I did have flowers and lanterns."

"Sounds beautiful compared to what I endured."

Margaret took a sip of her lemonade, then laughed out loud. "During college, you and I talked about the weddings of our dreams. I would have been horrified to think of the back side of a filling station as a wedding venue. But it was really nice. And the Threatt family are some special people. I'm thankful I was with them for my nuptials."

"I love my husband, but I am not thankful for any part of our wedding." Gayle sighed. "My one saving grace was joining the National Association of Colored Women's Club. They have helped me to see that colored women can make a difference in this country."

"I've always admired that organization, especially Mary Church Terrell and the way she fought for Black women to have the right to vote, same as white women."

"You should join. Being a part of this organization has really lifted my spirits." Gayle put a hand to her mouth as a thought occurred to her. "With the new baby and running the store, you probably don't have time to join our women's club, and here I am going on and on about it."

"Evelyn and Elijah are a great help to me. And like I said, I've wanted to be a part of this organization since college. Let me talk to Elijah and see if Evelyn can take on a few extra hours at the store from time to time."

"We have a meeting this coming Saturday. I'll introduce you to the ladies if you're interested."

Was she interested? Or did she already have enough on her plate? Henrietta was so young, she needed to spend as much time with her as possible. So she would only join the organization if she could make a difference.

Work was a bore. They had been back in Greenwood for six months and Evelyn was already tired of Margaret telling her what to do and when to do it. She needed a break from the grocery store, a break from home, and a break from Margaret.

Henrietta had started on small bits of food like grits or porridge, so she didn't have to pump as much milk these days. But she'd still left three bottles in the icebox. So she didn't have a reason to return home before nightfall.

There was a jazz club just outside of the business district. One of the customers at the grocery store told her about it. Evelyn hadn't reconnected with any of her high school friends since being back in Greenwood. Didn't see a point in idle chatter when she had nothing good to chitchat about. So on Friday night after receiving her pay from Elijah, she started walking toward the jazz club.

As she turned the corner, she caught sight of a man with the same broad shoulders and same height and skin color as her daddy. Her heart raced. She sped up.

"Hey! Hey!" Evelyn waved her hand in the air as she ran toward him.

The man put his hands in his pockets and kept walking down the street. He looked as if he was in no particular hurry. Like he had no place to go. Had her daddy lost his memory during the massacre and hadn't been able to find his way home? Could that be what had kept him away from them?

Evelyn's eyes lit with excitement. "Daddy!" she called after him as she reached out a hand and touched the man's shoulder.

His head swiveled around to face her. Sharp intake of breath. Evelyn put a hand to her heart.

"I'm sorry, do I know you?"

Her shoulders slumped as she let out a long, deep sigh. "No, you looked like someone. I-I apologize." Evelyn turned away from the man and tried to steady her racing heart. She leaned against a building and sucked in air, still holding a hand to her heart. It was no longer racing, but it ached. Ached really bad. She needed to soothe her pain. Needed something, or she was going to lose her mind.

She continued down the street toward the jazz club. The beat of the music could be heard even before she opened the door to gain entry. People were on the dance floor doing the Charleston, the Swing, and the Lindy Hop. This was her kind of place.

A piano man, saxophonist, and drummer played in the back of the room while a woman sang Ethel Waters's "There'll Be Some Changes Made."

I loved a man for many years gone by.
I thought his love for me would never die.
He made a change and said I would not do,
So now I'm going to make some changes too.

Evelyn tapped her feet. A trumpeter joined in with the piano man, saxophonist, and drummer. Someone came up behind her and grabbed her hand. "Come on, dollface, dance with me."

She turned around to see Clarence Jones, one of the guys she went to high school with. Brenda had a crush on him, so he'd been off-limits to her. "Hey, Clarence, how've you been?"

"Making it as best I can." He tipped his head toward the dance floor. "Let's do the Lindy Hop."

The musician played "Mama's Gone Goodbye," and Evelyn let the beat of the music guide her to the dance floor.

Fare thee well, mama's gone, goodbye.
No use to cry, no use to sigh.

Catching the rhythm of the beat was important for doing the Lindy Hop. She and Clarence bounced, stepped, bounced, stepped. Then he picked her up and swung her over his back. They went back and forth on their bounce, step, swing rhythm until they danced themselves right off the floor.

Evelyn laughed, enjoying the moment. Dancing was good. Dancing helped her forget. She wanted to dance all night. So when Clarence led her off the floor, she said, "Let's go back. I'm not tired yet."

"We kicked up a sweat, and I'm thirsty."

She fanned herself with her hand. "I'm thirsty too." She looked around. "Can we get a glass of water or lemonade in here?"

"Got something better than that." He took Evelyn to a door on the other side of the dance floor. He knocked on the door.

A man as tall as Elijah with a bulky build opened the door. He grimaced when he looked at them. "What you want?"

Evelyn turned away. "Let's go back to the dance floor."

But Clarence held on to her arm. He looked at the man, who held the door close to his chest, and said, "Swing night."

The man smiled and opened the door wide. Patted Clarence on the shoulder. "Come on in."

Evelyn had heard about speakeasies that required a password to enter but had never been to one in her life. As they walked down the steps into the basement and saw all the people milling about with glasses in their hands, she knew exactly what she had walked into.

"I don't drink," she told Clarence.

"I didn't either before the massacre. But after what we've been through in this town, every now and then, I need something to take the edge off."

Something to take the edge off. She liked the way that sounded. Maybe a drink was exactly what she needed. Margaret would say she was being impetuous again. Not thinking about the consequences. Prohibition meant no alcohol. If she was caught in a place like this, they might lock her up.

Remembering the man on the street who looked like her daddy but wasn't, she asked, "What do you suggest I try first?"

Clarence grinned, showing his missing front tooth. "Walk over here to the bar with me. Let me treat you to the finest liquor in all of Greenwood."

Chapter 37

During the immediate days after the riot, over four thousand people were housed and fed in detention camps.

—*Maurice Willows, Red Cross Disaster Relief Report*

JUNE 1923

The Coca-Cola truck pulled up in front of the store. Margaret rang up her customer and then went outside to greet the driver. "Hey, Mr. Daniels, good to see you on this fine day. We've been out of Coca-Cola for two weeks. My customers been craving this drink."

"I hate letting you down, Mrs. Margaret, but I don't like driving into Greenwood. I'm always watching my back, wondering if another attack is getting ready to go down."

Putting her hands on her hips, Margaret rebuked him. "You're a truck driver. I'm sure you drive into some bad neighborhoods to deliver these sodas. So don't start trembling when it's time to deliver in Greenwood." Her chin lifted as she took on the airs of yesterday. "We have always been a respected community."

Mr. Daniels took two crates of Coca-Cola out of the back of his truck. "Y'all good people. I ain't never said nothing different."

He glanced up the street and then looked back at Margaret. "And the neighborhood is clean and respectable. But I still get this eerie feeling every time I drive over here."

The idea that they might be attacked again once they moved back to Greenwood had played out in her head, especially since Evelyn had warned of such things. But the fear of further attacks had subsided as each day passed and the white folks stayed on their side of the Frisco tracks and left them alone.

However, when the new year rolled in several months ago, Margaret had noticed that it wasn't only the white folk leaving them alone. Ever since Booker T. Washington declared Greenwood the Negro Wall Street, Black folks traveled across state lines to view the business district. But they hadn't had many visitors in Greenwood since the massacre. Evidently the delivery drivers weren't the only ones afraid to drive through.

While Margaret pondered that, Mr. Dorsey came into the store. He milled around a bit but kept glancing over at her out of the corner of his eye. Margaret hadn't seen him since he and his family left the Threatt farm. She tensed, then called for Rose, their part-time worker and next-door neighbor now that Mrs. Pearl was gone.

"You need me?" Rose peeked her head out from the back, where she had been counting inventory.

"Can you take over at the cash register? I'm going down the street for a minute." She came from behind the counter and was headed outside when Mr. Dorsey put his items on the counter and ran after her.

"Margaret, hey, wait a minute. I came by the store so I could talk to you."

Closing her eyes, Margaret took in a long, deep breath, then turned to face the man who told Elijah that he'd seen her father get shot. Even though she knew where Mr. Dorsey lived, she had never sought him out, and she'd been thankful he hadn't come into the store since they'd reopened. But now he was here, and he wanted to talk to her.

"What can I do for you?" Her lips were tight and twisted to the left.

He hesitated, seeming to have second thoughts. "I know I'm the last person you want to see—that's why I've stayed away from the store."

She didn't respond. Couldn't respond, when he was so right about her not wanting to see him.

"I was one of the last people to see your dad alive. I have been a coward not to tell you myself what a brave and honorable man your daddy was in the face of all those white men who came with guns blazing."

She lifted a hand, exhaled, needing a moment before putting the final nail in her daddy's coffin. "Elijah said you saw Daddy get shot."

Mr. Dorsey's eyes shadowed over with sadness as he nodded. "If it wasn't for your dad, I don't know if I would be alive today. When those white men attacked, several of us were unarmed. Your dad ambushed a group of them so we could get away."

"If you were running away, how do you know for sure my daddy got shot?" She was grasping at straws. There was no way her daddy had survived. He never would have stayed away from his family this long.

"I hadn't run very far before more shots rang out. I turned and saw three, maybe four men shooting at Henry." He lowered his head, took off his cap, and pressed it against his chest. "He was dead before his body hit the ground."

Margaret's hand went to her heart, her eyes growing wide as the horror of that moment played in her head . . . Her daddy had been gunned down, with no chance for survival. "I-I have to go." She turned and ran away from the truth that Mr. Dorsey spoke. Her daddy was the kind of man who would give his life fighting for those who couldn't fight for themselves.

That fact made her proud, but she still missed him with every fiber of her being. "Why, Daddy?" she moaned to the wind. "Why didn't you come home with me that night?" Her eyes filled with tears. She wiped them away. She couldn't think on this right now.

Trying to push every bit of her conversation with Mr. Dorsey from her mind, she met up with Gayle and told her friend about what the Coca-Cola truck driver said to her.

Gayle frowned at that. "What he said is nothing new. My own mama won't come to visit me. She says we're some fools for staying in Tulsa. Says we should come to Ohio with her and get away from these racist people who want to kill us."

Greenwood was back in business. They were flourishing despite what their enemies tried to do to them. Margaret had built a garden behind Justice for All Grocery Store and was selling fresh vegetables to her customers. Her daddy would be proud. "Well, your mother is wrong, and so are all the rest of these people who act as if we've suddenly developed leprosy."

Gayle put a hand on Margaret's arm. "Are you okay? This man couldn't have disturbed you enough to put tears in your eyes."

Margaret sniffed, wiped the tears from the corners of her eyes. "I'm fine. It just makes me mad how we're being treated after so many men sacrificed their lives trying to protect us."

"Hey." Gayle snapped her finger. "Since you're so passionate about this, why don't you bring up our dilemma with tourism at the next meeting?"

Margaret nodded at that. It had taken a few months, but Gayle finally talked her into joining the National Association of Colored Women's Club. The first thing she learned was that the ladies wanted to talk about anything but the massacre. The massacre was bad for business, so it was better to forget and move on. But the people outside of Greenwood weren't forgetting what happened to them by a long mile.

Twenty women with businesses in Greenwood gathered to discuss the way forward. Their meeting was held in the basement of the Mount Zion Baptist Church. Mrs. Loula Williams was rarely at these meetings anymore, but she was in attendance today, which made Margaret think that something mighty important was at hand.

Betty Sue brought the meeting to order. "Good afternoon, ladies. I am so thankful that you were able to join us today. The main issue for discussion is our trip to the National Negro Business League Conference this year. Our local association hasn't participated since 1920, and our national president, Miss Hallie Q. Brown, has requested that we attend."

One of the members stood. "That's all well and good, but we've spent these last couple of years recovering and rebuilding. I don't know about everyone else in this room"—she pointedly glanced at a few of the ladies—"but I don't have the necessary funds needed for travel right now."

"Neither do I. My family is barely making ends meet, so I won't be doing any traveling. And besides, the Negro Business League hasn't held much clout since Booker T. died back in 1915," another member said.

Betty Sue frowned at that. "They may not have as much influence with the White House and the like, but the Negro community appreciates the work Mr. Moton has done for Negro businesses since he took over as president."

Margaret stood. She put her hands on the table and leaned forward. "They haven't done much for business here in Greenwood. They ought to be speaking up for us, letting others know that it's safe to travel to Greenwood again."

"Darn tooting," Betty Sue agreed. "We need someone to serve as our spokesperson." Betty then glanced at Loula Williams.

Loula stood up and addressed the women. "Greenwood has suffered severely due to the actions of those who would do us harm. And we are yet and still suffering due to safety concerns. Yes, someone needs to serve as our spokesperson." Her eyes traveled around the room until they landed on Margaret.

Loula smiled at her, and for a moment—only a moment—Mrs. Loula's eyes looked hopeful, as if she were looking into the future and seeing better days for Greenwood. Then the sadness returned. "I don't believe I'll be able to make this trip, but I select Margaret Justice to go in my place."

Margaret couldn't bring herself to correct Mrs. Loula on her last name. She stood and accepted the nomination. Someone had to represent Greenwood at that convention. And if Mrs. Loula trusted her to do it, then she would do everything in her power to ensure their concerns were heard.

By the time the meeting concluded, five women committed to attend the conference. "I promise you all . . . we will not leave that meeting until the Negro Business League makes a commitment to uplift the name of Greenwood as Mr. Booker T. Washington did," Margaret assured them.

Cheers went up around the room. At that moment, Margaret understood exactly what Elijah meant about filling up the soul. But the fuel Margaret was riding on wasn't spiritual. Hope for better days fueled her soul. Greenwood would rise again. And she would do everything in her power to ensure it.

Margaret went home and told Elijah that she would be attending the Negro Business League convention in Hot Springs, Arkansas.

He had been reading the *Tulsa World* newspaper with his feet propped up on the table in front of the sofa. He placed his feet on the floor, folded the newspaper, and put it down. "I don't remember us discussing this."

She chewed on her bottom lip. She thought he would be as gung ho as she was. Elijah knew how much Greenwood meant to her. "It just came up in the meeting today. The women picked me to represent us at the convention."

"You're a married woman with a child. You can't go running off without discussing the matter with me first."

"It's for the good of Greenwood. We need more business brought into Tulsa. But people still don't feel safe visiting this town. There has to be something we can do to let the world know that we are back in business."

"You're too anxious. Just keep doing what you're doing, and things will turn around."

Waving an outstretched hand, she said, "Open your eyes and look around. Eighty percent of the homes have been rebuilt, but we're doing thirty percent less business than we did before they burned down our homes and businesses."

"Keep your voice down," he told her. "Henrietta just went down for her nap."

At eight months, Henrietta was crawling and getting into everything. Naps gave them the break they needed to get things done around the house. Margaret went to the kitchen and chopped collard greens, then threw them in the pot with her ham hock.

Elijah followed her to the kitchen. "Maybe one of the single ladies in your women's group can go to that convention in your place."

Chopping the next batch of greens like she was chopping down a tree, Margaret eyed her husband. "You expect one of the women in my organization to go to that convention and fight for what we need?"

"Why wouldn't they?"

"Women in this town don't even discuss the massacre. I've tried to get a group to go in with me on a lawsuit so we can get some of the money that's owed to us by some of those bomb droppers, but nobody wants to fight for what's right around here."

Elijah came up behind her, put his arms around her. "Or maybe they just want to live their lives in peace and forget."

Margaret put the knife down, leaned against Elijah's chest. "Too many images run through my head for me to ever forget."

"I'm praying that God heals your heart and cleanses your mind of all you suffered."

"That's a tall order, so you might be praying a long while." She stepped out of his embrace, put the rest of her collards in the pot.

He reached out for her. "Margaret, you've got to acknowledge God's hand at work. I mean, look at all that has been accomplished in Greenwood, even with all the obstacles. Only God could have done this."

She stared at him without responding, then headed out of the kitchen. "I'm going to check on Henrietta."

"Don't walk away like this. I only want you to see God's hand in the rebuild."

She turned back toward her husband. Seeing the frustration on his face didn't quiet her anger; it ignited it. "You talk of God's hand as if He cares about what happens to us . . . so answer this for me. If God is so caring, then why isn't my daddy here? Why did Mrs. Pearl die before seeing her home rebuilt?"

"The thing I'm trying to show you—"

She lifted a hand, halting him, her voice raised. "No! Don't try to clean it up or explain it a different way. If God is so good, then why . . . so . . . much . . . pain?"

He turned away from her. "I don't know how to answer that."

Hands on hips, Margaret kept shouting at him. "That's what I thought. And that's why I'll be the one to go to the convention. I'll get us the help we need." She jabbed a finger toward her chest. "Me . . . Not some God who doesn't care anyway."

Elijah's eyes filled with fury. Margaret couldn't recall a time when he had ever looked at her in such a manner. He stood, and his full height dwarfed her as he said, "You're not going, and that's final. You're a mother. A child needs her mother at home."

Was he insinuating that she wasn't a good mother since there were other things she enjoyed doing outside of this house? Her hands went to her hips. "I'm also a member of the National Association of Colored Women's Club, and we aim to get that organization and the Negro Business League to do some good for Greenwood."

"And you're a wife . . . my wife."

They went round and round until Henrietta started crying. Margaret left the room to go take care of her child. Just her . . . Evelyn wasn't home, as usual. And there was no benevolent God anywhere in the house to help her with the things that needed doing.

Chapter 38

By a flexible system of family case work, each family
was encouraged in helping itself.

—*Maurice Willows, Red Cross Disaster Relief Report*

Margaret felt terrible about the way she'd spoken to Elijah
the night before, so she got up that Sunday morning,
dressed Henrietta, and went to church with him. Elijah hadn't
told her that he was delivering the message this morning, and
that made her sad.

Her husband had been elevated to minister, and he hadn't
told her a thing about it. Did he not think she would be happy
for him?

This was an important morning for Elijah. As far as she knew,
Pastor DeLyle hadn't allowed him to preach the Sunday message
before. Elijah mostly visited the sick and shut-in and handled
church business or whatever Pastor DeLyle needed of him.

"This thing called faith has been troubling me lately," Elijah
began as he stood before the congregation. "I look out at this
world and see so many injustices. Our people have gotten the
short end of the stick for far too long. And yes, sometimes I
wonder why God allows bad things to happen to good people.
But then I read my Bible, and I am reminded of His goodness.

"So now I'm going to ask you to turn in your Bible to Psalm 77, and I will begin reading." He flipped a few pages in his Bible and then began:

"Will the Lord cast off for ever? and will he be favourable no more? Is his mercy clean gone for ever? doth his promise fail for evermore? Hath God forgotten to be gracious? hath he in anger shut up his tender mercies?

"And I said, This is my infirmity: but I will remember the years of the right hand of the most High. I will remember the works of the Lord: surely I will remember thy wonders of old."

Elijah closed his Bible and looked out at the congregation. Margaret noticed his hand shaking. She smiled up at him, hoping that would give him all the strength he needed to finish his sermon.

"So, my brothers and sisters, even though life hasn't been easy for us, I still see goodness in the world. I still remember the good things that God has brought into my life."

His eyes pierced her. "Yes, trouble came to us. No, God did not turn it away, but He has lifted our heads and renewed our spirits. Hallelujah!"

Elijah gripped the sides of the podium and leaned forward. "I choose to believe that God is good. What do you choose to believe?"

After service, Margaret stood in front of Vernon A.M.E. with Elijah while Henrietta bounced on her hip. "A preacher, huh?"

He shook his head. "Just a man who loves God."

Her eyes held questions as she looked at him. "Why didn't you tell me about your sermon?" It didn't seem right that he was holding this part of himself from her. But in a way, she understood it since they clearly didn't believe in the same manner. But still . . .

"Reverend DeLyle was called away this week and asked me to give a word." He put a hand on her arm, looked at her with those eyes that read her. "I should have told you, but I didn't think you'd want to hear about it."

Guilt pricked her heart. "I'm sorry for the way I spoke to you last night."

He nodded, but when he didn't say anything further, she was compelled to add, "If you don't want me to go to that convention, I won't go. You and Henrietta are the most important things to me, and I don't want you thinking otherwise."

Elijah lowered his head and planted a kiss on his wife's lips. "Let's discuss this trip after supper."

"Okay." A smile creased her lips. Sounded like there was still hope for her, like her husband might be softening to the idea of her going to the convention. "Let me go check on the store, and then I'll meet you at home."

They parted ways, but Elijah and his sermon stayed on her mind. Pushing Henrietta in her baby carriage, she kept turning Elijah's words over in her head. *"What do you choose to believe?"* Was it really that simple? Could she just choose to believe something and then that would make it so?

When she was a child, she believed in fairy tales. But that didn't make any of them real. When they arrived at the store, Margaret was surprised to see Rose standing behind the register. "I thought Evelyn was supposed to relieve you this afternoon."

"She never showed up."

Evelyn had been doing a lot of no-shows lately. Her sister was spiraling, and Margaret didn't know if she could rescue her this time. When she arrived at home, Margaret took note of the black Studebaker in front of their house again. She went inside and found Evelyn stretched out on her bed snoring so loudly, it seemed like the middle of the night rather than one o'clock in the afternoon.

Henrietta put her hands over her ears.

Margaret took her daughter to her bedroom. "Let's get you out of these church clothes. Then you can lay down and take a nap like a big girl."

"No."

Henrietta never wanted to nap but was normally out two seconds after Margaret laid her down. Margaret unbuttoned the back of the purple velvet dress Evelyn had made for Henrietta. She then put Henrietta's pajamas on. "Mommy needs you to take a nap so I can go see about Auntie Evelyn, okay?"

Henrietta shook her head.

Margaret laid her precocious child in the bed. Henrietta folded her arms against her stomach as if in protest. Margaret kissed her on the forehead. "Do this for Mommy, and I'll give you a slice of lemon cake when you wake up."

Henrietta made a show of lying down and shutting her eyes tight. Margaret pulled the cover up and then left the room. Walking back to Evelyn's room, she shoved her sister awake.

"Wh-what's going on?" Evelyn raised her head and quickly scooted herself off the bed. The whites of her eyes were wide with terror, her pupils dilated and darting around the room. Margaret immediately regretted waking her sister in such a hurried manner. "Calm down, Evie. No one's attacking us."

Evelyn took a few deep breaths, tried to back up, tripped over her foot, and fell onto the bed. "Whoa!" she said, then started giggling as if the funniest thing had just occurred.

Margaret glanced around the room. Her eyes connected with the bottle of bootleg whiskey on the floor next to the bed. She whispered as if the police might be passing by outside and overhear her. "You drinking?"

"Just a little bit." Evelyn used her index finger and thumb to indicate the amount of liquor she drank.

"That's illegal." Margaret grabbed the bottle off the floor. It was half empty. "You're not going to bring shame on this house by drinking and gallivanting around like a loose woman."

"Who you calling loose?" Evelyn snarled.

Margaret took the bottle to the bathroom and poured the contents down the drain. She then came back to Evelyn's room and wagged a finger in her sister's face. "Alcohol is not allowed in this house, and you know it."

Margaret pointed toward the front door. "And whose automobile is that in front of the house?" At first Margaret hadn't concerned herself with that car. But now she was wondering what Evie had going on.

"It's mine. I bought it last week."

"You bought an automobile? And didn't tell me!" Margaret's hands went up. "I don't know what's wrong with you, but you'd better get it together."

Evelyn rubbed her forehead but said nothing.

"You don't want to work at the store. Fine with me. But you got to figure something else to do . . . anything but what you've been doing."

"What else am I supposed to do? I'm trapped here. When I'm not working at the store, you've got me being a good little aunt and babysitter while you run to all these business meetings."

"Oh, well, don't worry. You won't be babysitting Henrietta anymore, not if you're going to be drinking."

Evelyn burst out crying. "I'm not good enough to watch my own . . ." She almost said "daughter" but clamped her mouth shut.

"I wouldn't be good enough to care for her either if I carried on the way you've been doing lately."

What was she going to do with her sister? Maybe she should choose to believe that Evie wasn't spiraling out of control, and then things would just magically be the way they used to be.

In Elijah's world, that's the way things worked. But in the world she lived in, Margaret didn't know if anything would ever be right again.

"What do you want from me? I came back to Greenwood like you asked. I watch Henrietta whenever you ask, and I haven't harmed her in any way—I would never."

Margaret rubbed her forehead with the palm of her hand. "Don't you get it, Evie? You're harming yourself . . . Please, grow up."

Margaret turned to leave her sister's room when Evelyn's words knocked the wind out of her.

"I saw a man who looked like Daddy a couple months ago. I chased him down the street and everything." Her lips pursed together. She shut her eyes tight, then choked out, "It wasn't him."

"He was dead before his body hit the ground." She hadn't told Evie what Mr. Dorsey said to her. Had kept it bottled up inside, not wanting the image of her daddy falling dead in the street, like so many other men that night, to play in her head.

Not wanting to face the pain this world had inflicted on them had only caused Evelyn to sink deeper into despair and confusion. As she opened her mouth, her words caught in her throat, but Margaret pushed them forward. "Daddy's dead."

Evie shook her head. "We don't know that for sure. We don't have a body. He could have lost his memory and can't find his way back home."

It would be so much easier to allow Evie to keep hoping that Henry Justice might one day find his way back home. But her sister was now drinking on top of everything else she'd gotten herself into. She had to make her see the truth so they could move on.

"I should have told you, but with all the nightmares you've had about that night, I didn't want to put one more image in your head."

Evelyn put her hands to her ears. "No, no. Don't tell me. I don't want to hear it."

Margaret wished she could let Evie continue to believe there might be hope, but would she chase another man down on the street? Would she hurt herself due to the not knowing? "Mr. Dorsey came to see me. He wanted us to know how brave and honorable Daddy was during the massacre."

Evie kept her hands pressed against her ears. She turned away from Margaret.

But Margaret wouldn't let it be, wouldn't let Evie continue in her delusions one day longer. She sat down next to her sister and pulled one of her hands from her ear. "He saw several men shoot Daddy all at once. He told me that Daddy was dead before his body hit the ground."

"Nooo!" Evie screamed. "No!"

With her words, Margaret not only crushed Evelyn's illogical hopes but broke both their hearts. Both women sobbed as Margaret pulled Evelyn into her arms. "I'm so sorry, Evie. I'm so sorry, but he's dead."

"He's not coming back. We'll never see him again, will we?" Evelyn asked as if she needed one more confirmation before she could mourn her beloved father.

Margaret let out, "He's gone," on a long-suffering sigh. Pain assaulted her body. She released Evie and folded within herself, sobbing from the aching in her heart.

"It's not fair!" Evelyn screamed. She got up and pounded her fist into the wall. "He never had a funeral . . . We don't even know where his body is buried."

Margaret went to her sister. They wept together until they were all cried out. When Margaret wiped the tears from her face, she told her sister, "We might not have Daddy's body, but we can have a memorial to celebrate the life Daddy led."

Wiping her eyes, Evelyn asked, "We can do that?"

At that moment, laughter bubbled up in Margaret's heart. She had hated that Elijah spent so much time down at the church, but her husband was yet again the man she would turn to in order to make this happen for her daddy. "Of course we can. We have a preacher in the family."

Chapter 39

That riot cheated us out of our childhood innocence.

—*Beulah Loree Keenan Smith, Tulsa Race Massacre survivor*

AUGUST 1925

The years rolled on. Margaret, Elijah, and Henrietta settled into life in Greenwood. Evelyn tried to turn things around but still floundered from time to time. It was now 1925, and the community was all aflutter about the National Negro Business League convention. Margaret should have been gleeful, but her body had betrayed her.

"What are you doing out of bed so early this morning? The doctor said you need rest." Elijah took her hand and tried to pull her back toward the bedroom.

"No time to rest. The menfolk are meeting over at Security Life Insurance as we speak, patting themselves on the back and congratulating each other on a job well done. Now the womenfolk have to make sure the job gets done."

"Let someone else take care of it. You've had a bad week."

Margaret had suffered two miscarriages since the time she had spoken up at the Negro Business League Conference in 1923 and demanded that they bring their convention to

Greenwood. Three days ago, it happened again. She'd thought for sure that this last pregnancy would hold since she'd made it to the third month.

"I promised President Moton a parade, and the Tulsa Association of Colored Women's Club will make sure it gets done."

"Exactly." Elijah gave her a pointed stare. "The Greenwood residents and even the white officials in Tulsa are working hard to make sure this convention goes off without a hitch. So you can lay back down and rest a little longer."

All he wanted her to do was lie down and rest, as if rest would bring back one of the babies she'd lost. She had failed to give Elijah any more children. The truth of that ate at her heart whenever she stood still long enough to think on her failings.

"I'm on the welcoming committee. I have to be down at the train station when the delegates arrive on those private Pullman cars." Margaret wouldn't miss that sight for anything in the world.

Oklahoma had a segregated train law, so when the Tulsa officials arranged to have the Pullman cars bring the delegates into town, she simply couldn't believe that they were doing such a thing. She had to see this for herself.

Margaret and Gayle stood at the train station holding signs that read *Welcome to Greenwood* as the Pullman cars rolled in. The doors opened, and beautiful, elite Black and Brown men and women stepped onto the walkways. The men wore suits and top hats. The women wore fine dresses and big hats with flowers.

It was a sight to see. The hotels in Greenwood would be full for the next few days. The hundreds of visitors coming into the city would be shopping at the stores in the business district. Many of them would attend a show at the Dreamland Theater.

Thinking of the Dreamland Theater caused a pang of sadness. Mrs. Loula's husband had placed her in a sanitarium this year. They were all hoping and praying that she would get better. But Margaret's joy at seeing the elite men and women arriving in town mixed with sorrow as she thought on the good people Greenwood had lost.

Mr. O. W. Gurley was now living in Los Angeles, California. He and his wife ran a small hotel. J. B. Stradford was living in Chicago, Illinois, where he owned a candy store, barbershop, and pool hall. And A. J. Smitherman had moved to Buffalo, New York.

A. J. Smitherman and J. B. Stradford were still fighting extradition requests from Tulsa on indictments of causing the race riots. Thankfully, most states ignored Tulsa's request, as the whites in this town had been labeled as the kind of racists even other racists didn't want to be in cahoots with.

Although having the National Negro Business League Conference in Tulsa was a win for the Greenwood community, a spark of sadness ignited in Margaret's heart.

"Hey, this is a good day. No frowns," Gayle told her as the delegates approached them.

Margaret nodded. "This day is for those who built this community from the ground up the first time—men like my daddy, O. W. Gurley, and J. B. Stradford. And women like Loula Williams. They may not get to see Greenwood rise in triumph, but I will hold them in my heart today."

Robert Abbott, editor of the *Chicago Defender*; C. C. Spaulding, president of the North Carolina Mutual Life Insurance Company; and Maggie Walker, the successful banker from Richmond, Virginia, were the first delegates to reach them.

"Welcome to Greenwood. We can't wait to show you around town this week," Gayle said as Margaret tried to compose herself.

"We have cars waiting to take you to your hotel." Margaret waved Simon Berry over to them as she said, "And Mr. Berry will be doing aerial tours of the city in his biplane before the parade begins. Please sign up with him before going to your hotel if you're interested."

Simon Berry held up the clipboard. "Step right over here if you'd like to fly the friendly skies and tour Greenwood."

Simon Berry was a licensed pilot and local entrepreneur. He used his topless Ford Model T for jitney service and gave nickel rides to Greenwood residents. He also owned a bus line and the Royal Hotel, and he owned a charter airline service with his business partner, James Lee Northington Sr., by which they flew wealthy oil barons around the country.

Mr. Berry was a big deal in Greenwood, and the fact that he was spending his day providing aerial tours added to the pageantry to which visitors would have a front row seat all week long.

A few hours after getting the delegates settled, Margaret stood on Greenwood Avenue with Elijah, Evelyn, and Henrietta watching the parade.

The procession was a thing of beauty and defiance. The parade stretched for miles down Greenwood Avenue. Visitors were a bit taken aback to see Black military units marching in formation with rifles in their hands.

Henrietta pointed. "Mama, look."

"I see them, baby. I see them."

The Colored Women's Club had spent an entire year planning this parade. But Margaret hadn't imagined in her wildest dreams how her emotions would run off the deep end at seeing this beautiful sight coming down Greenwood.

Tears blurred her eyes to the point that she could barely see the cowboys sauntering down the street on their horses. She wiped away the tears in time to see the automobiles that had been covered from hood to bumper with all types of colorful flowers and banners and flags.

Amanda Robinson had recently been crowned Miss Oklahoma. She stood in majesty as she rode on a beautifully decorated float, which was guided by a team of horses. She waved to the crowd of onlookers. Margaret and Elijah waved back.

Henrietta put her hands over her ears as the Tenth Cavalry band marched down the street beating on their drums in unison. Evelyn picked Henrietta up and walked her away from the beating drums. Kids were dancing in the street. Women smiled, and men clapped their hands to the beat.

The automobiles at the end of the procession honked their horns, loudly proclaiming that Greenwood would not be buried. It would stand in triumph as the world saw for itself that the massacre hadn't destroyed them. Negro Wall Street was back in business.

The first night of the National Negro Business League Conference was unlike anything Margaret had ever witnessed. The white officials in Tulsa mingled with the Black elites of the Business League. Smiles, handshakes, and mutual respect were on display for the countless reporters who'd come into town from places like Chicago, New York, and the like.

The newspapers would speak of unity between Blacks and whites in Tulsa, which was what they wanted, but Margaret couldn't help but grit her teeth as Mayor Herman Newblock stood behind the podium and addressed the hundreds of people in attendance.

He smiled and looked happy to be with them as he proclaimed Tulsa the most beautiful city and a great place to live.

Then he guaranteed, "There will be no more racial troubles in Tulsa."

At his words, the crowd cheered. But Margaret couldn't bring herself to clap. Newblock was the same man who voted in favor of the fire ordinance that had been put in place after the massacre to stop Blacks from rebuilding their homes. He had been a city commissioner at that time. Now that he was mayor and standing before reporters who could get his message out to the world, he acted as if he was all for progress in Greenwood.

Then Governor Martin E. Trapp, the same man who had stood by and let the National Guard treat the colored residents of Greenwood like refugees, now stood behind the podium and declared, "It's so wonderful to see Tulsans and the Greenwood community coming together in unison." As if Greenwood wasn't a part of Tulsa.

But not once while he held the microphone in his hand did his mouth split to talk about what Oklahoma or the city of Tulsa owed the Greenwood residents. Would anyone ever pay for what was done to them?

Greenwood had risen out of the ashes that these white politicians and others in Tulsa had left it in. Colored folks in Greenwood took back what belonged to them despite efforts to thwart their rebuild. If there was any silver lining in whites and Blacks coming together and being friendly at the opening ceremony, it was that the same men who watched Greenwood go up in flames now saw clearly that they didn't break the community members.

Then it was Robert Moton's turn at the podium. As president of the National Negro Business League, he had the final say of the evening. Before he began his normal "pull yourself up by your own bootstraps" speech, he asked the Negro League baseball players to stand. The men were seated in the second and third rows. They stood and waved.

"Our entry into Greenwood has been unlike anything we have experienced in the twenty-six years we've held this convention. And the festivities will continue this evening as the Chicago American Giants and Kansas City Monarchs go at it on the baseball field."

Cheers went up among the crowd.

Mrs. Alberta walked over to Margaret. On her hip was the newest addition to the Threatt family. Ella Mae Threatt was born in May 1924, and Margaret had gone back to the farm to witness the little girl make her entry into the world. Margaret hugged Mrs. Alberta and kissed Ella on the cheek.

"You did it!" Mrs. Alberta said, gleaming from ear to ear.

"Not just me. The ministers in town and everyone in the local chapter of the National Association of Colored Women's Clubs worked just as hard as I did."

"I'm sure they did. But not all of them lived in my home. I got a chance to watch you grow into the woman you are today, and I'm so proud of you." Mrs. Alberta gave her another hug.

Margaret hugged her back. This woman had been like a mother to her during the time when she most needed a mother, and she was grateful for her. "I'm glad you and Mr. Allen were able to make it. This week is going to be the best thing Greenwood has seen in a long time."

"All you had to say was 'baseball,' and Allen was going to be here."

Margaret's lips curved into a smile. She was about to exhale after the months and months of work they put in to make this convention a success, but when she scanned the second row and her eyes connected with Tommy Brooks, suddenly she didn't feel so good about the Negro League being at the convention. There was bound to be trouble.

Chapter 40

No law-abiding citizen, regardless of color, need fear
to come to Tulsa. As you will find the best of feelings
existing between races.

—*Theodore Baughman*, Oklahoma Eagle *newspaper, August 1925*

The Kansas City Monarchs and the Chicago American
Giants, two Negro League baseball teams, played against
each other all three nights of the convention. Evelyn wasn't
interested in the business league meetings, but she was on the
field for the baseball games.

Margaret was so busy with the convention that she'd asked
Evelyn to look after Henrietta. So on the second night, Evelyn
brought Henrietta with her. When the game was over, Evelyn
waltzed down to the field, stood on the diamond, and waited
while Tommy shook hands with his admirers.

She hadn't received so much as a note or letter from him.
Evelyn thought Tommy was still playing for the Dayton Marcos
until she saw him swinging the bat for the Kansas City Monarchs and heard, "Go, Tommy!" being hollered all around the
stadium.

She wanted to grab the microphone from the announcer
when Tommy came up to bat and tell everyone how he aban-

doned her and left her with no choice but to become an auntie to her own child.

"You were great, Tommy. We couldn't have won without you," one of the fans said.

Tommy shook the man's hand and looked over his shoulder, and then his eyes sparkled with familiarity as he glanced in Evelyn's direction.

There was no sparkle in her eyes. But she kept waiting, even when Henrietta pulled on her skirt, saying, "Where's Mommy? I'm ready to go."

I'm Mommy, Evelyn screamed from within. *I'm Mommy!* Her chest heaved. She waited until the last handshake. Tommy walked over to them.

"Well, aren't you a sight this evening," he said, standing a foot away from Henrietta, but he kept his eyes focused on Evelyn.

"You can't even look at her, can you?"

Tommy glanced around the field. Eyes shifting one way and then the other. "Don't make a scene. I see her."

Henrietta pulled on Evelyn's skirt again. "I want Mommy. Let's go, Auntie Evie."

Tears formed in Evelyn's eyes. She hated herself for showing such vulnerability. The weight of embarrassment and shame consumed her, overwhelming her heart, causing an overflow of wetness on her face. She didn't want Tommy to see her like this, but she couldn't control the emotions bubbling up inside of her.

He lifted a hand and wiped the tears away. "This . . . is . . . Margaret's child?" he asked cautiously.

Her bravado gone now, she turned, not able to face him. "Margaret got married not long after you left. She and Elijah are good parents to Henrietta."

Tommy bent down in front of Henrietta. He studied her for a long moment. Touched her nose. "Hey, little one."

Henrietta stepped back, tightened her hold on Evelyn's hand.

"Don't be afraid," Tommy said. "I'm not really a stranger. I'm . . ." He looked up at Evelyn, then held a hand out to Henrietta. "I'm just like your Aunt Evie . . . Call me Uncle Tommy."

Henrietta glanced in Evelyn's direction with questioning eyes. The child was almost three years old, and this was the first time she'd laid eyes on this man. Of course, he was a stranger. "It's okay. This is Uncle Tommy. You can shake his hand."

Henrietta shook Tommy's hand but kept her distance as she observed the situation.

Evelyn took a step backward. "Well, thanks for taking time to speak to us. I need to get Henrietta back to Margaret."

Tommy reached out and touched her arm. "Don't say it like that, Evie."

"Evelyn," she told him, not wanting him to use her special name even as his touch set a fire blazing within her.

He lowered his head. Repentant, he took the baseball cap off his head and held it in his hand. "I know I hurt you. I'm sorry. I really am."

"What do you want me to do with that? I'm not in a forgiving mood today . . . just ain't." She moved out of his reach. Let the fire in her belly die down.

"You don't have to forgive me. But you've got to eat, right? Have supper with me."

"We've got to go." As Evelyn started walking across the field with Henrietta, she saw Margaret standing by the gate with her arms folded, glaring at her as if she'd just had her way with Tommy in the middle of the field.

"What's your problem?" Evelyn said as Henrietta ran to her mother.

"Why'd you bring Henrietta down to the field? You should have known better than to do something like that."

"I wanted him to see her."

Margaret put Henrietta on her hip. "He doesn't need to see her. She doesn't mean anything to him."

"You don't know that. You're just being selfish because you can't have any kids of your own."

A sound of pain—no, anguish—escaped from her sister's lips, and Evelyn immediately regretted her harsh words. "I didn't mean that."

Margaret put a hand to her mouth and walked away.

Evelyn was about to follow, but Tommy ran over and put his lethal hand on her arm again. After that, she tuned out the rights and wrongs of the world and allowed Tommy to slide right back into her heart.

Margaret wanted to slap the taste out of Evelyn's ungrateful mouth. She'd never imagined that her own sister would say such a hurtful thing to her.

Three miscarriages . . . Three miscarriages . . . *Three* miscarriages. Margaret closed her eyes, shutting out the pain. She wouldn't allow the defects of her body or her sister to ruin the wonderful day she had experienced. Greenwood was alive and thriving, just as it had been when her father built his grocery store and declared it to be the beginning of a whole new life for them.

She looked to heaven. "I hope I've made you proud, Daddy."

"It's not only your daddy that's proud. All of Greenwood is proud of what you did. The hotels are full, and the visitors are shopping in the stores, getting their hair done at the beauty parlor, and catching a movie over at Dreamland." Elijah took her hand and swung her around. "You made all of this happen. You were right all along. And I'm thankful my wife had the gumption to convince the big cheeses at the Negro Business League to hold their convention in Greenwood."

She waved that notion off. "It wasn't only me. We have a whole association of women who worked tirelessly to ensure the success of this convention."

Elijah handed Margaret the *Oklahoma Eagle* newspaper. She grinned while reading the report of Theodore Baughman: "No law-abiding citizen, regardless of color, need fear to come to Tulsa. As you will find the best of feelings existing between races."

She put the paper down. "Exactly what we want our visitors to think." But Margaret wasn't so sure if the words of the reporter rang true. The white folks in Tulsa had put on happy faces and joined them for the opening ceremony, but that was for their own interests.

With the wealth from all the oil that had been found in Tulsa, the city government wanted Tulsa to be seen as one of the greatest American cities. But with the race riot hanging over their heads, other cities and states didn't want to acknowledge a place that stood for lawless retribution and Klan violence.

So the white business leaders stood shoulder to shoulder with the National Negro Business League members and pretended that all was well in Tulsa. Margaret smiled as they pretended, since it did her and other business leaders in Greenwood no good to call the white leaders on their hypocrisy. Better just to play nice and let them all live in their separate spaces.

Margaret needed to get dressed and head out for the last night of meetings, but Evelyn hadn't come home. She put Henrietta to bed and then went to her own bedroom.

Elijah's eyebrow arched as he looked at her. "Have the events of this week been too much for you? Do you need to stay home tonight?"

"I'm fine, but I may have to stay home since I don't have anyone to watch Henrietta."

"Why can't you leave her with Evelyn?" Elijah asked.

"Evelyn hasn't bothered to come home. She's probably running around with Tommy, letting him fill her head full of empty promises again."

Elijah frowned at that. He unlooped his tie. "You go on to the meeting. I'll stay here with Henrietta."

"You sure?"

He nodded.

Margaret kissed him. "You're a good man, Elijah Porter. I am forever thankful that you married me."

"You'd better be." He playfully smacked her bottom as she passed by him.

She was. But she wasn't sure if he was as thankful to have her for a wife, especially since she couldn't manage to give him the one thing a wife should be able to give a husband.

Chapter 41

The Red Cross has assisted, with the use of funds from the National Association of Colored People, in the erection of 13 homes.

—*Maurice Willows, Red Cross Disaster Relief Report*

On the third and final night of the convention, after the last baseball game, Tommy took Evelyn dancing at the Nails Brothers Pavilion. In its heyday, they had an orchestra with all of the musical instruments you could think of. Rebuilding had been costly, so there were only a few instruments for tonight's dance, but enough for her and Tommy to get on the floor and do the Charleston.

Tommy smiled as he danced next to Evelyn. "I forgot how smooth you are on the dance floor."

"It's like the music is calling my name," Evelyn told him while swishing her feet as if she was squashing a bug and swinging her arms to the music.

They danced the night away, but when the dance hall closed, Tommy wasn't ready to let go. He took her arm and guided her to the car. "You know where we can dance until two in the morning, right?"

Evelyn's eyes brightened at the thought. "The Threatt Juke Joint?"

He opened the passenger door for her. "Give me your keys. I'm driving."

With complete abandon, Evelyn threw him the keys. Then she remembered her lot in life . . . "Wait, it's nighttime. We can't drive through that sundown town. It's not safe."

"You got gas, don't you?" He got behind the wheel, turned on the automobile, and checked the gas. "We'll drive through that little Podunk town before they get wise to us."

She hesitated, but the moonshine she and Tommy had consumed earlier brought out the adventurous side of her. Evelyn got in the automobile and let him lead the way. Her head fell back against the car seat as she laughed. She honestly hadn't enjoyed herself so much since Tommy left for that Dayton baseball league. "You shouldn't have left me. Things would be so different if you had stayed."

He drove down the street. When they stopped at the red light, Tommy glanced over at her. "I got regrets. Ain't thought about nothing but you and Henrietta all week."

Evelyn's lips twisted with doubt. She shoved his arm. "Cut it out. You love hearing the crowd call your name while you slide into home base."

"Okay, I'll admit that the roar of the crowd and the bright lights of the field are addictive. Being a part of the Negro League is all I've ever wanted since the first time my dad put a bat in my hand."

"You don't have to explain to me. You made your choice, and then I had to make mine."

As he kept driving, his eyes shifted from the road back to Evelyn. "I saw your face when Henrietta called you Auntie.

That's when I knew how much my decision had cost you. I'm most sorry for that."

His apology the other night didn't hold much weight, but for some reason, it meant everything tonight. She placed a hand on his arm. "Thanks for understanding."

He pulled up to another red light, looked her way again. Their eyes spoke volumes. "I promise I do, Evie. I truly understand."

They were just outside of Tulsa, passing through Edmond, Oklahoma. Two Negroes in a sundown town in the dark of night. An automobile pulled up behind them. The bravado the moonshine had given Evelyn wore off. She prayed for the light to change back to green so they could get away from this small racist town. Why her dad ever thought Oklahoma would be better for them than the South, Evelyn just didn't get at all.

The light turned green. Tommy took his foot off the brake. The car started moving down the street, and she saw him glance in the mirror a few times. They'd passed two side streets, but the automobile behind them didn't turn off.

Squirming in her seat, Evelyn asked, "Are they following us?"

Tommy put a hand over hers. "Calm down, Evie. They're probably just headed up the street a little further." But when they reached the next traffic light, the car moved from behind them and drove up beside them. "Don't turn to look at them—keep looking forward," Tommy mumbled from the side of his mouth.

"Oh my Lord." Flashes of the white men who chased them down the street and out of Greenwood plagued her mind. Why had she let Tommy drive her out of Greenwood this late at night? She should have gone home. Why all these wrong choices? Why couldn't she be more like Margaret?

"Who told you to drive down this street, boy?" Despite Tommy warning her not to look at them, Evelyn snuck a peek over toward the other automobile. The white man looked to-ward the sky, then back at them. "I don't see a speck of sunlight."

"We just have a little further down the way to travel, and we'll be off your street." Tommy patted her hand.

Evelyn wasn't comforted by the gesture. The light was still red, and the white man was now holding a gun. "You'd better turn this car around and get back to Little Africa where you belong."

Tommy lifted his hands. "Now hold on, we don't mean you folks no trouble. We're just passing through."

"Well, you found trouble now, boy, 'cause you passing through at the wrong time."

Evelyn's head slowly swiveled toward the white boys. There was something about the voice . . . something in the man's tone. She locked eyes with the man on the passenger side, and everything in her trembled. Evelyn would never forget those evil green eyes. Eyes that blazed with hate and bad intentions.

"Get out of here, Tommy. He's not playing around. He'll kill us." Dr. Jackson never stood a chance. He'd come out of his house with his hands raised, no threat to anyone. Yet this evil man who was now holding a white hood and pointing a gun at them had shot Dr. Jackson anyway.

"He's going to shoot us!" Evelyn screamed.

Tommy's foot pressed down hard on the gas. He drove so fast the automobile swerved and skidded as he turned down the next street.

Evelyn held on to the door handle as moments of her life flashed in her head. She was supposed to be so much more, but at twenty-two she was still floundering. Not knowing which way to go or which road was right for her. Life had become so clouded.

Pow. Pow.

The devil who had met Evelyn in her nightmares was now chasing them and shooting at them. Would she make her next birthday? Would she ever have a chance to get life right? To become something that Henrietta could be proud of . . . even if she was only proud of an auntie?

"Help us, Jesus! Help us!" Evelyn screamed as another bullet shot past the car. "Why do they hate us so? What have we ever done to them?"

Evelyn had tried to shut out the horrors of the things that happened to them. When she was on the dance floor, nothing else mattered, only the rhythm of the beat. When she was drinking, she didn't care about the hate directed at her. Didn't worry about how the color of her skin might cause people to do her harm.

Margaret didn't understand why she partied so much. But it was better than what her sister did, which was dwell on all the hate and harm in this whole big, evil world.

She slumped down in her seat as Tommy drove like the devil himself was behind them, turning and turning, trying to get some distance between them. But no matter which way he turned, the evil was still following and taunting them.

"Oh God, just take me away . . . take me away from a world where a man can't drive down the street in peace. Just take me away," she cried.

"You're not leaving this world. Not tonight. I'm taking you home."

Evelyn shot up in her seat and looked around. They were back in Greenwood. She smiled, but then images of people running down the street as their homes burned to the ground invaded her peace, and she screamed and screamed and screamed.

†= =†

"What's wrong with her?" Margaret asked as she let Tommy and Evelyn into the house.

"We almost got run off the road by the Klan. They were shooting at us," Tommy told her.

"Shot at you? In Greenwood?" Margaret squinted, trying to make sense of what she was hearing.

"We were headed to Luther. I was taking Evelyn to the juke joint on the Threatt property."

Margaret turned to her sister. "You know better than to ride out of Greenwood at night."

"I wasn't thinking!" Evelyn whined like she was a little girl being scolded by her mother.

"When will you ever think before you act?" Margaret shook her head.

Elijah came into the living room. He tied the belt to close his robe. Wiped the sleep from his eyes. "It's too late at night for all this noise."

"I'm sorry, hon. Tommy was just leaving." Margaret put her hand on the doorknob to open it.

From outside they heard, "Get out here, boy. We ain't finished with you."

Evelyn jumped out of her seat, shaking like somebody had thrown ice-cold water on her. "They found us! God, help us!" She turned to Margaret. "It's that same one who shot Dr. Jackson."

Margaret glanced out the window. She turned back to Elijah. "Go get the rifle. This ain't 1921, and I ain't running away from this house 'cause them crackers want to start trouble."

"You can't go shooting white folks. Them boys out there with the Klan, and you know the Klan connected with the police," Tommy said.

Evie started crying and shaking. Shaking and crying.

"Hush up, Evie. You done brought this trouble to our house? Maybe I should just open the door and give them boys what they want." Margaret looked Tommy up and down like she was sizing him up.

"But it's him!" Evie lifted trembling hands and pointed toward the door. "The same boy who shot Dr. Jackson is outside right now. He'll kill us for sure."

A rock hit the front door, and then she heard a man say, "Don't make me burn this house down."

That shook Margaret. Her eyes darted from one side of the room to the other. Evie fell back against the sofa, rocking back and forth. Henrietta . . . Oh God, Henrietta was in her room. Margaret ran toward her daughter's room.

Elijah went to the back of the house and got the rifle. "I'll take care of this."

Margaret opened Henrietta's door. With all the noise going on in the front of the house, her child was snuggled up with her teddy bear, sleeping soundly like evil didn't exist in her world.

Elijah came through the hall toting the rifle. She had wanted him to get that rifle, but now fear clutched her heart at what might happen once he opened the door. Her daddy had gotten a gun to fight against those men who wanted to lynch a young boy without benefit of a trial. And he'd gotten shot and thrown into an unmarked grave.

"Wait, Elijah. I don't know about this."

"Fear not, my love. God is going to fight this battle for us."

She wanted to believe what he said, but what good were prayers against guns and fire? She'd witnessed firsthand a battle when God didn't show up. They'd lost everything, and Margaret didn't know if she could start over again or if her heart would just plum give out.

Elijah opened the door while Margaret stood behind him wringing her hands. He aimed the rifle toward the men who were hanging out the car window. "It's late, and it's time for you boys to go home."

"Who you telling what to do?" the guy on the passenger side with the gun said.

Elijah stepped onto the porch, his rifle still trained on the men. "I'm Reverend Elijah, which means if you force me to kill you tonight, I'll be able to preach your funeral in the morning."

"Over my dead body," one of the men said.

"If you don't get out of here, it will be." Elijah lifted the rifle to eye level, aimed and ready.

"We'll be back. We'll teach you a lesson about talking to white folks like that." The driver revved his engine, then took off down the street.

Margaret's eyes grew wide at the driver's words. "They're probably coming back with a mob. They'll wait until we're asleep, and then they'll set our house on fire."

Elijah came back into the house and closed the door. "It'll be alright, so stop worrying."

"How can you say that? Remember what men like them did to your grandmother . . . what they did to my father . . . what they did to Greenwood?"

Elijah put a hand on Margaret's arm. "I know, because I trust God." He looked to Tommy and Evelyn and said, "Let's join hands and pray."

When they were standing in a circle, hand in hand, Elijah began calling out to God. "Father, we come to You boldly in Jesus' name. According to Your Word, we know and trust that You will never leave us nor forsake us. And we know that the prayer of the righteous avails much. Father, we thank You for our assigned angels that are always fighting for us and protecting us.

"For we know that You have not given us the spirit of fear, but of love, power, and a sound mind. Get us through this night, Father, and help my wife to see that it was by Your mighty hand that we are not consumed by evil. In the name of Jesus Christ I pray. Amen."

Tears flowed down Evelyn's face, but she managed to say, "Amen."

Tommy said, "Amen."

Margaret let go of Elijah's and Evelyn's hands, mumbled, "Amen." Then walked away from the group. She was thankful that her husband hadn't been shot but didn't know if she could trust that God would protect them from further wrath. What if those men came back?

All her hard work getting the National Negro Business League to come to Tulsa would be for nothing. No one would ever come to this town again. She wanted to curse Evie for her impetuousness. But the fear on her sister's face looked as if one wrong word might send her over the edge. So Margaret left it alone.

Chapter 42

Relief work in the Tulsa disaster differed in many respects from that ordinarily followed in other large disasters in that NO provision was made for money grants or loans.

—Maurice Willows, Red Cross Disaster Relief Report

After the prayer, all Margaret wanted to do was get Henrietta to safety. She went into the child's room and put socks and shoes on her.

Henrietta opened her eyes, rolled over onto her side, and said, "Sleep," then closed her eyes again.

"That's right, baby, you sleep." Margaret took her next door to Rose, who had turned out to be a godsend. She not only watched Henrietta from time to time but also worked at the store when they needed extra help.

"Can Henrietta stay with you tonight? Trouble's brewing, and I don't want my baby getting caught in the middle of it."

"What's going on?" Rose asked as she took Henrietta out of Margaret's arms.

"A few white boys followed Evelyn home. Elijah chased them off, but they might come back."

"Oh no." Rose poked her head out the door and looked around. "You wouldn't expect them boys to show their faces in Greenwood after them white city officials talked about racial harmony at the Business League convention."

As Margaret walked back to the house, Rose's statement about the city officials replayed in her head. In fact, Mayor Newblock had said there would be "no more racial troubles in Tulsa." She was going to make him live up to those words tonight.

Things became clearer to Margaret as she stood in the living room giving direction to her sister. They wouldn't be sitting ducks, just waiting on those white boys to go get the rest of their hooded demons. Greenwood would not be destroyed by the hateful actions of men again. It would continue to rise and thrive. They were going to fight for what was theirs.

"Get back in your car and go to Mayor Newblock's house. Tell him that the KKK showed up on our street tonight, threatening to dust up some trouble."

Evelyn's eyes widened in fear. She shook her head. "I can't go back out there."

Margaret grabbed hold of her sister's shoulders. Made her stand up straight. "This is no time to shrink. I've told you before how special you are. I pray that one day you see what I see."

"But, Margaret . . . ," she started to whine.

Margaret put a finger to Evie's lips. "I need you tonight . . . Henrietta needs you."

Evelyn closed her eyes. Inhaled and then blew out a whoosh of air. "Okay . . . okay, I'll do it." She grabbed her keys and headed out the door.

Tommy stood. "I'm going with you."

Elijah piped in. "Tell the mayor that them New York and

Chicago reporters who attended the convention are still in town. The last thing he wants is for the Klan to bring those airplanes back to Greenwood."

When Evelyn and Tommy drove off, Elijah and Margaret ran down the street, knocking on doors and warning neighbors, "We got trouble."

The residents of Greenwood would not be taken down again. They would ban together and fight this evil. Margaret prayed that the mayor's words at the convention weren't just lip service but that he would make sure those hateful men didn't get their hands on airplanes and bombs. If it was a fair fight, then they had a chance. All they needed was a chance.

Within an hour, Detroit Street was packed with gun-toting, broom-swinging, and shovel-carrying men and women who aimed to fight to the death if need be.

"Just let 'em try to burn down my house tonight," an elderly woman said while swinging her broom.

"I got six bullets for anyone who's brave enough to try," one of the men declared.

The scene on Detroit Street was so very different than when everyone was running and screaming and begging men with torches not to burn their homes down. Margaret didn't see fear in anyone's eyes, but resolve.

No one came to their rescue the night of the massacre. If nothing else, that taught them to band together and rescue each other.

"We're in this together," another man shouted. "If one of us goes down, then ten of us need to pick him or her back up."

The last thing Margaret wanted was for word to get back to all of the out-of-town visitors that a racial war had broken out on Detroit Street, but if these boys were bringing trouble to them, there was nothing for them to do but fight.

True to his word, that little weasel who'd shot Dr. Jackson drove back onto their street with five other cars following behind him. They could only drive so far. The street was full of armed Greenwood residents, which took a bit of the bravado away from some of the night riders.

But the green-eyed devil was not deterred. "Told you we'd be back."

Elijah and Margaret were on the front line of the Detroit Street army that had come together in the space of an hour. Elijah pointed his rifle between the boy's green eyes. "And I told you there would be a funeral. You ready for that?"

God help her, Margaret wanted Elijah to pull the trigger. Some men needed killing, and the one getting out of the passenger side of that Ford, pointing a gun at them as if this was his world and they didn't belong in it, was one of them.

"Get behind me," Elijah said to Margaret while keeping his eye on the white men who didn't belong in Greenwood. Once Margaret positioned herself behind her husband, he yelled out to the men. "Y'all on the wrong side of the tracks, aren't you? Turn around and go on back home."

"We came for that boy who rode through our town tonight," one of the white men a few cars back said as he got out and walked toward them.

"We ain't letting you out of here with nobody. You best turn around and get. Remember, the sun is down on our side of the street too."

Margaret heard the man speaking. She turned to see Mr. Clifton standing tall and barking threats at the white men, who, as he said, found themselves on the colored side of town in the dark of night. If white men could invent sundown towns, why couldn't colored folks do the same?

She lifted the shovel she'd taken off the back porch and shouted, "If y'all don't get out of here, we're going to start shooting and swinging. Now, which one of y'all wants to die in Little Africa?"

She wasn't going to tremble against their actions one day longer. She would stand up and fight for the betterment of Greenwood, for a better America for Henrietta. She would fight so that others could live in peace in this land that had never been beautiful for colored folks.

"You boys go on home now."

The shovel was raised high. She was getting ready to move toward the men when she heard the sheriff's voice on the bull-horn.

Evelyn and Tommy came running down the street. Evelyn picked up a big stick out of a neighbor's yard and stood next to Margaret, ready to go to war to protect what belonged to them. "I did it," she whispered in Margaret's ear. "I told the mayor to come and get his riffraff."

Despite the angry scene going on around them, Margaret's lips curved into a smile. She held out her pinky finger, and Evelyn wrapped hers around it. The bond between them would not be denied. Come what may, the Justice sisters stuck together.

"Y'all heard me. Ain't gon' be no problems tonight. The mayor ordered me to handcuff anyone who don't belong on this street," the sheriff added.

The men backed up. Most got in their automobiles. The sheriff gave one last warning. "Don't let me see y'all around here stirring up trouble again."

For all Margaret knew, the sheriff was a white-sheet-wearing Klansman himself, but tonight he was on their side, and she was happy to see those intruders turn tail and leave Greenwood the way they found it.

Shouts went up all around them. Margaret turned and looked at the people in her community. The people who had worked hard to rebuild their homes and restore dignity to Greenwood. She raised a fist and declared, "We're safe here! This is our home, and nobody is running us away from where we belong ever again."

Chapter 43

True, the disaster was not "an act of God," it was "Tulsa made."

—Maurice Willows, Red Cross Disaster Relief Report

Margaret let Henrietta stay at Rose's house for the night. Evelyn went to her room, Tommy stretched out on the sofa, promising to keep an eye out if anyone decided to come back this way. Margaret thought they should all stay awake, but Elijah got back in bed and slept like a man who hadn't known a problem that God couldn't solve.

Lying in bed next to her husband, Margaret tried to figure him out. How could he be so calm? How did sleep come to him so easily? Yes, they faced down the devil and he fled, but that didn't calm Margaret. She was exhilarated by the fight and how her community came together. However, she also remembered how one fight broke out in Tulsa in the afternoon and then Greenwood was invaded later that night.

Filled with what-ifs, she tossed and turned. When she could take the thunderous silence no more, she shook Elijah. Then shook him again. He rolled over, yawned the breath of deep sleep in her face. Margaret turned away, put a hand to her mouth. Then sat up, ready to drill him with questions.

"How can you sleep? We need to make plans. What if they try to slip back into Greenwood? What if they attack others who are unaware? Should we have woke everyone in all the forty acres of Greenwood?"

Elijah scratched the side of his head. His eyes fluttered, then closed again. "Go to sleep."

"I can't. Don't see how you can either."

"We prayed . . . stood our ground . . . they left." He shrugged. "Nothing left to do but sleep."

Hot indignation filled her at his words. "Don't tell me about prayer when the whole of Greenwood was praying and going to church every Sunday morning and yet we were still attacked by them demons."

Elijah sat up and put a hand at the base of his ear. "Do you hear that?"

"What?"

"Silence." He got out of bed, looked out the window, then turned back to Margaret. "It's quiet out there. No movement at all. So stop worrying and go to sleep."

But she shook her head and wrapped her arms around herself. "It was quiet that night too. I remember it as if it was yesterday. I told Evie that things had settled down so we should get some sleep. I was laying on the sofa dreaming when Mrs. Pearl woke me up."

Elijah got back in bed with Margaret and pulled her into his arms. "I shouldn't have been so glib about your fears."

She beat a fist against his chest. "I don't want to be like this, but I don't understand how you're able to trust God so thoroughly after all that has been done to us in this country."

"It didn't happen all at once," he answered truthfully.

Margaret scrunched her nose as an eyebrow lifted. "What didn't happen all at once?"

"My trust in God," he said, "but day by day, as I watched God come through for our people, I learned to trust Him more and more."

"How? What has God shown you?" Margaret knew that her husband was a man of faith. Sometimes she even appreciated that. But on a night like this, she wished he could be more like her and prepare for the worst. After all, sometimes the worst actually happened.

He answered her with, "When you look at Greenwood, you see the destruction, but when outsiders like me look at it, we see the glory in the story."

"What glory is there in being attacked?"

Elijah shook his head. "That's not it, hon. We see a group of people who refused to give up or give in to the evil that tried to consume them.

"Yes, Greenwood was destroyed, but then those same men who had a hand in destroying your homes and businesses had to stand back and watch everything being rebuilt, bigger and better than ever. Now, if you don't see God's hand in that, then I don't know what to tell you."

"There have been times that I wanted to believe that God was helping us rebuild Greenwood, like when those men wanted to rezone our area and push us out, but Mr. Franklin took them to court and won." As her mind tried to reason it out, she said, "Or was it just good luck that we had an attorney living in the community when the attack occurred?"

Elijah smiled at Margaret. "I've always thought that it was a move of God—a Black attorney winning in a court of law against powerful white men. Come on, now. That had to be God working in our favor."

Margaret was still processing things as she added, "Or when the insurance companies refused to pay out those claims, but we were still able to rebuild. Thank goodness those millionaires donated money, or the Red Cross wouldn't have been able to help with the supplies."

Elijah prodded, "And who do you think turned those millionaires' hearts toward Greenwood?"

She knew he wanted her to say "God." But Margaret had a question for him. "What I don't get is, if God was helping us after the attack, why didn't He stop those evil men from attacking us in the first place?"

Elijah leaned back against the headboard. He rubbed his chin, then scratched his head. "I will never be able to explain or understand why there is so much evil in this world. I know that God has given us free will. Since Cain killed Abel due to his jealous heart, people have been killing one another."

Margaret frowned at that. That was such a simple way of addressing the matter at hand. But life had a lot of problems that God didn't solve. Some of them had nothing to do with man killing man. "Okay, let me ask you this." She folded her arms across her empty belly. "Are you telling me that you've never questioned God about why I haven't been able to carry a baby to full term?"

"Of course I've questioned God on that matter—and many others."

His quick response left her wounded. Did he find her lacking? Did he regret their union?

Then he said, "But those questions don't take away from the faith I have in God. I trust Him with our lives. So whatever comes, that is what I will say amen to."

Margaret got out of bed and turned away from Elijah and his reasonable-sounding words. His words didn't bring her comfort, only pain. She wrapped her hands around her barren womb. "I'm sorry I've been such a poor excuse of a wife to you."

He leaned forward and pulled her back toward the bed. "What do I have to do to prove my love to you?" Wrapping his arms around her, he kissed the back of her neck. "Should I have rebuilt the whole town? Would you then have understood that my love for you had everything to do with the time I put into rebuilding this community? I did it for you." His eyes watered as she turned and looked at him. "For love."

She had been a fool. All this time, he had been loving her . . . and she loved him. She could admit that to herself now. She hadn't wanted love. Hadn't wanted to feel the hurt that came with it. But this man . . . She put her hands on his cheeks, bent down and kissed his beautiful, full lips. "You made me love you, Elijah. I just wish I could give you more."

He lowered her back onto the bed. Wiped a few strands of hair from her face. "You've given me everything, my love. Let God handle the rest."

Wrapped in his arms, cradled in his love, she allowed herself to let go of the things she couldn't control. The rest of the world and the inner workings of her body didn't matter, just this man and this moment and this love they showered on each other.

When they parted and Elijah fell back to sleep, she fluffed her pillow and laid her head on it. She closed her mind to all the unanswered whys and what-fors running through it, and finally . . . finally, she went to sleep.

The next morning Margaret walked to work as if they hadn't just experienced a showdown with the Klan in the middle of the night. The fact that the neighborhood was still standing and nobody was in the hospital or in jail gave her peace.

But the way Elijah talked, you'd think God was somewhere in the background orchestrating things to make them work out for their good. As she passed each home and each business, she took note of the fact that each one had been rebuilt from the ground up, against all kinds of obstacles. She stopped walking and looked across the street, seeing homes and businesses and people walking, not running in fear of their lives. Walking . . . and smiling.

She asked herself, if it wasn't God, then who? Who could have brought this community back from the rubble and raised them up? When she turned down Greenwood, Margaret smiled as she remembered the parade that had come down this very street just three days ago. Did they have God to thank for that triumph?

"Hey, Mrs. Margaret, that convention was something special. Greenwood sure needed that," the postman said as he handed her a stack of envelopes.

"It was like the Greenwood of old, wasn't it?" she acknowledged as she took the mail from him.

But he shook his head. "It was even better. My mama cried when that parade came down Greenwood. Said she never thought she'd live to see something like that after what we all went through."

Good feelings flowed through Margaret as she sat on the stool behind the counter and reviewed the mail. When she was on the Threatt farm, she looked forward to receiving letters from Mrs. Pearl, but this mail was just bills from suppliers. She flipped to the last envelope and was taken aback to see it addressed to Henry Justice.

The letter was from New York School of Fine Art and Applied Art. The same school that Evelyn had been enrolled in before everything changed. Why were they writing to her father? Then Margaret realized they had no way of knowing Henry Justice had been killed.

She opened the envelope and read the first few lines. They had an opening, and they were inviting Evelyn to reapply. Margaret had just been wondering what she could do to stop her sister's destructive behavior, and then this letter showed up.

She looked heavenward, wondering if this was another thing God was orchestrating to make things turn out for their good.

Chapter 44

Mobsters had knocked a hole in the side of the store and had set it on fire.

—*Beulah Loree Keenan Smith, Tulsa Race Massacre survivor*

Evelyn had gotten through the night, but the daylight brought new challenges. As she was basking in the part she played to keep her neighborhood safe, Tommy was yet again making his escape.

"I don't want you to leave. You should stay and get to know Henrietta." Evelyn held on to Tommy's arm as if she were trying to hold on to what used to be.

She'd thought that if Tommy got to know Henrietta, he'd do what he should have done in the first place and marry her. Then the two of them could take Henrietta and be a family. But he didn't want that . . . had never wanted that.

"I can't stay in Greenwood. My team is heading out today. If I miss our bus, I'll be stuck here."

"You're not even going to stay until Henrietta comes back home? Don't you want to see her before you leave?"

Tommy stood. Shoved his hands in his pockets. "I'm not cut out for this family life you keep dreaming about."

"I don't understand." Evelyn's eyes were filled with confusion. "Why have you been spending time with me if you don't want to be a family?"

Tommy's hand went to his head. He turned away from her. "I don't know . . . After seeing that little girl, I thought . . . maybe. But then those guys chased us last night." He turned back to her. "I just want to get away from this place."

"And get away from me . . . again." She was a fool. The queen of fools. How had she thought that Tommy would ever do right by her?

"I've never wanted to get away from you. But the confining feeling of being a family man and having to plant roots in a place that don't even want me around is too much."

After seeing Tommy in his element this week, she understood him better than she ever had. "You like the sound of people calling your name and being the hero on the baseball field."

"I'm alive on that field." His eyes sparked with joy, then went dim again. "When I'm not on that diamond, I'm just another colored boy. And white men get to tell me when I can come and where I can go. That ain't no kinda life for a man like me."

His lip quivered as tears ran down his face. "I don't ever want Henrietta to see me with my head bowed low to another man who thinks he better than me, based on the color of his skin. I'd rather die than have her think less of me."

"She wouldn't think less of you. That's just the way things are." Evelyn walked closer to him. "You play in the Negro League. Henrietta would be so proud of that."

She thought her words would bring him comfort, make him see that he wasn't thinking rationally, but the pain etched on his face told a different story.

His shoulders slumped. His eyes brimmed with shame. "My daddy was a giant among men to me. He was strong, and he took care of his family. I never thought I could look down on him. Until the day some white man crossed our path and got in my daddy's face." Tommy balled his fists. "I thought my dad was going to lay him low when that man spit on him and called him 'boy.'"

"Some of the spit dripped from my daddy's face onto that white man's shoes. He told my daddy to clean it. I said, 'Don't do it, Daddy. He spit in your face.'" Tommy lowered his head as his tears fell to the ground. "That man called him 'boy,' but my daddy called him 'mister' as he bent down and cleaned the man's shoes." His head lifted, eyes full of the injustice of the world, as he bitterly said, "And I have never looked at my dad the same since."

She let him cry until he had cried out his pain. When he left, she didn't go after him. Tommy had accomplished more than most men dreamed of, but he was still broken. This whole racist world, where white was right and Black was a crying shame, had broken him, and she didn't have it in her to mend those broken places.

They were two broken people, running away from the things that had crushed their souls. Evelyn was tired of running, but she didn't want to stand still either. Just didn't know what to do to take away the pain this world had brought her way, so she lay in bed and kept lying there for two days with no thought of what to do next.

Then Henrietta opened her bedroom door and got into bed with her. "Whatcha doing, Auntie Evie? Why haven't you been playing with me?"

Auntie . . . she was Auntie.

"Don't you like playing with me?"

Say something. Talk to her. Tell her the truth. But as Evelyn turned to Henrietta and saw the look of concern on the child's face, she recognized that Henrietta didn't belong to her. She was the aunt, and she would never be anything more. Becoming more than that would probably leave Henrietta broken, and she couldn't do that to this child she loved.

A tear rolled down her face. Henrietta wiped it away. "You sad?"

Evelyn nodded.

"I'll get Mama." She got off Evelyn's bed and ran out of the room.

Evelyn didn't want to see the look of terror on Margaret's face. Whenever she was sad, she could see the wheels turning in her sister's head as Margaret wondered if she was thinking on killing herself again.

Evelyn didn't want to die, but she didn't know how to live either. Didn't know what use it was for her to get out of bed and go . . . where?

Margaret leaned against the doorpost. Evelyn avoided eye contact. "You sad that Tommy left?"

"No . . . I understand why he left."

Margaret walked over to the bed and sat down next to Evelyn. "I tried to warn you about him."

Evelyn turned to her side, put a hand under her head. She was all cried out, all dreamed out. She had messed up her life and would have to live with the fallout. "I know you did. But you were scared that we might take Henrietta away from you. That's why you were bad-mouthing him."

Sharp intake of breath. Margaret's hand went to her heart. "How can you say such a thing? My concern was only for you. Tommy broke your heart. I knew he would do it again."

She didn't have the strength to argue with her sister, nor did she want to. Margaret had been like a mother to her, and now she was Henrietta's mother. "I'm just letting you know that there's nothing to fear. Tommy doesn't want to be a family. This world beat that desire out of him."

And as she lay there, stuck between what could have been and what was, Evelyn reckoned with the fact that she was also too beat down to be any kind of mother to Henrietta. She would destroy any potential the child had of ever becoming anything in this world, just as all her dreams had been taken away from her.

Evelyn turned toward the wall, resigning herself to the hand life had dealt. She would find a way to get out of this bed and live her life. If not for herself, she would do it for Henrietta. All little girls needed an auntie to play with them and keep them safe when their mother couldn't.

Chapter 45

The bodies were hurriedly rushed to burial, and the records of many burials are not to be found.

—*Maurice Willows, Red Cross Disaster Relief Report*

Weariness and sorrow etched Evelyn's features, her once-vibrant eyes now dull and lifeless. Her body seemed to shrink, as if slogging troubles through a field of mud.

Margaret could kick herself for not telling her sister about the letter from New York School of Fine Art and Applied Art. But that school was in New York, and if Margaret was being honest with herself, she was terrified to have Evelyn so far away from her.

Elijah was still at the store, which was perfect. Margaret needed to talk to him, but she didn't want Evelyn to overhear their conversation. "Come on, Henrietta, let's go visit Daddy at the store."

"Wanna stay with Auntie Evie," Henrietta complained.

But Margaret put Henrietta's shoes on her and tied them. "Auntie Evie needs some rest. You can see her when we get back."

Margaret took Henrietta's doll baby off her bed, and the two headed out. When they arrived, she sat her daughter behind the checkout counter with Rose and said, "Play with your doll. I need to talk to Daddy."

"Okay, Mama."

Elijah was sitting behind his desk in the back room of their grocery store when she walked in. He looked up, and she immediately saw the concern on his face. "What's wrong? Did something happen at the house?"

She laughed. "Do I look that distraught?"

Sighing in relief, he said, "You actually do. What's bothering you?"

"I needed to talk to you."

He pointed to the extra chair that was against the wall. She brought the chair closer to the desk and sat down.

He gave her his full attention as she said, "I'm just wondering if my own personal fears are hindering Evelyn." She rubbed her hands across the arms of the chair. "I don't know . . . maybe I haven't done the right thing by keeping her with me all this time."

"It feels like part of this conversation is missing. What don't I know?"

She hadn't tried to keep secrets from Elijah. From the moment he married her, she'd tried to share with him her fears and her aspirations. But had she considered Evelyn's aspirations in the last few years?

"When we first moved back to Greenwood, a letter came to the house for Evelyn. It was from New York School of Fine Art and Applied Art. This is the school she was accepted to after high school."

"And . . ."

"Well . . ." Margaret squirmed in her seat. "Henrietta was only a week old at that time. We were rebuilding the grocery store and there was no money to send Evie to college."

"And now?"

His gentle prodding wasn't making this any easier. Margaret had kept something from Evie, and it was devastating her to think that life could have been better for her sister if she had gotten out of the way.

"And now another letter came. This was mailed to the store and addressed to Daddy. It feels like the school really wants to give Evie a second chance at her dreams."

"But?"

She squinted at him, getting annoyed with his one- and two-word sentences, like there was always an *and* or a *but* where she was concerned. "But . . . I haven't told her about either letter." Putting her hands over her face, Margaret declared, "She's going to hate me."

Elijah got up, walked around his desk, and knelt down next to her. "Hey, don't be so down on yourself." He patted her hand. "Evelyn will understand why you didn't tell her."

Margaret shook her head. "She's going to think that I'm trying to hold her back. She's accused me of that before."

"No, she won't."

Margaret ran a hand across her forehead. "The problem is, I think I have been holding her back, but not because I don't want the best for her. I just don't want anything bad to happen to her. She can be so hasty that she doesn't think about the consequences of her actions."

Elijah didn't say anything. He took her hand in his and squeezed it.

"I hate that I'm like this. I don't know how to stop thinking about all the terrible things that can happen." To those on the outside looking in, Greenwood had survived and was thriving again. But few who hadn't lived through that horrific night understood the type of trauma they lived with daily.

After a long moment, Elijah asked, "Do you want to change?"

She let his hand go. She sat up straight and put her hand on the desk. "I do, Elijah. I really do."

"Well then, you have to learn to trust again. Start with trusting Evie to take care of herself."

His words made so much sense, but the hardest thing in the world to do was to let go and believe that everything would turn out alright.

As she walked back home, Margaret did something she hadn't done in a long time. While holding on to Henrietta's hand, she looked to heaven and had a little talk with Jesus. "I need You on this one, Lord. Letting go isn't easy for me. But Evie needs more than I can give her. Promise me that You'll look out for her and keep her safe."

When they arrived home, Margaret fed Henrietta, then sat her child in her room to play with her toys. She then leaned her back against the wall, breathed in the courage to do what needed doing, and opened Evie's bedroom door.

It was time to let God be God and to let Evie go so she could grow. Margaret put the envelope from New York on Evie's pillow, then scooted onto the bed until her legs were straightened out in front of her.

"What's this?"

"New York School of Fine Art and Applied Art sent a letter to Daddy. They want to know if you're interested in attending for the winter semester."

Evelyn sat up, held the envelope in her hand. "They want me? After all these years?" Her eyebrow lifted. "Why?"

"They contacted you before." Margaret swallowed hard and let the truth of the matter have its way. "I was terrified that something might happen to you if you left here, so I didn't tell you about the other letter."

"That's stupid. Something already happened to us. And it happened while we were in our own home. So what difference does it make if I go somewhere else?"

"I know I'm not making sense. I've been irrational for a good long while now. I'm trying to pull myself back together. But I'm taking baby steps, and I hope you can forgive me."

Evelyn opened the letter and began reading. She held on to it as if studying each word on the page. Her eyes glistened with unshed tears. "So you're saying I can go?"

Margaret put an arm around Evelyn's shoulder and pulled her close. Her heart wanted to keep Evie right here for the rest of their lives, but that wasn't right. She had to let her go . . . She'd held on for far too long. "I've been taking care of you since Mama died."

"You act like you are my mama."

Margaret nodded. "I've smothered you, I know that. But I see now that I have to let you be who God created you to be."

Lifting the letter, Evelyn said, "All I've ever wanted was to be a clothes designer. I'm good at it."

"Yes, you are. I'm sorry if I've held you back. But it's your turn now, little sis."

"Where am I going to get the money to go to college?"

"Business has picked up at the store. Daddy would have sent you to school if he had lived. So it's my responsibility, and you can count on me."

The smile that had been missing from her face for so long stretched wide like Christmas morning. But in the next instant the letter dropped in her lap, and she bit down on her lip. "What about Henrietta? I can't just leave you with no one to help with her."

"I won't let you down, sis. Henrietta will want for nothing."

"She won't have me."

Margaret struggled with the fact that she hadn't been able to have a child of her own, while Evie struggled with giving one away . . . one she still saw every day. "Do you really think it's good for Henrietta to come into your room and find you drunk or so depressed you can't get out of bed?"

Evie opened her mouth as if she was about to say something, then closed it . . . eyes shifted toward the letter.

Margaret got off the bed and headed toward the door. But Evie's question stopped her. "What if you have another child—what happens to Henrietta then?"

As she turned back to her sister, Margaret's eyes filled with sorrow. She put a hand to her heart, looked back at the door, hoping her child wasn't lurking nearby. She whispered, "I love that little girl as if I birthed her myself. Nothing on God's green earth could ever change that."

Margaret pointed an accusatory finger at Evie. "What you need to decide is if you love her enough to be good to yourself." With that, Margaret left her sister to make her own decisions. She didn't totally trust that everything would work out okay for them. She would have to take things day by day and increase her faith as God kept showing her signs of His goodness.

It wasn't perfect, but it was what this cruel world had left her with.

Chapter 46

Instead of issuing ready-made clothing, cloth was supplied, sewing machines were provided and the raw materials turned into clothing by the Negro women and girls.

—*Maurice Willows, Red Cross Disaster Relief Report*

The cool fall breeze on a beautiful October day guided Evelyn to the other side of the tracks as she glided on a memory. She took the day off work and brought Henrietta to downtown Tulsa so she could let her look inside the window of a dress shop her mother used to take her to when she was young.

They never went inside the whites-only dress shop. But her mother used to sell a few of the dresses she designed to the owner. With traces of yesterday in the crevices of her mind, Evelyn could see her mother standing at the entrance of the store, handing Mrs. Oleander a long garment bag.

Mrs. Oleander then opened her pocketbook, pulled out a few dollars, and handed them to her mother. Evelyn's eyes shone with pride that day. Her mother had sold a dress to the nice white lady.

Now as she stood in front of the store, gawking at the beautiful dresses that hung on mannequins in the picture window, the door to the dress shop opened. A woman glanced over at Evelyn as she walked out of the store. Evelyn smiled then turned back to the powder-blue dress with fringes and the flapper headpiece that topped the mannequin's head.

She was so busy looking into that window that she didn't notice when Henrietta slipped inside the store until she heard the shop owner yell, "Oh no you don't! Whose child is this?"

Evelyn looked down. Henrietta wasn't by her side anymore. Her eyes got big. Looking inside the dress shop, she saw Henrietta headed for a frilly white and pink little girl's dress.

Evelyn snatched open the door and almost stumbled over her feet as she stepped into the shop. "No, Henrietta! Come here."

But childlike innocence propelled her forward. Henrietta touched the hem of the dress and said, "Mine."

Mrs. Oleander's hand went to her chest. She panted as if she were trying to catch her breath.

Evelyn pulled Henrietta away and then turned to the owner of the shop. "My apologies, ma'am. She got excited when she saw the dress. It looks like one I made for her."

Mrs. Oleander expelled a loud gasp. She glanced over at the two white women who were oohing and aahing over ball gowns on the other side of the shop and said, "My apparel is made from the finest of linen. I assure you, no Negro girl could afford to buy these dresses for her child."

That got Evelyn's back up. She stood at the door, gripping Henrietta's hand tight, lifted her chin as she glared at the owner. "Maybe we could afford these dresses if you didn't jack the price up so high after only paying the Negro women who make them a paltry."

One of the white women over by the evening gowns was holding up a beautiful yellow silk dress with lace around the waist and sleeves. At Evelyn's words, the woman snorted and then put the dress back on the rack.

Evelyn picked Henrietta up and ran down the street. When they reached her automobile, she looked to heaven and said, "That was for you, Mama."

Evelyn placed Henrietta in the back seat. As her hand grazed across the pleated blue jean skirt she had made for the child, she took note of the thickness of the fabric. Quality. And a Negro child wore it.

At that moment, it became as clear as day what she would do with the rest of her life. She leaned in and hugged Henrietta. "I love you so much, little girl."

"I love you too, Auntie Evie."

Her heart tightened at those words. But as the grip of sadness loosened, she smiled. "You know what Auntie Evie is going to do? I'm going to make bunches of pretty dresses, and I'm only going to sell them to Negro dress shops so little girls and women like you and me can wear them and look as beautiful as you do in them."

Henrietta was too young to understand the significance of Evelyn's dreams, but that didn't matter. What mattered most to Evelyn was that she said them out loud. She was going to that school in New York, and she was going to make a name for herself. White women would desire to wear the clothes she designed. But they'd have to watch Negro women prancing down the street in the finest frocks money could buy instead.

The smile on her face was as bright as the sun as she drove down the street. Her brother-in-law had once told her that the Bible and prayer were like a filling station to him. Evelyn finally realized why she hadn't been content since the day she'd discovered she couldn't go to college. She was always meant to be a dress designer . . . It was that dream that filled her up and gave her hope.

Chapter 47

In 2001 . . . the [Oklahoma] Commission found "strong evidence" that some local municipal and county officials failed to take actions to calm or contain the situation once violence erupted and, in some cases, became participants.

—*Randle v. City of Tulsa (decided: June 12, 2024)*

The house smelled like a good memory wrapped around wish-it-still-was . . . like her mother was in the kitchen bringing Christmas in with pancakes, hugs, and love. Those mornings had been special to Margaret—and not due to the presents she and Evie opened after breakfast. The love and joy that filled the house at Christmas set the mood for the year to come.

Her dad had been so busy building his business that he didn't have much time to spend with them. Christmas was different. Henry Justice loved the holiday as much as her mother had, and they made it special for the family.

It had been many years since Margaret had smelled pancakes on Christmas morning. The last time had been in 1921, when Mrs. Alberta made pancakes for the family. But she hadn't wanted pancakes without Velma Justice.

Her eyes filled with water as she got out of bed, threw on her housecoat, and went to the kitchen. Elijah was at the stove flipping pancakes while Evie and Henrietta sat at the kitchen table with plates in front of them.

"Hand me Henrietta's plate," Elijah said to her.

"I want to open my presents, Mommy."

Margaret took Henrietta's plate to Elijah. With her back to the kitchen table, she whispered, "Why are you making pancakes? You know I don't like them."

Placing the pancakes on Henrietta's plate, he said, "Evie said your mother fixed pancakes for you two every Christmas morning."

"Did she now?" Margaret took Henrietta's plate back to the table and set it in front of the child. She then scowled at Evelyn.

Evelyn shrugged. "Don't look at me like that. I'm leaving for New York next month. Who's to know when I'll see Henrietta again? I should at least be able to do something with her that Mama did with us."

It was Christmas, and Margaret should be happy and enjoying this morning with her family, but she had unfinished business with God. She walked away from the table without responding.

"Don't be like that," Evie called after her. "Sit down and have breakfast with us."

Margaret waved a hand. "I'll be back. You all go ahead and enjoy your food."

Back in her bedroom, Margaret sat on the floor at the foot of her bed. She put her head in her hand, trying to drown out the smell of pancakes and the sounds of good cheer coming from her family. She wanted to be happy and rejoice with everyone else, but life was so confusing to her at times . . . God was confusing.

Lifting her head to the heavens above, with tears streaming down her face, she told God, "I don't understand You at all.

Why are things so hard for colored folks? Why do we take so many losses and then thank You for giving us back what we never should have lost in the first place?

"Why do people hate us so much?" She went on and on with her list of "whys." God owed her some answers. She used to be happy. She used to dream of her future and believe that God was in the blessing business. All of that changed when she saw firsthand how blessings could be crushed in the space of a few hours.

But Margaret had also seen firsthand how she and Evie had been guided to the Threatt Filling Station after remembering their father saying it was a safe place to refuel at a time when they needed to feel safe in this world.

She'd also witnessed firsthand how a community came together and rebuilt itself even when so many obstacles stood in their way. She did believe that God had a hand in the rebuild. Only God could have restored Greenwood from the crushing blow it received.

But that was the reason she didn't understand God. Wiping her face, still looking to heaven, she screamed, "Why so much pain? Why do You leave us to suffer and then expect us to rejoice when You finally turn things around?"

The bedroom door opened. Elijah came into the room and sat down on the floor next to her. He pulled her into his loving arms, and Margaret wept like the gift of tears had been wrapped in a box for her this Christmas morning.

"I'm sorry," he said. "I didn't know those pancakes would upset you so."

She shook her head. "It was nice of you to do that for Evie and Henrietta. I'm not upset about the pancakes."

"Do you want to talk about it?" Elijah ran a hand up and down her back.

Exhaling, Margaret told him, "God is real. I do believe that. I see Him in so many things these days, but I still don't understand Him. And I don't know if I can ever trust Him again."

"That sounds like progress to me."

"Huh?" Margaret glanced up at Elijah. He was smiling. "I just told you that I still don't trust God."

Elijah planted a kiss on Margaret's forehead. "The Bible says this race is not given to the swift, nor to the strong, but to he that endures until the end."

Margaret was still looking at her husband as if he was some strange creature. "What does that Bible verse have to do with anything?"

Elijah continued, "There are people who can experience tragedy and bounce back immediately—they are the swift. Then there are those who shook off the massacre and started to rebuild their lives brick by brick—those are the strong. And then there are people who might waver and question, but eventually they end up in the exact right place—the place God prepared for them."

And maybe it was that simple. She just needed to keep moving forward, stay in the race, and allow God to mend her heart until that day she could put her whole trust in Him again. "I'm trying, Elijah. I really am trying."

"Day by day, my love, that's all God requires of us."

She nodded. Wiped her face again. Then got off the floor and went into the kitchen and ate pancakes with her family . . . It was Christmas, after all.

The new year rang in, and Margaret woke with reparations on her mind. Although Greenwood was in much better shape, not everyone in Greenwood had survived or been able to rebuild. There ought to be a price paid for the pain inflicted on others.

She folded the newspaper and put it on the table as Elijah entered the kitchen. "Good morning, my love."

"Good morning to you as well." He bent down and kissed her on the forehead as he glanced at the paper. "Is that last week's newspaper?"

He was so intuitive. She knew better than to hide anything from him. "I've been looking it over."

His plate of grits and eggs was on the stove. He took it, sat down at the table with her, pointed at the newspaper. "How long are you going to look at that city council position before you put your name on the ballot?"

An article had been written about the vacated city council position and the upcoming election. For the past six years now, women had the right to vote. If she could rally enough support with the help of her women's organization, maybe . . . just maybe. "I could do some good for our community on that city council."

"Yeah?"

"They owe us for what they did. You know it, I know it. Everybody around here knows it, but ain't nobody holding their feet to the fire. If I'm on that council, I'll be asking for reparations for Greenwood until they vote me out."

There was silence between them. Henrietta's bedroom door opened, and the pitter-patter of little feet bounded into the kitchen. Elijah lifted her onto his lap, and she laid her head against his chest. "What's got you hesitating? I can see you've given this a lot of thought."

Margaret leaned forward and put a hand on Henrietta's back. Her daughter's eyes were closed as she tried to grab the last bit of sleep. She was so precious to them. Margaret loved her family and was thankful for them. Her eyes met Elijah's as she gave him her truth. "I don't want you thinking I'm neglecting you and Henrietta."

Elijah shook his head, his eyes filled with compassion. "I could never take this from you. I know who you are. You're a fighter. Maybe lending your voice to this cause will actually do some good for Greenwood."

Excitement burst forth. Margaret leaped from her seat. "You don't mind if I busy myself with this campaign?" Before waiting for his response, she said, "I won't neglect you or Henrietta. I promise you that."

"And we won't stand in the way." He winked at her. "I know you need this."

She didn't start this. Hadn't wanted her community to deal with any of what had been put before them. But she would take this fight to the city council, the governor, Congress, and even the White House if she had to. She would wear this country out with her fight for reparations. This country owed her people something, and Margaret wouldn't rest until they got it.

She'd always wondered why her dad took up arms rather than come home with her. But she understood him more and more each day. Her father took a stand to show colored folks that they were worth the fight. Even if that fight brought war on their heads. Margaret was just like her daddy; she could never turn from an adversary . . . It was the thing that fueled her soul.

Chapter 48

Don't Let Them Bury My Story

—*Title of memoir by Viola Ford Fletcher,*
one of the last Tulsa Race Massacre survivors

Evelyn had spent Christmas and New Year's at home loving on Henrietta as much as she could. But now the car was packed with all her things, and it was time to go. Evelyn hugged Margaret and Elijah, then scooped Henrietta in her arms as the child ran toward her with tears in her eyes.

"Don't go, Auntie Evie."

Evelyn closed her eyes and tried to squeeze out the pain that flowed through her body and made every inch of her ache for things to be different. Sighing deeply, she put Henrietta in Margaret's arms.

She leaned forward and planted a kiss on Henrietta's forehead. "I wish I could stay, but I have to do this for me."

"Come back, okay?" Henrietta kissed her cheek.

Nothing would ever erase the bond she and Henrietta shared. Evelyn might not be able to mother the child she brought into this world, but she loved her, and she wouldn't let her down. "Nothing in this whole wide world could stop me from coming back to you."

Her emotions were all over the place. If she kept looking into Henrietta's face, which was a mix of her and Tommy, she would change her mind, unpack the car, and go back to her room, but she couldn't stay. She needed Henrietta to see her doing more with her life than drinking moonshine and passing out.

She rushed around to the driver's side and opened the car door. She jumped in and then blew kisses at them before speeding off. She had one stop to make before she headed down Route 66. Her plan was to drive that road until she got to Chicago and then turn off. She would make it to New York within three days.

Her gas was running low, so she pulled up to the pump at the Threatt Filling Station and honked her horn. Evelyn got out of the automobile and leaned against the trunk of the car waiting for Mr. Allen to come out of the store.

"What's all that honking for?" he said as he walked toward her with a smile of greeting. "You used to work here. I should make you pump your own gas."

She wagged a finger at that. "You used to tell the men who wanted me to pump their gas that I didn't do stuff like that."

"I didn't want them gawking at you like you was a piece a meat." He started pumping her gas, then mumbled, "I tried to keep you safe."

"Don't doubt what you did for us, Mr. Allen. Margaret and I were safe here with you and Mrs. Alberta. We never would've had the strength to go back to Greenwood if we hadn't been cared for by you all."

He put the pump back and walked over to her. "I just hate that you got mixed up with that baseball fellow."

She wanted to hate Tommy for the way he left her to deal with the fallout of what they did. But she loved Henrietta too much to hate the man who had a hand in bringing her into the world. "All of that is water under the bridge."

Mr. Allen nodded toward the back of her automobile. "You going somewhere?"

Smiling, Evelyn told him, "I've been accepted into a design school in New York. I'll be gone for a couple of years, but I'll be back."

"You sure about that?"

"Positive. Greenwood is my home, and I'm not running away from that." She hugged him. "How much do I owe?"

He waved that off. "It's on the house."

"Thank you so much for everything." She got back in her car.

Mr. Allen leaned into the driver's side window and said, "Now, you be careful on this road. Only stop during daylight hours and try to stop at filling stations that are either owned by colored folks or have some of us working there . . . Keep your eyes open."

He had taught her well about the ways Negro men and women stayed safe while traveling. She was excited to be driving down Route 66. She wouldn't have to turn off for a long way down the road. And she'd be able to stop for a rest and pull right back on the route. "I'll be careful. I promise."

"There'll be a few hotels and boardinghouses for Negroes along the way. You need to look for the signs and check in to one of them before nightfall."

"Yes, Mr. Allen. I'll do exactly as you say."

"I don't want you to be afraid on the road. Just want you to be watchful and stay safe."

Evelyn reached an arm out the window and hugged him again. She kissed his cheek. "Thank you for all you did for us. Tell Mrs. Alberta and the kids that I'll stop by and see them when I come home for my break."

"I'm gon' hold you to that," he said as he backed away from the automobile.

"You can count on it." Evelyn left the window down as she pulled out of the filling station, the place where she and her sister had found refuge from the storms of life, and turned right onto Route 66 to begin her new journey.

This road wouldn't take her all the way to New York—she'd have to turn off to get to her final destination, but she'd veered off course a few times already and yet managed to find her way back.

She thanked the good Lord that He hadn't given up on her when she wanted to give up on herself. Evelyn wasn't downing herself anymore . . . wasn't dwelling on the many mistakes of her past. Instead, she gripped the steering wheel as she kept driving down the road, breathing in the winter air and letting it fill her up with hope for tomorrow.

Evelyn didn't have life all the way figured out, but she knew one thing for sure. She was going to live big and loud and with purpose. This world would know that Evelyn Justice was here and that she didn't cave in when things got hard.

Her lungs filled with the refreshing air, and she exhaled all the hope and wonder she'd held in for so many years. With her automobile speeding down Route 66 and her adrenaline pumping, she shouted a warning to those traveling this way with her: "Look out, world, this Greenwood girl is still dreaming, and I'm coming to get everything God has for me."

Author's Note

What an honor it is for me to be able to write stories about African American experiences that have been forgotten, hidden, or omitted from our history books. The 1921 Tulsa Race Massacre was the most horrific attack committed by a white mob against Black people on American soil.

When I discovered that the Threatt family played a pivotal role in providing a safe haven for some of the Greenwood residents who escaped the Tulsa Race Massacre and that the Threatt Filling Station is now on the historical registry in Oklahoma, I knew I had to write this story and include the filling station.

The filling station was the first Black-owned station on the original 2,448 miles of Route 66, at least on Oklahoma's 375 miles of it. This filling station became an official Red Cross First Aid Station in the 1930s, with the first all-Black staff. The Negro Baseball League also played tournaments on the Threatt property.

Mr. Allen Threatt Sr. did all sorts of things on his property to take care of his family, such as expanding from the filling station to build a café, store, bar, campground, and roadside rattlesnake pit. They say that the actress Pearl Bailey stopped in during cross-country tours. But in 1921 the family farm also offered shelter to those fleeing the Tulsa Race Massacre in the Greenwood District.

The thought of needing a safe haven after going through a traumatic situation was something I wanted to explore with this novel, which is the reason this novel is not called *Greenwood* and the reason the Threatt family is highlighted. Allen and Alberta Threatt had nine children, only six of whom are named in this novel because of the time those children were born. However, in honor of what the Threatts did for a few of the people escaping the Tulsa Race Massacre, I have listed the names of all of their children on my website. Please go to vanessamiller.com for more information on the Threatt family.

If you would like to find out more about the Threatt Filling Station and donate to their renovation efforts, you can start here: lutherregister.news/2022/02/24/threattstationrenovation.

HOW GREENWOOD BEGAN

In 1905 Ottowa W. Gurley sold his property in Noble, Oklahoma, and purchased land in the oil-rich town of Tulsa. O. W. Gurley became one of the richest Black men in Tulsa after buying forty acres of land and then selling plots of land to Black folks so they could build homes and businesses.

These forty acres of land, filled with almost twelve thousand Black residents, became so prosperous that folks from all over the country traveled to see this glorious place that Booker T. Washington dubbed "Negro Wall Street." Today people have substituted the word *Black* for *Negro*, but you get the gist. It was a mecca of home-grown pride and entrepreneurship. If you'd like to know more about O. W. Gurley, go to blackpast.org /african-american-history/o-w-gurley-1868-1935.

John B. Stradford was another man who'd made his fortune in Greenwood. Mr. Stradford owned the most luxurious hotel in

Greenwood, the Stradford Hotel. He also loaned money to residents of Greenwood who were interested in starting a business. These loans helped build Greenwood into the thriving business district it became. If you would like to know more about J. B. Stradford, visit blackpast.org/african-american-history/john-the -baptist-stradford-1861-1935.

The thing I want to make clear is that although I've portrayed two fictional main characters, Margaret and Evelyn, I've written this story about true historical events. Therefore, several people you meet as you read *The Filling Station* are actual people who once lived in Greenwood, such as Mrs. Loula T. Williams. What happened to her was a travesty of the highest degree. If you would like to know more, go to blackwallstreetwomen.com /loula-t-williams.

I don't have space to list the names of all the real people and businesses I have named in this book here in my author's note, but to honor them, I have listed those names in the research link on my website.

I read countless books and articles in order to deliver this story. I list the books and articles at the back of this book. But I also traveled to Tulsa to see Greenwood. My husband and I were amazed at the rich history that is still available to see. I took a lot of pictures and will be sharing some of them with you. If you would like to read my complete author's note or see some pictures from Greenwood, go to my website, vanessamiller.com, and click on the research links or join my mailing list for more information.

Acknowledgments

As always, I must first thank God for the gift of writing and the ability to get out of bed each morning and do the thing I love so much.

Once again, I must thank Lisa Wingate. She has been such a good friend to me, and I appreciate her guidance. But this thank-you is for some information she passed on to me that sent me down another research trail and led me to this beautiful book.

The story of Greenwood is truly amazing all on its own, but adding the concept of a filling station and the real-life family who helped some Greenwood residents escaping the 1921 Tulsa Race Massacre was something I couldn't pass up. So THANK YOU, Lisa, for mentioning that you'd seen a documentary about the Threatt Filling Station on the Discovery Channel.

I would also like to thank Michelle Burdex, program coordinator at Greenwood Cultural Center, for being so helpful while I researched my novel and for allowing me to add a few words from the survivors to this novel. I will forever be grateful for your kindness.

Pictures of the Tulsa Race Massacre survivors along with the words from interviews conducted with them hang on the wall at Greenwood Cultural Center. If you would like to visit this center or donate to them, they are located at 322 North Greenwood Avenue, Tulsa, OK 74120. The website is greenwoodculturalcenter.org.

I have to thank my new agent, Emily Sylvan Kim, and my editor, Laura Wheeler, for being just as excited about *The Filling Station* as I am. And a big thanks to Chandra Sparks Splond for her insight during copy editing.

Each book takes close to a year of researching, writing, and rewriting. By the time I finish my books, I always feel as if I know the characters personally, but there are so many names mentioned in this novel that were not just made-up characters but real people who went through this massacre. Some came out on the other side, and some did not survive. I want to acknowledge the people of Greenwood. They had grit and resilience that should never be forgotten. I'm honored to have written their story. The people of Greenwood taught me what "never quit" looks like.

There is one more person at HarperCollins whom I simply must acknowledge. She has worked tirelessly to ensure that Black voices are heard in this industry. It is because of her that I was selected to be an Essence Author in 2023. She has helped me secure countless bookstore signings, and I am forever grateful for the advocate LaTasha Stewart Estelle is for not just me, but all the authors and their books.

I am so thankful for my husband, David Pierce, my daughter, Erin Miller, and my writer friends. You have all helped keep me on track with this book in one way or another, and I am thankful.

Discussion Questions

1. Did you know about the events that occurred in Tulsa in the 1920s before reading *The Filling Station*?

2. The 1921 Race Massacre was one of the most horrific crimes committed against Blacks in America and yet nobody was brought to justice for their crimes. The survivors and descendants of this massacre have been asking for reparations for over a hundred years, and yet neither the government nor the justice system has seen fit to honor their request. Do you think the people of Greenwood deserved reparations for what they endured?

3. Even though the author uses two fictional main characters, Margaret and Evelyn Justice, to tell this story, it is still about a real event that occurred in America. In light of this massacre, have a conversation on how we change the narrative on race relations. List a few ways that we can treat someone of another race with dignity. Does it start with the way we think about other races?

4. This was a time when Black bodies didn't matter. Those who died during the massacre were thrown in unmarked graves and families were left to wonder what happened to their loved ones. Could you understand the agony Margaret and Evelyn felt not having their father's body to bury?

5. Have you ever had a moment when you knew for certain that you loved God, but you didn't understand Him and

desperately needed answers? That's where Margaret found herself. Where would your trust level be with God and man after experiencing a massacre such as this?

6. Evelyn had a lot of growing up to do. Her character comes off as childish and selfish at times. Can you understand how someone's growth would be stunted after going through such a traumatic event?

7. Giving in to the love Margaret felt for Elijah was one of the toughest things she had to do. How easy do you think it would be to fall in love after experiencing such loss and pain?

8. Elijah asked Margaret, "Why do good things turn bad with you so quickly?" What did you think of Margaret and the way she saw life before and after the massacre? Do you have any bitter people in your life? Have you ever wondered what they endured to become so bitter?

9. Evelyn found herself in a situation where she was all out of answers and could only think of ending her life. Have you ever been so low where you thought of suicide? (I hope not.) If so, please know that better days are coming and seek help and support during this time. Please hold on to see the good that is bound to come your way.

10. Have you ever been so empty that the only reason you get out of bed in the morning is because other people are depending on you? How did you feel about Margaret when she made that statement in chapter 24?

11. Mr. and Mrs. Threatt provided a safe haven for some escaping the 1921 Tulsa Race Massacre. Have you ever needed a safe haven? Would the Threatts' place have been a comfort to you? Why?

12. In chapter 25, the author shares the story of W. A. Rentie, a man who struck oil only to then have a white man try to become guardian of his children in order to steal his profits.

This is something that actually occurred in Oklahoma. Many children were under guardianship because it was thought that Blacks and Indians needed help handling their finances. Would you have been willing to go to jail to keep your child from this so-called "guardianship" or would you have allowed your profits to be taken?

13. Sometimes trauma cuts so deep that even the smell of a certain food can trigger depression or anxiety. For Margaret it was pancakes. Could you understand her issue with pancakes on Christmas?

14. Between Tulsa, Oklahoma, and Luther, Oklahoma, there was a sundown town that Blacks could not be caught in at night. Had you ever heard of sundown towns?

15. With other disasters of the same magnitude as the 1921 Tulsa Race Massacre, the Red Cross gave out monetary assistance and loans. But they chose not to do so in Tulsa. Why do you think they chose not to help the Greenwood community get back on their feet with monetary assistance?

16. At the end of the book, Margaret has learned to love God again, but she is still struggling with trusting Him with her life. How about you? Have you experienced anything in your life that was so hard, you decided to fix it yourself? Or was there something you stopped praying about because you no longer believed God could fix it?

17. The author's prayer for this country is that we learn to love or at least accept one another no matter the color of our skin, that nothing like what occurred in Greenwood would ever happen to another community, and that we could all see the humanness of each other. What is your prayer for this country?

Sources

BOOKS

Colbert, Brandy. *Black Birds in the Sky: The Story and Legacy of the 1921 Tulsa Race Massacre.* New York: Balzer + Bray, 2021.

Johnson, Hannibal B. *Tulsa's Historic Greenwood District.* Mount Pleasant, SC: Arcadia Publishing, 2014.

Luckerson, Victor. *Built from the Fire: The Epic Story of Tulsa's Greenwood District, America's Black Wall Street.* New York: Random House, 2023.

Parrish, Mary E. Jones. *The Nation Must Awake: My Witness to the Tulsa Race Massacre of 1921.* San Antonio, TX: Trinity University Press, 2021.

ONLINE RESOURCES

"Allen Threatt, Sr., Named to Oklahoma Route 66 Hall of Fame." *Luther Register,* July 31, 2022, https://www.lutherregister.news /2022/07/31/allen-threatt-sr-named-to-oklahoma-route-66 -hall-of-fame/.

Anderson, Sydney. "John, Loula Williams: Massacre Survivors Who Shaped Greenwood." *The Black Wall Street Times,* July

13, 2022, https://theblackwallsttimes.com/2022/07/13/john -loula-williams-massacre-survivors-who-shaped-greenwood/.

Associated Press. "Tulsa Race Massacre Survivors, Advocates Testify Before House Committee." PBS News, May 19, 2021, https://www.pbs.org/newshour/politics/watch-live -tulsa-race-massacre-survivors-advocates-testify-before-house -committee.

"B.C. Franklin." The Victory of Greenwood, October 20, 2020, https://thevictoryofgreenwood.com/2020/10/20/the -victory-of-greenwood-b-c-franklin/?v=7516fd43adaa.

Briggs, Kelsey. "After the Massacre." In *Women of Black Wall Street*, ed. Brandy Thomas Wells, 2021, https://blackwallstreetwomen .com/after-the-massacre/.

Clark, Alexis. "Vernon A.M.E. Church Continues Its Mission 100 Years After the Tulsa Race Massacre." *Preservation Magazine*, Fall 2021, https://savingplaces.org/stories/vernon-ame-church -continues-its-mission-100-years-after-the-tulsa-race-massacre.

Desai, Mihir, Suzanne Antoniou, and Leanne Fan. "The Tulsa Massacre and the Call for Reparations." Harvard Business School, 2021, https://courseware.hbs.edu/public/tulsa/.

"Greenwood and Black Wall Street Tour." Tulsa Tours, accessed July 27, 2024, https://www.tulsa.tours/greenwood-black -wall-street-tour.

Greenwood Cultural Center. https://www.greenwoodculturalcenter .org.

Hinton, Carla. "Route 66 'Refuge' for Black Travelers Now Listed Among 'Most Endangered' Historic Places." *The Oklahoman*, June 10, 2021, https://www.oklahoman.com/story /news/2021/06/10/route-66-oklahoma-luther-gas-station -named-endangered-historic-place/7603608002/.

Johnson, Hannibal B. "The Ghosts of Greenwood Past: A Walk Down Black Wall Street." May 11, 2009, https://www

.hannibalbjohnson.com/the-ghosts-of-greenwood-past-a
-walk-down-black-wall-street/.

Luckerson, Victor. "#027: The Myth of an Impervious People."
Run It Back, April 23, 2021, https://runitback.substack.com
/p/027-the-myth-of-an-impervious-people.

National Park Service. "1921 Tulsa Race Riot: Reconnaissance
Survey." November 2005, https://www.nps.gov/parkhistory
/online_books/nnps/tulsa_riot.pdf.

Oklahoma Historical Society. "Threatt Filling Station." An
Oklahoma Story of Place: Voices of Preservation. YouTube
video, June 13, 2019, https://www.youtube.com/watch?v
=pjL0kKymIio.

Parks, Katrina. *Route 66: The Untold Story of Women on the Mother
Road*. Documentary, August 2, 2022, https://vimeo.com
/ondemand/route66women.

Pendleton, Todd, and Mason Callejas. "'Dodging Bullets' and
Coming Home to 'Nothing Left': An Illustrated History
of the Tulsa Race Massacre." *The Oklahoman*, May 26, 2021,
https://www.oklahoman.com/in-depth/news/history
/2021/05/26/tulsa-race-massacre-centennial-illustrated
-history-black-black-wall-street-destruction/5237930001/.

Randle v. City of Tulsa, 2024 OK 40, __ P.3d __. https://law
.justia.com/cases/oklahoma/supreme-court/2024/121502.html.

"Renovations Begin on Route 66 Threatt Filling Station." *Luther Register*, February 24, 2022, https://www.lutherregister
.news/2022/02/24/threattstationrenovation/.

Summers, Juana. "Survivors of 1921 Tulsa Race Massacre Share
Eyewitness Accounts." NPR, May 19, 2021, https://www
.npr.org/2021/05/19/998225207/survivors-of-1921-tulsa
-race-massacre-share-eyewitness-accounts.

Taylor, Candacy A. "Allen Threatt Interview Conducted by
Candacy A. Taylor, 2019-01-07." Library of Congress audio

recording, January 7, 2019, https://www.loc.gov/resource /afc2018029.afc2018029_05462_ph/?st=gallery.

——. "Postcard of the Royce Cafe in Edmond, a Sundown Town Next to Luther. 'No Negroes' Is Printed on the Front." Library of Congress, January 7, 2019, https://www .loc.gov/resource/afc2018029.afc2018029_05462_ph/?sp =3&r=-0.188,-0.031,1.382,0.706,0.

Thibert, Keshler. "O. W. Gurley (1868–1935)." BlackPast.org, September 19, 2020, https://www.blackpast.org/african -american-history/o-w-gurley-1868-1935/.

Thomas, Elizabeth, and Makayla Swanson. "Loula T. Williams." In *Women of Black Wall Street*, ed. Brandy Thomas Wells, 2021, https://blackwallstreetwomen.com/loula-t-williams/.

"Threatt Filling Station." Wikipedia, last edited September 27, 2023, https://en.wikipedia.org/wiki/Threatt_Filling_Station.

"Tulsa Colored Business Directory." *Tulsa Star*, February 14, 1920, https://tile.loc.gov/storage-services/service/ndnp/okhi /batch_okhi_delaware_ver01/data/sn86064118/00237281020 /1920021401/0019.pdf.

Tulsa Race Massacre Centennial Commission. "Tulsa County Courthouse circa 1921." PocketSights, 2023, https:// pocketsights.com/tours/place/Tulsa-County-Courthouse -Circa-1921-49103:4905.

Whitney, Wanda. "How to Research the 1921 Tulsa Race Massacre." *Timeless* (Library of Congress blog), May 26, 2021, https://blogs.loc.gov/loc/2021/05/how-to-research-the -1921-tulsa-race-massacre/.

Willows, Maurice. *Disaster Relief Report: Riot June 1921*. Tulsa Historical Society and Museum, accessed July 27, 2024, https:// www.tulsahistory.org/wp-content/uploads/2018/11/1921 -Red-Cross-Report-December-30th.pdf.

SONGS

Armstrong, Louis, vocalist. "Dardanella." Lyrics by Fred Fisher. Composed by Felix Bernard and Johnny S. Black. Recorded November 20, 1919.

Piron's New Orleans Orchestra, performers. "Mama's Gone, Good-Bye." Lyrics by Armand Piron and Peter Bocage. Recorded 1924.

Smith, Mamie, vocalist. "Crazy Blues." By Perry Bradford. Recorded August 10, 1920.

Waters, Ethel, vocalist. "Kiss Your Pretty Baby Nice." Lyrics by Corrine and Edgar Dowell. Recorded 1922.

___, vocalist. "There'll Be Some Changes Made." Lyrics by Billy Higgins. Composed by Benton Overstreet. Recorded 1921.

About the Author

Sean Evans Photography

VANESSA MILLER is a bestselling, award-winning author and playwright. Her writing has been centered on themes of redemption and books about strong Black women in pivotal moments of history.

Several of Vanessa's novels have appeared on bestseller lists. *The American Queen* won the prestigious Christy Award and was the 2024 American Fiction Award winner for Historical Fiction. *The American Queen* was also the Woman Evolve Book Club Pick for October 2024; is a North Carolina Reads pick for 2025; and has been featured in GMA, *Washington Post*, and *Essence* roundups. Her novel *Something Good* was the 2022 Best Christian Fiction Award winner at the African American Literary Awards. Vanessa's books have received countless favorable reviews.

Vanessa is currently published through HarperCollins/Thomas Nelson. She lives in North Carolina with her husband and family. She graduated from Capital University with a degree in organizational communication.

Connect with her online at www.vanessamiller.com
Facebook: @Vanessamiller01
Instagram: @authorvanessamiller
X: @Vanessamiller01